Sword Across Time

Treble Heart Books
1284 Overlook Dr.
Sierra Vista, AZ 85635-5512
http://www.trebleheartbooks.com

ISBN: 1-931742-87-1

Thank you for choosing
A Treble Heart Books
Selection

Sword Across Time

Catherine Anne Collins
Treble Heart Books

Dedication

With all my heart, I thank Lee Emory and Treble Heart Books for giving me the chance that I so longed for. This is just the first step in a journey. I thank my editor, Kathleen Wells, for having so much patience with my first time author mistakes and learning curve. I promise to do better next time.

I have to thank my husband, Fred, for his total belief in my abilities, and for urging me to write, write, write. I appreciate his understanding when I disappear into my world of fantasy and forget (briefly) that he exists.

To Marjorie

Enjoy

Catherine O. Collins

Prologue

Thunder and lightning crashed above, sending my beard flying wildly about my face. I swore and peered into the backdrop of midnight sky and billowing clouds. My searching gaze came to rest on the woman who dared challenge me, the Great Merlin. Taunting and defiant, she stood arms arched to the heavens above and dark hair swirling about her exquisite features.

The battle began.

Unsure as to the extent of her power, I knew the battle would most likely be one of equal ability. Majestically Nimue stood, shooting blasts of flashing light from her fingertips and challenging words from her lips.

"The ways of Avalon are deeply ingrained in me, and my powers have developed in ways you cannot imagine. Besides, Merlin, you are old and your powers are waning." Harsh words spoken in a lyrical voice to melt a man's heart.

I rose to the challenge that Nimue's words flared within me. "Do you think I do not know all that you do? Do you think that I have not spent my time connecting with nature and the elements? I have powers for tasks you only dream of in your wildest imaginings. I will draw on these abilities to destroy the evil which has grown within you."

Nimue hesitated only a split second and cast out an arrogant challenge. "Merlin, life away from Avalon has not only aged you, it has blinded you to my recent activities. You have no clue to the powers I have tapped into from the Universe around me. I will destroy you and all you stand for. I am tired of your frequent lectures about acceptance. What about Avalon? Do we not deserve consideration for our ancient ways and knowledge? Without Avalon, the Christians would not even exist, and the outside world would be naught but heathenish churls. With your lies and manipulations, you have helped, as much as any Christian, to destroy the old ways of worship and respect for all life. I am tired of arguing and trying to hold Avalon and our beliefs in the face of your power and opposition, as well as the beliefs of the staunch Christians and their condemning God."

"Nimue, my heart aches that I have wasted so much time despairing for your soul. You have become warped in your desire to save Avalon. Your lies and deceit have brought you low."

"Speak not to me, you wizard of deception. Priests and their unforgiving, cold ways have turned you into a coward. You no longer stand for the same beliefs, and that is why we stand here in battle."

Hurtful words echoed high upon the craggy hill and fell like stones upon my heart. How could such a warped view of past events come from the woman I once loved?

I watched as Nimue reached within the folds of her velvet clothing and slowly pulled forth an object carefully hidden until then. A stab of fear forced itself into my heart. It astounded me that Nimue possessed such an item.

The Crystal of Light. Normally used only for the most holy of ceremonies, the Crystal of Light held the power of the ages.

She held within her hands an energy that was quite possibly more powerful than even I. Becoming a mere shadow of dust could likely be my fate before the end of night. Deep inside my soul, an aching dullness of pain took root.

Time ran short as I watched Nimue focus her abilities to draw in the energy from the air around her. Her body glowed and became translucent, while the wind over the Tor blew fierce enough to hurt one's senses with its intensity.

Deep inside I still harbored hope I could rise triumphant from this confrontation, yet I worried about the sanity of the sorceress. Sincerity of Nimue's emotions and her desire to save Avalon were not in doubt, but she was so driven by revenge for the natural passing of the ways of Avalon that her lust for revenge would either decrease or enhance her abilities. Unfortunately, I did not know which.

I needed to protect myself. Nimue may be pulling her energy from the surrounding air, but I would focus on the heavens above and use the storm for my power. Drawing the energy to me, I aligned my senses with the forces of nature. I took in more energy than I believed possible, but the circumstances called for extreme measures. Nimue would not be easily stopped, and if I did not stop her tonight on this summer solstice, the future of the world would be greatly changed for the worse.

Nimue's power increased, and I felt the edges of my protective shield being battered and growing weak.

"Focus, Merlin." Whispered words I gave up to the wind, and I felt my energy rising. What a glorious feeling it was.

Intent upon my task, I was barely aware of Nimue who seemed to be looking for a path to lead her closer to the Tor. "Yes," I muttered. "Her only salvation lies in the ancient stone that stands as a beacon on the Glastonbury hilltop."

Energy locked within the secrets of the monument would enhance her power and the power of the crystal she held in her hand.

With a burst of speed, Nimue fled up the winding path toward the Tor that stood like a sentry to the Otherworld. My heart pounded as I realized that if Nimue reached her destination, she might yet rise above my own power. I needed to draw upon the power of the stone from where I stood. Nimue's distress pulsed strongly within me. I could not let her sense my steely fear. Only now realizing the full extent of her power, I realized I might not be able to destroy her, but if I could stop her for now, I could work on a way to destroy her in the future.

Feeling more powerful than ever before in my many years of life, I felt now was the time. Turning to face the towering stone, I saw Nimue outlined against the sky. Somewhere deep in my subconscious, I took a second to appreciate the beauty of the woman and how the power she called to her command only enhanced her beauty.

The air around me became mute, and time stood still as Nimue turned to face me across the distance. At one with the stone monument she stood beside, Nimue smiled at me and reverently arched the crystal to the heavens.

I watched, waited. My former love stood, waited. Her hesitation gave me hope. If she mastered the crystal, I would not still stand alive upon the hill.

A slight smile of triumph lifted the corner of my mouth and I raised my arms to the heavens. The sleeves of my dark robe slid gracefully up my arms, energy crackled hot between the palms of my hands. These same hands I turned toward my nemesis. All my knowledge, powers, emotions, and beliefs were centered upon destroying this woman before her destructive hate could spread.

My bleary eyes watched as Nimue raised her arms in preparation. Shining like polished diamonds in the moonlight, the beauty of the Crystal of Light dulled the flash of lightning streaking the night sky.

A twinge of unease grew in my stomach. Was she yet more powerful than she presented so far this evening? Time for doubt was gone. I needed to act.

With a mighty roar, I threw all I possessed towards Nimue. Our energies met and the battle, which ensued, was fierce. With so much at stake, I was motivated to exert beyond my limitations.

Nimue was thrown backward. She was losing, but I knew she was stubborn and angry enough to continue fighting although she was depleting herself beyond any quick recovery.

Angry words flew down the hillside to my ears as Nimue cursed my strict values and morals. She weakened, and I felt her energy retracting until it became naught but a dim spark.

Knowing her mind so well, I assumed she was counting on my strict values forbidding me from destroying her if she were not fighting back.

I increased my power until I knew I overwhelmed Nimue. Sensitive to the forces of energy, I lived her experience. When her lungs heaved in an attempt to bring life-giving breath into her body, mine did as well. When she crumpled to the ground, my knees came to be like water. For a moment, I wondered if I misjudged her power and my own as well.

Then, suddenly, breath returned and I regained my strength.

Nimue stood. With shaking limbs, but emanating relieved triumph, she faced me and shook her fist. "I will be back stronger than ever. When the stars are again aligned as they are tonight, you can expect me to destroy you, old man. Then I will find the sword and use it against you. In the meantime, I curse your descendents to suffer at the hands of their greed and lust for power. They will seek to attain the sword and all it entails only to find death within the confines of their greed. This I do to keep the sword safe from the bloodlines of the Great Merlin."

Like quicksilver, Nimue vibrated her energy and sent herself to another dimension where she would heal and plan her future revenge.

Quivering, I fell to my knees. I knew Nimue relied upon my goodness to let her live once I was able to deplete her energy. What she did not realize was that I pulled my energy from her because my strength was gone. If she held out much longer, I would have been the one disappearing into nothingness in an attempt to save myself.

Feeling slowly returned to my legs, and my heart beat at a more normal rate. I stood, took a deep, cleansing breath of ozone charged air, and contemplated the stone monument. In the future, Nimue would return here to the stone from which she drew her power. The question was, how and when would she return? When she did return, would she have found the Sword Excalibur?

I would have little control over these circumstances. The stars and Nimue's studies would dictate her return for vengeance. All I could do was prepare for the eventual battle.

"Ahh, Nimue, my once lover, I ache for what is lost and yet to be." My voice was low, barely a whisper over the receding storm. "I also place a curse on your descendents. They will search for love never to find fulfillment. This I do to keep others safe from the manipulations of your bloodline."

Unheard by Nimue, my words danced with the breeze to be heard by the spirits of the ages.

If only things were different. If Nimue could have been patient, she would have seen that the new ways and the old could be melded together in harmony. That was all I wanted. Not the total destruction of Avalon. Instead, she demanded use of my powers and abilities, expecting me to destroy the new religion growing outside Avalon. She lied to me and used me for her own selfish purposes. How my soul cried for the waste of time and energy spent on my lover. I hoped she would understand that sometimes the world needed to change.

Weary and disappointed in my failure, I vibrated my energy and disappeared into the inky darkness of the starry night.

Chapter One

T amara suppressed another sneeze and questioned, again, why she was crawling around this dusty, cramped attic. Oh, yes, nostalgia. Making use of her well-deserved vacation time, Tamara found herself drawn to the attic with its hidden secrets and past memories.

Since her mom's morning included a trip into town to sell her herbal concoctions at the local new age store, the morning belonged to Tamara. So far she had spent three hours digging up schoolbooks, trying on old clothes—at least those that still fit—and discovering unread books and clipped newspaper articles.

So far she found nothing of much interest.

Oh, well, it relaxed her. Tamara needed relaxation and time away from her hectic job writing for a small, New York magazine.

Funny, after the noise of the city, Tamara found the quiet of the Vermont countryside almost deafening. Although she would never admit it to her mother, Tamara actually missed home with its ever-present music of songbirds, the rustle of wind in the surrounding trees, and the beauty of nature in full glory.

Tamara gave herself a mental shake and chastised, "Settle down, you're starting to get sappy."

With a glance at the afternoon sun, which shifted slowly across the sky, Tamara decided to end her journey into the past. Stifling a yawn, she stretched her stiff muscles and began to stuff dusty clothing back into old cardboard boxes.

Trying to maneuver the boxes back under the attic window proved more difficult than moving them in the first place. Unfortunately, the largest box didn't want to co-operate. It was stuck. Peering behind the box didn't show any obstruction, so Tamara set her shoulder in place and gave one powerful shove. Her efforts were greeted with a wrenching, ripping sound that made her cringe in dismay. Definitely not a good sound.

"Oh, no. What now?" Hesitantly, she risked a look behind the box and found it stuck on one of the floorboards, a floorboard she neatly managed to crack down the middle. Great, Mom is definitely not going to be happy. Tamara gazed at the broken piece, trying to wish it into repair.

"What's that?" Tamara just barely detected a glint of silver underneath the floor. "Well, well, what have we got here? Maybe this treasure hunt will turn up something interesting after all."

Being careful not to hurt herself on the jagged edges, Tamara reached her hand into the crevice. With some minor shuffling and wriggling, she was able to dislodge the hidden object slightly, but it remained stubbornly stuck in the crevice. Known for possessing her own stubborn streak, Tamara shifted her rear end, braced her shoulder against the wall, and gave one hard yank. Unexpectedly, the object came free and sent her tumbling across the smooth hardwood floor.

"Ouch!" Slowly she sat up, pulled her long auburn hair into the elastic, and made sure all body parts were still attached. The only thing bruised was her ego, and thank goodness no one had seen her rolling around the attic like an uncoordinated geek.

The mysterious object turned out to be a book. Lifting it to her lap, Tamara stared in wonder. She brushed her fingertips over the smooth surface and traced over the gold inlay of an elaborate clasp. Although covered in dust, the ancient looking text was still legible.

Carefully blowing on the cover, Tamara sent a cloud of dust dancing about the attic. Blazing through the octagon shaped window, the afternoon sun reflected off the strangely shimmering dust and shone on the worn leather of the old book.

Through fits of sneezing, Tamara tried to focus her now watery eyes upon the heavy, brocade book that glowed with a light of its own. Heavy in her hands, the book radiated an authentic timeworn appearance.

Worn thin from handling, the cover was made of rough, dark leather embossed with gold flecks that shone dimly in the form of words that Tamara couldn't quite make out. A magnifying glass would be the only way to read those words.

Elaborate and slightly bent, the gold clasp spoke of history and past artistry. Tamara realized the clasp was actually a lock, leading her to believe the book was some kind of journal. But whose? Her investigative juices simmered. She loved a mystery.

Tamara barely noticed the sound of wheels crunching on gravel below, but her mind registered the fact that her mom was home. Great, she couldn't wait to show her the book. Between the two of them, maybe they could figure out who it belonged to and why that person would hide it in the attic, under the floorboards.

Tamara sprinted down the worn, burgundy carpet on the stairs, through the living room, and grabbed the door handle to open it for her mom who was gathering up groceries from the back of her vehicle.

"Dear, there's more here. Would you mind grabbing a couple of bags?"

"Sure, Mom." Tamara laid the book on the oak preacher's bench that graced the front hall and ran to the car to help.

"How did your day go at the bookstore?"

"Fine, I sold everything and have orders for more next week." Diana's arms were full as she turned to her daughter. "How is your first day off going?"

Tamara could hardly keep the excitement from her voice. "It was quiet until I found something. Actually, I'll wait until we get inside and show you."

Diana raised her eyebrows. "Sounds interesting. I've got all I can carry, so I'll see you inside."

Tamara reached into the back seat of the Cherokee her mother drove and grabbed as many bags as she could. With a grunt, she shuffled up the walk to the cabin mumbling about how her mom always spoiled her when she came home, which meant twice as many groceries as were actually needed.

Her good-natured grumbling was interrupted by her mother's unusually high-pitched screech. "Tamara, what have you done?"

Tamara frowned. Now what? She was always doing something wrong.

"Tamara, get in here now."

Tamara tripped up the stairs with grocery bags in hand, and kicked open the screen door only to be greeted with chaos. Congealing on the floor and running toward the cream colored carpet was a slimy mess of broken eggs and chocolate milk.

"What happened?" Tamara looked to her mother, who stood amidst the mess with a flushed face and silvery eyes full of fear.

"Mom, it's all right. I'll help clean up the mess."

Confusion lit Diana's eyes. "I don't care about the mess." Her voice trembled. "The book…"

"The book?" Tamara was perplexed until she saw that her mother pointed to the bench. "Oh, that book. That's what I was telling you about. I found it up in the attic."

Her mother's fists unclenched and fell to her side. "You found it?" Her voice no longer trembled. "How in the devil did you find it? I hid it."

"You hid the book, why? Mom, your face is like chalk. Are you all right?"

Silence greeted her words. Diana stood so still that she resembled one of the stone statues decorating the garden. Her mother's lack of words worried Tamara. "Mom!"

Diana snapped out of her trance and answered her daughter with a sigh. "I'm fine, Tamara, but I think we need to talk. Let's sit down."

Stepping over broken eggs, Tamara settled into the corner of the old couch she loved so much; sinking deep into the welcoming softness was always a comfort to her.

Diana paced the small room.

"Tamara, I know you've never accepted my beliefs or way of life, but there are things at play here that you have no idea about." Fevered footsteps were silent upon the thick, braided rug.

"Okay, Mom. Why don't you explain after we clean up the mess."

"No! This can't wait. You've never listened to me before, and I have always given you freedom to find your own way. Well, now I insist that you listen to what I have to tell you, and then you can do what you will with the information. My responsibility will have been fulfilled."

Not even her father's desertion caused her mother to be as upset as she was now.

"Okay. Go ahead, I'll listen." Maybe one of her mother's visions caused her nervousness, or was it fear?

Diana took a deep breath and spoke. An amazing story of magic, deception, Kings, and magicians, the words fell into the warm air of the cabin, while Tamara sat straighter and listened carefully.

"You see, Tamara, we are descendants of Nimue, Lady of the Lake. Her lineage is a royal one of priestesses who are responsible for the well-being of a place called Avalon."

Suddenly, Tamara experienced the most overwhelming urge to put the book back and pretend she'd never found the hiding spot in the attic. She made a move to stand. "I really think that..."

"Sit down, young woman." Diana's voice rang strong and true in the suddenly small room of the cabin. "Say nothing until I am finished speaking."

Shocked at her mother's commanding tone, Tamara sat back in her chair and listened in silence to the rest of the story. As far as she was concerned that's exactly what it was, a story. In fact while growing up, Tamara became used to a freedom not usually enjoyed by other children. Seeing her mother so out of character was enough to set Tamara back

Diana continued, and as she did her voice grew soft, gentle, and filled with a wistful longing, almost as if reciting from memory. "Avalon was a truly beautiful place with lush growth, bountiful wildlife, and a way of life that survived in harmony with the energies of all living things. Merlin and Nimue were part of this world, and only ones who understood the old ways could actually gain access to the world of Avalon."

Tamara found herself caught up in the story in spite of her disbelief. "I heard somewhere that Merlin and this Nimue person were lovers?"

"Yes, they were lovers and cohorts. The two of them were responsible for the placing of King Arthur upon the throne of Britain. The woman who was Lady of the Lake before Nimue planned the birth of Arthur with all intentions that child would rule once he came of age. Legend has it that Merlin and Nimue were ageless. Their love grew and flourished in the place called Avalon for so long, no one could remember a time they did not exist."

Tamara was entranced. "What happened to them?"

Diana's voice now held a hint of sadness and regret. "Something happened between them, nobody is really sure what, but they began to rebel against each other. The myths tell of the rivalry culminating in an intense battle of power and energy, a battle in which there was no victor." Diana turned to look directly at Tamara, once she was sure her daughter was enthralled, she continued. "The battle was fought centuries ago at a place called Glastonbury."

Not giving Tamara a chance to remark, Diana finished her tale. "They battled for the Sword Excalibur and the right to continue governing Avalon. It is said they swore to return one day when the stars where aligned in the sky the same as they were that evening. Descendants of both Merlin and Nimue would be used as instruments for the final battle to determine who would rule in Avalon."

There was no sound. No birds sang in the trees; no wind rustled the leaves. Tamara felt as if she were in a vacuum, until she regained her sanity. "Mother, you should write that down. It would make a great novel."

"Tamara, I swear upon all that I know, what I tell you is the truth. Please don't dismiss this lightly."

"Mom, I believe that you believe. I'm sure when Granny told you the same story, you took it quite literally when she only meant it to be a bedtime story or something."

"Don't patronize me, Tamara. I am your mother."

"I realize you are my mother, Mother. I just don't see how you expect me to believe that we are descendants of the Lady of the Lake. I always thought she was a fictional character from the time of King Arthur."

"She existed."

"Fine, she existed, but in Avalon? I know that place never existed. It was a mythical place that the people of the time dreamed up. As for Merlin the Magician, well, he was some kind of advisor to King Arthur, but there's no way he possessed the kind of power he is credited with."

"Oh, power coursed through his blood, Nimue's as well. I told you they came to some misunderstanding and ended up battling against each other. Being of equal strength, neither could win the fight." Diana frowned. "It's all in the memoirs."

"Memoirs?"

"The Lady's, of course."

Tamara's gaze flew to the innocent looking book. "Memoirs, I thought it was something like that."

"Yes, it's been passed down through her female descendants until the time was right. Don't you understand, Nimue and Merlin are destined to confront each other again."

Throwing up her hands, Tamara exclaimed, "Now I know you're crazy. Mom, Merlin and Nimue are dead. How can they possibly confront each other?"

"There are ways. Please, Tamara, stop patronizing me."

Tamara sat back and watched her mother's fingertips reverently brush the cover of the book. In an abrupt movement, Diana thrust it into Tamara's lap.

"Tamara, it's time for me to stop mollycoddling you and explain a few facts of life."

Knowing there was no stopping her mother when she got off on this tangent, Tamara sighed deeply and settled herself back for some kind of lecture. Her mind barely registered the sound of her mother's voice as Diana spoke.

"I realize that you've never shown interest in the ways I was raised. You never could understand anything unless it stared you in the face. I think that has a lot to do with your father's influence, but we won't get into that right now."

Thank God for small favors.

Her mother's voice droned on. "It's time you accepted the legacy that has been passed down through the females of our family. It's my fault that you are so disconnected from the natural wonders around you. I felt guilty when your father left, and I allowed you too much freedom. Oh, there are so many things I should have taught you, now I fear it is too late."

"Mom, aren't you being a wee bit melodramatic?"

As Diana spun on her heels, silver hair flew about her face and snapped with electricity. Her blue-gray eyes lit with fervor. When she spoke, her voice crackled with emotion. "There is nothing melodramatic about what is going to happen and the role you are to play."

Tamara was tired. She stood abruptly, letting the book drop to the couch. "Mom. That's enough, I don't believe that our ancestor is Nimue, and I don't believe I have to fulfill some destiny. What I do believe is that when someone is dead they are dead. Now, I'm tired so I'm going to clean up the mess, then have an afternoon nap."

They worked in silence cleaning the mess. With a weary yawn, Tamara made her way toward her bedroom. Before she made it from the room, Diana called, "Don't forget to take this. It's yours now." She stood, like an ancient goddess herself, the book extended in her quivering hand. Tamara hesitated but, noting the look in her mother's eyes, grabbed the book with both hands and retreated to her room.

She tossed and turned, her mind insisted on re-hashing the events of the afternoon. Of course, Tamara didn't believe her mother's tale of lost love and curses, but what about the book? It lay on her dresser, large as life and as authentic looking as any antique she had ever seen. Tamara couldn't bring herself to open the pages and read anything. Three times she rose and stepped, hesitantly, that direction.

Finally, she punched her pillow and mumbled to herself, "I don't need this in my life right now. I'll just leave the book behind and get on with my life." Satisfied with herself for deciding her course of action, Tamara closed her eyes and gave in to sleep.

Chapter Two

Dinner consisted of roast beef, gravy, potatoes, fresh corn on the cob, and homemade biscuits. Tamara was in heaven; she never ate like this unless she was home. She'd made sure to keep the conversation steered toward catching up on local gossip and not a word was spoken about her discovery.

No problem.

Until the telephone rang.

Now she was locked in an argument with her boss.

"Damn it, Rod, I don't want to do the story. I'm on holiday, remember. England yet, jeesh. Where exactly did you say?"

"Glastonbury. Look, Tamara, you're the most qualified, that's why I need you to do this."

"Best qualified, why, because my mother's a quack?" She glanced over her shoulder to make sure her mother was still in the kitchen.

"No, because you're the best damn writer at this magazine, that's why, and show some respect for your mother."

"Puhleese. Rod, I love my mom but I'm the one who grew up with her and put up with her chanting, herbs, and strange visitors coming to see her at all hours of the night. I could tell you stories about how the other kids at school used to tease me about her being a witch. They'd tell me how they saw her flying over the moon on a broomstick, or there was the time they saw her on Halloween drinking the blood of some dead animal. As we got older and my classmates discovered boys, then the tune changed. I'd get asked all the time if my mom could tell a certain boy liked them or if they'd be asked to the dance. You know, stupid stuff like that."

"I'm sorry, Tamara, I know kids can be cruel, but whether you want to admit it or not, your mother has a special ability to see beyond what most people can see. She's learned over the years to block out the skeptics and focus on her beliefs and needs. Why don't you take a good look at your mother? I think you'd be surprised at what you see."

"Rod, I see my mother every weekend. What am I going to see that I haven't already?"

"You look at her through the eyes of a kid. Try looking at her with the eyes of an adult, or at least someone who's reasonably mature."

"I tell you, Rod, if you weren't my boss…"

"Sure, you just don't have the balls. Now, about this assignment?"

"Fine, I'll do it!" Tamara's reply was short and definite. "It's the least I can do for you after all you've done for me, right?"

"Right. You never know, maybe you'll change your mind about a few things while you're over there."

"I highly doubt that. Okay, so fill me in on the story. What do you want? What's the angle?"

"Summer solstice is approaching. I'm sure you understand the importance of this?"

Without breaking stride in her writing, Tamara remarked, "Don't assume anything, I'm not my mother."

"Well, you are a reporter, so do some research."

"Okay, I will. But at least tell me why this year is so special you feel the need to send a writer to cover the story. I mean summer solstice happens every year, right?"

"Yes, but this year is special, something to do with the alignment of the stars that only happens every few hundred years or so. But there is a catch."

"Oh, no, why do I feel as if the other shoe is about to fall?"

"Because it is. Based on the alignment of the stars, and the believed energy of the Glastonbury Tor, there is a certain group of people in England who will be present for certain rituals. This is the angle I want you to cover."

Tamara's voice was tinged with weary irony. "Let me guess. This group of people wouldn't happen to be witches, would they?"

"Well, actually…"

"I knew it. Tell me again how this has nothing to do with my mother and her abilities."

"Tamara, just hear me out. This coven is made up of some very powerful and influential people. We're talking surgeons, judges, even someone in political office. These people have come out of the closet, so to speak, and admitted to practicing witchcraft. Even if it is a recognized religion, it's not what you would call mainstream." Without waiting for a reply, Rod kept speaking. "They're planning some kind of a ceremony at the Tor on the night of summer solstice. I have a feeling this Wicca stuff is getting to be a big thing. In fact, I think it may be something that's been sitting on the back burner for a long time and only now becoming an accepted part of society again."

"You're starting to sound like my mother."

"Look, Tamara, I don't have time to verbally spar with you now. You've got your assignment. You know what my expectations are, so please just do your job." Although mild confrontation was a usual part of their routine, exasperation tinged Rod's final words.

Feeling she'd pushed her boss as far as she could, Tamara acquiesced. "All right, Rod. After all, you are the boss. So when do I leave, and where do I stay? I'll also need the names of any contacts you may have for me once I get there."

"Your flight leaves from Kennedy Airport on Friday. Your ticket will be waiting for you at the counter. You'll be staying at a B&B in

Glastonbury." The sound of shuffling paper crackled over the phone as Rod checked his notes. "It's called The Will-O'-the Wisp. You have a reservation for six nights, which will give you a few days before the solstice, and a day or two after. That should be long enough for you to get the information you need. If not, give me a call and we'll talk, other than that, you're on your own, kiddo."

"Fine. Can you do me a favor and call my roommate, Joanne, to let her know I won't be back for a week or so."

"Oh. Can't you do it yourself?"

"I'll be too busy packing. Thanks, Rod, bye." She chuckled and hung up before her boss could protest. Rod had a crush on Joanne, and his tongue couldn't focus when he spoke to her. It was just Tamara's small way of getting revenge for his sending her off on a wild goose chase.

Her musing was interrupted by the sound of a car pulling up the driveway. Her mother called out from the kitchen. "That will be Mitch. Could you tell him to call and book another time."

"Sure, Mom." Tamara frowned a she made her way to the front veranda. Mitch. If it was the same guy she dated in high school, he left town to find himself, but returned last year and now ran one of the local food markets. What would he want with her mother?

She stood on the porch and waited for the mysterious Mitch to get out of his car. Yep, it was definitely the Mitch from high school. Her curiosity grew.

"Well, if it isn't Tamara."

He possessed a deeper voice than before, and his features now looked more ruggedly mature than boyish. Tamara appreciated his looks and felt a tinge of regret at letting him get away so many years ago.

"I haven't seen you in quite a few years."

"I'd say. Probably about fifteen of them. You're looking good Mitch. How is life treating you?"

"Life is great. I guess you heard that I came back to town and bought Food for Thought?"

Tamara needed no further explanation. Food for Thought held the honor of being the one and only grocery store for as far back as Tamara could remember. Mitch wanted to live up to the store name by importing a variety of organic, upscale foods.

"I heard. I understand you're married and have two kids."

"Yeah. Marie and I got married about five years ago. We actually met in New York on a street corner. We recognized each other from school, started talking, and, shortly thereafter, fell in love.

"School…you don't mean Marie Hodgkins, do you?"

"The one and only."

"Wow. Congratulations. I'm working in New York now, maybe I'll be lucky enough to meet someone on a street corner."

"Still single, eh?"

"Yes, I'm just so busy with work, you know, there's no time left for dating." Her excuse sounded lame, even to her.

"Take a word of advice and don't get so caught up in work that you forget to live."

These words came from someone so career-driven in high school that he wouldn't spend money on so much as a movie. He saved all his money so he could go to the big city and make it big on Wall Street.

"I'll be sure to keep that in mind."

Now the amenities were out of the way, there was a pause of awkwardness until Tamara spoke the question that was burning in her mind. "If you don't mind my asking, why are you here to see my mother?"

Without a twinge of embarrassment, Mitch spoke words that stunned Tamara into subdued silence. "I'm here to get a tarot reading." The world stood still. Choking slightly, Tamara repeated, "Tarot card reading…you're kidding right?"

"No, why would I be kidding? Diana is one of the best readers I've ever been to. She doesn't fortune-tell. She just tells me what the cards say, and I interpret the meaning based on my present situation in life. In fact I'm not the only one of our old crowd who comes to see her once in awhile."

"Jeez, Mitch, do you realize what you're saying? If you remember correctly, you used to tease me just as mercilessly as the rest of the kids about having a 'wicked witch' for a mother."

"Oh, come on, Tamara. We were kids. Kids tease and make fun of what they don't understand. Truth is, I grew up and did some searching of my own. I landed back here in Woodstock, because I find the energy here invigorating. In New York, I started feeling suffocated, drained, and edgy. You know, there are more important things to life than making money or being seen at all the 'in' places."

Butterflies began a dance of uncertainty in the pit of Tamara's stomach. She couldn't believe what she was hearing. She was barely able to get out the words that her mother wouldn't be able to see him today and he should call for another time. With a wave and admonishment to drop by to see Marie and the kids, Mitch was gone.

Profound changes can happen in a split second. Tamara heard that somewhere, but never believed it possible. A large part of her outlook on life was based on opinions expressed by other kids while she was growing up and kids can be so unintentionally cruel. Now, one of her staunchest tormentors showed up to see her mother for a reading. The world suddenly flipped upside down, taking Tamara and her beliefs along for the ride. Deep in the seat of her soul, a realization began that other people no longer held the prejudices upon which her own morals and beliefs rested. So why was she hanging on to them? The question was, if she didn't have those morals or standards to believe in, what did she have? Who was she? Panic was not far from lodging itself in her throat. She was saved only by the intervention of her mother.

"Tamara, are you all right? You look a little pale."

"No, no, I'm fine." She choked the words out. Her mother only looked at her with a frown of disbelief.

"Hmmm. Well, have some tea with dessert. You'll feel better."

Diana sat on the couch across from Tamara, who slumped down in her favorite chair.

"Did Mitch tell you why he was here?" Although the words were deceptively simple, Diana's voice was tinted with her awareness of Tamara's discomfort.

"Yes, he told me." The damn burst. "What is going on here? I leave town and all of a sudden, my old classmates are coming to you for readings. Don't you know what they used to say about you in school?"

"Sure I do, but they were kids. Now that they're adults, they've come to realize I'm not so crazy after all."

"I suppose you're saying that because I don't believe, I haven't matured yet?"

"No. I'm saying that everybody has to find their own way and what works for them. Why do you think there are so many religions in the world? It's because people are different. They need something different to fulfill them. The truth is that everybody needs something. It just may not be the same thing that would satisfy his, or her, neighbor. In any religion, you will find the central theme is, or should be, compassion and love. The way this is put across to the followers will be through history or stories and legends. Depending on the culture, these stories will be of varying adventures, or people, or prophets, but it will be based on what works in that culture, in that civilization to get the point across."

Out of breath from the long speech, Diana sighed deeply and then continued. "Tamara, you're obviously still unsure of who you are and your place in the world, so you're still searching. I promise you that there is a reason for you being here, just as there is for everyone. When the door is presented for you, you will walk through into a world that suddenly seems like home." Diana's face reflected a smile of sympathy and understanding. She brushed her hand over Tamara's cheek. "Now, enough philosophy for the day, tell me all about your new assignment."

Shaking off the uncertainty of her encounter with Mitch, Tamara focused on her new assignment. "You'll love it. It deals with witches, summer solstice, stars in the sky. All the kinds of stuff you're into."

'That "stuff,' as you say, is very powerful and important. What exactly are you supposed to be doing?"

"It seems that at summer solstice the stars will be aligned in a way they haven't been in centuries. A powerful, and influential, coven of witches has received permission to hold some kind of ceremony at the Tor. Since this is so unusual, Rod wants me to find out why it's being allowed. Maybe even talk one or two of the witches into an interview."

The look on her mother's face stopped her from explaining any further. "What, Mom? You look strange."

"Listen to yourself, Tamara. The stars will be aligned a certain way, the Glastonbury Tor, special ceremony. Doesn't any of this sound familiar to you?"

"Oh, come on, it's just coincidence, that's all." Tamara's voice quivered with slight uncertainty.

"Some coincidence, I'd say. Damn, Tamara, why do you have to be so stubborn?"

"Probably because I take after my mother."

"Flattery won't work with me, young lady."

Diana rose.

Tamara noticed how the worn jeans and denim shirt made her mom look so young and slender. Sometimes, Tamara wished she'd inherited her mother's fair looks and tall slender figure, rather than the auburn hair and more full figure she was born with.

"Come on daughter of mine, time for dessert and tea. I think it's going to be an early night for both of us."

Tamara followed and even managed to make some polite conversation for the rest of the evening, but under the surface her mind raced and emotions bubbled. Her carefully planned life suddenly plunged her into the unknown.

Chapter Three

Silver moonlight gleamed off the shimmering water and bathed the night in a luminous cocoon. Blanketed in the silence of the night, there was a sense of calm and peace.

The water rippled. Tamara felt her heart beat with impending fate. A figure rose, slowly, emerging from the life sustaining water of Mother Earth.

Rivulets of mercury-like liquid ran down the naked splendor of the male form. Tamara knew that she was about to face her destiny, her soul mate.

He stood like a still life portrait, a creation of the Moon Goddess herself. Outlined behind his masculine figure, a temple of Greek-like characteristics rose atop a sloping hill. Its stone columns graced the earth and arced to the heavens above.

Tamara's eyes roamed the length of hard masculine body. Her eyes came to his face and in that moment, she became overwhelmed with the fullness of emotions, her heart jumped to her throat, and her emotions stirred in ways she never could have imagined.

She was complete, and he was the reason. Dear God, could

there ever be such strength, such sureness, such wonder? With an aching need to feel his flesh, she reached out her hand.

Closer. Closer. Ever closer. Just as her shaking hand touched the cool water on his skin, the man disappeared.

"No! Please don't leave me. I've just found you." With a sob, Tamara fell to her knees, and tried to soothe the empty ache inside. As her first tear slipped into the dark water, Tamara jolted awake. Tears she cried in her dream rolled down her face.

"Damn. Not again." With a quick snap of frustration, Tamara threw back the covers and sat up. Intruding on her sleep more than once, that same dream wrenched her emotions more each time. Was that what love was like? This hodgepodge of conflicting emotions, each one trying to overtake the other.

A glance to her bedside clock showed her it was after 7:00 am, no sense in trying to get back to sleep.

Her head throbbed with the restlessness of her sleep. Having your whole life turned upside down could do that to a person, she supposed. How she longed to get in her car and leave yesterday, and all its events, behind.

Why couldn't she? Her flight wasn't until tomorrow afternoon. She could pack in the morning and then make the five-hour drive from Woodstock to New York in plenty of time. That left her all day today to do whatever she wanted.

Feeling better already, Tamara jumped from bed, threw on a pair of jeans, her favorite green T-shirt, and sneakers. She pulled a brush through her hair, splashed water on her face, and sprinted down the stairs.

Sounds of dishes rattling from the kitchen let her know Diana was up. Not ready for a confrontation, Tamara hollered on her way out the front door. "Mom, I'm going for a drive. Don't expect me back for awhile."

"But, dear, what about breakfast?" Since Tamara was half way down the front stairs, she barely heard the question as it drifted out the window.

"It's okay, Mom, I'll stop for something. See ya." Tamara climbed into her classic, baby blue Mustang, revved the engine, and tore out of the driveway. She winced and knew she'd be raking gravel when she got home. She didn't care.

Rolling hills of lush green melded with spiked mountains and craggy rock against the hazy blue of the horizon. Tamara pushed her car to the limit. She loved the exhilaration and freedom of racing down the highway, watching the scenery blur into a single smudge of color.

Her speed of travel was a reflection of the state of Tamara's mind; the last twenty-four hours caused her to question a lot in life. This assignment placed her smack in the middle of a way of life she grew up with and tried to avoid. Not that Tamara didn't love her mother, she just harbored some serious doubts as to her sanity. Witches, potions, earth energy, guardian angels, herbs, and rituals, the list went on. Now she found out her childhood friend was coming to her mom for tarot card readings.

Tamara could find no fault in her upbringing; she hadn't suffered in any way. In fact, her mother always went out of her way to allow Tamara to explore all beliefs and religions. When she was nine years old, Tamara insisted on attending the local Sunday school. It was the popular Sunday morning activity, and she didn't want to be left out.

Through the years of attending church on Sunday, she also read about other religions, without telling her minister of course. Instead of after school activities, she would go to the library and study Buddhism, Hinduism, Catholicism, basically anything she could use to convince her mother to quit the way of Wicca she followed so intently.

The result was a mind so full of facts and beliefs, judgments and denials she finally gave up trying to find something she could believe in. She quit her local church and became an agnostic. She also gave up trying to sway her mother from her rituals and beliefs.

Tired of the past, Tamara focused on the emerald green lushness of countryside and the low-lying mountains. Pangs of homesickness struck her, and she realized that New York could never take the place of home.

Her move to New York took serious thought, but Woodstock held nowhere for her to advance. Her job at the local paper held her for a while, but the need for independence grew, so had the need to break free from her upbringing. As long as she was in Woodstock, she would be referred to as the daughter of the local witch.

She contacted a friend of her mom's, who ran a magazine in the city, moved to the city, and came home to visit only on weekends. She wanted to make something of herself, become the best at what she did, and thereby win the acceptance of other people.

So far, she'd managed to fulfill her ambitions. Her breaking story came in the form of the tactics of a network religious show pastor. The self-proclaimed pastor fleeced his followers with promises of salvation, and took their money to spend on his own sinful pursuits. Exposing his deceit won Tamara the respect of her colleagues.

Even with her fame, Tamara still experienced an emptiness inside that was obviously not going to be filled by her career. She knew she was in the middle of her own search. She just hoped she wasn't as gullible as the poor, misguided people taken in by promises of redemption and forgiveness.

She sighed with conflicting emotions. Mom's driveway was just up ahead, but Tamara's mind still spun with questions.

Wheeling into the driveway, she soaked in the sight of the field of brilliant hued wildflowers that greeted her. Her mother lived in the middle of the wildness of untouched forest, and wouldn't change it for the world. Tamara appreciated the sense of natural peace. Birds twittered in wild abandon about bird feeders, glimpses of colored wings flashed in the sun as they chased each other about, sweeping and darting with not a care in the world.

In the middle of all this sat a roughly hewn log cabin awash in the rays of the sun. Wrapped around the small house was a veranda, obviously meant for sitting on, with its rocking chairs and throw cushions. Plants and herbs of indeterminate origins grew lushly in planters on the railing and hung from the overhang.

Tamara soaked in the energy. Yes, even she would admit there was a certain sense that filled a person with an indescribable feeling of belonging. Her mother claimed the Earth was a living creature that needed love and nurturing, just as people. Tamara scoffed at her, most of the time.

"Tamara, dear, are you going to sit in the car all day, or would you like to come in for some lunch?" Her mother's mellow voice entered her reverie.

Delighted to be home, and loving her mother, Tamara jumped from the car and engulfed her in a hug.

"Sorry I'm such a bitch. I just needed to clear my head some."

"Don't worry, I know you're confused. I just wish I could help somehow."

"You can help. How about a cup of tea? Plain, regular tea, none of the fancy herb stuff."

While her mother clattered about the kitchen, Tamara plopped down into her favorite chair. Thick and soft, it reflected a security she never felt growing up. Her mother provided her with a stable home and a lot of love and support, just not a father. As far as Tamara was concerned, her father deserted them because of what he considered the strange ways of her mother.

Somewhere, deep inside, Tamara knew she held that against her mother, whether she wanted to or not.

The day passed quickly, filled with gardening and polite conversation. Neither Tamara nor her mother spoke of the book, Mitch's visit, or Tamara's assignment.

Early morning sun glinted off the busy bird feeders and a warm breeze signaled the start of another hot summer day. "Okay, Mom, I'm ready to go." Tamara slugged her suitcase into the trunk of her car and wondered if she could have gotten away with fewer clothes. Probably not.

Her mom appeared on the front veranda. "I think you're forgetting something."

"No." Tamara took a quick inventory of her car. "I have everything." She turned to face her mother, and her heart sank when she saw what was being held out to her. Accusing and conspicuous, the book glowed with subdued sunlight bouncing off its worn cover.

"You have to take the book and promise me you'll take the time to read it before summer solstice."

"Mom, come on, this is ridiculous."

"Tamara, I expect you to take the book and read it." Before Tamara could protest, her mom spoke. "I'm not asking you. I'm telling you. I have never demanded anything of you, so you owe me, and I'm collecting."

A heartbeat passed, then another. The birds suddenly stopped fluttering and sat in the trees expectantly. Tamara saw a fog rise before her and engulf the cabin and her mother in a fine mist. For a moment, she felt as if she were alone in the world and all else ceased to exist. The pulse of her heart that sent blood through her body was all that reassured her she still lived.

Panic seized her insides, along with the certainty that her world was rapidly changing and spiraling out of her control. In the midst of the swirling mist, Tamara could see only the book as it shone with an otherworldly glow. Unaware of even moving, Tamara reached out to grasp the book and hold it firmly in her hands.

A split second later, the mist was gone and the world was normal. Tamara was not sure what happened; the book was in her hand and she heard herself promise to read it as soon as possible.

In an unexpected gesture, Diana reached out and wrapped her arms around Tamara in a fierce hug. Tamara found herself relaxing and enjoying the scent of her mother's lemon shampoo and lavender skin cream. Moments like this made Tamara realize how much she loved her mother, despite their differences. Maybe, just maybe, she could be more understanding to her mother's way of doing things.

Not that they argued or anything, but Tamara was willing to admit that she was deliberately provoking and close-minded.

"Mom, I love you, but I've got to go or I'll miss my flight."

"I know, dear. I just have this strange premonition that when you return home you won't be the same person who left. I'm just saying good-bye."

Oh, no! Here Tamara thought they were doing so well.

"I'm only going for a week. I'll come home the same logical, irritating daughter who left. I promise."

"Haven't I raised you better than to make promises you can't keep. Go. I'll make sure to say a prayer for you."

It was definitely time to go. Tamara got into her beloved Mustang, revved the engine, waved to her mom, and ventured out on her cross-country journey to the New York airport.

Nimue's words sat on the seat beside her all the way. It taunted and tantalized her. Damn her mother for making her promise to read it. Having no idea how the words had been wrested from her mouth, Tamara knew that she would keep her word.

As the city became visible on the horizon Tamara's insides tightened ever so slightly. That was normal, the pace of the city was much quicker and more cutthroat; a person needed to prepare for the shock. For the first time, Tamara doubted she actually wanted to live in the city.

Par for the course. These last few days seemed to have caused her to question everything in her life. Oh, well, she her job waited, and a book beckoned. Hopefully, she'd make it through the next week with a little of herself in tact.

Chapter Four

Gavin Calder swore that Glastonbury air was better than any. He inhaled deeply and enjoyed the mingling of nearby pasture and hay with the cinnamon scents drifting from the bakery across the street. Stepping back from the bookstore window, his eyes sparked with mischief as he asked for reassurance, again, from the bespectacled shopkeeper. "You are absolutely, positively, sure that this book is authentic? I mean there's no doubt in your mind, whatsoever?"

"Gavin, I can't be makin' myself any more clear than the words I've already spoken. The book is older than these wrinkles on my face."

"I knew it."

"Well, I'm glad yer so smart. Now could you leave me to go about my business. An old man needs to make a livin', you know."

"Right. You probably have more money hidden away in these musty old books of yours than most people will ever earn." Gavin teased his old friend and mentor.

"And pigs can fly," snorted the shopkeeper. "Tell me, Gavin, I didn't get to read much, but what I did see made my blood tingle. Are you sure you couldn't be leavin' the book with me so I could peruse it further?"

"Mac, as much as I love and trust you, there's no way these memoirs leave my hands until I have figured out exactly what it means." The sound of a bell alerted the two men to a customer. "Now, I can see you need to go. If you don't mind, I'll hang around a few minutes and check out some of your latest stock."

"Yeah, yeah, whatever." Mac waved his hand in dismissal and ambled over to his latest conquest.

Gavin watched Mac fondly. Their friendship spanned many years. Mac rescued Gavin from a street fight he had the misfortune to wander into when he was only a young teenager. Just as one of the boys was about to bop Gavin for daring to wander into the middle of their brawl, Mac tore out of his small bookshop and threatened physical injury to any who dared hurt the innocent lad.

Mac brought the young boy into his shop and proceeded to berate him for not being more careful. "Couldn't you see there was a fight in progress, laddie?"

At that moment, a friendship formed. Mac introduced Gavin to the wonder of books, a whole world that Gavin never imagined he would enjoy. He found he loved the feel of the leather bound first editions, the smell of musty pages, and the energy that leapt off the pages and inundated him with history and nostalgia. The bond of friendship that cemented that afternoon only strengthened over the years.

While Mac's customer browsed the rickety, dusty bookshelves, Mac continued the conversation. "Gavin, my boy, how are your parents faring? With your pa retiring, it must be a whole new way of life for them."

"Yes, well, let's just say the last month has been a period of adjustment for Mom. She's finding a new vein of patience she never knew she possessed. She's used to doing her own thing without him, and Dad's following her around like a puppy dog looking for someone to entertain."

Gavin chuckled at the thought of how his mother complained that her life no longer belonged to her. Something as simple as shopping became an echo of never ending questions and suggestions. Gavin reassured his mom that things would settle down. He suggested trying to find Dad a hobby to keep him busy so he'd quit breathing down her neck.

Mac's voice broke into Gavin's reverie. "They'll settle into a routine. They love each other, you know."

"Oh, I know. I've never seen two people of their age act quite the way they do, kissing and hugging. They can't keep their hands off each other."

"If that's your worst complaint, I feel no sympathy for you. You'd be lucky to find love like that."

"I know. I'm not complaining."

A shadow fell across the counter. It seemed the customer made up his mind what book to buy. While Mac was dealing with the sale, Gavin glanced around the store that housed so many childhood memories. Nothing much changed over the years. Gavin smiled as he glanced around the small store with three rickety steps from front door down to the first shelf of books. From there on, shelf upon shelf of books lined the store. Old ones mainly, with a few newer ones here and there. Mac's latest project involved trying to draw in a younger crowd. The whole ambience of the store was of peace, a place where nothing could go wrong. Rather like the fantasy worlds of Avalon and Lyonesse Gavin used to read about when he was younger.

A tingling bell signaled the customer's departure. Mac was quick to return to Gavin and begin questioning. "I'm still waitin' for you to tell me where you got that book from. It's a strange one."

"To tell you the truth, I found it in our attic a couple of weeks ago. When Dad retired, he got on this cleaning binge, probably from boredom. Anyway, he ended up talking Mom and me into going through both the garage and the attic and throwing out anything we not used in over five years. Let me tell you, there was a lot of stuff. I found this book in an old trunk. Mom and Dad said they had no idea where it came from. They had no interest in it, so I started reading it myself." Gavin hesitated, unsure of how much to reveal to his friend.

"Well, don't stop now, lad. Tell me more."

"No, I need to try and authenticate some of what it says. If I just blurt it out with nothing to back it up, you'll think I'm crazy."

Mac snorted, "I already do, that's beside the point."

"You can talk like that now, but if it turns out I'm a descendant of Merlin the Magician, you'd show me some respect."

"Merlin?"

"Yes. It seems there was some kind of battle with a woman he loved or something. Anyway, he's supposedly an ancestor of mine."

Instead of the teasing he was expecting from Mac, Gavin watched his friend's face turn serious. A sensation of uncertainty crept up from his toes to his throat.

"Mac?"

"Quiet, let me think." Mac stood in pensive silence for a moment and then rushed over to a bookshelf. Mumbling to himself, he rummaged around and pulled forth an old edition of some indiscriminate heritage. Flipping through the pages, he apparently found what he was looking for as he began to read. The solemn tone of his voice beckoned Gavin to lean closer and listen intently.

Upon the hill they stand, two timeless forms, they wage a fight
Below lies the Well of Life, doorway to the forbidden world
The Priestess cries into the night, I fight for my world
The Magician echoes across the hills, I fight for what's right
Once true love they held; now only hate casts Dark in Light
No victor, No glory, Retreat is the cry of the night
Stars of the Heaven shine brightly into the distance
Fading away, they leave only lonely existence
Silence reigns 'til stars shine again across the plain
Legend tells across passages of time
The Priestess, the Magician will return
All is written in a book of rhyme
This book of life Merlin passes to his own blood kin
While his Lady rests to resume her battle for Avalon.

Mac closed the book and sat in silence allowing Gavin time to digest the words. It only took a moment for Gavin to start asking questions. "So what exactly does all that mean?"

"It means, my boy, that the mighty Merlin and his Lady of the Lake, Nimue, came to a disagreement and duked it out on some hill. Neither won, but they vowed to return when the stars were lined up the same as that night. According to the poem and legend, they wrote it all down in some books."

Gavin was stunned. "You mean this could be the book? Come on, I was only kidding about being a descendant of Merlin's. I thought this was an authentic antique, but I also figured it was just a fairytale." Gavin studied his friend. "You're just pulling my leg. The book is worth something but only because of its age, not for any other reason."

Mac still sat in silence and stared at Gavin as if waiting for him to weed his way through his own thoughts.

"Mac, tell me you're kidding. There's no proof that Merlin ever existed. I was raised to be open-minded, and I've heard plenty of stories of Avalon and Lyonesse for that matter, but don't try to tell me they existed."

"I'm not tellin' you anything." Mac sat back and crossed his arms.

Gavin picked up the book and looked at it with new reverence. "Maybe I'd better read some more."

"Yeah, and while you do that I need to think. I have this niggling in the cobwebs of my brain, and I'm not sure what it means. Hopefully, my brain will be clear next time I see you.

"I still don't believe it's any more than a story, but we'll see." Subdued, Gavin stood and stretched his lithe body. "Time to go. If I'm not home for dinner, Mom will have a fit."

"Don't you think it's time you got your own place again?"

About seven years ago Gavin moved to the big city of Bristol and began his own detective agency. Although fully trained as a police officer, he wanted some freedoms that wearing a badge wouldn't provide. So, he took a course that earned him his detective license and trained for a black belt in martial arts.

Never a big fan of city living, he stayed long enough to build a solid reputation and find trustworthy people to work for him. He then moved home to Glastonbury. For the moment, he was running his detective agency long distance. Luckily, his manager could be trusted with just about anything. Besides, there was only just over an hour between Glastonbury and Bristol. He made the trip a couple of times a week. If he needed to stay for a day or two, any of the local hotels were more than adequate to suit his needs.

"I've kind of been spoiled living at the manor, but now Dad's retired, I've put the word out. Something'll turn up soon."

Mac waved at his friend and turned to greet his next customer, another tourist wandering in off the street looking for some local color.

"Can I 'elp you?"

Gavin laughed at his friend. Born in America, Mac enjoyed putting on the thick, heavy cockney accent for tourists.

"The tourists expect it. I'd hate to disappoint them."

As usual, dinner with his parents was an interesting affair. His father was a perpetual tease and his mother enjoyed playing along. It was a ritual, a testament to the ease of the love they shared.

"So, Mom, are you sure you can't tell me anything about this book?"

"Why are you asking her? What about your old Dad? Maybe I know something?"

"He asked me, Ruddy, because he knows who has the brains in the family."

"What? You've got the brains and the beauty. There's got to be something unfair in that."

"All's fair in love, my dear."

"Ahhh, Caroline, you wound me deeply." He covered his heart with his hand and feigned pain, which only earned him a slap on the shoulder.

"You'll heal quickly enough when you see the dessert."

Gavin and his dad laughed and helped clear the table. Along with dessert, makings for tea were brought to the dining table and placed on the cream-colored lace cloth. With a flourish, Gavin's mom lifted the lid of the round cake tray.

"Chocolate truffle cheesecake." Gavin moaned in appreciation. "You're going to spoil me so I won't want to leave home, even if I find the perfect place."

"Well, if you also happened to find the perfect wife and have some children, I wouldn't mind you moving out at all. I just hate the thought of you out there all on your own."

"Caroline, leave the lad alone. You'll spoil him worse than you already have."

"Fine, fine. I'll just sit here like a good little woman and keep my mouth shut," she replied while gracefully slicing the creamy cheesecake.

"That'll be the day."

Gavin was getting dizzy with the ongoing repartee, so he attempted to steer the conversation back to the book. "Would you two quit fooling around and tell me what you know?" He punctuated his question with his first bite into the cheesecake and moaned aloud at the rich flavor of chocolate.

"Why, Caroline, I do believe our number one son is growing impatient with your mindless chatter."

"My mindless chatter?"

In an attempt to get order at the dinner table, Gavin tapped his knife against his water glass. The ringing sound produced the desired effect, and both parents quietened.

"Great, now that I have your attention, what can you tell me about the book?" He forked another mouthful of creamy chocolate into his mouth and almost missed the look that passed between his parents. Suspicion aroused, Gavin questioned, "You know more than you're telling me. I can see it in your faces. What's up?"

His parents exchanged another look and seemed to come to a mutual agreement. Placing his blue china teacup on the table, his father heaved a sigh and began to talk. "These are only legends and talk passed from generation to generation you understand, so you mustn't believe all that I say. I'm not even sure what I believe myself."

Impatient, Gavin sighed in frustration. "Stop beating around the bush. I'm growing old sitting here."

"Well, we both know who you take after with your lack of patience."

"Dad."

"Okay, okay, I'm talking. As you know the journal, or book, is supposed to be Merlin's, and yes, we are supposedly descendants of the Great Magician. Ancient legends tell of some kind of misunderstanding between Merlin and his love, the Lady of the Lake.

"What kind of misunderstanding?" Gavin questioned, only to have his father wave his hand for silence.

"I'm not quite sure what this disagreement involved, but some stories talk of the Sword Excalibur and the land of Avalon. The sword, as you know, was given to Arthur in order to assure his acceptance amongst the knights of Britain. Well, it has always been understood that the Lady Nimue gave the sword willingly to Arthur with the help of Merlin. Others would say that the sword was stolen by Merlin from Nimue and given to Arthur without permission from the Priestess of Avalon."

"The Priestess of Avalon meaning Nimue?" Gavin was confused with all the titles being bandied about.

His mom clarified. "Yes, Nimue was the Lady of the Lake, which is a title given to the priestess who rules in the land of Avalon. Of course, there were many priestesses with varying degrees of abilities and duties, but Nimue was the head priestess at that time."

"Yes, quite." His dad cleared his throat, obviously uncomfortable with talk of priestesses and mystical lands. "It seems there is more to the story than we are able to find out through Merlin's writings."

"You mean you've read it already?"

"Yes, both your mother and I have read the book." That same uncomfortable look passed between his parents.

Gavin eyes narrowed and he took a deep, calming breath. "You told me you'd never seen the book before."

"We only wanted to protect you, Gavin. Besides, we only get Merlin's side of the story, an incomplete one at that. He only knows what transpired, he never knew how, or why Nimue turned against him. However, the battle that ensued was one that left scars upon the land and on the energies of history. On a dark, stormy night…"

"Oh, come on Dad, and a shot rang out, and the maid screamed. Now you sound like you're telling some ghost story to kids on Halloween."

"Sorry, but it was on a dark stormy night. How else do you want me to say it? Anyway, the two of them fought on a hilltop at the Glastonbury Tor, which, by the way, is supposedly the doorway to Avalon. Neither won the battle, but each swore to return when the stars where aligned in the heavens in the proper manner." His dad hesitated and cast a look for help.

"It's all right, dear, I can take it from here." Her voice was soft and gentle. "Do you remember a few years ago when a skeleton was found at the site of the Tor?"

Gavin considered for a moment. "Yes, barely. It was said that the body and head were found separate. Supposedly someone beheaded the poor chap."

"Yes, well, that poor chap was your great-great grandfather. He also read the book, and he experienced the misfortune of being alive when the stars were aligned in the heavens properly. No one is sure what really happened, but he got caught in the middle of strange events and, somehow, ended up dead at the Tor."

"But how do you know for sure it was him? The identity of the skeleton was never made public."

"When your great-great grandfather disappeared, no one ever knew what happened to him, until the skeleton was found, along with the family ring he always wore on his finger. The identity was kept quiet only through a large payment to the government by your great-grandfather. He knew that the speculation and publicity would tear the family apart. All those nosy people poking around in our family history, asking questions, invading our privacy."

"All right, so why all the secrecy now? What are you trying to hide from me?"

His dad interceded in the conversation and continued the story. "This year at summer solstice, the stars will be in the sky as they were at the time of the battle and the time of great-grandfather's death. We were avoiding the whole situation, but we know you and your curiosity. We knew you couldn't leave this whole thing alone. I guess we're just trying to protect you."

"Protect me, from what? Neither one of you have any idea what happened to great-great grandfather. I can't believe it's connected to anything that happened centuries ago. To think there's a connection is ridiculous. Don't you see that?"

His mom spoke up, her voice sharp and demanding, a side of his mother Gavin rarely saw. "Gavin, we have always raised you to know that there is more to the world than we can see in front of us. We have given you knowledge of different religions, beliefs, and cultures to help you be open minded and non-judgmental, so don't start closing your mind now, not when you need to be receptive and accepting."

His father interjected his objections into the conversation. "Listen, Gavin, we only have one side of the story in Merlin's memoirs. There's more going on than we know about and that's what makes it dangerous for you. Please, do us all a favor. Put the book away and pretend it never existed."

"If you two are so dead set against this book, why haven't you thrown it out or burned it or something? I mean, that way I never would have seen it."

His words evoked an eerie reaction. All color drained from both their faces, leaving them pasty white.

When his mom spoke, her voice was merely a whisper. "We tried. We tried to throw it away. We tried to burn it, but every time we think it's gone it shows up in our attic. That is why we want you to just leave things as they are. We have no idea what we are up against. We don't want to know. As long as we ignore it, the summer solstice can come and go. The next time the stars are aligned in the sky, we won't even be alive and the worry can become someone else's. Please tell me you'll let things lie as they are and not get involved."

Gavin didn't know what to say. His parents were obviously upset by this whole book thing, but couldn't they see how ridiculous it sounded? He looked into their faces. His father's features showed handsome with a square-jaw and weathered skin, while his mother's, once sleek, now showed maturity with a soft roundness of features. His heart filled with love. They were only worried because they loved him.

"Mom, I can't just forget about it." He reached out, put his arm around her shoulder and gave a squeeze. "Think about what I do for a living. I investigate. It's in my nature." He shrugged. "It's who I am... How can you ask me to ignore what could possibly be the biggest mystery in my lifetime, not to mention lifetimes before me?"

"The lad's right, Caroline."

"How can you say that, when all he'll do is put himself in danger?"

"Think, Caroline. You believe in fate or destiny. How many times have we tried to rid ourselves of that damned book, but it keeps returning? There is obviously more going on here than we can comprehend. Powers have been put into play, and forces are at work that we have no control over. We no longer know the old ways, none of our family has for a long time, but these ways are stronger than what we can deal with. We've always encouraged Gavin to follow his feelings and search for himself, can we do any different now?"

"Curse you for making sense. I knew it would come to this. You never understood my fear of the inevitable, and that's because you don't know the whole truth." She hesitated. "You know my ancestors were of the old ways, what you don't know is that I still retain a weakened ability to see things. Oh, sure, it only comes in flashes now and then, but I see enough to know that trouble lies ahead. What I can't see is the final outcome." Her hands were shaking as she sat in her chair and drew her hands over her face. "No matter how hard I focus, this end is denied to me." Pleading eyes turned to Gavin and his father. "That is why I worry so much."

Unsure how to deal with this side of his mother, Gavin could only question, "Mom, are you all right?"

"I'll be fine, just promise me you'll be careful."

"There's no need to worry. I'll be careful as always, besides I still think you're blowing this book thing out of proportion. Some roving bandit or something probably killed our ancestor. I'm sure there is no relation with the stars in the sky or the curse."

"That would be your first mistake. Never assume anything, and never believe all you see or hear. There is something going on and you're right smack in the middle of the danger. Promise me you'll be careful."

"Of course, I promise." The distant bell of the telephone ringing interrupted the tension that grew steadily in the dining room.

"I'll get it." Gavin was hasty to offer. Picking up the telephone, he recognized the voice of Mac greeting him. "Gee, Mac, did you miss me that much? I just left you a few hours ago."

"Listen, Gavin, can you come here tomorrow? I found something I need you to see."

Gavin frowned at Mac's tone. He sounded worried and that emotion was usually foreign to his friend. "Sure, I'll come over in the early afternoon sometime."

"Great, see you then." Mac hung up without any of the banter in which he and Gavin usually engaged.

Feeling drained from the confusion of the day, Gavin bid his parents goodnight and made his way to his suite of rooms.

His father's inheritance included the ancient stone castle, a family heirloom passed through four generations. Consequently, their home was rather large, and Gavin's wing consisted of a sitting room, bathroom, and a large bedroom.

Gavin stretched his large, muscular frame on his bed, crossed his arms behind his head, and contemplated the new information gathered that evening. He found it all so confusing and unreal. To think that his great-great-grandfather was killed because of some battle for power between Merlin and Nimue.

His gaze wandered around the room that used to be his great-great grandfather's, but was now his. A tingling sense of awareness mingled with feelings of apprehension. A gentle light fell across the darkened windowsill, spilled onto the floor and drew Gavin's gaze. The hue of bluish-white light grew and pulsated until it became a form not unlike a person. Weaving across the burgundy Aubusson carpet, the form drifted to the nightstand to illuminate the finely carved, marble topped, mahogany table. Most importantly, it illuminated the book that lay there, unopened.

Gavin was stunned. His hand was no more that a foot from the table and strange light. He moved ever so slowly, lifted his arm, and reached out to touch the light. As if on cue the light flickered and disappeared, leaving Gavin's room lit only by the bedside lamp.

A moment of disbelief froze Gavin, and then an awareness of the message of the light formed in his mind. Of course. He needed to read the ancient text. The question answered itself before even being spoken or thought. Merlin's memoirs would be read. Now.

He propped himself up with his pillows, reached out his hand, and touched the worn leather cover. Encompassing warmth welled up his arm from the pages of time. Was he really an ancestor of Merlin? His parents believed. How could they know for sure? There was no positive record of Merlin or what happened to him after he left King Arthur's court. Maybe, just maybe, the book would hold the answers.

Gavin untied the cover ribbon and, hesitantly, opened the book. Written in a flowing script, and faded in some spots more than others, words filled page after page. Dark black ink seemed to have weathered well over the ravages of time. With a grunt, Gavin settled himself into a comfortable position and began to read Merlin's words.

Chapter Five

Here I sit, Merlin the Magician. A disillusioned old man putting his life to page and word. It is imperative I do this because there is much my family who comes after me must know. Stories of love, deception, cruelty, and misplaced beliefs that placed my world and all I fought for into jeopardy. I suppose I shall begin at the beginning and take you from there.

The first time I saw Nimue, I was but a child, wild and untamed in the mysterious country of Avalon. Innocent and careless, I did not understand that the world I lived in occupied a different realm than other worlds. Knowledge of forces that would threaten me and all I love, also eluded the understanding of my innocent youth.

Being young and bearing few responsibilities, I used to wander the hills pretending to be a stag, stamping and snorting at the delicate does. The countryside surrounding me was beautiful, alive with animal forms, effusions of colorful flowers and a sun that shone intensely upon the life below.

One fine summer day, I came upon a never before seen path. Had I but known the life path it would set me on, I may have turned back and resumed my innocent play. Alas, I did not.

This is how I came upon Nimue.

Setting my feet upon the path and following the twists and curves, I eventually found myself in the middle of a dense forest. Above me, the sun was barely able to break through the branches and leaves, save for a single, lonely ray that illuminated to my eyes an unexpected sight.

Standing in the clearing was a young girl so beautiful that my breath left my chest with difficulty. Ethereal and glowing, it seemed that a single ray of sunlight found its way there to purposely bask in her beauty. A sound reached my ears, the sweet sound of the young girl's voice as she hummed an unfamiliar tune. I was drawn to her voice, to her presence; I was not the only one.

Before the vision of beauty, stood a slender fawn and her golden colored mother. Alive with the fluttering of birds' wings, the trees also seemed drawn to the voice that rang in the deepest darkness of the pungent forest.

Sensing my presence, the vision turned to me and spoke. "I have been waiting for you." Enhanced by the sweetness of her voice, the surrounding air shimmered.

I quivered and this emotion crept into my reply. "You must be mistaken, how could you know of me?"

A secret smile lit up a face that already glowed with light and beauty. "Ahh, there are ways for ones such as myself. I have seen you in my mind. You, as well, have ways that you will begin to understand shortly."

Uncertain as to her meaning, I blurted out the only question I cared about at that moment. "How are you named?"

"I am Nimue."

I answered her unspoken question. At the time I did not wonder how I sensed her words before she spoke. "I am Emrys, although my mother says that one day I will have a new name."

A far off voice intruded on our world and brought Nimue to attention. "I must go." She spoke. "But we will see each other again one day, when you are a great man and I a High Priestess."

With those words, she danced from the clearing, her movements graceful and flowing. The place was empty without her presence, even the animals left quickly, melting into the safety of the surrounding forest.

It would be many years before I ran into Nimue again. I came to realize our destinies were intertwined, which they still are.

As I look back to that time, I believe that meeting Nimue in the forest was an omen; my life began to change after that encounter. My mother decided at that time to inform me that I was not her son, but someone left me on her doorstep when I was a babe. You can imagine the shock of hearing such a thing from the woman I thought gave me life.

The story deepens from there. Left alongside me in my basket was a note declaring that I was to be the savior of Avalon and Britain, but needed the powers of a magician to help me. The woman whose doorstep I appeared on, my supposed mother, was a powerful woman in the magical realm. It was the knowledge she held that enabled her to live in the land of Avalon, as this was not a place for ordinary people. At least, not in the era I was raised.

As I grew, I heard stories that the land of Avalon used to be open to all people, until the time of Christians. Their beliefs, or their God, would not allow them to understand the ways of Avalon, although to one raised there the daily rituals were quite natural. What was wrong with worshipping the Earth that gave life or the life sustaining air? How could it be wrong to sense the mind and the feelings of the people you loved? The ability exists in us all, why choose to shut it off?

It seemed that some advocates of the Christian God demanded total obedience and a humble demeanor to your superiors. Many innocents were tortured for following other beliefs, or merely questioning the Church of Christ. I could never understand how one God could rule all people. Are not people different? Do they not all have different beliefs and rituals? Does it not follow they would have different Gods to follow?

Although, if you really think about it, all the Gods are really the one God worshipped by people in a form they can understand. One energy that takes on different forms, just as when we die, we change form and become one energy in the Universe.

Ahhh, it gets so complicated and I digress from my story. As I said, my life changed from the day I found I was not who I thought. My foster mother taught me all of her healing knowledge. I learned that it was wrong to manipulate my powers for personal or evil reasons. It was instilled into my very being to only use my powers for the good of others, otherwise there would be dire consequences as the Earth Mother did not allow negative use of her energies.

As I grew, I learned that the time that passed here, in Avalon, wasn't the same as time in the outside world, so I have no way to relate how many years I actually lived.

This lack of concept of time caused me to be taken quite by shock when I found out that the woman who had raised me was dying. With my magical arts and scientific knowledge, I tried to heal her to no avail. Upon her deathbed, my foster mother grasped my hand and bade me come closer.

Whispered words sent like arrows into my ear gave me just an inkling of my destiny. Barely able to speak for weakness, her final words etched themselves in my mind.

"I take leave of this earth and set you free to fulfill your destiny. Avalon comes upon troubled times. It is almost too late. You must find your other half to help save this land of mystery. I warn you not to believe all you are told. Mists can cause your sight to fail. Trust only what you feel."

At this point, my foster mother raised her hand to touch my forehead and spoke one last sentence. "From now on, you will be known as Merlin the Great."

As the life force passed from her body, I saw mist rise into the air and disappear into a place we can only wonder about.

A knock on the doorframe startled me from my mourning and I turned to gaze upon a cloaked figure in the doorway. Wreathed in pale blue silk, the figure lifted her arms to push the concealing hood back and reveal the fine features of a woman. The words the apparition spoke shocked me more than I thought possible, especially in light of my lifetime of learning.

"My name is Niobe. I am sorry for your loss, Merlin. It is time for you to come with me and learn more of the old ways. Your mother was well-versed in those ways, but I am much more adept, and you will need my knowledge to fulfill your destiny."

I was confused, and it must have shown on my face, for the woman reassured me. "You will be fine, as will your mother." The heavenly creature gestured toward the body on the bed that used to be my mother. "She goes now to continue her life in another place, but she will always watch over you."

It was at that point I came to the realization that we have no control over our lives. Whatever we believe, there is a pre-ordained destiny, a greater power or purpose, as you will.

I followed the woman, Niobe, through the forest. We walked for most of the afternoon until my legs shook and my breath caught in my chest. Finally, we came upon a place I remembered from my dreams.

The sun shone, as always, but a fine mist melted into the landscape. Soft and fine, the mist swirled about my ankles and wafted gently upon the warm breeze. We came to see water. Sparkling and blue, it lapped at the shores with a loving caress only to retreat again to a never-ending horizon. A slight incline in the pathway led us to, what seemed to me, a castle in the clouds. It beckoned to me. How could a building made of cold hard stone, seem so warm and inviting?

Bubbles of excitement rose in my chest. I knew I was in the company of one of the priestesses of myth that haunted the forests of Avalon. What purpose did Fate hold for me? What purpose held the priestess for teaching me her arts?

At that moment, I saw Nimue for the second time in my life. A throaty laugh drew my attention to the water's edge below me, just a little farther on where the hill declined into the lake. There she stood, a contrast from head to toe. An angel with a devilish laugh, a dark-haired beauty who, somehow, reflected only light. I knew I was in trouble, even if I wasn't sure how or why.

Niobe's tug upon my arm broke my reverie. "Come child, we have a lot of work ahead of us." She must have seen my longing gaze return to Nimue because she admonished me. "You have much to do before your path will cross with hers again. The sooner we begin, the sooner you may spend time with Nimue."

She pulled my arm more insistently, leaving me no choice but to follow. As we left the water's edge, the tingling sound of laughter warmed my ears and shortened my breath.

My life took on a relaxing monotony. My days were spent in learning and perfecting many, many spells and rituals. I learned how to make use of all that was around us, as well as some things that were not visible to the normal human eye. I trained hard because I knew there was a greater destiny in store for me. Not only because of my mother's dying words, but also because the priestess prepared me for my role in history.

One day, when I stood by the water trying to call upon the creatures to help me fish, I heard a twig snap behind me. I knew who approached but, not wanting to seem over eager, I stood my ground. That was a mistake, as two hands landed in the middle of my back and I flew, headlong, into the lake.

I sputtered to the surface to confront the one who dared. Upon seeing her face my resolve weakened, and instead I splashed her with water, a move she was not expecting.

For a moment she stood, beautiful as a doe in peaceful repose, and then brilliant laughter chimed across the water. "I suppose I deserved that, did I not?"

How else could I answer her? "Of course, you did."

"I told you we would meet again."

I dragged my soaking body from the water and shook like a dog, spraying the Lady Nimue. "In the forest that day, yes, you did say that. I wondered then how you could know such a thing, but since studying here, I have come to realize there is much that is possible."

I saw sadness or resignation come over Nimue and settle into her soul. However, when she spoke, her voice was bright. "I am being trained to become Head Priestess, you know."

"Yes, I know. That is quite an honor, also a responsibility. Are you sure that is what you desire?"

The sadness in her flamed to the surface and sparked her face a dull red. "It does not matter what I desire. Do you not know yet that you cannot direct your destiny?"

I did not like to see her upset, so I tried to soothe her. "I am sorry my words upset you. How can I make it up to you?"

"You cannot, but do not worry, I am all right. I just have a tendency to overreact. The other priestesses are trying to help me overcome this small deficiency in character."

"I do not see it as a deficiency. In fact, when the color spread to your face, I found you quite beautiful." The words were spoken with no thought, but I meant every one.

Nimue blushed again, upon realizing this she became more embarrassed, and left me watching her retreating form as she fled to the part of the castle where I was not allowed.

I remember how I searched daily for just a glimpse of Nimue. Opportunity abounded, as part of my training entailed scouring the countryside for healing herbs and certain substances used in my spells of magic.

Unfortunately, it would be a couple of years before I saw Nimue again. The day I saw her was the same day that a visitor arrived in Avalon. A man who entered by way of the barge we used for emergencies.

Oh, there was much ado centered around that mysterious visitor. Initiates guided him to our Lady's chamber and scrambled about carrying food that was prepared in the most glorious of fashion.

In the sky, the sun passed slowly until there was naught but a golden glow on the horizon. The Lady summoned me to appear in her chambers. This was an unusual request, not that I had not been in Niobe's chamber before, but never when she entertained a visitor.

All people in Avalon knew the Lady of the Lake planned strategies. Yes, even here in Avalon, political bargaining occurred. Of course, that only became necessary when the incoming Christians threatened our way of life and beliefs. Like a disease, they savaged the rituals and values that we held sacred for so many centuries, and then condemned any whom still practiced the old ways. We worshipped God, but we also worshipped the Goddess. Does not all life need both in order to be born and survive? In the greater scheme of things, we are all one, so I could not understand why these priests hated us so.

There I go again, off the subject I began. As you can no doubt tell, this matter of religion and Gods, or God, is one that rests close to my heart. I ache because of the hatred and petty squabbling that ruins the lives we live.

With all this weighing on my mind, I made my way to the Lady's chamber and knocked gently at the door. Bid to enter, I stepped into the large chamber and found my senses immediately drawn to Nimue, who sat in the corner shadows.

Her presence caused my heart to beat faster and my head to spin as if affected by a whole keg of mead. Mature now, her essence no longer echoed that of a young girl, but a beautiful and desirable woman. I knew that both Nimue and Niobe felt my thoughts. Each of them was far too advanced and full of the wisdom of the priestess for me to hide anything.

I tore my eyes from the vision of my love incarnate and focused instead on the surroundings of the room. Although sparsely furnished, warmth welcomed all who entered. Windows east and west beckoned the sun at all hours of the day; the half of the room reserved for greeting guests was separated from the bedchamber part of the room by a hanging velvet curtain. Rich burgundy augmented the gold candlesticks that sat on the fireplace mantle. One simple, wooden table with four plush chairs sat on a thick braided rug. No bearskin or sheepskin here, animals were meant to live and be respected just as humans.

"Greetings, Merlin, may I present Uther Pendragon, my guest for a day or two."

"Good eve to you, sir." I tried to speak in my most formal manner. The man sitting in the dark returned my greeting with the nod of his head.

"Merlin, please seat yourself, we have much to discuss. Are you hungry?" Niobe inquired as she motioned to the abundance of fruit and vegetables upon the table.

In truth I was far too nervous to eat, so I forewent.

"Merlin, you have been raised here many years and learned all that anyone can possibly teach you. It is time for you to go out in the world and fulfill your destiny."

"But, my Lady, I don't understand. I have no desire to leave Avalon." My glance flew to Nimue. The thought of leaving her was the first one to my mind. At that moment, I knew how much I cared for her.

"What you desire, and what must be, are often paths of different directions. You know that best of all, Merlin." The Lady gave me a gentle pat upon my hand. I noticed how white was her hand, with spidery blue-veins running in criss-cross fashion. Had her hand always looked so?

In a wavering voice, she continued her story. "You know there is much unrest in the land, for over the years Britain has grown weak. The time is ripe for change, and Uther is that change."

Surprised, my glance flew to Uther. There he sat, so sure of himself, as if he knew something others did not. Of course, with our Lady of Avalon behind him, I suppose he could be sure of winning whatever battle he fought. He was not a mean looking man, just cocky enough to make me worry.

The Lady Niobe spoke, breaking into my contemplation. "Uther has been under my scrutiny for some time, and I believe he is the one to replace Vortigern on the throne. He will ensure Avalon's safety by seeing that the Christian's do not completely obliterate the old ways."

"Of course, if that is what you wish, but how can I help with this?"

"You are to become advisor to Uther. There are things that need doing, and only you are capable of these deeds." Niobe glanced to her guest. Uther remained silent all this time. "Our guest is tired and ready to retire. We will excuse him so he may rest." Summoning a priestess, Niobe gave instructions for Uther's care.

I stood to leave as well, thinking all was done, but Niobe motioned me to sit. The door shut firmly, and the Lady turned to Nimue and me. A heavy silence descended over the chamber.

Patiently, Nimue and I waited. When Niobe finally spoke, we almost wished she remained silent, for the words she spoke were such that the course of Britain, and an untold number of lives, was altered forever. It was there, in the chamber of the Lady of Avalon, that destinies were wrought, and fates decided.

As if all this were not enough, what happened next set my blood to pounding, and I could see in the blue eyes of Nimue she was feeling as I. My Lady Niobe crossed over to the fireplace and stood, back to us, hands raised in a holy gesture of respect. Nimue glanced at me, her eyes questioning. I shrugged. What was our Lady paying homage to? Nothing appeared unusual about the fireplace. Velvet rustled against velvet as the Lady Niobe lowered her hands to a stone on the fireplace mantle. Fire snapped and crackled, and then all noise stopped. Softly, in the distance, I heard the sound of thunder rumble across the night sky. Gently, the Lady pushed until the dull, grinding sound of stone on stone echoed out above our heads. I was surprised to see the upper part of the mantle slide to one side and disappear into a recess.

Tension knotted my stomach as firelight flickered orange-blue shadows within the dark hole. Revealed before us was a sword of such overwhelming beauty and nobility, I gasped in reverence. I remember that Nimue's reaction was much like mine. We both fell to our knees and touched our fingertips to our forehead in a gesture of respect.

Lady Niobe reached to the sword and brought it forth from its resting-place. The glow from the sword transferred itself to the Lady until she was bathed in a warm, luminescent aura. When she spoke, her voice changed. She no longer sounded like our Lady did; she was somehow different.

"This is the Sword Excalibur, one of our few holy relics remaining from times of old."

No words were needed, as all in Avalon knew the tales of the sword. However, no eyes ever rested on it, or knew where the relic came from, or what kind of powers it held. Whispered legends spoke of a land of immense beauty and wisdom that long ago disappeared beneath the ocean waves.

"I know there is much wonder surrounding the sword. You are the first to lay eyes upon this relic in many lifetimes. Sword Excalibur is from ancient days, days I no longer hold very much in my memory, it has been so long."

I could not hold my silence. "How could you have lived so long?"

"Merlin, there is so much I don't remember. What I tell you both must remain here, not that it matters, I suppose, since I am the last one from those days. Once I am gone, there will be none to protect.

"Yes, I lived on an island called Atlantis, a world of beauty, peace, and learning. We lived in harmony with nature's creatures and laws, and our hearts vibrated with the tune of the Universe. Gods ruled in benevolence and love, in fact…" Her voice trailed away into memory.

Sensing Niobe's reluctance to finish her sentence, I prompted her, "In fact what, Lady?"

Her face took on a rosy hue. "In fact, one of the Gods took me as his lover. It was said that I was his first human lover, until then the Gods loved only amongst themselves. Back in Atlantis he was referred to as The Thunder God. Why he chose to honor me with his love still mystifies me. It was about that time that visitors appeared from another land. Their teachings began to cause doubt among our people, like a poison seeping through our society. Slowly, greed, lust, and a desire for power took over the minds of many. Chaos became rampant, so did killing and bloodlust. Some of us could see what was coming, so we took a few items of importance from our places of worship."

"You built places of worship back then?"

"Of course, Merlin. All civilizations have places of worship. We left ours open to the skies above and the animals of the forest.

We used these places to gather and share knowledge and love. Not like the churches here, where all is cut off from nature." Niobe paused, took a deep breath, and continued her story. "Some of us made it away before the final destruction—barely. From our ship we watched the death, and heard the screams of men, women, and children as the world was consumed by fire. There was naught we could do but save ourselves."

Enthralled, and repelled by the tale, a thousand questions haunted my mind. I tried to ask them all. "When did this happen? Is this where the Sword Excalibur is from? What happened to the others on the ship with you?"

"Merlin, Merlin, please, I will tell you what I can. It is from this place of destruction that we made our way to Brittany, where we chose to settle. We carried with us our blessings of the Earth Mother. The land began to change as we created a special place where all creatures of mystery were drawn. As the many life forms drew together, they altered the very atmosphere, pulsing with the vibrations and enabling Avalon to shift away from the world around it. We are here, yet not here."

"That is why only some people can find their way here."

"They must contain within them a higher energy to be able to see the way."

"Tell us more of the Sword Excalibur." Nimue's hushed voice broke into the conversation.

"Being a symbol of the harmonious balance of all energies in the Universe, Sword Excalibur is not of one god, but of all gods. It is a symbol of the harmony of the Earth Mother, the giver of life, and all that she holds dear.

"Any who hold the sword, must be pure of intent, strong of will, and willing to fight any injustice, whether it be perpetrated in the realm of mankind or any realm beyond. The sword was of Atlantis, but now is strictly of Avalon, given only on rare occasion to a mortal who may fulfill the desires of this land.

"You must now see why the teachings of the Christians are such a threat. I have seen one place of harmony destroyed by narrow-minded men, and will not allow Avalon to be lost the same way."

In the dim light of dying fire, the Lady of the Lake shimmered with pulsing energy. Out the window I heard the faint sound of thunder grow closer as Niobe held the sword in front of her, extended toward a stunned Nimue.

At this point Gavin's legs tingled into numbness. He needed to stretch. Damn, but didn't his heart ache with longing for the absolute love that Merlin felt for Nimue. It was the same kind of love shared by his parents, and it was the only kind of love he would settle for.

He chuckled as he placed the book on his nightstand and stood. Mac's words rang in his mind. He'd be damn lucky to find love like that. Relieving his full bladder in the toilet of his overly opulent bathroom, Gavin mused that many people would envy his life just as it was. But for him, it wasn't enough. Not if there wasn't someone to share it with.

Returning to his bed, he pondered whether or not to read more. So far, nothing explained his parents words of warning. On the other hand, he found himself inexplicably drawn to the bond shared by Merlin and Nimue, as well as by the appearance of the Sword Excalibur. The story reeked of fantasies and legends from his childhood. Now, those same stories were presented to him in memoirs written by his ancestor. If this book were to be believed, his bloodlines ran back to the Arthurian times. That tie, as well as the promise of timeless love fulfilled, drew him back to the yellowed pages of the ancient words of love.

O nly the approaching rumble of thunder and occasional flash of lightning interrupted the breathless silence. Within my very soul, I felt Nimue's conflicting emotions of joy and fear.

When Lady Niobe spoke, her voice no longer carried her usual regal tone. "I now pass my mantle and this sword on to you, Lady Nimue. I believe it is time, and that you will rule justly, always staying true to the ways of those who came before us, and those who will follow after. For we are all one in the same."

Stunned, I could only imagine how Nimue felt. Neither of us expected so momentous a gesture this evening.

Nimue opened her mouth to protest, but the Lady would not listen. "Quiet, Nimue. You are now Lady of the Lake. You must carry on for me, as I grow too old and weary. Do not feel sad, time passes more slowly here than elsewhere, and I have lived a long and fruitful life. I am also lonely, as there are none but I left who remember how things used to be. I pass my mantle on to you, but there are certain events already set in motion you must be made aware of."

Nimue rose to her feet and stood in silent nervousness. Niobe reassured her. "Come, Nimue, you are now Lady and this is your chamber, therefore this seat is yours." With her bony hand, Niobe led the trembling younger woman to the throne-like chair. Nimue looked fearful, and I felt her pain.

Once Nimue took the place of Lady of the Lake, we knew that Lady Niobe would no longer have reason to be with us. We would probably not see her after that evening. I was enveloped by an overwhelming sense of sadness, and saw the same emotion reflected within Nimue's eyes.

Niobe sat herself in one of the smaller chairs and waited for Nimue to take her newly acquired position. Once all was as it should be, Niobe spoke. "You know that the border lord Gorlois covets the throne after Vortigern. This will not happen. I have seen this with my Sight. Instead, Uther will rule."

"But that is good, Uther is a fine man." Nimue found her voice.

"That he is, but that is not the problem. His infatuation with Gorlois's wife, Igraine, is the problem. Any issue coming from a union now made by Uther will be a cause for confusion and rebellion in the future. Can you imagine the battles that would wage, if a male child were born to Igraine? There are those who follow Gorlois who would try to sit the boy upon the throne, and if it were to be known that the child were Uther's, the results could be just as horrific. The people of Brittany would not tolerate their king to be cuckolded, especially by one of the lesser Kings. In fact, the Christian Church that many have come to follow would revile both Uther and the child that would be produced for the sin committed. The throne and the strength of Britain are at stake."

"Can you not just deny Uther the woman, Igraine?"

"He will not listen. He is enthralled with her for some reason. I have woven many spells, but there is something greater at work. We must do the best we can with circumstances presented us. Uther's inability to see the danger weakens him in my eyes as the savior of Avalon. However, he must still rule. Events have come too far, and there is no one else. We must form his obsession to fit our needs. Have either of you any ideas?"

I think Niobe knew what needed to be done, she was merely allowing Nimue to feel her new authority. Breathing deeply, I watched Nimue close her eyes and begin to hum a low chanting melody. Her lithe body began to sway, and the palms of her hands wound around each other in a familiar motion of energy gathering. Flames flickered in the fireplace and leapt in crackling accompaniment to Nimue.

Finally, her wavering voice fell upon the room, slowly and surely gathering certainty and intensity. "If Uther must go to Igraine, we must set the time so that we can ensure the death of Gorlois before any child is conceived. This will end any doubt. He must then make Igraine his Queen, which will ensure the child is heir."

Certain in her appraisal, Nimue's voice ripened with strength. "Of course, we must also ensure that the child is a boy, and exact a promise from Uther that he will give the child to us to foster in Avalon. That way, the boy will be of our ways and strong enough to stand against the single-minded destruction of the Christian priests. He will be our savior, since Uther is showing himself to be more concerned with other pastimes."

To say the least, I was stunned. I stared uncertainly at the beautiful young woman as she casually discussed murdering a King.

Niobe knew my thoughts because she answered sharply. "Do not be so stupid, Merlin. Of course, we must make plans. If we leave events up to the eccentricities of mankind we are doomed. We must ensure that the man who sits on the throne is of our choosing. As history has passed from future to present to past, we have always set the ruler of Britain upon the throne. As long as this continues, Avalon will be safe. With the onset of religious bigotry and hatred we find this harder to do, so we must become more secretive and creative."

The Lady paused to catch her breath. She did not have the strength she used to, and I noticed her weakness increasingly those days.

"Nimue is right in her perceptions, and her plans. You see that the trust I place in her as my heir is not misplaced. Uther will rule well, but it is his son, through Igraine, I have seen as the savior of Avalon. All this and more, I have seen with the Sight."

Niobe softened her voice and instructed me, "You will guide Uther, but he will not be long on the throne. Uther's son will be your main purpose. You need to be with the child from the day he is born. Your guidance will ensure that he is wise in the old ways and sympathetic to our people. A promise will be extracted from Uther to allow the boy to be raised here when he is of an age to understand. This way he will see our ways first hand. Then, when the time is ripe, he will be placed upon the throne in place of Uther. He will rule strongly, mercifully, and with understanding of all beliefs. This I have seen in my dreams and wanderings to the Otherworld."

Tired from the long speech, the Lady's face took on the look of age and her shoulders bent ever so slight, as if the responsibilities were too much to bear.

"I read your thoughts, Merlin, I am not yet that old."

"I am sorry, my Lady. I was lost for a moment."

"No, you were correct. I am getting old, that is why Nimue is here to listen to my plans, and that is why I pass this responsibility to you. I will not be of this world long enough to see Uther on the throne, let alone his son. My plan, the salvation of our very world and beliefs, rest on the actions of you two. As of tonight, Nimue is Lady of the Lake, Ruler of Avalon, High Priestess of all we hold dear. Merlin, you will be her guide in the world of mankind. Together, the two of you will ensure the preservation of the worship of our Earth. Our ways, which have been passed on through our ancestors from the lost continent, are in your hands."

Beyond anything I imagined, these words fell like a hammer. I always thought to spend my days in Avalon, and harbored no desire to go out into the world of man. There was too much pain and hatred in that world.

"Merlin, it is your destiny. It is why you were born with the powers you have. We cannot allow the same mistakes as our ancestors who developed avaricious, destructive ways. They paid dearly for their arrogant mistakes, and I would like to think we have learned from the course of history. If our way of life is to be preserved, you must make yourself as mortal man and forge into their world. Never fear, your ability to return to Avalon will always be part of you. I have prepared your way, many people already talk of you and your many abilities. You will fit in and be respected, except by some of the more narrow-minded."

"I care not if they accept me, but I will do what I can to help preserve Avalon and all we hold dear." At the time I meant all the words I spoke, though I dreaded the thought of leaving Nimue.

Niobe, vigilant as always, read my emotions. "Do not worry my Merlin, you and Nimue have a destiny to fulfill as well. You will be together, as you were before."

These words of prophecy caused Nimue to blush. How beautiful she looked with the faint tinge of pink creeping up to color her cheeks. I should have remembered that Nimue was as adept at reading minds and emotions as the Lady.

"Now, I am tired, and I need rest before I begin the next part of my journey. Merlin, you will leave tomorrow with Uther. Remember, you need to guard the boy child when he is born. He will be your responsibility until he is old enough to come here. Nimue, you and I need to work some spells to ensure our plans come to fruition. Come back to me as the sun tops the hilltops. For now, I need rest."

Before I was able to say good-bye to the woman I considered a mentor, I found myself on the outside of her chamber door. Nimue and I stood looking at each other. The dim hallway sparked with tension as well as shock at the speed of all that had taken place within the chamber of the High Priestess.

"Merlin." Nimue's rested her soft hand lightly upon my arm. Her touch burned through the light cotton of my mantle. Like a whisper, her breath touched upon my face and caused my heart to beat. I remember how I had to brush my palms against my pants to discard the sweat.

"Merlin, we have only tonight, time that I think Niobe has given us on purpose."

At first, the truth of her words failed to register. When they did, my face burned. I know it must have turned scarlet but Nimue said naught, she simply waited for my move. I took hold of Nimue's hand and bade her to follow me.

Fallen leaves crackling under our slippers was the only sound heard in the stillness of the dusk's cover; even the birds were silent. Through the darkening forest, our stealthy steps carried us to a place I knew of that was private and holy. Nimue never questioned. She must have sensed our journey would take us where we needed to go.

Even with darkness approaching, I remember how the clearing glowed. Upon the ground lay a newly fallen blanket of fresh leaves, and the stream where I usually bathed was an orchestra of nature's music.

Nimue was enthralled by the beauty and peace of the place. "Merlin, I have lived here my whole life and never seen this place. How is it you have been so blessed?"

"I know not. Some days I look and cannot find my way, other days, I feel as if I am called here. My magic increases, and I feel more in tune with all around me when I am here. I think it is not really part of Avalon, so it does not surprise me that you have not found it on your wanderings. It is a special place, the perfect place for this eve."

Under the munificence of the Rose Moon, with the blessing of the earth and sky, Nimue and I became as one. Intermingling in a passion beyond this world, our spirits filled with wonder and soared above any earthly bounds. We ceased to be ourselves as our joining caused a rift between worlds. A part of our minds understood our past as distant memories of the ancient world and its destruction burst forth in a flurry of senses.

Exhausted, yet revived, we lay in each other's arms with spongy moss for our bed. The positive emotion from our joining faded as we both accepted this would be our last time together for a long time.

"The sun rises. We must return to the keep."

Nimue's words were unnecessary. We needed to fulfill our duties, so we returned. In no time, we found ourselves standing in the bailey.

Muffled sounds of early morning life drifted on the still present fog, accompanied by the smell of bannock and oatmeal.

A brief touch of hands, a spark in the rays of the rising morning sun, was our unspoken goodbye. I cast one last, longing glance to Nimue and felt her sadness reach me as I crossed the courtyard. Upon reaching Niobe, I thought how unwell she looked and doubted that she would be here when I returned. She placed a hand upon my arm; the warmth of her love radiated into my body.

"We will not see each other in the world again, Merlin. You know what needs to be done to ensure the survival of our world. I count on you, and Nimue, to carry this out."

"I vow that naught will get in the way of my duty." Suddenly feeling brave, or simply foolish, I leaned forward to kiss the Lady upon her cheek. This gesture of respect and friendship pleased her greatly.

"Go! Go now before the tides turn against you." With a tear in her sad eye, Niobe bid me ado.

With the barge rolling gently beneath our feet, Uther and I departed from the shores of Avalon. All that was familiar to me became naught but a shimmering vision beyond the mist.

Short and uneventful, the journey was soon over. When we approached the opposite shore, I could make out the dim shapes of men and horses breaking through the mist.

"Those would be my men awaiting my return." These were the first words spoken to me by Uther, the future King of Britain. I was still uncertain, and more than a slight bit nervous, until we came closer to shore.

Breathing deeply of the crisp air, I was reassured that all would come to bear as Niobe predicted. After all, she predicted my birth and training? Did she not have the future King of Britain as an ally? Was she not a more powerful priestess than anyone? Yes, Niobe's plan was in my mind, Britain's destiny at my fingertips, and the love of Nimue in my heart.

As I watched the Red Dragon of Pendragon waft in the breeze, I secretly wondered if Uther was a fool or just so sure of himself he felt no fear.

"Lord, do you not think it overly soon to be boldly dancing the flag of Pendragon amongst your men?"

Distracted, Uther replied briskly. "As we speak, a battle is being waged among the invading Saxons and Gorlois's Marcher Lords. My men tell me that Vortigern has passed from this life, and Gorlois will surely perish this day in battle. Is this not what Lady Niobe has promised?"

"Most assuredly, yet it is disrespectful to flaunt your new position before the bodies of the King and his choice of succession are even cold. It is not wise to let your ego rule your mind. Why not put the flag from sight as we head to Tintagel? Besides, I have come with a plan already in mind, and it does not involve a show of force."

"How else am I to claim the vacant throne? You know that as the news of Gorlois's death reaches others, they will rush to his manor in an attempt to overtake his place on the throne. The throne he will never have the good fortune to sit upon. Our only advantage is our foreknowledge and ability to hold the manor and lands with a strong show of force."

"No. There is another, far easier way to take the throne. You have demanded of the Lady of Avalon the possession of the Lady Igraine. She is your way to the throne. She will be the mourning wife of the man named to succession. He who wins and weds her will be the next King, especially if he can back up his claim with a strong army. But better to take over quietly rather than battle with the men from whom you desire allegiance."

"But how can you accomplish this? She will believe her husband still lives. We are the only ones who know he will die this day."

"Trust me, she will accept you in her bed thinking you her husband. When she wakes, she will find she loves you, and believe she gave herself willingly. You will wed within the week and Britain will be yours to rule. None will gainsay your right to the throne, and none will gainsay the boy child born to Igraine nine months from this day."

"The child you will take to Avalon."

"Yes, just as we agreed." I hesitated. I needed to make sure Uther understood the severity of not keeping his end of the bargain sealed in the land of Avalon. "Uther, once you join with the Lady Igraine, events are in motion that cannot be halted without severe reprisal. You must know that your promise to give your son to Avalon, and to rule with the old ways ever in your mind, must be kept."

"I understand, Merlin. May we proceed now? I find myself tasting for the delights of the Lady Igraine."

Uther's ascension to the throne came about with little fuss. Of course, there was rumbling amongst the more loyal knights of Gorlois. The word was that magic was at work for Vortigern and Gorlois to both perish so close together, enabling Uther to become king. To listen to the priests, one would believe that some kind of evil had been perpetrated. They preached from their Holy Houses of the coming of a dark time unless all people prayed to their Christ, as His way was the only way. This narrow view bothered me, but I was sure this was not the view held by all that followed his way. I found myself advising Uther…King Uther, to appease them with offerings of worship at his place of living, as well as donations to the local orders.

Festivities of Uther and Igraine's wedding kept the worst of the dissenters at bay. Nothing like the joy of a union of love, and all the encompassing details, to keep tongues from wagging. Servants were kept busy stocking up on food for the incoming crowd. Kings and knights, from the nearby regions, were to assemble for the merry day. In fact, the crowning of Uther, which was to take place on the same day, took a back seat to his marriage.

Finding myself with a day off, I was at a loss as to what to do, so I wandered about the feasting hall, eyeing the building array of food. The table was filled with piglings stuffed with nuts, cheese, eggs, and spices; a tasty chicken dish of rice, almonds, and sugar, called blackmanger; as well as capon and venison to finish off the array of meats. Tempting fruits, figs, cheeses, cakes, and jellies, along with spiced wine to drink, completed the day's menu.

"A person would be wise to practice restraint with such a feast before them."

The breathy, singing quality of the voice set my senses to flying and my heart to pounding. I knew instantly who spoke. My beloved stood beside me, leaving the familiarity of Avalon. My furtive gaze quickly found the glowing beauty of Nimue standing beside me.

"My love, how come you to be here? No one spoke of your presence at the feast."

"That is because none knew of my arrival. In fact, I did not decide to come until today."

Comprehension dawned within my mind. "So you are still in Avalon with only your thought projection here." I knew this was the only way Nimue could accomplish a five-day journey in less than a day.

"Yes, I am here in thought form, and thus cannot hold this place for too long without draining myself. Of course, to others I appear as a noblewoman. It would be hard to explain my presence in two places at once. Would that not give your priests cause for mutterings of evil?"

"They are not my priests, and all are not bad. I have seen much good come from their teachings."

As the evening passed in good cheer and delicious foods, Nimue and I put aside our difference of opinion to enjoy ourselves.

"How long will you remain here?"

"I cannot stay much longer. My body will need nourishment, and the longer I hold this form, the more stiff I will be when I finally come from my trance."

"However you disguise yourself, I still recognize the essence of your energy, Nimue." Soft, dulcet tones of the Lady Igraine interrupted our words. Nimue turned to the bride and offered her congratulations.

"I do not accept your well-wishes. You think mayhap you have fooled me with your magic and illusions, but you need to know that I was aware of who Uther was from the moment he stepped into my bedchamber. The only reason he sits upon Gorlois' throne and pleasures me, is because it is my desire, not yours. Look around, is there a single man here that could cause your heart to beat and your loins to burn? I think not. Uther is the best of the lot, that is why he is king and not another."

The venom of Igraine's tone stunned me, but I was impressed with how Nimue handled the woman.

"If he is your desire, then why do you hate me so for placing him in your life?"

"I hate what you stand for and your manipulations just to preserve a dying land and beliefs that none care for anymore."

Dryness filled my mouth with cotton, and pulses of uncertainty ran through my veins. Igraine's feelings of Avalon worried me. How was Uther to fulfill his promise if his wife detested the sound of the word Avalon? Where did the hatred grow from? I'm sure I heard naught of any disservice visited upon her by the people of Avalon.

"There are many who still practice the Ways of Old Igraine, do not fool yourself into believing otherwise." Nimue's full voice rose to the stone parapets above. She was playing the role of Lady of Avalon, not simply my lover.

"I will make certain their ways are not tolerated. If I must give up my son, I will at least have my people about me."

Lightning struck in my mind; this was the source of her anger. Uther told her of the deal, and she had not recognized him upon entry to her chamber but found out the truth afterwards. Add the truth that she must give up her son, and she became a woman filled with poison.

Nimue replied, since it was her place as the Lady of Avalon. I needed to remain as uninvolved as possible, as I would be living here over the years to come. It would better be served that Nimue antagonize the woman.

"You may hate all you want, Igraine, I am sorry for that, but you cannot understand all that transpires, and the reasons for such. Yes,

Uther came to you under disguise, but there was no other way for him to assume the throne with no bloodshed. He wanted you, and would have taken you regardless. Is this not a better way? Yes, we will take your son when five summer solstices have passed, but he has a future determined long before being born. He will be great. Would you deny your son his full potential?"

"Oh, you are good at twisting to suit yourself."

"I speak but the truth. We will have your son, but he will be returned to you the better for his time in Avalon."

"Better according to your beliefs, but he will be living in a world ruled by the Christians. They will not accept a ruler raised in the heathen ways of the Priestess."

Nimue's voice snapped the air about us, causing heads to turn and brows to furrow. "How dare you speak such...you...who were also raised in the ways of Avalon? How can you forsake what you know to be true?"

Raised in Avalon? Igraine? These words shocked me. I did not know she'd ever been to Avalon, let alone learned the ways of the land.

The growing tirade was put to an end by the appearance of Uther. Placing his arm about Igraine's shoulders he jested, "Do not wear yourself out in argument, my love. I have many plans for the evening."

His ribaldry drove the sparks from the air and allowed a forced calm to fall over us. His eyes found Nimue and narrowed slightly. "Is that you Lady? I am sorry I did not recognize you. Is all well here? My love, the Lady of the Lake is an honored guest. Why do you argue?" His voice was uncertain. Obviously, he did not like to see his new bride arguing with the people who put him upon the throne.

I watched Igraine speculate how far she could push her husband. She chose the safe path. "We argue not, just jestful banter my husband." I was surprised that Uther could not see the ice daggers emanating from her eyes. Was he blind?

"Yes, and it is time for me to leave." Nimue's voice returned to normal as she bid her good-byes. "My well wishes to you both. I trust the ways of those who went before to you, King Uther. To you, Igraine, I wish you a healthy and fruitful breeding."

"You would." Igraine sulked just loud enough for me to hear. I worried that she was so against the ways we hoped to hold onto, she would make our attempts very difficult. My path seemed to be cut from granite.

Upon Nimue's wishes, I accompanied her to the bailey where we could see the stars in the sky. I reached out and brushed my hand across her cheek. Warm, pulsing light engulfed the coarseness of my hand. For a moment we were connected on a level other than what can be seen with the human eye.

Nimue smiled. "It will not be long and we will be together again. I know that Igraine already carries the boy child of Uther. He will be brought to Avalon when he is five as Uther agreed. The years he spends in Avalon will be our time together."

"Then what happens?"

"With the help of the Sword Excalibur, he will return here to rule in place of his father, just as Niobe decreed. You need to be by his side guiding him. You still plan to follow the way as set by Niobe on our joining night…do you not?" Her eyes were sharp, they pierced into my mind, searching and probing. I was bothered by the air of distrust suddenly appearing as if on wings.

"Of course, I still follow the vows made that eve. I am hurt that you think otherwise."

Even as the words passed my lips, Nimue's form dissolved into a mist. She became ethereal, and her voice faded along with her essence. "I will look forward to our time together."

"As will I, my love, as will I." I reached out to touch the air were my beloved stood but a moment before. Tingling echoes of past times, promises, and deceptions throbbed throughout my hand. A song of ancient rituals and beliefs rang in my ears and warmed my soul. Our history was a long one, longer than either could remember. We were destined to live the wheel of life, making decisions to shape our future.

However, all was not so easy; I came to realize that Fate did lead a ruling hand in many cases, we were but to react to what was passed our way. With all the uncertainty, I still looked forward to future years together in Avalon. All that needed doing was to ensure Uther kept Britain from being torn asunder with conflicting beliefs. At least until his soon to be born son could be placed upon the throne. The son who would be the savior of the ways of the People Who Came Before.

A luminescent moon rose high in the inky blackness and disappeared over the hilltop, causing shadows of rowan trees to dance upon the earth. I shivered as I recalled the words cast about that evening. Nimue's questions of doubt and mistrust were to hold themselves in my mind for a very long time.

The ringing of the church bells in the distance brought Gavin abruptly from the past to the present. His clock showed three hours gone by while he read Merlin's memoirs. His eyes were tired, and there was no way he could read any more tonight.

It made for an interesting story. Gavin found himself fascinated by the intrigue and mystical sense that was prevalent throughout the tale. So far, nothing he read would incite the fear and reticence in his parent's faces at the dinner table earlier that evening.

Oh, well, tomorrow is another day, he thought. With a stretch, Gavin turned out his bedside lamp, fluffed his pillow, and rolled into an almost instant slumber.

Chapter Seven

T amara woke to a consistent background rumble of powerful jet engines and the fading light of late day sun as it reflected off cold steel. The strange sounds and a stiff neck quickly made her aware that she was not in her own bed; she was headed to England. A fuzzy look at her watch warned her there was only about half an hour until the plane arrived at the Bristol airport.

The half hour passed quickly, and Tamara's stomach fluttered with uncertain butterflies. She'd never been across the ocean before, but that wasn't the problem. Tamara wasn't sure why her nerves decided to cause her discomfort, but the closer the plane came to touchdown, the more her butterflies fluttered. She tried to distract herself by reviewing her plans upon landing at the airport. Hopefully, there'd be a car waiting to take her to The Will-O'-the Wisp, where she could settle into her room and relax for the evening. Heck, maybe she'd even pull out Nimue's memoirs and do some light reading.

All went according to plan. She slid through customs no problem and spotted the chauffeur waiting patiently with her name emblazoned on a placard. With a sigh of relief she gladly gave him possession of her bags.

Tamara knew the trip would take about an hour, so she took the time to organize a plan of action for the next couple of days. She needed to find out more about the ceremony, find someone involved to interview, and get some local people's slant on the event. The human-interest aspect of any story was usually popular.

Tamara looked up from her laptop and rubbed her stiff neck. The hustle and bustle of the city melded into rolling, green hills dotted with cows and sheep. Here and there, gray rocks jutted up from the grassland meadows and demanded attention. A sigh of relaxation wound its way through Tamara's tense muscles.

"We're almost there," the driver informed her.

Tamara was impressed with the view that greeted her. The dirt driveway was narrow and took a meandering course through a wooded ravine. A spring fed creek flowed from the side of the hill, its pathway winding gently below the driveway. Tamara's first view of the inn was breathtaking. Silhouetted against the sun sinking below the horizon, the inn was bathed in the paling oranges and pinks of the sky. Set on either side of a cedar shake roof, two stone chimneys spiraled toward the sky. Large and roomy, the inn still managed to exude a cottage-like feel with its abundance of flowers and herbs growing in the surrounding gardens.

The black limo rolled to a stop in front of the picturesque building. Tamara smiled at the familiar sight of bird feeders in a garden filled with wildflowers. She immediately felt at home.

Thanking the driver for his help with her suitcase, Tamara stepped into the front lobby. She was greeted by the ardent attention of a rather large calico cat that insisted upon rubbing himself against her pant legs. The feline's gentle purring was punctuated by the crackling of the fire burning in the stone fireplace. Tamara inhaled the scent of lily-of-the-valley from an unseen pot-pourri, and her tension instantly dissolved into a pool of relief.

"Crikey, ye startled me poor heart." An older woman with graying hair and a pleasant, grandmotherly appeal shuffled forward and relieved

Tamara of her suitcase. "I suppose I've been faffing about, so I missed your arrival. Well, no worry, I've been known to be slightly daft now and again. At least, that's what me dear departed husband used to accuse me of. Now, to matters of business, my name is Mrs. Harlow. The dosh has been taken care of, and we're empty 'til tomorrow, so why don't you bagsie a place to settle your stuff. I'm sure you'd like a quiet evening and then some kip."

Tamara's mind tried to work its way around the unfamiliar words. Analyzing and calculating, she still couldn't come up with anything even resembling a meaning to the words spoken. The numbness in her brain must have converted to a stunned look on her face, because the woman promptly apologized.

"Oh, there I go again forgetting how you Americans can't fathom our language. I'll try to tone it down. Sorry, I can't do much about the accent."

"Thank God, for a moment I wondered if I'd landed on another planet." Tamara breathed a sigh of relief that the woman spoke a language she could understand. "My name is Tamara Camden."

"Yes, of course it is. Come, and I'll show you a couple of rooms. You can have your pick."

Tamara chose a room on the upper floor. Small and cozy, it boasted a fireplace and deep-soak tub. The décor was slightly on the frilly side, but in a homey way. In fact, it reminded Tamara of home, boasting a down comforter decorated with purple pansies, lavender colored walls, and cherry wainscoting. Yes, this was definitely the room.

With the help of Mrs. Harlow, Tamara lugged her bag and camera equipment up the stairs and onto the bed. In a brief struggle of might and muscle she picked up her suitcase and threw it onto the queen-size bed. To her dismay the lock snapped open and spilled the contents onto the bed. Clothes fell in disarray, and toiletries scattered about the floor and rolled under the bed. But, worst of all, the offensive book sat on top of it all looking as inoffensive as any other book.

"What a lovely book," commented Mrs. Harlow. "It's obviously an antique. What beautiful engraving and leather work." Mrs. Harlow's finger traced the pattern of smooth leather and gold trim.

"I'm not exactly sure how much of an antique it is. I'm sure it's old, but I haven't really looked it over closely, so its age is up for grabs. Not that I'd be able to tell how old it is, anyway."

"Dear, if you're looking for someone to look at the book for you, I know just the person. A sweet, little old man. He's right in town. Oh, he runs the most adorable little bookstore. If anyone can tell you about this book, it'll be him. My guess would be that it's genuine, as they don't make books like this these days, besides…" Mrs. Harlow closed her eyes and ran the palm of her hand just over the cover of the book, "I can feel the energy coming from the book. There's so much emotion and heartbreak." With a choked cry, Mrs. Harlow practically threw the book to the bed. "Oh, dear, I'm sorry. I just couldn't handle the energy, there's just too much."

Tamara kept her voice light, but tension stretched her jaw when spoke. "Now you sound like my mother. She's always talking about auras, energy, and stuff."

"Don't tell me you can't feel the emotion just wafting off that book? My Lord, it's so powerful, it just about knocked me over. Well, be that as it may, I suppose I should let you unpack your trunk while I go see about some food for you. Would you like to eat downstairs or would you like a tray in your room?"

"If it's not too much bother, I'd really like to just take it easy in my room for the night. Maybe I'll even take some time to do some reading." Tamara was only half kidding, but she found herself intrigued by Mrs. Harlow's reaction to the book. Maybe it was worth checking out. In fact, maybe she should take it to the "sweet, little old man who ran the bookstore." "Mrs. Harlow, when you bring my tray, could you also bring me directions to that bookstore you told me about? I'd like to check it out."

"Sure I will, though, it is far enough away, you'll need a car to get there. If you'd like, I can lend you my car. She doesn't get out too much, but she's a brick, so she'll get you where you're going."

"Thank you, I wondered how I would get around. Maybe I should rent a car while I'm here."

"Don't be daft, you can borrow mine for the week." With the matter of transportation settled, and a cheery wave of her hand, Mrs. Harlow went to prepare dinner.

After a delicious feast of grilled fish and salad, Tamara relaxed in a hot bath overflowing with lavender scented bubbles. She figured she might as well relax now, because the next few days were going to be busy.

The promise she made to her mother stood uppermost in her mind, and the journal sat on her night table just waiting to be read. While she was having the authenticity of the book checked out, she could do some research on the summer solstice and witches at the same bookstore. That way the day wouldn't be a complete waste.

Feeling a chill from the cooling bath water, Tamara knew it was time to vacate the tub. She appreciated the thick, softness of the towel as she rubbed her skin dry. She wrapped herself in the warmth of the terry robe she'd found hanging on the bathroom door, and reveled in the luxuriant feel against her skin. With a smile, she sent her hostess silent thanks for her appreciation of the finer things in life.

With a final sigh of relief and comfort, Tamara curled up under the down-filled comforter and began to read the journal supposedly written by Nimue, Lady of the Lake.

Chapter Eight

I remember the mists swirling about my feet the morning I saw Merlin off on his journey from Avalon. I knew Niobe gave him no choice, yet my heart broke to see him leave. It was as if Fate worked of its own accord, and there is naught we could do to alter the course. The more we rebelled the more the Fates forced us to follow their ways.

As Merlin and Uther disappeared into the mists, I knew not how long it would be before I saw Merlin again. Many years may pass in the other realm, but only a short time would pass here in Avalon.

I could not believe that I was Lady of the Lake Where had the years gone? Fear and self-doubt plagued my mind, until I forced myself to soothe those negative emotions. Niobe would not have chosen me as Lady if she did not have total faith in my ability to preserve our way of life and beliefs. I needed to ensure that her faith, and the faith of all who dwelled here, and the outer world, was fulfilled.

I shook myself out of my reverie. There was much to plan for Britain's future. Avalon would place a King on the throne, an act manipulated by Avalon since the beginning of all.

The beginning was a time so long ago that it turned into a haze. Most possessed only distant memories passed down from their ancestors, and Niobe remained the last of those there during the Great Destruction. What was clear was that the values taught and revered must be preserved, and we must not make the same mistakes. That is why it was so important that we keep Avalon from disappearing the same as other places before us. We must keep the peace, harmony, and understanding alive or all could be lost forever this time.

I sighed deeply. How I missed Merlin already. I ached with the emptiness of his place beside me. My only reassurance was his worked with me in the world beyond Avalon. He would ensure that our plans for Uther and Uther's son take the proper course.

Looking back I see how young and untried I was. I lacked the experience of the outside world that would prepare me for all that transpired over the years. I had no idea of the pain and disillusionment that went along with the throne of Avalon.

Niobe left with the morning mists. She could have warned me, but I suppose that is part of being the High Priestess. I needed to learn and experience for myself, for life is what tests a person and makes them worthy or not.

My life as Lady of the Lake was only slightly different from when I was a regular priestess. I still rose early to perform the rituals of our people. Rituals of contemplation under the natural energy of the sky and giving of thanks to the Earth Mother. These morning rituals were relaxing, and many times we found the creatures of the forest gathered around us as they sensed the energy emanating from our bodies and minds. They feared us not, as we lived in harmony.

Where my life did change was the responsibility I held. The lives and learning of all who resided in Avalon was in my hands. Quickly, I learned the desires, abilities, and station of each person here. It was up to me to assign tasks and judgments.

The Book made my job easier. Passed down from one Lady to another the Book of Avalon was a record book of all that transpired, and a history of all incantations and rituals as far back as any could remember. The first time I came upon the Book and began reading, a thrill coursed through my veins. In my hands I held knowledge of power enough to do anything I wanted, and no one was strong enough to stop my desires.

My mind clouded with dark thoughts, and I breathed deep to clear the energy. I never did know why Niobe had not told me of the Book. I suppose I was meant to find it on my own. Maybe it was another test. If so, I suppose I passed, as I never did use the knowledge for anything but the good of Avalon and Nature's energies.

Time passed, I have no idea how long. Word came to us that Gorlois was dead, killed by the arrow of an unknown assailant. The messenger expressed concern at the fickle hand of fate, as it seemed that King Vortigern passed away on the same day as Gorlois perished by the arrow. I sent a silent prayer to the heavens, yet felt relief that events unfolded as necessary for the fulfillment of our plans.

It was about that time that I began to doubt the strength of Merlin's resolve. I held no doubt as to his love for me, but stories filtered to Avalon about how willing he was to accept the priests who littered the countryside, squelching our ways and killing our people. I could only offer prayers to the Goddess that he would uphold the bargain sealed with the Lady Niobe before she left to become One with All.

The messenger returned within the same year to announce the birth of Uther and Igraine's son, the future King of Britain. He was to be called Arthur.

Time passed until one fine misty morning the boat arrived unannounced and caused quite a commotion among the initiates and priestesses. Who summoned the boat to Avalon? No one but someone of this place possessed the power. I knew even before the boat touched upon the shores I sensed Merlin.

I saw in my mind a young boy as well. Blond and blue-eyed, the boy was the hope of our world. Along with the boy came a young girl. I could not be sure who she was, but from the look of her features, I guessed she was the daughter of Igraine and Gorlois.

I made my way quickly to the shore. All before me stepped from the pathway to allow my passage. Like a wave they parted, allowing me access to the boat and Merlin. When our eyes met, I felt a familiar shock bolt through my system. No words were spoken, yet I knew we would be together as we were before he left. As Lady, I was allowed to take a lover of my own choosing. One who could enhance the power within and work with me to protect Avalon and the ways of our people. Merlin was the one I was destined to choose. Together, he and I would know no bounds. Together, there was no obstacle we could not overcome. Our bloodlines were of the ancestors. We honed our abilities over time and would now persevere into another generation.

Merlin understood the bond we shared. He would come to me that evening. No words needed speaking, so I turned my attention to the young boy who stood at his side. Only five years old, the boy's demeanor was of a much older child. I saw that he was afraid, but he hid the fear well. Good, that showed the strength of character necessary for his purpose in life. A purpose he would learn much about over the years.

"Mistress," the boy named Arthur spoke. "Merlin would tell me naught except that I would find out all in due course. Could you tell me why I am here? I miss my mother." His lip quivered, and my heart ached for the boy who held so much responsibility.

Silently, I cursed the Fates that made it necessary to place a lad in such a position. I quickly revised my curse and spread it to the priests who were slowly wreaking havoc on our countryside. It was their denial of others to worship and practice as they desired that was the cause for all this manipulation.

I kept my voice soft and musical so as not to scare the boy. "All will be revealed to you in due course, just as Merlin has said. I will tell you that you are a special boy, and you have much to learn over the next while. Tonight you rest, for tomorrow you begin your lessons."

Obviously not satisfied with my answer, but being well mannered enough not to question further, young Arthur bowed his head in acquiescence. "Yes, mistress."

I then turned my attention to the girl who remained silent all through my discourse with Arthur. "You are Morganna, I assume."

The girl, who I knew to be only ten years old, curtseyed in a very grown up manner and replied, "Yes, mistress, I am Morganna. It seems my stepfather desires not my company to remind him of my father, so he has sent me with Arthur."

So much left unspoken. Black eyes flashed from the not quite innocent face of the child. She held an obvious dislike for the man who would cast her out for a situation beyond her control.

"He presumes much to think I will take you in as an initiate, does he not?"

"He cares not if you take me in or thrust me alone into the forest. I think he is only pleased to say he did his duty by me. I will understand if you do not want me here."

My heart ached for the young girl, so proud, noble, and mature for her age. I saw more grace and honor in her than Uther ever displayed. Cast into an uncertain situation, she barely wavered, yet I sensed her emotions, and she was terrified. Underneath the fear, I also sensed hate. A hate I assumed she held for Uther, but there was a block against my gentle mind probe, so I could not be sure.

I was interested. The girl was preventing my thoughts from reaching her. Was she aware of what she did? I thought not, but thought it would be interesting to develop her skills.

"I see no reason not to accept you into Avalon. After all, you do have blood of the ancestors flowing in your veins. Your mother, Igraine, is of Avalon you know?"

Speculation crossed the girl's face. "I knew not. If she is of the Old Ways, why does she practice the ways of the New Religion?"

"Ahhh, so you know of the Old Ways, do you?"

Morganna looked worried that she may receive punishment for her words. I wondered what events transpired that learning the Old Ways would promote fear in a person. I placed my hand upon Morganna's head. "It is all right to speak of these ways. In fact, that is what we learn here. Not the ways of the Christian God."

Realizing she was allowed to speak of such things without getting herself in trouble, Morganna said, "My maid would tell me of such things, but one day, when I spoke to Mother of this, she slapped my face." Morganna touched her face in remembrance. "She told me never, never to talk such again, or I would be greatly punished. If Mother is so much against these ways, why would she let me be sent here?"

"She does so by her husband's urging. Uther gave his word to send his son here for fostering. He is not so against the ways as Igraine. If he also insisted that you come here, then Igraine would have no say in the matter."

Morganna's next question surprised me as to her mature grasp of political maneuvering. "What did Father owe you that he risk the displeasure of my mother, whom he greatly loves, to give you their son?"

"Why, I think that is something for older and wiser minds than yours."

"Yes, mistress."

Merlin spoke his first words since arriving on the shore of Avalon. His voice poured over my body and made my skin heat. "From now on you must both address the lady before you as Lady Nimue, for she is the Lady of the Lake, High Priestess of Avalon, and Protector of the ways of the Old Ones."

Arthur's eyes grew round in astonishment. His whispered words fell upon the swirling mists. "I have heard tales of Avalon and the Old Ones, but thought them fairytales."

I frowned at these words. Addressing Merlin, I snapped rather harshly, "What is this? Is Avalon not given due consideration in the outside world? Are we to perish so easily into a forgotten land?"

My fury built at the thought that those who used to revere the Holy place, now placed Avalon in such low esteem. I waited while Merlin looked for an answer to placate me.

His voice soothed softly. "No, Nimue, many people still jump the fires at Beltane. There are still those that believe the ways of Avalon. It is just that Arthur has not been exposed overly much to this. Igraine became quite adept at Christian ways while she was married to Gorlois. It seems her beliefs have been passed on to Arthur."

I was so incensed I ignored the small ears that still stood with us, soaking up all that we spoke. "What of Uther, does he not teach his son and heir the ways of Avalon? After all, it was we who put him upon the throne and gave him the wife he so desired."

"Uther is so enamored of Igraine he does naught to aggrieve her. She has woven the spell of love, and it wraps itself around Uther, causing him to act like a love sick lad."

"Well, it is good that we have Arthur with us now. Morganna, as well. She may prove useful. Niobe was right about Uther not being the one to bring peace to the land of Britain. He is too weak if he is ruled by his cock instead of his responsibility and promises to us."

I knew I spoke harshly, especially in front of the young ones so swiftly torn from their family. I suppose I lost patience with those who would give their word and then go about their own way as if nothing mattered. Uther owed Avalon, but to be fair, he fulfilled his promise to give his son over for fostering. He made no such promise to keep Avalon and the ways of the Old Ones alive in Britain. That would be up to Arthur when he became King. Thank the powers that the lad was now in our hands.

I directed my priestesses to the care of Arthur and Morganna and went back to my chambers to prepare for the arrival of Merlin. It was to be a special night. I would give of myself again to Merlin, and we would come together in a physical joining to signify the timeless joining of forces. Our union would bring about a development of higher consciousness in an evolution of better understanding of the forces around us.

The occasion was austere and serious. As we came together, time stood still. The reasons for our joining became meaningless. For a short time, we both lost control and became one in each other. If Avalon ceased to exist that night, I would not have cared. All I cared for was the feel of Merlin and the love we shared. Nothing else I ever felt overwhelmed and overpowered me, as did our joining. Could anything even compare? I almost understood Uther's preoccupation with Igraine. If that is what he felt when they were together, I would have a hard time faulting his actions.

When our joining was complete and we lay beside each other watching the flames from the fireplace dance upon the wall, I came back to my senses. Losing control like that scared me. The fate of Avalon and many people rested on my shoulders, and I not cared. For a few moments I gave in to the passion that was Merlin's and mine. How could I have done that? My duty remained clear, my burden to carry from the day I was born, as it was Merlin's. We could not allow ourselves to be carried away down the path of passion or much would be lost. The Old Ones, who passed on their ways and beliefs, would cease to exist in our minds and our world if I allowed myself to waver from my destiny.

Merlin must have sensed my discomfort for he spoke to calm me. "Do not feel afraid, my love."

"How can I not? We lost ourselves and our destinies. That cannot happen again."

"We lost nothing. We experienced a beautiful union of two energies, and now we are back to a more stable mindset. Nimue, we both know what needs to be done, that does not mean we cannot enjoy each other as well. The Earth Mother would not wish us to be miserable." He took my face gently between his hands, kissed my lips, and whispered in my ear. "We are meant to be together or we would not be here. You are the High Priestess of Avalon, and I am Merlin of Brittany. Our destiny is to see to the salvation of our beliefs and the beliefs of all who are different, even the Christians."

Shocked at his words, I bolted up in bed. "What say you? It is the Christians who will not accept any way but their own."

"Yes, and it is up to us to help them understand the ways of peace, harmony, and acceptance. We will not make ourselves as them and destroy a religion just because people believe differently."

His words confused me. He made sense, but somewhere deep inside, I felt doom plant itself in my chest and begin to grow slowly.

"But they seek to destroy us. They know nothing of our ways, and they do not care to even try. They call us evil, revile us, and say we will be cast into the Holy bowels of Hell. How can you defend such a belief? They use their God to control the lowly farmer or shepherd who knows not better."

Merlin was visibly upset that his words upset me so, but I cared not. I needed to know that he was with me in this battle or not. He took my hand in his; his magic worked in my mind and my heart as he weaved his spell with words of comfort and explanation.

"Nimue, my love, not all Christians are as you say. Many of them are giving and loving people who want only what is best for their people. They truly believe there is but one God and this God gave his son for their sins. To them, they must pay this debt by teaching of love and harmony. Are these beliefs so different from our own?"

I almost killed him there in the bed where we created love but a moment ago. As much as I loved Merlin, my mind could only recall the carnage and horror that occurred but a few years earlier, and I wanted to kill the man who lay beside me telling me the innocence of the invading Christians. Visions of words void of honor, sly threats, and then the blood—oh, the blood—was terrible to behold.

"Nimue, Nimue, what is wrong? My heart is breaking with reflections of your pain, and I know naught what is wrong. Please tell me so I may help you."

Merlin's loving voice and words of reassurance dragged me back into the present. My tears began to fall. I could not help myself; I needed someone to confide in. Someone I could show weakness to. So I confided in the one person I thought I could trust.

"Merlin, I will tell you of the day of horror in Avalon that we are only now recovering from. About five years ago a visitor came to us. We were expecting no one, but I awoke one morning and, in my meditations, was told to send the boat to the other shore. This I did. All the while curious as to whom possessed the ability to send thoughts for the boat. No one I knew of was gone from Avalon, and I knew you were still at the King's summer retreat in Tintagel. I was most heartily surprised when the boat returned with a man dressed as a Christian priest. I could not recall ever seeing any Christian in this land. He said he was from a faraway land and brought a message from the man who led the Christians."

I was thirsty and found it hard to continue my story. To gather my thoughts I paused to sip some nectar squeezed from peaches grown nearby. The cool, golden liquid ran down my throat leaving a sweet, sticky taste on my lips. I ran my tongue over my lips and enjoyed the taste of the fruit drink.

"Come, Nimue, you are holding back, what happened?"

I sighed heavily, placed my glass down, and began to recite my tale. "The priest stated briefly that the message was one of peace. The man who led them was interested in coming to Avalon to learn of our ways, maybe even learn to work in peace and help each other if our goals were similar. There was more to the message and arrangements to be made, but the priest claimed to be tired, so he asked if he could rest for the eve and continue our talk the next morning. Of course, I let him. My heart was singing that the newcomers to our land would attempt to understand us and the ways of our ancestors rather than destroy us out of fear and misunderstanding."

"Obviously, something happened or I would not still be out in the world using tact and politics to try to save the Old Ways." Merlin prompted.

"Yes...yes. You could say something happened, and it is my fault. I was so pleased at the promise of a bond between our worlds that I neglected to scry before retiring to bed that evening. I saw no need to consult the crystal and its energies for signs. I could not have been more wrong."

I stopped my tale there, as my voice was shaking and my throat was dry. I finished the last of the peach juice, took a deep breath, and told Merlin of the events of that eve.

"It was a night of a dark moon. The energy of the Goddess was low and the women of Avalon each spent the night in their room for relaxing or a meditation of solitude. This is how he was able to kill so many before we knew what was happening. He went from room to room with his axe and he killed them. There was no sound, no cry for help, no warning.

"Sometime in the night, I was awakened by the cry of Ebony, a raven I healed some years back. I instantly felt all was not right. Pain ripped through my body, such intense waves of emotions that I can recall no such experience. I stumbled to the door and beckoned my maid to sound the alarm, something was wrong. I gathered my energies and used my mind's eye to see where the disruptive energy was. I was sorry my powers are so strong. I saw the so-called man of God covered in blood. The light of madness glowed from his eyes. His axe swung from his hand in pious abandon, and I heard him pray in the name of Christ as he let the blade loose on the slender neck of our newest and youngest initiate. The blood, oh, Merlin, the blood was everywhere. I never saw first hand as others cleaned up the bodies and all their parts, but I witnessed enough to make me sick, and sorry, for the rest of my life."

Merlin's face was stark. I believe my story shocked him. Good, he should have been shocked at the evil perpetrated in the name of the one God. He was trying to speak, but his voice failed him. After a couple of attempts, he finally was able to speak.

"I assume the man no longer lives?"

"You would assume correctly. He was sacrificed in the name of our God and Goddess. Such a sacrifice has not been done in many, many years, but the souls of the butchered cried out for retribution."

With the end of my story, talk between us was non-existent as we both gathered our thoughts and feelings.

"Tell me, Nimue, how many did he kill?"

"He slay fifteen priestesses in all levels of their training. Thank the powers that there were enough with advanced knowledge to re-teach new members. We are still returning to our former strength and abilities after the desecration and destruction."

A bright sliver of light found its way through the window, signaling the beginning of a new day. I could not believe the eve passed us by so quickly. Having recited the tragedy, I needed to know how Merlin stood on the matter of religions.

"Do you see now, Merlin, why I cannot accept the ways of the Christians into our land?"

"Will not is what you mean. Nimue, I am ashamed and disgusted for the actions of that man. I feel heartfelt aching for the pain and suffering of the women, but you have to understand he was probably some zealot. His actions would have been his own. The Church would not allow such butchering in the name of their God, of this I am sure."

"I am glad you are sure, because I am not. You were not there. You did not see the madness of his mind all in the name of his God. The acts of horror he committed were because of what he believed. How can any kind of religion that is supposed to be about love and harmony teach its followers to kill and torture innocent people because they are different?"

"You killed him. Was that an act of love and harmony, or vengeance?"

My heart pounded deep in my chest, and each word Merlin spoke was like a hammer beating on my heart. My head began to spin, and a dense wall of fog rose to separate us. As the sound of ringing increased, I felt as if I were slipping upon a smooth, wet surface until I could not stand any longer. As I fell, I reached out for Merlin to save me, but he was not there. Nothing but silence greeted my pleas for help.

I awoke sometime later that day to the worried face of my maid. I pushed away the cloth she held to my head and attempted to sit up. Where was Merlin? How long had I been unconscious? These questions I asked of the young girl who waited upon me.

"Milady, Merlin has left for the other world. He says he leaves Arthur and Morganna in your competent hands, but Uther is in need of his council. The sun has passed over the earth and its golden rays disappear behind the hills. That is how long you have been laying abed."

I cried, not aloud but deep inside my head where no one could hear but me. The cry turned to a scream. A wailing, aching cry for the loss of something so newly found. From now on I would be on my own. I was sure I could not count on Merlin to help Avalon, or me.

Tamara was jolted from the yellowed pages of the journal by the sound of a train whistling in the distance. The lonely echo sang a song that beat with the rhythm of Tamara's heart. She wiped away the tears that flowed unheeded. Tears for the sadness of a love gone awry.

Moaning, she stretched her stiff body and made her way to the bathroom for a quick pee. Her senses were muddled with the emotion of Nimue's words, and she found herself anxious to return to the story of the past. Ironic, considering her reluctance to read the journal.

She flushed the toilet, washed her hands, and returned to bed, where she lay for a moment in consideration. Love! An emotion she had little experience with. Sure, she loved her mom. Despite their differences. But that's not the same thing. She'd never experienced the kind of love that happens between a man and a woman. Based on what she just read, maybe she was better off.

Trust. As far as Tamara was concerned, that would be the hardest part of a relationship. She sighed and settled back into a comfortable position. Since there were no prospects on the horizon, she figured she didn't have to worry too much that trust was one of her weaker traits.

Her fingers tingled to return to the story. Anxiously, she picked up the book and opened the pages to the past.

As time passed slowly in Avalon, news from the outside world seemed slow as well. In truth, events happened quickly. I was able to use my Sight to watch the reign of Uther and determine the right time to take steps to place Arthur upon the throne. It would take careful consideration, as I wanted the lad with us as long as possible so he could develop the understanding and loyalty of our ways he would need. I also didn't want to let the state of affairs in Britain slide so far that there would be no hope of rescue. As it was, I felt the thin thread that connected our worlds stretching.

Arthur himself was a polite lad. Interested in learning of our ways, he was more interested in climbing the throne and doing what he could to help his people. I shook my head that his mother and father spoiled him and treated him as a king before his time. He felt he need not work hard to attain what was already his. Do not misunderstand me. He was a lad with a true heart, but his mind was not sharp enough to question and see what was beyond his eyes. I would need to prepare him for a battle, not on the battlefields of so called honor, but a battle of wits and souls. I was not sure if I would be able to in our short time together.

I often cast my mind to Morganna, I wished she had been born Arthur, and he her. She was intelligent and possessed strong abilities in the ways of the Old Ones. The way she grasped the situation on her first day here was only the tip of her talent and abilities. She should have been the one to be on the throne. I knew I would have to take a special hand in her teaching, as I would with Arthur.

I probably should have listened to my inner urgings at that time, but after the massacre of many of our powerful priestesses, I was grasping at the abilities I could see in Morganna.

In hindsight, I should have sensed the darkness, but at that moment, I saw only what I wanted to see. Actually, I foolishly believed what I saw when I put my scrying to practice. With a candle flame, I went easily into a state of relaxation by watching the dancing flames of orange, blue, and gold. When I asked the powers to show me the future, I saw Morganna as a priestess and Arthur as a king much loved by his people. Merlin and I stood together at the doorway to Avalon. I was satisfied and relieved that all seemed to go so well.

I curse myself for not following a basic rule of following through and not always believing things as they appear to you. I should have looked further to see that yes, Arthur was loved much by his people, but not his wife. I should have understood that although one becomes a powerful priestess, it does not ensure that her heart is pure. Happiness and relief upon seeing Merlin and I together at our place of power, blinded me to the fact that we were locked in mortal battle.

Yes, if I used the knowledge and ability entrusted to me by Niobe, I would have saved much grief for many people. So, I suppose you could say that all that followed is really my fault. As it was, I continued to teach Morganna the ways of Avalon. In fact, I taught her much that was not shown to others. I continued with Niobe's plan to place Arthur upon the throne, and I continued to believe that Merlin would uphold the ways that he was raised with.

Thus, history was written.

Chapter Nine

A slamming door startled Tamara from the mythical world she entered. As her tired eyes re-adjusted, she rubbed her stiff neck and glanced at her bedside clock. It was past midnight. "Wow, I can't believe I read for that long."

She stood and stretched, attempting to return to a normal state of reality. The haunting story of her ancestor hypnotized her, and Tamara was having difficulty shaking off the heavy, lethargic feeling that crept inside her. For a brief moment the room swayed and Tamara grasped the dresser for support.

Just then, her attention was captured by a gentle hum from down the hallway. Curious, and feeling stronger after a couple of deep breaths, Tamara crossed to her door and listened. The humming turned to a low, continuous chant. Hoping to see the source of the noise, Tamara tied her robe tighter about her body, opened her door, and peered down the dim hallway.

Hmmm, nothing jumped out at her. Silently, she padded through the carpeted passageway. Behind her, shadows from her still open bedroom door arced in dancing forms upon the walls.

As she approached the staircase, the sounds became clearer, and Tamara paused to determine their exact location. They came from Mrs. Harlow's bedroom. Maybe her hostess wasn't feeling well. Should she check on her? But it was after midnight, if there was nothing wrong, she'd just be intruding.

Oh, well, in for a pence, in for a pound or something like that. Tamara knocked lightly on the door. No one answered, but the tempo of humming increased, which worried Tamara enough to push the door open a crack.

Her gaze was met with the sight of Mrs. Harlow sitting cross-legged on the floor. Incense wafted a gentle aroma upon the air, and candle flames bounced their reflection into the mirror. Barely visible were pale forms of a canopy bed, a couple of chairs, and a dresser. Innocently upon the dresser sat a crystal wand, a gleaming copper chalice, a deck of tarot cards, and a small gold pentagram. The rest of the items sat in the shadows.

Tamara knew this scene. She'd seen her mother's rituals often enough. "Great, it must be a full moon or something." Assured that nothing was wrong, Tamara closed the door with a soft click and made her way back to her room.

With her own door closed behind her, Tamara mumbled, "Figures I'd end up staying somewhere that's run by a witch. Wouldn't Mom love this irony?"

Overcome with extreme exhaustion and tired from the day's excitement, she yawned and stretched. Bouncing onto her soft bed, she curled up under the down comforter and drifted off into dreamland.

Morning came in the form of bright sunlight that drenched the room in warmth. Not one for rising early, Tamara was tempted to cocoon under the covers and shut the sun out. But the journal piqued her interest, so Tamara was prompted to pull herself from the comfort of her slumber.

Uncomfortable about seeing her host after the glimpse into her personal life, Tamara's plan was to sneak out before anyone was up.

No such luck. Mrs. Harlow's chipper greeting was the first thing Tamara heard upon descending the stairs.

Maybe she could just avoid the subject and make her getaway without any uncomfortable scenes. "Good morning, Mrs. Harlow. Breakfast smells great."

"Ahh, yes, when I saw you yesterday, I said to myself, that girl needs fattening up. So, I set about to make you a good ole-fashioned English breakfast. I must say, girl, you do look so much more rested this morning. Did you sleep well? Are you hungry?"

Without waiting for a reply, Mrs. Harlow set down a plate filled with sausage, eggs, home fries, pancakes, and toast. "Now, as soon as you've eaten a good breakfast you can set about your day's work."

"Oh, but I can't eat a breakfast like this. I usually only have yogurt and some fruit."

"Then it's time you start eating proper and put some meat on those bones of yours. By the way, I hope I didn't disturb your sleep last night? It was a full moon you know."

The question would have confused Tamara, if she hadn't been raised by a mother who swore by the power of a full moon and regularly performed her own rituals. As it was, she didn't want to get personal, so she shoveled a forkful of food in her mouth and mumbled a response.

Unfortunately, Mrs. Harlow seemed to have no compunction about continuing the conversation, as if it were an everyday subject. Her landlady settled herself down across the table, elbows propped on the table and chin resting on hands. "Yes, I do tend to get carried away when I celebrate an Esbat. Oh, I'm sorry, sometimes this brain of mine doesn't stop and think. An Esbat is a Wiccan moon ritual where we honor the Goddess."

"I know." Damn, the words were out before she could stop them. Now there'd be a whole conversation about how she knew about such things.

"My dear, that's wonderful. I'm so pleased that you practice the Wiccan traditions. Oh, we have so much to talk about."

"Mrs. Harlow." Her hostess continued to ramble about introducing Tamara to her coven. Raising her voice, she repeated. "Mrs. Harlow."

"Yes, Tamara."

"I'm not a witch, my mother is."

A crestfallen look perched itself upon the woman's face. "Oh." She was obviously disappointed that there would be no long discourses on the wonders of witchcraft.

Now seemed as good a time as any to make her escape. Tamara stood. "Breakfast was great, but I'm afraid I really have so much to do today."

"The keys are on the table. Tizzy'll give you no trouble."

"Tizzy?"

"My car."

"Oh." Tamara wasn't sure what she thought of people who actually named their cars, but she was willing to keep an open mind considering Mrs. Harlow was lending the car free of charge.

With directions in hand and a quick lesson on driving the wrong side of the road, Tamara set off with a sigh of relief. Pleased at the comfort and luxury of the borrowed car, she promised herself to enjoy the countryside, unlike yesterday's speedy trip from the airport.

With a careful eye on directions and staying on the right, or wrong, side of the road, Tamara's mind still wandered. She couldn't believe the spectacle of her hostess performing a ritual last night. Why was it that she couldn't seem to get away from all that hocus pocus stuff? Between her mother, her current assignment, Nimue's memoirs, and Mrs. Harlow, she was facing something Wiccan at every turn. If you believed in fate, or karma, you'd almost think there was some lesson that needed learning. Sure, and next there'd be little faeries flying around the air.

It only took about fifteen minutes for Tamara to reach the downtown area of Glastonbury. The quaint, yet regal, beauty of the city's ancient stone churches and downtown shops instantly enraptured her. Merchants obviously cared for the appearance of their stores, as the sidewalks were kept clean and the windows sparkled. Some merchants even went so far as to paint their buildings cheery colors of blue, red, and yellow. These brilliant colors provided a dazzling contrast to other whitewashed buildings that lined the street.

In an impromptu tour, Tamara traveled down one side road after another, searching out the churches belonging to the spires that crested the landscape. She found herself in awe at ancient arched doorways, iron rod fences, and roughly hewn stone structures. Realizing she could spend all day sightseeing when there were things to do, she headed to the main street and pulled her borrowed car into an available parking spot. Parking in Glastonbury was much easier than parking in New York.

Tamara gathered her purse and Nimue's journal. With the tingle of fresh air and the mild aroma of coffee and baked goods assaulting her nostrils, she turned her attention to the bookstore she'd come to find.

Not quite as well maintained as some of the other shops, Mac's Books exuded character nonetheless. Lead crystal glass filled the arched window frames, albeit slightly dusty. Smooth faced, white brick walls long past better days, but the hand drawn welcome sign and baskets of fresh flowers on the front walk made a person comfortable.

She must have looked lost, because a passer-by asked if she needed directions.

"No, I'm fine. Thanks for asking."

Before she even made it to the door of the shop, she'd been greeted and wished a good day by two more people. Helpfulness seemed to be the normal way of things in this quaint town. Tamara was used to the abruptness and impersonal attitude of the big city, so she found the casual attitude rather strange. In New York, if you even so much as looked a stranger in the eye, they'd figure you for a mugger or something worse.

A small bell on the door jingled Tamara's arrival, and she found herself immediately under the scrutiny of two people. Both looking as if they'd been caught in the middle of something they shouldn't be doing. Although she turned her attention to the gnome-like man approaching, she felt her senses highly attuned to the other person standing in the shadowed recess of the small store. For some reason she felt drawn to him and stopped herself from, literally, leaning his direction.

"G'mornin miss. It's a fine day in the makin' today, isn't it?"

Her response was automatic. Her pulse raced in reaction to the stranger in the corner. She forced her glance to remain on the man who stood in front of her. "Hi." She took the offered hand and shook. "I assume you're Mac?"

"The one and only. How can I help you, Missy?"

Mac's gaze quickly fell to the book held under her arm. Only a small part of the cover was exposed, but for some reason Tamara felt the need to shift her arm to hide even that from the piercing gray eyes of the shopkeeper. "I was told that this is the best place to come to get an appraisal on a book. Is that true?"

"Of course, it is." Mac chuckled. Tamara relaxed and decided the small man was kind of cute, and seemed nice enough.

"Is that the book you brought me to appraise?" Mac gestured to the book Tamara still held clutched under her arm.

Flustered because she found her gaze wandering to the still silent giant in the shadows, Tamara's speech was hurried. "Yes. Oh, yes, this is the book…I…" Her voice lowered to a whisper. "Is there an office or something where we can have some privacy?"

Mac's eyes flew to the unidentified man in the corner. "Don't worry about him. He's like a son."

"Still, I'd really like this to stay between us."

"Fine. Gavin, you'll have to get lost. The lady wants to be alone with me." Bushy gray eyebrows wriggled up and down to accentuate the statement.

"No, that's not what I meant."

"I'm only joshin' you. Gavin knows a pretty lady like you wouldn't have any interest in an old geezer like me."

Tamara now knew the name of the silent figure. Gavin. Silently, she rolled the name on her tongue and found she liked the feel. Gavin took a step forward, and Tamara's world suddenly fell apart. Her free hand flew to her suddenly constricted throat, and she took an involuntary step backward.

The man from her dreams. How could that be? Her senses were assaulted with a flashback. Memories of a sculpted bronze body stepping from crystal water and standing splendid, wet and naked. Dream and reality melded together until Tamara could no longer tell which was which. Her gaze wandered to a face of granite chiseled with the layers of life. Unshaven, Gavin's jaw was strong in a way that spoke of a streak of stubbornness, yet his lapis blue eyes, instead of looking hard like the crystal, shimmered soft and gentle.

Gavin thrust a hand in front of her. Tamara couldn't move; her mind refused to send the proper signals to her hand. Finally, she reached out and found her hand engulfed in the heat of Gavin's larger one.

"It's nice to meet you." Why did her voice sound so shaky? And why did her hand refuse to obey her mental command to return to her side?

The two of them stood locked in a handshake. Gavin was the first to move. A cool breeze and emptiness were the only sensations Tamara felt on her hand now released hand. For some reason, she couldn't look straight into the eyes of the man just introduced to her. Instead, she stared at his chest. Curls of dark hair peeked out from beneath the faded denim shirt. Tamara's eyes searched out the pearl buttons and frayed edges only to return to the chest hair.

"Pleasure's all mine. Umm, is there something on my shirt?"

Oh, God, what an idiot. "No, sorry, I was just thinking about something. I tend to drift every now and again." That was the best she could come up with to cover her dazed state.

"Don't drift too far, you might get lost." Gavin's voice teased her senses and caused Tamara's heart to beat a swift staccato.

The moment was broken by the merry jingle from the door, and Mac excused himself to see to his latest customer. Tamara forced herself not to laugh at the most recent occupant to Mac's bookstore.

"Is it the orange spiked hair or the ring through his nose that makes you want to laugh?"

Gavin's question registered in Tamara's mind, but it was his voice that shot quivers of sensation through her stomach. Come on, it's a simple question. Don't freeze up like some schoolgirl with a crush, she admonished herself.

"More likely it's his pants that look like they're about to fall down around his ankles." She congratulated herself on coming up with a witty answer. Why did this man make her feel so ill at ease? Did he really look like the man from her dreams, or was that her imagination?

Loud, angry voices from Mac and the teenager made Tamara tense. It sounded like there was trouble brewing. But Gavin didn't seem worried, and Mac wasn't kicking the kid out, so Tamara relaxed.

Just then, the kid took a book, threw it to the floor, and stalked out of the bookstore. Mac stood for a moment and then followed. The heavy silence in the store was equaled only by the uneasiness beating in Tamara's chest. The room felt very small and stifled.

In an attempt at conversation, Tamara remarked, "Okay, I'm lost. Any idea what's going on?"

"I'm not exactly sure, but it looks like Mac's gone to reason with the lad."

"Why? I mean the kid was rude and disrespectful. Why doesn't Mac just let him go on his way?"

"Ahh, you don't know our Mac very well, if you think he'd let one of his protégés leave in anger."

"Protégé?"

"Yep. Mac has a tendency to take a punk off the street and under his wing every now and again."

"Oh. Why?"

"He likes to help them see a better life through books and learning.

By making sure they don't get unduly influenced by some of the street gangs, he can help steer them down the right path."

"That sounds a little philanthropic."

"Maybe, but Mac believes if more people paid attention to the welfare of others, the world wouldn't be in such a state."

Tamara was curious as to the source of the defensiveness that threaded Gavin's voice. Then it hit her.

"You're one of his protégés, aren't you?"

"Yes, and look how I turned out." His eyes twinkled in a way that reminded Tamara of the moonlight reflecting in the still water of her dreams.

Before she could reply, Mac marched back in the store. "Kids these days, I don't know how they can think with brains like Swiss cheese. Now, where were we?"

"Mac, we still need to have a talk about the reason you called me last night." Gavin prompted.

"Oh, I'm sorry," Tamara said. "I've interrupted something. I can come back in a while, there's no hurry." She was glad of an excuse to get out of the suffocating store.

Mac's reply was quick and sharp, in contrast to his original happy go lucky demeanor. "No, stay. Gavin and I can finish what we were doing later. Really, it's all right."

The tensing of Gavin's jaw and the narrowing of his eyes told Tamara he was not exactly happy with the arrangement, but after all, it was Mac's store. It was up to him how he wanted to do business.

"I'll be back, Mac, and no more stalling." The sentence came out almost as a threat and served to heighten the tension in the small room.

Involuntarily, Tamara turned to watch the movement of Gavin's hips and, yes, his butt, as he walked out the door. Mac's eyes settled on her, causing her to blush profusely.

"Don't be embarrassed. Gavin's a handsome lad. I'd be surprised if you weren't finding yourself attracted to him even a little."

"He sounded kind of upset."

"Don't worry, he'll get over it, and it'll do the lad good to wait. Gavin is a man used to getting his own way. Not many people have the nerve to come up against him. Not many except me anyway." Mac's chuckle placed him back in character as the cuddly, old shop owner. "Now, why don't we get down to the reason you came to me in the first place." Mac moved over to a decrepit table and was clearing books and papers, strewing them carelessly onto a desk in the corner.

"To tell you the truth, I'm not sure if I'm wasting your time or not."

"Let me do the worryin' about that. I mean, if you knew what you owned you wouldn't be here asking for my advice."

"Of course. I'm sorry, it's just that my mother thinks this is some ancient book that holds special powers. Personally, I think she's been drinking a little too much herbal tea."

As soon as Mac heard the words ancient book, his pulse raced and his throat tightened. Arthritic fingers itched to touch the book under the woman's arm, and he silently warned himself to remain patient. For some reason, she was hesitant to give it up. While part of his mind listened to her explain about her mother and her eccentricities, another part of his mind was calculating the odds that two out of the supposed three journals in existence would show up in his shop within two days of each other. Mac wasn't much of a believer in magic and such, but his faith in fate and the powers that be would need to be re-evaluated if the book Tamara held was a mate to the one Gavin showed him yesterday.

"So, would you like to have a look?"

"Please." Mac rubbed his hands on his pants to wipe off some sweat. He couldn't remember the last time he'd experienced so much excitement in his life. Taking the book reverently in his hands, he placed it on the scarred wooden tabletop and proceeded with his examination. Thinking aloud, he provided Tamara with a running commentary.

"It's definitely old, and it's definitely a journal of sorts. I can't be sure how old it is, or whether it's actually the memoirs of— Lady of the Lake, you said?"

"Yes. Supposedly, she was one of my ancestors."

Mac knew the book was authentic. His bones ached with the certainty. He didn't know what to do about it, so he needed to buy some time. Between talk he heard, and what he'd read about last night after Gavin left, he was worried enough to proceed with caution.

"I'll need to keep it overnight and do some further inspection, as well as some research into the history of such an item."

"Research. How would you research something like this?"

"There could be references to such an item in other texts. My personal library is rather large, so I'll start there. The old timers at the local pub and their drunken tales of old may provide a clue. Maybe we'll find out there's something to the stories the old geezers tell when they're in their cups on a Saturday night."

Mac didn't want to fill her in too much. How could he be sure the book even belonged to her. If he could get her to agree to leave the book, he'd fill in some pieces of the puzzle, check on her credentials, and know better how to proceed.

"Tell me where yer stayin', and I'll give you a call tomorrow when, hopefully, I'll have some news."

"I don't know if I like the idea of leaving it overnight. According to my mom, it's been in the family an awfully long time."

"I promise I'll guard it with my life."

Tamara chewed her lip as she weighed leaving the book against being able to do some more reading that night. Suddenly realizing the grasp the ancient book held over her, she decided. "It's only a book. Of course, I'll leave it with you. It'll be nice to find out a little more about its history."

"That's the girl." Mac felt relief at having time to read and compare the books. He noticed Tamara hesitate and glance around as if looking for something.

"Was there anything you were looking for?"

"You wouldn't happen to have any books on witchcraft or the Glastonbury Tor would you?"

"Ahh, you're interested in the Ceremony of the Stars?"

"Yes, but only from a business point of view. I'm doing a story for my magazine and was hoping you could fill me in."

"Only if you'll have a cup of tea with me."

"Twist my arm, and it's done."

Relieved to be off the subject of the journal, Mac set about to prepare tea. He kept up a constant line of chatter to Tamara who sat on the wooden bench at the nearest table.

"The Ceremony of the Stars is part of the history of Glastonbury. No one is exactly sure when it began except that it was many centuries ago. Since the event only happens once every few hundred years, you can well imagine the bruhaha surrounding that particular night. People come from all over the world, and the Tor is lit up like a Roman candle with all the different groups of people. It's become so busy that organizations need to apply for permission to worship on the Tor on the night in question."

"Hmmm, that's interesting. Do you know any witches who are in the ceremony this year? I'd really like to interview them."

Tamara's words barely registered in Mac's confused mind. He found his mind working over the appearance of two journals at the time of the Ceremony; it seemed too much a coincidence. He'd never been one to believe in coincidence. All sorts of possibilities assaulted his mind, but the questioning look on Tamara's face brought him back to the present. What was the question the young lady asked of him? Oh, yeah. "I'm sorry. They'd be mighty upset if I handed their names out, and I can guarantee none of them would speak to you. Especially you being a reporter. No offense."

"But I don't write for one of those rag mags. My magazine has a good reputation or else I wouldn't be working for them."

"That may be, but folks involved in Wicca like to keep their ceremonies secret. Not because they're doing anything wrong mind you, but they open themselves up to all kinds of prejudices and condemnations, so they keep to themselves."

"I promise I'll be respectful and won't push any of them if they don't want to talk with me. Please."

Mac considered himself a fairly good judge of character, and he hoped his judgment was right in this case or else he'd have a whole lot of witches ticked off at him. "All right, you talked me into it, but mind you've got to respect their wishes."

"Oh, I will, thanks, Mac."

"Your best bet is Lady Divine. She has a place just outside town where she does readings. You know, tea leaves, tarot cards, you name it, and she does it. Here," Mac pulled a card from the desk drawer, "this is her address. Tell her I sent you. You'll be assured of a warm welcome that way."

"Thank you, Mac, you're saving me a lot of trouble. I guess I'll come back tomorrow for my book."

"Sounds good. I'll find out what I can."

Mac watched the sway of Tamara's hips as she climbed the three stairs to the sidewalk. What the heck, he wasn't dead, and she sure did have a nice body. She was a sweet girl, too. Mac chuckled as he recalled the sparks jumping about between Gavin and her. He wasn't sure if either of them was aware of how they affected each other, but they would certainly be seeing more of each other over the next while. The memoirs of Merlin and Nimue appeared for a reason. Mac was absolutely certain of that.

Chapter Ten

Gavin hadn't wandered far. From across the street, he appreciated the sway of Tamara's luscious behind as she exited the store and made her way down the street. Her appearance threw his thoughts into turmoil. Gavin tried to decide whether it was her luscious, tightly compacted body or the emerald green gaze that flickered to his and then turned away. Maybe it was the silky, auburn hair that touched her shoulders and made his hands ache to run through the curly thickness.

Whoa, get a hold of yourself you idiot. She's just a woman like any other. But even as he admonished himself, he felt a nagging sensation that she was more than that. It didn't matter, because she was gone, and he'd probably never see her again. Giving himself a mental shake, he loped across the street, threw open the door, and stood for a second while his eyes adjusted to the dim light.

Mac must have been intent on what he was doing, because Gavin's entrance surprised him enough to drop the book he was dusting onto the hardwood floor.

"Sorry, Mac. Damn, I thought that woman would never leave. Can we talk now?"

"Calm yourself. What were you doing, standing across the street waiting?"

"Well, since you kicked me out of here I decided to wait in the Market Café."

"Lad, you never were one for patience."

"Come on, old man, quit giving me a hard time and fill me in."

Gavin chuckled at the familiar exchange of insults. Anyone listening would probably think he was being insulting. But years of friendship and respect that allowed the two of them to insult in a caring way. Mac was always trying to teach him a lesson or two, and it looked like today would be no exception.

"That woman was quite attractive, wouldn't you say?" Mac teased while he waved a duster over books and shelves. Mac never dusted anything in his store. In fact, until now Gavin hadn't even known Mac owned a duster.

"Yes, I suppose so, but what does that have to do with Merlin's memoirs?"

"Nothing, just that she was an attractive woman."

"Fine, she was good looking. Now would you quit puttering about, sit down, and talk."

Gavin was eager to return to the journal for a couple of reasons. First, because he wanted to know, second, because he wanted Mac to quit teasing him about Tamara. He found himself at a distinct disadvantage in her presence. The disadvantage being that he'd never felt so ill at ease with a woman before. Usually, he could steer the conversation with some gentle sexual teasing and innuendoes. With Tamara, his tongue felt like raw meat, and his brain about as much use as the Swiss cheese Mac mentioned earlier. What really worried him was the way he wanted to reach out and touch her. Anyway, anywhere, anyhow, he ached to make contact with her naked skin.

"Okay, okay. What's wrong with the young today? Ordering an old man around, anyway. No respect, I tell you, no respect." Mac grumbled as he took a seat across the table from Gavin.

"Now, where would you like me to start?"

Gavin growled. "You're pushing it. How do I know where you should start? You're the one telling the story."

"Oh, yeah, that's right. Well, I suppose I'll start with why I called you last night."

"Great. Why don't you?"

Mac laughed, and Gavin could tell that today's lesson was going to be one of patience. Mac reached under the table and pulled up a large book. The text crackled ominously and left a cloud of dust in its wake. To Gavin, it looked as if the book would fall apart in a strong breeze. He watched as Mac carefully handled the ancient book.

Voice hushed in reverent tones, or maybe fear, Mac spoke. "You won't believe what I found. In fact, my boy, you won't believe what's happened. I have to tell you I've been quite a cynic, but over the last day I've developed a new respect for the supernatural, or fate."

"Stop being so mysterious and tell me what is going on, or am I going to have to start finding out on my own?"

"Like I said, my boy. Patience."

The only response was a low growl as Gavin made an effort to control his emotions.

"First of all—"

"Finally."

Mac raised his eyebrow and then continued. "First of all, yours isn't the only journal. In fact, since you left yesterday, I've found out about two more."

"What! So what you're saying is that it's a fake? Not even a good one since they seem to be showing up all over the place."

"Will you sit still, keep quiet, and let me talk. Two more have shown up, written by different people, but intertwined in their origins."

"Okay, now I'm confused."

"Nothing confusing about it. Merlin wrote the book in your possession, I have no doubt as to its authenticity. When you left, I researched some of my older texts that I hadn't looked through in a while. I stayed up most of the night researching, pouring over books I forgot I even owned. Something kept nagging at my old brain, a quote or paragraph I read. It took half the night, but I finally found what I was looking for in an old museum catalogue. Here, let me show you." Mac rummaged through old newspapers and half read books. He never proclaimed to be a well-organized person.

"See." He thrust the yellowed catalogue under Gavin's nose. "It has a date of 1923 on the front, at least if you look through a magnifying glass. Illumination Point Museum had a display of old books and relics from the fifth century, the time of King Arthur. On display was an old journal of memoirs, supposedly written by Morgan le Fay, half sister of King Arthur."

"One of the other diaries."

"Yes. While this book was on display, the museum got broken into, and the thieves stole the book."

"Just the book?"

"Yep. Now, this is where things get weird."

"I think they're already there."

"Not yet. Wait till you hear the rest of the story."

Silence reigned in the small bookstore until Gavin couldn't stand it any longer. "Mac, I am about to take you over my shoulder and throw you off the top of the nearest hill. That should jar your tongue loose."

"Give an old man his due. This one time I get to hold information over your head, let me savor the moment."

"The moment has been savored enough, spill the beans."

With a feigned sigh of frustration, Mac continued. "Okay, the supposed memoirs of Morgan, or Morganna, never showed up after being stolen, but another book of memoirs, written by the Lady of the Lake, showed up. Earlier today."

"Who is the Lady of the Lake? How does she relate to Morganna and Merlin? What do you mean it showed up today? How is that possible? Where is it?"

Frenzied questions fell from Gavin's mouth until there was nothing left for him to ask.

Mac's voice remained calm as he answered the questions in order. "If you think back to your Arthurian history, Lady of the Lake was the title given to the current High Priestess of Avalon. This particular one, the author of the third journal, was Nimue, the lover of Merlin the Great." Mac paused for effect. It took only a second for Gavin to absorb the facts.

"Merlin and Nimue were lovers, and they both wrote journals?"

"Yes, and even better, I also read last night that Morganna supposedly trained as a priestess in Avalon. If that was the same time that Nimue ruled as High Priestess, it would tie the two of them together."

"We need to read the journals. This could get interesting."

"You're in luck, I have the journal right here."

Gavin frowned as Mac placed the book on the table. "That's the one that woman just brought in. That's Nimue's memoirs?"

"Yep, can you believe the coincidence?"

"No, not really. Are you sure it's authentic? That woman gave off strange vibes right from the start. Do you think she knew about my book? I mean what are the odds of her bringing hers here the day after I show you mine?"

"Slow down, Gavin, use your detective skills. How could she have known about your book? She's a reporter from New York?"

"Well, that explains it, she's a reporter, a vulture, and she's here to do a story. Are you sure her book is real?"

"First of all, yes, her journal seems to be authentic, and secondly, she didn't even arrive in England until yesterday. Think about it, Gavin, how could she have known about yours? And what would she have to gain from coming here? I'm not sure what's going on here, but I'm a bettin' man, and I'd say that some kind of karma or something is at play here."

"Come on, now you're starting to sound like my parents. They seem to think there's some big mystery involved. In fact, they're adamant that some ancestor of ours was killed because of some curse or something."

"And they'd be right."

Mac's words floored Gavin. He convinced himself that his parents overreacted to Merlin's scribbling, but now Mac's words lent credence to their fears. Small knots of tension wound their way around Gavin guts, and apprehension crept its way from the tips of his toes to mingle with the heat of his blood.

"I think you better explain yourself, Mac."

"The reason I called you last night was not that I found another journal." Mac rifled through files, discarded papers, and let out an exclamation of satisfaction as he pulled a tattered paper from its hiding place. "This is why I called you." With gentle hands of an experienced connoisseur, Mac laid the paper upon the table and carefully flattened age-old creases. "This paper was part of a lot that I bid on at an auction a few years ago. Since it's just a single page from a book, I figured it was no good, but something kept me from throwing it out. I'm a sucker for old stuff, and it seems somehow sacrilegious to throw things like this out, kind of like I'm destroying a piece of history."

Gavin could relate to what Mac was saying. This quirk of never throwing anything out resulted in the bursting at the seams, dusty bookstore that was Mac's trademark. It might also turn out to be what solved the mystery of the memoirs.

"So, what are we looking at that has your shorts in a knot?"

"What we are looking at is a page from an ancient text written by a Druid priest, at least that's what I can figure from how it's written. The page is written on both sides, and from what I can piece together, this Druid priest was paying tribute to the God and Goddess at the time of summer solstice. He describes the place he worships as, a large obelisk-like stone, standing proudly to the heavens and reflecting blue in the moonlight. My guess would be the Tor. He also tells a story of, a ferocious battle of lightning and thunder crashing across the heavens. Maybe the Gods offering their energies to the fertility rites of

Beltane. His writings tell of the battle that raged across the hills and plains coming closer to the Chalice Well where he and some others offered themselves to the Goddess of fertility. As the storm increased, so did their apprehension. Instead of being powerful and all encompassing, the storm was destroying the surrounding rowan trees and vegetation and sending animals of the forest scampering from their homes. Devastation was the mainstay of this storm and the worshippers quickly dispersed from the magical circle. Here's the passage that worried me.

"My eyes gazed upon the familiar figures so revered by our people, Merlin of the Magical Way and Nimue of Avalon. They battled upon the plains and fought with the energies of the surrounding heavens. Coldness ran through my veins, as the disruption of their relationship could naught but cause a rift in the energies of Britain, on all levels. I cringed as the words they screamed carried to my ears. Words of revenge and destruction. A curse of each other's descendant's to stand through the ages of time. I was in fear for my own unworthy life and then…suddenly, they were gone. The storms settled. Rain fell from the thunderclouds, and animals returned to their homes. Ahh, but I pity the people born to these bloodlines, as they will need to deal with repercussions of this battle fought.

Both men sat silent, lost in thought. Traffic could be heard outside, but in the dimness of the store there was an air of unreality.

Gavin took a deep breath, ran his hands through his hair, and asked. "Does it say anywhere what they were fighting about?"

"No, but there is one minor reference to a third figure standing on the sidelines watching the battle."

"One of the Druid worshippers?"

"The priest didn't think so. He only saw a brief flash of a hooded figure, and his senses prickled at the aura of evil as the person passed close by. He seemed to feel it was a woman, other than that he knew nothing."

Confused and frustrated, Gavin stood and began to pace the small room. "Right, so if there is some kind of curse, it seems to have started then, and if Merlin and Nimue were involved, then they may have written some clue in their memoirs." Gavin couldn't believe what he was saying. He was actually beginning to get raveled up in this curse business. The detective in him was on full alert, and there was nothing he could do but follow the story through to some kind of conclusion, even if that made him a fool.

"Okay, Mac, you've got me hooked. I think before we do anything else we should each take a journal and spend the afternoon reading. Maybe we'll find a clue to all the mystery that seems to be surrounding the history of these books."

"I guess maybe you're right. We won't know much until we find out exactly what's in them."

Still confused, but anxious to solve the mystery behind the disappearance of Morganna's memoirs and the fear he sensed in his parents, Gavin settled down to read for the afternoon.

Since he'd already read most of Merlin's journal, he decided to read the one brought in by the woman. Nimue, Lady of the Lake, he liked the unusual name and found her words interesting. In many ways her view was in contrast to Merlin's. One thing they were both sure of was the love they held for each other. The unwavering emotion and overpowering sense of fulfillment that filtered its way through the pages of the ancient journal moved Gavin.

About an hour passed by when the bell above the doorway jingled the arrival of another customer. Silence settled into the bookstore long enough for Gavin to feel prickles on the back of his neck. Looking up, he found himself looking directly into the thunderstruck face of the woman whose book he held in his lap.

"What the hell is going on here?"

Gavin jumped up as the woman—he couldn't remember her name, just her body—stomped down the stairs and headed directly for him. She reached out, grabbed the journal from his hands, and cut off any possibility for him to offer an apology by turning her back on him.

Directing her anger to Mac, the woman snapped, "I'm sure I made it quite clear this was a private matter. I trusted your professionalism to keep it private, not to give it out to the first red-neck that comes along looking for a cheap thrill."

Gavin was stunned by the accusation. He understood her anger, but her insults were uncalled for. For some reason the fact that she was the one doing the insulting bothered him even more. His warped sense of male pride made him want to impress her.

It was probably residual emotion from reading the journal entries, but he wanted to reach out and stroke her cheek. Her lips, so full and soft looking, stimulated an urge to take her in his arms and kiss her until she couldn't speak.

He felt like an idiot standing there unable to say a word. His mind stopped working, but his traitorous body responded to the passion in the air, even though the passion was anger.

Mac spoke first. "I'm sorry. There is an explanation, if you'd only take a second to calm down and listen."

"There can't be any explanation for going against my explicitly expressed wishes. You're just lucky I don't bring some kind of charges for invasion of privacy or something. Good day to you both."

Gavin and Mac stood in helpless confusion as she left the store, slamming the door behind her. Amidst the merry tinkling of the bell, Gavin cursed himself for not being aware enough of his environment to hide the book when the woman entered the store.

"We need that book, Gavin. I'm afraid you're going to have to make peace with her and convince her of the importance of being on our side."

"Me. Why me?"

"I'm the one she trusted, and I'm the one that broke that trust, not you. I'm sure you'll have an easier time getting close to her."

"I'm the red-neck, remember."

"It doesn't matter. Besides, I think she's attracted to you. You can use that."

"Mac, you're crazy. What in God's name makes you think she's attracted to me?"

"Men's intuition. Gavin, we really need that journal back. I'm afraid you have no choice."

"We could just forget this whole curse thing."

"Not a good idea. Along with everything else I found, I also did some research on your family history. I don't like what I found."

Gavin's sense of unease increased to a roaring tempest. He'd knew that Mac held something back.

"What did you find?"

Mac sighed. "I suppose you have a right to know. Heck it could mean nothing, but with everything else that's happening, I'm beginning to think it might mean a lot. It goes back to your great-great grandfather and the alignment of stars in the sky. It…"

"I know the story, all about his remains with no head and the curse." Gavin felt a twinge of satisfaction at the look of surprise on Mac's face; let him think it was due to detective work and not his parents passing on the information.

"Well, I'd be bettin' you don't know about any of your other ancestors."

"For example?" Gavin asked the question not sure if he wanted an answer.

"There have been three times in history where unexplained deaths have plagued your family. Each time the stars were aligned in the sky the exact same way written of in both the verses I read you and the page written by the priest we just read. Certain male members of your family died on these nights, and their deaths were not by natural means."

"How the devil do you know that? I don't even know my family history that well?"

"I have some friends at the Hall of Records. I knew the time period I was looking for based on the stars, so all I needed were recorded deaths on those days. The rest was easy."

Tendrils of fear laced themselves in Gavin's stomach. He was having a hard time grasping everything. "All right, since my mind is not working clearly at the moment, let me recap what we've got." Gavin's detective ability to analyze took over. "We have two journals, written by two people who were once lovers but ended up hating each other for some reason. We have a third journal, stolen seventy some odd years ago, written by someone somehow tied to the other two people. The existence of all three journals shows up within twenty-four hours of each other, just days before the stars are aligned in the sky in a way that has somehow been responsible for the death of three of my ancestors. We know there was some kind of battle at the Tor many centuries ago. The answer may be in the journals, one of which we don't know the location, another is in the hands of a woman who distrusts us immensely, and the third only gives one side of a story. Am I with it so far?"

"Yep. That's about it."

"So, basically, what I'm hearing is that we have got bupkiss."

"Well, if yer wantin' to think negatively."

"Mac, we have nothing, unless you want to believe that some curse has followed my family since the time of Merlin and Nimue."

"Explain to me the appearance of the journals, and the timing."

"Coincidence."

"No such thing."

"Look, Mac, you know I love to detect. My suggestion would be that you finish reading Merlin's memoirs for any possible clue. I'll see what I can find out about the third journal, maybe we'll get lucky."

"I still think you should be tryin' to make amends with that pretty young lady. She'll give in to you, especially if you turn on yer charm."

"I'm not turning on any charm. I'm better off trying to find a book that's been missing for the last seventy years."

"Whatever. Why don't you try asking Lady Divine? She's been doin' readings for people for the last fifty years. She knows most people here about. It's possible she's heard something over the years."

"I guess that's as good a place as any to start. I'll get back to you later today. I have a couple of other ideas where to start checking."

"I'll be here. By the way, be careful. I have a funny feeling about all this stuff. As much as you scoff, there are strange things happenin' in the Universe we lowly human beings can't explain."

"I'll be careful, Mac."

As Gavin left the store he'd practically grown up in, he felt a gentle prodding in his mind, like an irritating mosquito. Too busy, with too many things on his mind, Gavin swept the prodding unease to the back of his mind to deal with later.

After giving Mac a piece of her mind, Tamara stalked from the bookstore. Reluctance to leave the book with Mac still prodded her, she only did so because she felt at ease with him. Besides, it gave her an excuse to go back tomorrow and maybe see Gavin, with his haunting blue eyes that warmed her blood and tugged her senses. Now, she was sorry her senses overcame logic.

She wondered how much of the journal Gavin read. She'd only been gone long enough to peruse a couple of the local shops. Good thing she went back to the bookstore to pick up some books on witchcraft, otherwise, she never would have caught Gavin reading her book.

Reaching the car, she got inside and slammed the door behind her. "Sorry, Tizzy," she mumbled. She was frustrated with herself for her intense reaction to Gavin when she entered the bookstore. She found her gaze immediately drawn to him. He pinned her with his magnetic eyes, and teased her with his hard body. Okay, maybe that was her fantasies working overtime. Actually, his nose was buried in her book. What gall! And there was Mac, with all his attention being poured into another book. Somewhere deep in her mind, it registered that the book was extremely similar to her own, but the thought was lost as anger pushed to the forefront.

Turning the key in the ignition, Tizzy's engine roared to life and Tamara pulled from her parking spot with more zeal than was necessary.

She knew she made herself clear that the journal was private. She would assume that meant no one else was to touch it, let alone read the ancient text.

Her anger abated as she recalled how Gavin's blue eyes clashed with her pointed gaze. Maybe she overreacted, but the book was hers, and that man, as handsome as he was, had no business reading what belonged to her. Obeying a stop sign, she rolled to a standstill, and found herself pondering her reaction when she snatched the book from Gavin's grasp. Her fingers touched lightly upon the heat of tanned flesh. That had been her undoing.

She remembered their eyes clashed, this time with a flare of passion. Tamara wanted to berate the man for invading her privacy, but all she could do was wonder what it would be like to touch her lips to his.

Thank God, Mac broke the sexual tension. "Please, let me explain." His voice sounded from a distance. "There's a good reason that Gavin's reading the journal. I think there are a few things that maybe you ought to know."

Sexually flustered and not willing to listen to any explanation for invading her privacy, Tamara gave the shopkeeper a piece of her mind about his business practices and then stalked from the unassuming bookstore.

Tamara snapped back to the present and wheeled Tizzy around the corner and out of town. She'd realized that she'd been rude to both Mac and the mysterious man from her dreams, but she didn't care. Or did she? What nerve. Why did she find herself wanting to go back and apologize to Gavin? Why did she care what he thought of her? What had Mac meant about there being things she should know about? Damn, why was life so complicated? It never used to be, before the journal.

At least Mac proclaimed the authenticity of the book, not that it mattered. Light, entertaining reading was about all it was good for, whether or not it was actually written by the Lady of the Lake.

Speaking of reading material, she forgot all about picking up a book on witchcraft or the Ceremony of the Stars. Oh, well, she did have an address of a witch. That should be enough. With a deep sigh, Tamara decided the only thing to do was return to The Will-O'-the Wisp for a nice dinner, slide into a hot bubble bath, and then do some reading.

She'd also make sure to set up an appointment with the witch for tomorrow. After all, she was here to work, not investigate a book she'd found in her attic.

Chapter Eleven

Morganna deliberately chose to rent a loft apartment on a side street just around the corner from Mac's Bookstore. Outside the window, traffic became a mere trickle in the inky darkness of the night. Fools, did they think to stop events set in motion centuries ago? What power did they have that could compete with her knowledge learned over the ages?

Bright eyes, like hard sparkling sapphires, reflected against the smooth, clear surface of the crystal ball. Hands of alabaster cream ran sensuously over the globe, gently caressing forth an image. Warmth radiated from the now misty crystal. Morganna knew the image she called upon was about to take shape.

Earlier today, when she saw the woman enter the bookstore with the journal, Morganna fought to control her delight. With both journals in the same place, it would be so easy for her to steal them. But then, the stupid woman returned, only to leave again with the journal.

Let the Hounds of Hell curse the bitch for making things difficult.

Her own book of memoirs, stolen from the museum years ago, sat upon the table beside her crystal ball. Actually, since it was her memoir, one could say she hadn't really stolen anything. But try explaining that to the cretins of the world today. None would believe she was able to still be alive after all these years. Morganna was disgusted that abilities, once so common amongst people, slowly became nothing but legends and folklore. The stories she could tell if one were so inclined to listen. Oh, well. Their loss.

Vibrations from the crystal transformed Morganna's hands into glowing energy, the connection made. Before her very eyes, shapes and forms appeared. A smile of satisfaction curled her lips into an obscene mask of evil.

The old man lay in bed reading the journal. Perfect! In a corner of the downstairs room a window stood open to the warm, night breeze. Even better. A scan of the small bedroom showed that he was alone. Morganna sneered; the stupid man made her task so simple. All she needed to do was wait until the moon rose to its highest point, present an offering to the Moon God, and then go get the book. She'd deal with the woman tomorrow.

Once she held all three memoirs, she would hold the power and knowledge she deserved and worked for all these years. This time she wouldn't make the same mistake as in Avalon. Then, her arrogance caused her to believe all she needed to do was turn Merlin and Nimue against each other and she could reign supreme. Now, she realized she would have to destroy them. Blast them into an eternity of shapeless form and thought.

The journals offered her the chance to do just that.

Nimue's words would offer the hiding place of the Sword Excalibur. Merlin's would offer the knowledge of how to destroy Nimue. Once Nimue was destroyed and the sword was in her own hands, Merlin would be easy to dispose of, which would leave her as the ruling power. Anything could be hers. There would be no restriction of her power or ability. She would no longer need to hide, or have the need to be careful of using her spells.

Merlin was a very skilled magician. If he became aware of her role in past events, and the fact that she still lived, he would destroy her. As it was, neither he nor Nimue were aware of her existence. Unknowingly, Nimue presented Morganna with the knowledge necessary to transform her energy to different levels of denseness. This enabled Morganna to become light and ageless, until such time as she desired a physical form. Of course, once she assumed this form, she began to age at a normal rate, so she would be very careful how long she remained dense.

The secret lay with the Chalice Well. Morganna knew this. The Holy Waters of the well were the ones she drew upon for her energy transformations. What she didn't know was how to make her shape shifting permanent. Once she achieved her goal, she would have Nimue's knowledge, and then she would never age. No matter what.

A wave of her hand dimmed the eerie glow of the crystal. She'd seen all she needed. Morganna estimated about three hours before the moon was at its optimum, and her own journal beckoned her. The yellowed pages may hold something useful in the scribbling of her past.

She lifted the heavy volume of blue leather into her hands and felt the emotions of her writings vibrate deep within. So much hurt, so many misunderstandings.

Dust from the yellowed pages tickled her nose and caused a sneeze to disturb the quiet of her room. Without realizing it, her mind began to return to past times, and her emotions became taut, as if everything was happening to her all over again. The words swam before her eyes until they became nothing. Instead, she began to feel her memories.

Britain is mine!
Avalon is mine!
Arthur is mine!

I lived with those desires for so long, along with my naïve belief that I mattered and that my life held meaning. Where once I blessed the birth of my brother, I now curse his name upon my lips to the endless, bitter void of being yet not being. I also curse that wench who came to us. She was the cause of such upheaval. Her, with her limpid blue eyes and hair of spun gold. Whispers among the other maidens proclaimed that she was a child of the faeries, but no one really knew at the time where she came from. One day she appeared in the land of Avalon. That day I wish never happened. The slut took Arthur from me along with all my dreams.

When I first came to Avalon, I blamed Arthur for my being here. From the day I watched his fragile head emerge from the uterus, he was mine. Mother and Uther paid him no mind, as if they cared not if he lived or died. It was I who became his caretaker.

I eavesdropped upon a conversation between Mother and Uther. That was when I came to understand the reason for such indifference. I hid in the parapet outside their bedroom window, even as a young girl I thirsted for knowledge, even then realizing that with it came power. Voices of anger drifted on the still air to reach my ears

"I care not what deal you made with that Temptress of Avalon. I will not give up my son to her evil clutches."

"We have not a choice, Igraine, you know the power she wields. Besides, how can we deny our son his birthright?"

"He has that right by right of succession. We need not send him to Avalon. What good serves such an action?"

"I made a promise and sealed my word within a circle of fire blessed by the faeries of the Netherworld."

My mother made the Christian sign of the cross upon her breast. "How can you speak such blasphemy? You are not expected to keep any vow spoken in that place. Our Lord will not condemn you for ignoring that part of your past. In fact, he will condemn you if you seek to follow such pagan ways."

"Igraine, I will hear no more on the matter. The Lady of the Lake gave me all that I now have. I must keep the promise I made." A shiver passed through the sturdy body of Uther. "I am afraid to think what would happen to us if I did not. Igraine, you may deny the way of life that leads the people of Avalon, and many of our own people, but the power Nimue possesses is beyond any we can withstand. You cannot deny this."

Silence sat heavy in the bedchamber. Mother hesitated. Uther saw her moment of vulnerability and took advantage. He moved close and gathered her in his embrace.

"My love, we have no choice."

Mother narrowed her gaze and spoke. "This I will do only if you promise to give up your worship of the Goddess and all that the old ways stand for. You must take the baptismal with Father Thomas and cleanse yourself of your sins."

Sharp knives of breath pierced my chest. Give up the ways of the Druids, the people of Avalon, and all who came before? My blood kin had not taught me in these ways, but many villagers were willing to show me. I could not imagine that Uther could give up his beliefs so easily, for I knew he was devout to all the rituals.

"I will agree to all that you ask, Igraine." The words left his lips as molasses poured on a cold winter day.

I crept from my hiding place. My legs flew over the dew-covered grass of the meadows until I could run no more. My mind tried to understand the implications of what I heard. Arthur was leaving for a very long time. Uther was giving up the ways I was only coming to understand. Even with my young, untried mind, I sensed the powers available to me through the old ways. Energies and powers that became stifled within the confines of the Christian churches. I needed to explore what I sensed inside me, but now it would not be possible as long as I remained with Mother and Uther.

That night, the way became as clear as the starry sky of the evening. I would go to Avalon with Arthur. There, I could learn the ways only a priestess could teach me. There, I could stay by Arthur's side as he matured. When he took his rightful place upon the throne of Britain, I would sit by his side, ever loyal and loving.

When did all start to go wrong? Yes. I remember. It was at my first joining with my brother on Avalon. One day, an exuberant knocking at my door interrupted me.

"Enter." I spoke.

Arthur entered my chamber. Ruffled from childish horseplay, twigs and leaves were still tangled within his hair.

"Sister, why did you leave so suddenly? Were we not having fun?"

"No, you and that harlot were having fun. I was merely an obstacle."

"Guinevere is not a harlot, she is but a lonely girl who wandered into the land of Avalon. She is the one I plan to marry. I wish you would treat her with respect."

Arthur's voice cracked. He was at the age of transformation, making it hard for me to take him seriously. However, his words tore into my heart and caused emptiness in place of desires and wishes. This emptiness needed to be filled. In a slow rise of bile, I felt the ooze of hate gradually fill the hole of my heart.

When I spoke, my words were harsh and my voice condemning. "I care not who you have by your side when you are king, that is, if you ever become king."

"Of course, I will be king. That is my destiny. It is what the Lady Nimue trains me for."

"Things can change, Arthur. I'm sure your studies have taught you that the future is never certain."

"I have learned that, among other things. Though, I confess I think you have learned more. You have a natural gift."

"Not if you allow yourself to be smitten by that wispy faerie-child."

"I do not understand you, Morganna. Why do you hate Guinevere so? She has done naught to you. I hoped that you two would care for each other. I will rely on you both for advice when I become king."

"I do not want her to sit with you. I want to be the one!"

My private desires flew from my mouth before I could stop them. Arthur would know I was jealous. I should have learned better control over myself in the years of training as an initiate priestess.

Arthur was mortified to have offended me in some way.

"Morganna, I had no idea such thoughts visited themselves upon you. I do not know how you could think to sit upon the throne beside me. It is forbidden for brother and sister to join." His face flushed pink at the thoughts of such a thing. A glimmer of possible hope warmed me. As yet, Arthur was untried in sexual passion. I thought to be the one to awaken those emotions. I knew spells to bind him to me.

In a seductive move meant to stimulate, I swayed across the room. Subconsciously, I put all my powers and knowledge into making myself sexually attractive. With a silent prayer to the Enchantress, I placed my energy thoughts before me and presented a vision of lust for Arthur.

His tongue licked his lips when I began my chant of binding. I saw his pants swell at the crotch, a sure sign my spell was working.

My palm caressed his cheek and scratched against the stubble of new growth. I lowered my hands down his body gently, keeping eye contact and mentally reciting my words of binding. I felt strong and beautiful. There was no way Arthur could deny me. He was mine, and as soon as our bodies intertwined in a gift to the Enchantress, he would be mine forever.

Somehow, we became naked; time ceased to mean anything. Vibrations began to shake my body and meld themselves into Arthur. His eyes were vacant, but it mattered not, he was about to take a step there would be no returning from. Wetness leaked from between my legs. It seemed I waited for this moment all my life. Arthur's cock stood up hard and big, bigger than I could have imagined. I remember how he was hung like the studs Uther bred at home for his knights to use in battle.

I touched the quivering flesh. As young and untried as he was, he could not hold his seed for long. I took him inside me quickly. I lay him on the bed and straddled his body, so I could be in control. With a moment of hesitation at the pain that awaited me, for I was also a virgin, I took his hot, throbbing cock inside me. The soaring of my senses and Songs of the Sirens replaced the split second of pain. Our joining was more than I could ever have imagined, as we rode the crest of pleasure to a place not quite of this world.

Triumphantly, I took my brother's seed into my womb in a confirmation of the powers building within me from the day we came to Avalon. I felt as if no one could stop me. Arthur was mine, and, therefore, Britain would be mine. As my breathing returned to normal I wondered how to make sure that Avalon became mine as well.

In the afterglow of our lovemaking, I was sure that Arthur would now see my way. How could he not? That is why surprise took me when he jumped from the bed thrusting me from his naked body.

"What have we done? Morganna, what magic have you used to seduce me into giving what should have been saved for my bride?"

"I have done naught that you did not desire, Arthur."

With thought forms, I focused on Arthur and sent them to convince him of this truth. It was not easy, as my half-brother's will was stronger than I imagined.

"No, Morganna, you cannot bind me with your spells again. You have abused my trust this day. Henceforth, I will still call you sister and show you courtesy in public, but that will be all. We will no longer share the closeness we have shared until now, and we will never, never, join our bodies as one again."

Arthur stormed from the room, not quite a child, yet not quite a man. I sat and meditated upon the night, looking for a hint as to my future path. The Goddess deserted me. I no longer felt her presence in my heart. I wavered in fear for a while until I felt a new energy replace the old.

All sound left the room, and darkness overcame the brightness of the moon. Small figures of undetermined origins flitted about the shadow of my room. They couldn't be faeries, for I sensed staleness in the air. A fetid aroma assaulted my nose, and I looked for the source. I didn't have to look far. Before me stood a wavering form of the blackest depths.

I sensed, rather than heard any words spoken. My mind was

able to decipher the meaning of the demon presence.

"I can give you all you desire. In return you must promise to take me into your life and give me obedience and unquestionable loyalty."

"How can you know what I desire?" I was terrified at this force that found its way into my room, but I did not show my fear.

The stone walls of my chamber shook with laughter that resembled rumbling thunder. "I know all, Morganna. I can give all, or I can take all."

"You cannot be strong enough to stand up to the powers of Merlin and The Lady of the Lake."

"With your help I can be. With us together, your life will be whatever you want, and no one will be able to gainsay you. With the influence of Herne, God of the Underworld, we can rule together over both lands. You will not need Arthur."

"How can I do this without him? He is to be the King of Britain."

"I know that which you do not. If you bind yourself to me in ceremony, I will tell you the secret that will enable you to rule without Arthur."

"Bind myself to you…how would this be done? And how do I know you can offer that which you say?"

"You do not know for sure except to feel the power within this room that I bring with me. The binding ceremony will be done with a circle of fire and thorn branches, where you will dance about within the circle allowing your bare flesh to be pierced by the burning branches. Only then will I be able to enter your body and add my force to yours. Then, we will become as one, but your allegiance must always remain with me, or I will destroy you slowly and painfully from your very insides."

I was horrified. I only heard sketchy tales of such kinds of possession, but I never really believed any of them. Now this demon offered me all I desired, but at what cost?

"Hurry. The moon dances across the sky, and it will be another year before this act will be able to be consummated. Decide now!"

The demon's command reverberated in my bedchamber.

He gave me no time to think through what would change my life forever. With a throbbing pulse in my temples I couldn't think straight. What was I willing to give up for my lifelong dreams? My soul? Yes, yes I was willing and damned be to Arthur and all others who would seek to limit my powers.

"Come, demon, let us join in your ceremony." I knew that once a bond was made in the circle there would be no going back.

That night I became a priestess. Oh, not the priestess I dreamed of being as a naïve young girl, but a Priestess of Darkness. I would have powers of the night as my mantle. As the moon rode the breath of the night sky, our fire burned brightly, a beacon to all the dark forces that came to watch our joining. My body throbbed in tune with the drumming in my ears. Dancing naked in the ring of fire, I felt the demon in all the pores of my skin. Each beat of my pulse brought him to be more a part of me until, in a burst of fire from the circle, we became one.

With the presence of the Underworld God, Herne, the cool night air became unbearably hot. Eyes of unknown creatures gleamed just outside the circle, as my demon and I writhed in a parody of sexual union. In the dimness of my mind, I heard snarls and growls until the very moment when all came to end.

Exhausted, I remember how I lay on the cooling grass within the dying circle of flames. Once we were one, I asked what was next. The demon's reply angered me.

"We wait and watch until the time is right."

"Wait and watch…what do you speak of? You promised me all I desire, and I want it now! You must tell me of the secret you spoke of earlier as well."

"Do not ever demand anything of me. Without me you are nothing. With me, you will rule the world."

His words and tone scared me. The thought that he was inside me and could hurt me from my most private areas was not a pleasant one. I realized patience would need to be learned on my part. The answer to my questions came quickly.

"You hold within your belly the answer to all you wish. Arthur's boy child quickens within you. That will be the weapon by which you can command Arthur."

I touched my belly in wonder. A child inside me, Arthur's child. Yes, even in my naiveté I saw the possibilities of such a deed. "But what of the children he will have with his bride?" I spat the words from my mouth. "And what of Avalon? I want ultimate power here, in the land of faeries and priestesses."

"Arthur will have no children with his future bride. She cannot bear children. That is why we sent her here."

"You sent the wench knowing Arthur would fall in love with her. It is your fault he goes from me."

"No, he could not marry you no matter how much you wanted that, but if he marries another who is weak willed and cannot bear children, she will have no control over him. Your child will be his only offspring, and the right of succession will put him upon the throne after Arthur. As for Avalon you…we will rule here as well. The source of control lies in a chamber only the Lady knows of, this secret place holds the symbol of the ancient Gods."

"The Sword Excalibur."

My muted voice echoed and filtered through the branches of the willow trees, causing them to stir with the essence of my words.

"Yes, Morganna," whispered the demon in my ear. "The sword is your path to all you desire. Your one obstacle will be the strength of the love held by Merlin and Nimue. Their past is long and mighty, built through passions of the ages. As long as they are together, they are unstoppable. We must separate them and take the sword for our own."

"That will not prove a simple task."

"No, but we can do it. There are things I need to show you, magic that is forbidden within the walls of Avalon. None will know how to battle the spells you cast because none know of their existence."

"Even Nimue." I refused even then to allow the woman the title she bore. It was because of her that Arthur left me behind.

"She will know of the spells. Some of them she is responsible for from the times of old, but there are ways to keep her mind from comprehending what is happening. Her love for Merlin is her weakness."

"The last act needed of you to complete our union is a bond of blood. Tomorrow you will sacrifice a living creature to the God Herne. Now let us retire, the eve has worn me out."

Morganna came to a slow awareness of her present surroundings. A horn honked outside her window, and the distant hum of voices and laughter mingled with the night. Strange, she reached a hand to the dampness on her face, I've been crying.

After all these years, her brother's betrayal still managed to tear at her emotions. After all the time that passed into the obscure shadows of history, her thirst for revenge and supreme power surged strong within, suppressing her emptiness. Memories haunted her, drove her forward to complete her mission. Only then, would she be free of the past.

"This time, I will not fail." She whispered the oath to a darkened room. Then, slowly, with a smile, she lifted her journal and continued to read.

Chapter Twelve

My sacrifice of blood turned out to be a hawk. A Merlin actually, which I thought appropriate. Arthur, Nimue, and I were herb gathering since our stores ran low. Aglow with my secret knowledge of all that transpired last eve, I was unaware of the hawk that lay on the ground. Arthur found him first. The creature became tangled in some thorn bushes and struggled to exhaustion.

"Lady, is it permitted for me to nurse him back to health?" Arthur's voice cracked with the sound of boyhood to manhood.

"If you take this bird from the forest Goddess, you must realize that the responsibility for his life will be yours."

"Yes, I understand."

"Fine, first you must give an offering to the forest in thanks for providing you with such a friend, for he will become a friend if he lives."

I watched Arthur gently lift the bird to his arms. The stupid creature looked to him with such trust. One more thing to distract Arthur from my side. I knew at that moment the blood sacrifice I would make to the God Herne.

Later that night when all fell into slumber, I cloaked myself in invisible energy and crept into Arthur's chamber. I almost turned and fled as that bird, obviously unaffected by my spell, squawked a warning. I stood absolutely still as Arthur stirred, looked around the room, and then bade the bird be quiet so he could sleep.

As soon as I heard the sound of light snoring, I commenced to the bird and cloaked his head so he would be silent. In the silence of night under the rowan tree, I delighted in slitting the throat of the bird and drinking his blood in a final gesture of bonding with my demon and a tribute to the God Herne. There was no turning back now.

I awakened the next morn to the sound of Arthur's voice calling for his bird. I smiled. The sweet sound of my revenge, and it tasted sweet like honey mead. Arthur never knew for sure what happened to his bird, but I think he suspected me. Every now and again, I would sense his eyes peering at me as if trying to figure me out.

Time passed quickly, I would be showing my state soon, and Arthur would be leaving for Uther's to assume the role of his son. I needed to find a way to turn Nimue and Merlin against each other.

One day, only a few weeks after my binding ritual, my chance came. My demon taught me in the ways of dark magic. I was now able to put myself in the same room as Nimue and not be seen. She may have felt a twinge, but when she used her powers to search for unseen forces, she could never find me. I was elated.

Then, Merlin returned to Avalon. None had seen him here since he left Arthur and myself ten years ago, so many wondered at the reason for his return. Of course, with my ability to creep about unseen, I was easily able to intrude upon their privacy. At first, I wasn't sure if Merlin would be able to detect my presence. After all, he was a powerful magician.

No need to worry. So locked in their conversation were they that I would have gone unnoticed even in my true form.

I sat in Nimue's chambers and listened to the two of them reminisce. There was tension between them, and I always wondered why they parted so suddenly many years earlier. I understood that Merlin was to stay here with Arthur for his training. They argued muchly over Christian religion and tolerance, or lack thereof.

"Nimue, you cannot sever all ties between Avalon and the outside world. Already, I feel a distance when I try to return. Soon no one may be able to reach here from there."

"Fine, then we will remain safe."

"But you will soon wither away and die like a plant cut off from the sunlight. You need outsiders to mate with and keep the people of Avalon strong."

"We will mate with those from the Netherworld."

"Bah! They are too flighty and unpredictable. In some ways they have advanced beyond us, in others, they seem savage. We know little of their life and world."

"You may argue all you want. I will not allow outsiders to taint Avalon anymore. We live a quiet life, and I wish it to remain so."

Nimue's face colored red with her protests, while Merlin's became sad. No one spoke. I heard the trickle of the river passing by outside the window as it carried life from one end of Avalon to the other then disappeared somewhere into the Netherworld.

"Fine, then there's naught else I can do here. The time has come for Arthur to return to Britain. I will take him, Morganna and the Sword Excalibur."

"No!" Nimue's response was abrupt and sharp.

"No, what?"

"You may take the two children, but the sword stays here in Avalon. This is where it belongs, and you said yourself the ties are becoming weaker. What would happen if no one could return here with the sword?"

"Nimue, I will always be able to return, no matter how weak the ties. The sword will be returned when Arthur completes his rule. Lady Niobe laid the plans before your rule. You cannot change them to suit yourself."

"I can if I believe they will be harmful to Avalon, and I do believe Arthur's rule will not go as Lady Niobe ordained."

"What have you seen?"

"Nothing in my scrying, but I know Arthur. He is a good lad but easily influenced. Britain needs strong leadership. A king who will uphold our ways and the ways of the sword. If he cannot rule with this in mind the Sword Excalibur does not belong in his hands."

"If he does not have the sword to proclaim himself king, he will not become king and the land will fall into vast devastation at the hands of all the border kings trying to claim the throne."

"He is son of Uther, so the throne is his by right of succession. He needs not the sword."

"He does need the sword. Arthur is unproven as a warrior or leader. Few will accept him just because he is son of Uther."

"I'm sorry, Merlin. I will not give the sword from the land of Avalon."

I sat anxiously, enthralled by the conversation and the manipulation of a nation that was going on within these very walls. Oh, how I craved the power to control as these two were doing. There would be no question as to whether or not to use the power of the sword; I would use it to rule a nation.

As it was, Merlin and Nimue faced each other, none too sure as to the next words to speak. Two angry energy shields collided and battled on a plane not of this world. Overwhelming suffocation almost made me leave my spot. How could they stand there so unaffected with no air to breathe? Lightning flashed in the sky, and thunder rumbled menacingly closer until dark clouds burst in a downpour of liquid. Still they faced each other, unmoving.

Finally, the pressure receded. Merlin and Nimue began to breathe, and their eyes focused into this world. Merlin snapped his cloak from the chair and stocked to the door. Turning to face Nimue, his last words to her were, "This is not over."

Nimue's shoulders dropped, she moved to the door, and waved her hand as if placing a locking spell. I was right, she did not want to be disturbed. I thanked my demon for the knowledge and ability that made me able to be here now.

Outside the window, the storm subsided, and the sun dipped just below the horizon causing shadows to dance upon the stone walls.

Nimue stood before the fireplace with tears upon her face. If hate didn't rule my senses, I may have felt sorry for her.

She raised her arms and hummed a verse I was unfamiliar with. Her essence began to glow, and the fire flames jumped ever higher, licking at her dress. Reflections of orange flames intermingled in the sheer whiteness of flowing silk, beckoning for Nimue.

Stone grated upon stone and I watched in wonder as the mantle slid open to reveal a gaping, dark hole. Heart racing, I thought I knew what would be revealed. Seemingly unmoving, Nimue reached out and beckoned to the opening. A glint of steel flashed in the chamber, and the light slowly became almost unbearable.

The beauty of the Sword Excalibur was wondrous to behold. Shining silver, as unblemished and smooth as the day it was forged, shot flames of red and orange in the firelight. The hilt itself was plain leather, making it easier for a warrior's hand to wield. However, it was the cross guard of the sword that caught my eye. Its jewels reflected fire and rainbows through the small chamber. It was only through supreme effort I remained calm and, thusly, hidden.

Mesmerized, I watched the sword float from its resting place to settle in the hands of Nimue. Her chanting stopped and she began to speak. Her words bound her to the honor of the sword.

"By all I believe and all that have gone before, the Sword Excalibur will not leave my hands to be desecrated by those who will not believe. This I swear with my life."

The sword was the key. The instrument that could drive a permanent wedge between Merlin and Nimue. And I knew the verse to open the hiding place. When Nimue was otherwise occupied, I left the room. I collected some holy thorn, rowan branches, and druids bane. Along with a sacrifice of blood from my own palm and the allegiance of my demon, I was able to instigate my plan without problem.

I could not give Merlin and Nimue a chance to see each other again, for their anger against one another would be the fuel that fired my spell. Under the blessed power of the full moon, I cast my spell in the circle of rowan branches. I called upon the power of the darker Gods and Goddesses, and asked for protection and the ability to see my plan through to the end without reprisal or discovery.

The night gave life to my plan. Casting a sleeping spell upon Nimue, I stood before the fireplace and recited the verse I heard her chant earlier. Until the stone actually began to move I was not sure if this was to work, but the grate of stone upon stone set my mind at ease and raised my senses to a fever pitch.

I called for the sword and stood in awe as it floated into my open palms. Upon first contact, I was overwhelmed by the images that played in my mind. I saw how things once were in the land that disappeared beneath the ocean, and I remembered. I was tempted to let the images run their course, but I knew I must make haste before the spell wore off Nimue.

With a tight clasp on the sword, I hid it under my cloak and hurried to Merlin's sleeping chamber. Hesitating, I asked of my demon, "You are sure this is the way? Why not keep the sword for ourselves?"

"This is the only way. Do not question me further."

"So it shall be." Scratching upon Merlin's door, I was surprised when it opened almost immediately under my hand.

"What do you want Morganna?" Merlin did not sound as if he had slept.

"I bring you a gift from the Lady." I pulled the sword from under my cloak and presented it to the gaze of Merlin. His eyes rounded in wonder, and he reached out to touch the steel.

"She gives it of her own free will to me?"

"Her words are that you must take the sword and do what must be done with the promise you will return it here when Arthur no longer rules."

"What has made her change her mind?" He spoke without thinking. No one should know what had transpired between them, so I was careful in my answer.

"I am not privy to my Lady's mind, but I know she stayed up and paced all night. Early this morning, she called me to her side and bade me bring the Sword Excalibur to you. She then left for her monthly retreat into the Netherworld. She regrets there will be no formal good bye, but knows you will see each other again in the future."

"We leave today then?"

"Yes, all is prepared for our journey, and Arthur knows we leave."

"Thank you, Morganna." Before turning from me, he looked into my eyes and I was afraid. I sensed his power and worried that he saw through my ruse. But he turned without a word and began to pack.

Anxious to be on our way before Nimue recovered from the sleeping spell I placed upon her, I rushed Arthur through his packing and insisted we leave before the tide pulled back.

"But what of Guinevere? I cannot leave without her." Panic rose in his eyes, and I cursed the young twit who so enchanted him.

Inside my mind, my demon cautioned, "She serves the purpose we need. You needs be tolerant of her."

He was right. I settled my breathing before replying to Arthur. "By the dawning of the next blue moon, she will be finished her studies here. It will be time enough for her to join you at your side. You would not want to pull her away from her duties with the Goddess. It would not bode well for your future as king." I spoke the words all the while hoping that the wench would perish before her time came to join Arthur and me. With one last check of his chamber, we rushed to the water's edge where Merlin waited.

Exhilaration at accomplishing my goals pumped through my veins. As soon as Nimue awoke and found the sword and Merlin gone, she would be furious. My hopes were that she would be too wise to go up against the power of Merlin by trying to regain possession of the sword. I knew I would also need to keep an eye on Merlin. So far, he thought Nimue had given the sword willingly. He would return to Avalon sometime thinking his reception to be a warm one. I knew I would find a way to turn him against Nimue, so he would never again set foot here.

My demon whispered. I delighted in his evil and manipulative mind, and aspired to be even better than he one day. "Use your magic against Merlin. Make him think it comes from Nimue. Mayhap you can make it look like she gave up the sword but withheld its powers. Merlin will believe she plans for Arthur to fail, as she has already stated her desire to see him not ascend the throne."

"Yes," I whispered inside my head. "It can be done—oh, so easily—it can be done."

And it was! I must admit it was an impressive show. The border Kings stood within the walls of Tintagel, grumbling that a young, untried lad should not be set upon the throne. I think one wrong word or move would have started a battle of blood, yet Merlin handled the situation with extravagant ease.

His arms rose high in the air, stretching the sharp tip of the Sword Excalibur heavenwards. Heavy cotton sleeves of navy fell back to reveal tattoos of the Dragons of Avalon twining up and down both arms. Silence sat heavy in the courtyard, and uncertain fear stretched from man to man. In one move of grace, Merlin the Great turned the tip of the sword down and drove it to the hilt into a large boulder upon the ground. Sparks flew and men scattered from the force. Gasps of disbelief almost drowned the sound of rumbling thunder in the distance, yet I could see nary a cloud in the sky.

Merlin's voice was deeper and more resonant than ever. I thought he must be using a glamor spell for effect. Already in awe at the spectacle of the sword in solid stone, the men listened closely to his words.

"Within this rock lies the Sword Excalibur. Whether or not you believe in the Old Ways, I know you all are wary of the power evoked by this ancient relic. The sword may be wielded only by a true protector of the faith, a man true of heart and a savior to the land of Greater Britain. I urge any one of you to attempt to raise the sword into your hand."

Merlin stood aside and waited for the first man to attempt such a feat. Over the next hours many men tried, but none succeeded. Finally, when elation fell to disappointment, Merlin urged Arthur to have his turn. Arthur hesitated. Many tried and failed, and it was obvious he held little faith in himself, but Merlin did. Gently, he urged Arthur to the stone. Arthur placed a hesitant hand upon the hilt of the sword and gave a gentle tug. Nothing happened. A couple of self-satisfied snickers from the men rose to my ears.

Arthur placed both hands upon the sword, raised his face to the heavens, and whispered some words none could hear. Closing his eyes, he pulled hard. Sweat broke upon the bulging muscles in his arms, and his body began to shake. Just when it seemed impossible, and men became restless, a grating sound created silence in the watchers. Agonizingly slow, but moving nonetheless, the Sword Excalibur began to reveal its blade to the sunlight. Glinting, glorious colors it reflected in the eyes of the men. The Sword Excalibur rose from the stone and became one with Arthur.

None spoke. Hearts pounded, but not a breath of air moved. Merlin spoke first. "Hail to King Arthur." The border kings responded in an overwhelming fashion as they fell to their knees in supplication to the new king.

From there on, all was a blur. I retreated to my room to work on my spell to turn Merlin from Nimue. I would cast a spell to hide the power of the sword, so Merlin would believe Nimue betrayed him.

I gathered gems and herbs to make a talisman for Merlin's room. The rose colored rhodochrosite would enhance his dream state and allow me access to his thoughts. I would reverse the effects of a black colored jet crystal, which would cause unreasonable fears, distrust, depression, and negative energy. With a pinch of wormwood, I would have Merlin at my mercy. Any thoughts or dreams he experienced on that night, would be ones of my making. I also placed some herbs on the altar in the clearing. Offerings to the Goddess.

The moon's glow shone upon the offerings. Shadows of alternating luminescence and darkness filtered about the clearing. Dancing naked, clad only in the garland of foxglove, I chanted into the night. Like spider webs, fingers of darting figures touched upon my flesh, my mind rang, my senses sang, I danced evermore feverish in the sanctity of my clearing.

When I could no longer stand the increasing thunder in my breast, I finally saw the vision I sought. Merlin! On his pallet he laid, arms flung over his head, naked to the narrow shaft of moonlight shining in his window. Gathering my forces about me, I used the rays of the moon to send dreams into his mind and cause a long and disruptive night for the Great Merlin. Dreams of betrayal and lies haunted his sleep, mixing with the image of his love laughing at his naiveté, taunting him for trusting in her. Slicing into his subconscious the sword flew, useless, ordinary, holding only the power of any other sword. I created a battle of blood and gore to test the abilities of Arthur and the Sword Excalibur. Visions of clashing metal, screaming horses, and dying men. I slowed action and let Merlin toss in his sleep as he watched Arthur die a slow and painful death. Useless, the sword lay at his side, reflecting upon its blade the brightness of Arthur's seeping blood.

Merlin burst forth from his dreams, a profusion of sweat, doubt, and raging emotions ravaged into his face. Chanting ever more loudly, I danced around the clearing, shaking thorn branches at the sky, invoking the strength of the God of Darkness into my soul. I succeeded. Merlin thought the dream I sent him to be a vision. To believe he saw the death of Arthur, with the Sword Excalibur in his hand, he must believe that Nimue let the sword work until Arthur was upon the throne, and then deceived him by withholding the power of the sword.

Merlin doubted Nimue. He would now test the power of the sword and see that there was no power. My spell would hold for a couple of days. As long as Merlin completed his testing within that time, he would conclude that there was no power within the sword.

With Merlin and Nimue at odds, I then needed to accomplish the same feat between Arthur and Guinevere. Since he was king, I knew he would take Guinevere to wife. I knew I could not put a stop to such proceedings, but I made sure their marriage was not a happy one. I also needed to find a way to turn him from Merlin's side. As for Merlin, well—believing the sword held no power, being banished from Arthur's side and losing the love of Nimue—I guessed he would retire somewhere far from there, alone and weak. I would be left here with Arthur. Naturally he would turn to me for council and comfort. I would rule Britain through Arthur long before I sat our son upon the throne. I would also hold within my grasp the Sword Excalibur and all the powers of which it was capable.

The sound of a clock striking midnight wrested Morganna from her reading. In amazement, she noted the quick passing of time. Her written words truly gave life to emotion. She tasted her hate for her brother, and throbbed with desire to reign supreme over all.

The rise of the moon in the sky was such that she could carry out the next part of her plan now. The old man would be most vulnerable and her powers their strongest.

It was time.

Chapter Thirteen

Tense and weary from the day, Mac's senses prodded him to acknowledge the presence of a power. An ancient power of other worlds and forbidden knowledge. Skepticism still gnawed at his stomach, yet how could he explain the events of the last two days? Too many coincidences too close to the solstice to be coincidence.

Mac silently cursed losing the memoirs before reading the book, which would result in more research on his part. Considering the ancient curses left him with many unanswered questions. What form did they take? How would they affect Gavin and Tamara? Two men that they knew of perished from the curse, and Mac wanted to make sure Gavin's name wasn't added to that list.

Finishing Merlin's memoirs was his first step. Hopefully, a clue to his next step would come to light. If not, he'd start calling in favors from friends he helped over the years.

Only three days to solstice; he'd have to hurry. He just hoped that Gavin was successful in winning back the trust of Tamara so they could compare books. If they were lucky, Gavin would be able to find the third book of memoirs, everything would fall into place, and the solstice would pass without a ripple.

Making sure the lights were out downstairs, the door locked, and the alarm on, Mac made his way up the rickety steps to his apartment above the store. He prepared his usual midnight snack of cheese and crackers and placed it on the nightstand beside his single bed. With a couple of vigorous punches, he plumped the down-filled comforter, adjusted his pillows, and settled in for an evening of reading.

Anxious shivers of anticipation tickled his stomach. He was curious to find out more about the past, and these journals were the key. With shaking hands he reached for Merlin's book and opened it to a place near the back. He figured if there was anything to do with the curse it would be held closer to the back, after events leading up to it might have occurred.

My life! What has all I worked for in my life come to? The years in Camelot—Arthur's dream—passed quickly, and I stood at the gateway looking back upon the city. No longer was I be a part of the dream. Arthur threw me out, banished me, and left me to fend for myself. Years of counsel and friendship meant nothing to him, and my heart ached with the loss.

I feared dark magic at work, as I felt its cloying presence many times over the years. Nimue's magic. It had to be, as she was the only one strong enough to bend to her will the minds and will of others. First the sword, thank the Goddess there existed enough power to place Arthur upon the throne, because the next day Sword Excalibur held no power within its depths. I tried, and Arthur tried. Of course, no one else was present. The border kings needed to fear the power of the sword for Arthur to rule. At least, to begin with. I must admit that Arthur has been a great king. He thinks of the welfare of others above his own. He had only one fault.

His wife.

It seemed his wife, Queen Guinevere was staunch in her ways against Avalon and all the mystical land stood for. I think she tried to drive her faerie side from her by baptism of fire. None dared to openly practice their beliefs for fear of reprisal, and my heart ached for the desecration of the ways I had been sent to protect. Arthur was not the savior of Britain; he was the savior of Christian Brit's only.

How could Niobe have been so wrong in her visions? I doubt she was. I feared, as I said, magic at work. The spell had been cast upon Arthur and Guinevere. Queen Guinevere's gaze turned to another, while the king did all in his power to please his wife, whom he adored. Balance disrupted, causing the forces of the universe to compensate. Consequently, events changed.

I wonder that Nimue harbored such hate in her to ruin the lives of so many people as well as the fate of a country, all in the name of revenge. Why could she not harmonize? Why must Avalon be the one and only? I am constantly surprised by her unbending attitudes and the use of dark magic by the High Priestess of Avalon.

Well, she was able to drive Arthur from my side. I, at least, from his. Stories of bloody sacrifices and practicing of dark magic within my walls reached Arthur's ears. Since the subject was raised in the presence of Guinevere, it could not be ignored, which I think may have been Arthur's tendency if left on his own. The Queen bred again, and Arthur tried to console her by casting the evil demon, me, from Camelot. If I thought it would help the woman hold onto her child, I would have left willingly, but she has been unable to carry any child to full term. I wonder at this also. What purpose could Nimue have for this? I was sure it was Nimue. Magic: I felt its stifling presence.

Therefore, with the King and Queen at constant odds, myself banished from the kingdom and Nimue acting as all-powerful judge, I took leave of Camelot.

I traveled many days, led by my senses to a place I knew existed waited for me. At first I was unsure, as I found myself wandering closer to Avalon, a place I would avoid at all costs. As it came to pass, I was led to a place in the hills just a stone's throw from my nemesis and one time love. Far enough away for me to be comfortable, yet close enough to mayhap keep an eye on the evil workings of the High Priestess of Avalon.

I feared she would end up severing Avalon from the world for eternity, setting the magical place adrift on a plane not reachable by anyone ever again. Maybe that was her plan, for then she would have ultimate power and control. Then why did she still care what happened to the land of Britain? I suppose she wanted the sword back. Although it was powerless, maybe she could re-ignite what lay latent within its hilt and blade.

With a heavy-hearted sigh, I turned my attention to my new home, the place where I thought tospend the rest of my days. Upon the circular hill, buried within the confines of a lush forest and abundant wildlife, stood the dark opening of a cave. Like a magnet, I felt myself drawn to the opening only to hesitate before making my step forward. Could it be a trap? I did not feel so, but Nimue's powers were extreme.

With nothing else to care about and naught else to do, I took my first wavering step forward into a beauty so vivid it blinded my eyes. I cannot even begin to describe what seemed not of this world. Disguised as a threatening, dark cave, the place was, in fact, a crystal cave of seductive energy. Not needing the thin flame of my torch, I stomped it out beneath my foot and gazed in awe at nature's art on display before me.

Was there ever such beauty? Such fulfilling, invigorating energy of light and form? I was home; this was no trap. The place lay in wait for me. In the corner was a soft place to lay a blanket, to the side was a place to build a fire, and natural venting to the outside above. The crystals formed shelves upon the walls were I would be able to collect and store my herbs and medicines.

Like a fire slowly building, I felt my energy re-charge, and for the first time in awhile, I felt at peace. I set down my sack of extra clothing, dried fruits, and books, and began to organize what was to become my home over the next years of my life.

As I relaxed, I began to notice flickers of light dancing about the crystal cave. Teasing and flitting they slowly began to take on a more substantial form. Tickling my nose and pulling at my beard these figures presented a playful demeanor that, in my experience, signified them to be faeries.

"I'm sorry, have I taken over your home?" I questioned the flickering flames of light. My questions signaled the eruption of an onslaught of faerie chatter that made me almost sorry I even asked the question.

"Please slow down. One at a time. My mind cannot interpret all at once." For that's what faerie chatter was, not the spoken word, more like a language of the mind.

"Forgive us, Merlin, we are just so excited to finally have you here with us." The single thought voice spoke within my mind and was easy to understand, but the reply confused me.

"How do you know my name, and what does have you here with us finally, mean?"

Giggles exploded, and my faery friends put on a dance of dizzying proportions. "Oh, Merlin, there is so much to teach you and so much we can learn from you. It was written many lifetimes ago that you would come to us and be our connection to the outer world. You see we can no longer travel to places that you can, yet you are still able to come to our world."

"Is this cave not of the real world then?"

"All depends on how you perceive the real world. To us it is as real as anything, and it will be to you as well."

"But anyone can come up the hill and enter the cave, so why need you me?"

"Ahh, you are only one of a few who can enter the mouth of the cave and see what you see. Others who come here see naught but a dark, empty cave."

"Amazing!" My voice was barely a whisper amongst the chatter of the faeries. "But to what purpose? You spoke of teaching each other."

"The place you come from is what we call the primal world— fundamental, basic, primal, instinct driven. We are of the elemental world—relying on and melding with the powerful forces of nature. Humans are densely made, while we are light and able to change form. We were able to help those in your world understand and work with the forces at their disposal to make the shift to our world. This no longer happens. Energies have made a major shift until we no longer have access to your world. Ways are being taught that deny the natural ways of the universe. People have been set upon the wrong path and they will never become enlightened until your world becomes increasingly dense in form. This will end in ultimate nothingness."

"You speak of the ways of the Christ?"

"No, he was one of us and his spirit is devastated that his teachings have been so misunderstood over time. I speak of the people who speak on his behalf, who torture and kill in his name. There are others as well. Many of your kind have been led astray by the greed and ego of a few."

"I think I understand what you speak of, but what can I do to help?"

"We will teach you all you need to know and then set you back in the primal world to pass that knowledge on to others. This way you can ensure there is a chance for mankind. Will you help?"

"I think I have no choice."

Years passed with no upsets. I lived in the crystal cave leaving only to forage for food and supplies. Never once in all that time did I encounter another human being. I saw many, and I think some saw me, but only from a distance.

My pile of parchment paper increased ever much over time. I became a scholar of nature's wonders and discovered that there is much available to people if they only took the time to study and learn. Seasons and cycles of the earth became my schoolroom; the animals and all nature's creations became my teachers. As my knowledge increased, so did my powers. My abilities grew in magnitude until I no longer felt human. Feats such as shape shifting, floating on the breeze, and seeing of the past and future became as easy as breathing.

My mind returned now and again to Nimue. I remembered her ability to shape shift. I wondered what other abilities she possessed and how she came of the knowledge. One day I asked one of my faerie friends.

"The Lady of the Lake is a powerful and wonderful being. We have worked with her and taught her many things, much as we have you."

I was enraged. Did they not know of her evil nature? Was she so adept that she could hide her true nature so well from even the faeries?

"I see you are upset. Do not be so, Merlin. The Lady is not what you believe her to be."

Incensed, I snapped, "I have seen with mine own eyes what the Lady is capable of. How can you not see what is before your very eyes."

"All is not as it seems, Merlin. Please remember all we have taught you, and use your powers wisely. Always for the good of mankind, never for revenge. Good-bye, our friend." Thought forms became increasingly faint. A final good-bye spoken by my faerie friends settled panic into the pit of my stomach.

"Wait. Where do you go? Don't leave me."

So faint I could hardly make out the words, "Merlin, it is up to you. Trust what you feel, not what you know."

What in heavens did they mean by that final cryptic sentence? No time to figure it out, as I heard the crackling of branches and scrambling of stones down the hillside. Who found my cave? None ever dared come this close.

I stepped into the hot afternoon sun, and was stunned to come face to face with the Lady Morganna. I spoke first. "Lady Morganna, what do you here? How did you find this place? Are you alone?"

"Merlin, I'm so glad I found you at last. I have searched for many months. How long I know not even. When I came upon the last village, they spoke of a man upon the hill who lived in a cave. When they gave a description that matched you, I thought I would see if mayhap it was you. I guess it is, as here you stand before me."

"I'm sure the villagers also told you I was an evil sorcerer as well."

"Yes, they did say that. But I am not scared of you."

"Maybe you should be. It has been many years."

"I know you well enough to know that you love Britain and Arthur—yes—Arthur." She spoke such because I raised my eyebrow at the name not spoken in so long. "I know he banished you from Camelot, but blame Guinevere, not Arthur."

I paced across the grassy hillside, scratching at my long grown beard. "If he is not man enough to stand up to his wife for someone who has been his mentor and friend since childhood, then he is no one I care about." I sliced my hand through the air dismissively.

"Would you care if I told you Nimue was going to kill him and steal the sword back to Avalon?"

"What say you?"

"It is true." Morganna delicately sat down upon a large rock at the cave's entrance and spread her clothing about her as if seeking the right words. "I went to Avalon recently to visit the Lady of the Lake, and I was surprised to see how she has changed so. I think she has been practicing in the ways of dark magic, I could see it in the colors that surround her body. All she could do while I was there was babble about how she never should have given the sword to such a knave as Arthur. She was going to get it back, no matter what, no matter whom she needed to kill. Her words then took on a tone of singsong madness, and she swore that she would kill the man who held the sword from her all these years. I would assume she meant Arthur."

"Aye, she would mean Arthur. But why is she suddenly so desirous of getting the sword back? It holds no powers."

"She spoke of leaving Avalon and taking the sword back where it belonged."

"But the sword came from the People Who Came Before? How can she return it to them…unless…"

"Unless what, Merlin?"

"If she plans on ending her life form here and proceeding to the next plane, she does have that ability. She could take the sword with her, but they must stay where it is once it powers are restored."

"Oh? You speak as if you know something of the sword, Merlin?"

"I have learned much over the years, I do know that the sword must help retain the people's belief in the ways of old. Without such a symbol, or others like it, the people will be lost."

"I'm not sure I understand, Merlin."

"You do not need to. Did you try to warn Arthur of Nimue's threats upon his life?"

"Yes, and he just laughed at me. Merlin, he no longer believes in any of the powers and myths of Avalon. Though he saw for himself what is possible, he has forgotten over the years. I think Guinevere has done much to bend his mind against any but Christian ways."

"I need to go to him, what you must do is come with me to Camelot and help smuggle me to the King so I may warn him of the danger. I can make him believe me. I must then restore the powers to the Sword Excalibur."

"You have learned such things here?"

"As I said, I have learned much, Morganna."

"If it not be too forward, I would be humbled to be your student and learn such things as well."

With these words, Morganna knelt on the ground at my feet in supplication. I looked to her up turned face and wondered if she may not be my first student. First, though, we needed to make our way to Camelot and Arthur before Nimue got there and destroyed him, and Britain as well.

With these final words ringing in Mac's mind, he couldn't be sure whether he heard a noise or he was just being fanciful. "If it was anything, the alarm would have set off," he reassured himself in the dim light.

Focusing his attention back to what he read, Mac found it interesting that Merlin's disappearance had been of his own free will.

Rumors abounded, and stories written, about how his own true love, The Lady of the Lake, tricked him and forced him into an eternity of imprisonment. Others believed that after making him fall in love with her and teaching her all he knew, she actually destroyed him.

That didn't make sense. Though, according to Merlin's own words, most of his knowledge in the ways of magic and healing were learned during his self-induced sabbatical. His relationship with Nimue ended long before that, so it wasn't feasible that she used him to learn his powers. Oh, there was no doubting that he'd been a powerful magician and Druid before that time, but the powers that Nimue held as Lady of the Lake equaled Merlin's easily.

No, obviously. By Merlin's own written words, Nimue wouldn't have benefited in any way by getting close to him only to learn powers she already possessed.

Maybe if he read on there'd be some answers. Maybe Merlin did return to Camelot and renew his relationship with Nimue. However, if what Morganna told Merlin was true, Mac doubted they would ever have become lovers again.

Besides, he never heard of Merlin returning to Camelot once he disappeared. But then again, the poem of Merlin and Nimue battling each other on the crest of the Tor attested to the fact that they saw each other at least once more. Merlin must have returned with Morganna to help save Arthur's life and retain the sword for the people of Britain.

However, the battle was not won, and the Sword Excalibur disappeared forever, much like Merlin and Nimue. What transpired for them to face each other in battle? Was there really a curse? If so, what was it, and how could it be put to an end for good? Mac shook his head in confusion. There was so much more to learn before the pieces could be unraveled, and not much time left.

A familiar niggling began knocking itself at the base of his skull. The same sensation he felt yesterday when Gavin first showed up with the mysterious book. There was something he needed to remember. Maybe if he browsed his books, he'd remember what he was obviously forgetting.

Leafing through dusty, musty books with yellow pages and cracking covers, Mac was in his glory. Books were his passion. History, life, knowledge, love, hate, greed and wisdom, all within the covers of these books he cherished.

He was getting warm and felt as if he was just on the brink of remembering. Grasping the thick leather cover of a rather large book, he pulled it to his lap and tested his memory. Each book told a story, and Mac prided himself in knowing when and where he purchased each one. This one belonged to a box of books he bid on about two years ago. Most of them were not worth much, just old mystery novels and some romance, nothing old or valuable.

Except for this one, a first edition of a virtually unknown author from the late 1700s, the novel was a work of fiction. Unfortunately, Mac never got around to doing anything more than glancing through the pages. He did know the author had been a practicing witch, not the kind of thing you bragged about in those days. He also knew that the author disappeared never to be heard from again.

That's it. How could he have been so stupid? Mac felt the excitement of remembering turn his body flush. The author of this book disappeared on the night that the Ceremony of the Stars was acknowledged. People spoke of a deal made with the devil for a Sword of Fire. This writer, Reginald Cook, must be Gavin's ancestor. Of course, at the time he purchased the book, Mac didn't know of the blood relation. It wasn't until Gavin showed him the book and the possibility of his being a descendant of Merlin's that the memory wriggled itself in his mind. Another coincidence? No way! Things were falling into place a little too easily, almost as if some force wanted things to happen for a reason. Maybe it was better to leave the situation alone. After all, Reginald disappeared, and Mac didn't want anything happening to Gavin.

Curiosity overrode hesitation, and Mac's fingers began to tingle as he leafed through them again. What was that? Scraping his finger across the peeling inner cover he could feel a slight rise in the paper. Excitement rose in his throat.

Yes! The inner cover was loose, and he felt a piece of parchment tucked and folded. Carefully, he peeled the thick paper back with his nail, and was able to grasp the parchment and slide it from its hiding place. He knew he glanced over the paper last time, but hadn't enough time or interest to decipher the meaning. Now was the time.

He placed the parchment on his nightstand. Crinkling paper echoed in the room as Mac used his palm to flatten the almost two hundred year old piece of material. Words were faded, but still legible and Mac began reading. Words leaped off the page and finally made clear many of the questions Mac asked himself. Excited, he read aloud.

"As my great ancestor, Merlin, did before me, I will fight for the sword to return its power back to the people. I tremble to face the Lady on this eve, yet the Pinnacle of Power calls to me. I know Merlin is by my side; his presence haunts my every breathing moment. His hunger becomes mine. His anger and desolation I feel within each pulsing beat of my heart. No rest for those of our blood. No rest until the deeds of times gone past have been set into proper motion. If I should fail, I will perish, yet when the stars are in the sky as they are this eve the energy of Merlin will instill his mission onto another of our bloodlines. I write these words in case I fail. I have reason to doubt the course of history. Merlin will not hear of my reckonings, yet tonight I will attempt to speak with the Lady. I believe a falsehood has been perpetrated upon these two age-old lovers. I must set the wheel back on course. As Merlin and Nimue are made of sparking energy, there is a third energy. Though, she is as human as you or I. How can this be? I know not how, but she has come to me with her flashing eyes, thrusting the lushness of her breasts within my face. My honor she wanted, 'together we can rule the world,' she promised. I felt choked by her evil and cast her from me, but I fear she is

stronger than all, as she is here, in person, and not just a feeling as Merlin is to me. I feel not right about tonight, so I write these words and will place the parchment in my belongings so those of my blood can know these words of warning. Beware of the Dark Lady of evil!"

"It was signed, Reginald Cook 1786."

Mac shivered. Reginald wrote this as a warning that almost passed unnoticed into the hands of others. How had he come upon it two years ago only to remember it when the time was needed? Surely, there was some kind of force or energy leading the course of events. If that were so, Gavin would have no choice but to follow as events unfolded. No, Mac didn't believe that. There must be something that could be done.

Reginald spoke of another's involvement. After reading what Merlin wrote, the only name jumping to attention was that of Morganna. Right! He could almost accept the fact that the spirit of Merlin and Nimue were hanging around, but for Morganna to still be alive after all this time was insane. It would explain a lot, though. She had been in Avalon. Actually, according to Merlin, it was she who gave him the sword. Morganna searched Merlin out at the cave and warned him of Nimue's plans to kill Arthur and retain the sword. It all made sense. Damn, if they could only look at the book that Tamara woman brought in earlier. If it truly was Nimue's, it could answer many questions and maybe save a life or two.

A faint knocking at his downstairs door interrupted Mac's thoughts. Mac stood up, stiffly and slowly. He hated getting old. With his joints settled into place, he took a couple of steps toward his bedroom door, but no sooner did his hand touch the knob than the door flew open sending Mac staggering across the room to fall upon his ruffled bed. "What the…"

"I am here for the book."

Mac was flabbergasted. In front of him stood one of the most stunning women he'd ever seen. Not so much beautiful in her appearance, more stunning in her very presence. Mac was hypnotized by the energy flowing from her and swirling about the room. All at once she was fire and ice, more ice than fire. Light and dark, hot and cold. In a glow of energy pulses, the woman advanced.

Mac's heart raced in his chest.

He was terrified, yet entranced. Surely such a woman didn't exist.

Thoughts flitted about his befuddled mind as he stepped slowly back from the advancing woman. How did she get past his alarm? Why did she want the book? How did she even know about it? Who was she?

As if in tune with his thoughts, the woman answered Mac's unspoken questions. "I am Morganna."

Mac sat up abruptly on his bed while his mind worked at full speed trying to decipher the meaning behind those words. Reginald's words were becoming more believable by the second.

"You mean you're Morganna's descendant. That would explain how you know about the book. Maybe it was one of your family who snatched it from the museum back in the thirties."

"No, actually that was I."

Mac swallowed and whispered, "But you wouldn't even have been born then."

"I lied not, old man. My bloodlines are as pure of Avalon and Britain as anyone could be. Now give me the book." She thrust her hand.

Mac could not comprehend what was happening. The words the woman spoke made him think he was dreaming, yet everything seemed so real.

He must be dreaming, that would explain everything.

"It is not a dream. Now I lose patience." She read his mind again. "Give me the book and that parchment you were so busy reading when I entered. I'm surprised that Reginald had the forethought to write such a warning. He was more intelligent than I gave him credit for, yet still stupid. Did he think he could outsmart me? His attempt to warn Nimue and Merlin was that of a child against me. He did not survive and neither will any of his kind who interferes. Soon the Sword Excalibur will be mine, Merlin and Nimue will be gone forever, and I will rule as Most Supreme."

The hand that reached out to snatch the book from Mac's hands was as real as anything he'd ever felt. Maybe he wasn't dreaming. If that was the case, then this woman was either crazy, or actually Morganna, the Dark Lady of Reginald's writing, a woman from over 1500 years ago. Either way he was in trouble.

"Maybe I am slightly crazy, or maybe I am centuries older than you can imagine, but nothing can help you now regardless. I'm afraid your destiny was determined the moment you interfered in my affairs."

Cold air swept through Mac's room, brushed against his skin, and raised goose bumps on his arms. What the…? There was no chance to finish his thought before a band of pain clutched itself across his chest, squeezing harder and harder. Mac fell to his knees in weakness and panic, and reached out to the woman before him. His gaze traveled up her body to her face, and the look of self-satisfaction upon her features sent a stab of cold fear into his heart.

There would be no help there.

With a haunting laugh and the flick of her dark cape the woman left, but the tightness in Mac's chest continued until there was nothing but a spark of life.

Damn if he'd let the bitch get the last word. He reached for his pen and paper. Barely able to hold the pen upright, he was able to scratch, Dark Lady…danger. With his breathing labored and uneven, Mac gave a prayer to God, or whatever force existed in the Universe, to keep Gavin safe.

Morganna laughed at the ease with which she dealt with the old man. He might live or he might die, he definitely wouldn't be talking to anyone soon. Back in her small, dingy apartment, Morganna sneered at her paltry surroundings. Soon she'd be out of here and living in luxury with the future at her fingertips. The secret of the Chalice Well would be hers, Excalibur would be hers, and Merlin and Nimue would be destroyed. She grew weary of the constant replay of energies and prayed to the God Arawn this would be the last time such would be necessary. She had almost been discovered once or twice and knew her luck would run out. If Merlin and Nimue discovered her presence they would figure out her part in all that happened. As it was, they still blamed each other, each one not knowing the truth.

This time I am prepared. This time I will make sure they are destroyed. Merlin's journal was now within her hands, and all that remained was to get her hands on the memoir of that bitch Nimue. She needed to find the location of the final journal. Morganna reached out to caress an oval mirror resting upon her dresser. Yes, scrying would be the quickest and easiest way to find what she desired.

Her scrying tool was her crystal ball, an item gifted to her by the God Arawn. The stand was black obsidian with the outlines of white dolphins carved into its blackness. Nestled in the center was a crystal ball: smooth, round, and dark as midnight. Once used by the God Poseidon in the time of the ancient ones, the crystal ball with its obsidian holder was now Morganna's main tool in her rituals of darkness.

Surrounding herself in a circle of protection, Morganna placed her hands upon the crystal until she felt warmth. Humming a vibration meant to attune her to the crystal and what lay within, she rocked gently to stimulate energy.

She had no idea how long passed; she only knew that visions began to appear. That woman from yesterday was visible, as was the journal. Was it the past or the future? Morganna needed to find out. Surroundings became clear and Morganna recognized the bookstore she recently left. Upon surveying the small room, Morganna saw the books scattered about the floor. Books she threw about only a short while ago. Since the sun was shining in the crystal, Morganna made the conclusion that the woman would be in the bookstore during the day in the very near future. If it were more than a day or so, the books would not be still on the floor.

Awakening from her self-induced trance, Morganna smiled to herself. This was too easy. All she would do was grab the book from the woman, find the clues, and claim what was rightfully hers, the Sword Excalibur and all the powers it entailed. Of course there was the small matter of destroying Nimue and Merlin, but with the sword in her hand, and the secret of The Chalice... Well, that feat would be easy. Her disciples were already working on preparations for the Ceremony of the Stars.

Chapter Fourteen

Diana tripped as her feet carried her quickly over the rough terrain. The same branches slapping her face left the blood red streaks of scratches on her arms. Full and luminous, the moon barely broke through the foliage to light her way ahead. Moon shadows danced, contorting the shape of the beast she was trying to escape from.

With breath tugging sharply in her chest, Diana thought only of saving her daughter. The clearing loomed ahead. A combination of the uphill climb and terror turned her legs to quivering limbs.

Steel glinted in the moonlight. Hypnotized, Diana suddenly felt as if she were moving in slow motion. No! The word ripped from her throat, but she was too late. In a downward arc the sleek sword descended toward the altar, and her daughter.

Sobs wound their way from deep inside, expanded in her throat, and tore themselves from her mouth. The stifling presence came closer from somewhere close behind. She didn't care. Tamara was gone, which meant all her preparations, her whole life, amounted to nothing.

She failed.

Diana cringed as a large, horned hand closed around her throat and closed tightly. In a struggle for life, Diana grasped at the suffocating hand. Warm, fetid air blew into her face as the creature laughed at her pain and struggles. Just when she couldn't breathe anymore, Diana saw a light.

The light came closer.

Diana reached for the glowing beacon thinking she could be saved. A blinding flash saturated the clearing in a white haze, and Diana closed her eyes.

All became silent. The hand was gone from her throat.

Cautiously, Diana opened her eyes only to find herself looking at the furniture in her own bedroom.

"Damn!" she cursed aloud, startling her cat, Mortimer, who lay at the bottom of the bed. So real, yet somehow different from the dreams she experienced her whole life. It could only mean one thing. Tamara needed her.

In a swift, fluid movement, Diana jumped from her bed. "Come on, Mortimer, we have work to do." She swept the longhaired, black cat into her arms and hugged him. Meows of delight echoed in the subdued shadows of the room. The comforting sound helped clear the nightmare's energy from the room.

In the bathroom, Diana filled the tub with hot water and lavender bubble bath. Negative emotion could be washed away by the relaxing effect of lavender, and Diana needed to be able to connect with positive, heavenly energies for her ritual ahead.

Her skin tingled as she lowered herself into the water. Hot and soothing, the water wrapped itself around her like a silken balm. She only allowed herself ten minutes, and then she climbed out of the tub and into her favorite indigo robe.

Prepared now to cast her circle, Diana mentally inventoried her stock of herbs, candles, and crystals. The situation called for the proper use of color, scent, and magic. Tamara's life, and maybe others, depended on the visions and insight she received.

Climbing to the attic, scenes of her life flashed in Diana's mind. An awareness of her purpose for being born haunted her from the very first day of life. Of course, everyone's purpose was to grow and learn as beings of energy. But her destiny remained a desperate one that needed fulfilling. A past needing to be put right. Quiet desperation ruled her life, along with the worry that she wouldn't be prepared when the time came. She never knew what time or what purpose, she just felt a driving need for the unknown.

When she was about ten years old, she'd come across an old book in the attic. Upon showing it to her mom, she received a slap and a firm warning not to mess with things that didn't belong to her. But the dusty old book enchanted her. It tingled in her hand and made her heart beat quickly. That same night, while her parents slept, Diana sneaked the book from their bedroom and started to read.

History, betrayal, mystery, and magic enthralled her. From that night on, Diana knew her purpose was related to the ancient book. Her subconscious sensed the seriousness without realizing the magnitude of what she dealt with. Shortly thereafter, she began to have nightmares. Always the same battle between two people, a man and a woman. It took years of research to find out the man was Merlin and the woman was Nimue, her ancestor. The woman who wrote the journal.

Her Wiccan rituals, esoteric studies, and constant searching drove her husband away from her, as well as driven a wedge between her and Tamara. The hardest part had been losing the respect of her daughter. While the years drifted, so had Tamara's love and respect. Explaining things wouldn't have worked, as Tamara's closed mind and opposition to anything logical made that alternative impossible.

Diana sighed. She reached her altar room. Her shaking hand pushed the heavy oak door to reveal her sanctuary. Moonlight shone on polished hardwood flooring and reflected into Diana's eyes. The large window facing south was ideal for catching the movement of sun and moon as they made their journey across the sky.

Although usually recommended that altars faced north, Diana placed hers directly under the window for optimum visibility of the sky and the outdoors. Now, the forest below was bathed in gentle rays of moonlight, and the trees danced a quiet beat to the prompting of the night breeze. Sometimes, Diana found herself just sitting at her altar looking out the window. When the weather was warm enough, she'd open the window and breathe in the natural scents of the life all around.

Diana gave herself a shake and muttered quietly. "Enough foolishness, it's time to get to work." With her crystal wand, she cast her circle starting north and turning clockwise. Her abilities took her far beyond the need for props and could have used her finger instead, but she enjoyed the feel of the smooth crystal as it warmed her hand and emanated its natural energies.

Soft and melodious, her voice belied her nervousness. Good, that meant she was able to control herself despite fear. That was important. The familiar chant for casting her circle passed over her lips and resonated on another plane.

"I cast this circle once around
All within by magic bound
A sacred place, a healing place
Safe from harm by love's embrace."

She placed both hands around the crystal wand and raised it to the heavens. Songs of the sirens rang in her mind, her blood raced with energy, and her pulse beat a wild staccato in her veins. How she loved the uplifting feeling she experienced when connecting to the Universe and all its energies.

Safe in her circle, Diana settled down to her altar and began preparations. She lit silver and gold candles for the Goddess and God and rubbed her favorite lavender oil on her wrists for relaxation. Hopefully, she'd achieve a meditative state that would show her a sign of coming events and necessary preparations.

This fateful night required the use of nutmeg; Diana loved the scent that would allow her to reconnect with higher realms of spirit and help bring her dreams into a sharper focus. She inhaled the spicy smoke and bid her mind relax. Immediately, she felt the sensation of her physical body receding, her heart slowing, and the floor beneath her knees disappearing. The small room ceased to exist. Instead, Diana found herself floating in a world beyond the visible. A place of sensation, free from worldly problems and limitations.

A flash jolted her from the floating state, and her mind's eye brought her to unfamiliar territory. Puzzled by this new experience, Diana didn't feel threatened, so she let herself continue on this pathway. She stood in the center of a clearing peppered with stone trails leading into dense forest.

The defining feature in the slightly overgrown clearing was an ancient looking well. Built of stone and set in the ground in an uneven manner, the well drew her forward. From the center it glowed a luminescent, amber light that flickered and became brighter as she came closer. Heat and energy emanated from the well and upset Diana's equilibrium. One step closer and the urge to reach out and touch the light became overpowering. Without sensation, Diana watched as her hand rose toward the light. Fingertips brushed the heat of amber and caused streaks of gold to glimmer in all directions. Stone pathways became paved with gold and trees glittered with the light.

The ground beneath her feet rumbled, and Diana became scared. Leaving her no time to decide whether to advance or retreat, the well exploded in a glorious display of rainbow colors. From the center of this festival of light a solid object rose. Gracefully, gently, a gleaming sword of ornate and beautiful design revealed itself. Diana gasped. She'd never seen anything of such beauty and powerful energy. The need to touch the sword, which now hovered in the air before her, was strong. But before she could reach out, she found herself jolted back into her attic in a rude awakening. Just before she found herself fully aware of her surroundings, a voice whispered in her ear.

"Protect yourself and find your daughter. Your path will be led by spirits of light."

Heart pounding, Diana took a deep breath and a moment to digest her journey into the nether regions. Wow, in all her years, she'd never experienced anything quite so vivid. The sword had been amazing, and the well almost as beautiful with its show of light and energy.

Now, her next step was clear. With deft fingers and a quiet fierceness, Diana mixed together oils of juniper, vertivert, basil, and clove for protection. She gathered two strips of silver silk and dug out her bag of small crystals she used for making charms and amulets. Pouring the contents of the pouch onto her altar cloth, she took a moment to appreciate the display of color as the stones glittered and gleamed. Hmm, the best would be obsidian for protection, grounding, and balancing. Also rose quartz for healing and love.

Choosing two of each stone, she placed them on her altar to soak up the rays of the moon before it disappeared for the night. But something wasn't right. Slow down, Diana, she cautioned herself. What are you forgetting? She pondered her actions so far, and took inventory of her incense, herbs, and crystals.

It wasn't that.

A strong urge prickled at her to pick up two more silk squares and two more pair of stones. As she added the silk and laid the crystals in moonlight beside the others, the prickling sense of missing something disappeared. Strange, she mused, but certain that she'd be shown the reason for the extra amulets later.

While charging the stones in rays of lustrous silver, Diana sprinkled them with her mixture of protective oils. Her wand she circled above the stones and spoke the words she found coming from her mouth, if not her own mind.

"I call the Lord and Lady fair
Elements of Earth, Fire, Water, and Air
Your protection I seek for the task at hand
As I battle forces in another land
Also with my words I request

This Goddess to appear at my behest
Ceridwen, you know what is best
Your wisdom, your knowledge
Will be the judge
Upon the battleground far and away
I seek your protection, upon that day."

The stones glowed, filling the room with heavy, yet comforting, energy. Diana's final gesture was to enfold the stones into the waiting scraps of silk and close them with leather string. One, she placed around her own neck, the others, she gathered to place in her purse later.

Her next step was clear. A quick drive to New York and a plane to England. She could be there by afternoon if all went well.

Diana just hoped that she wouldn't be too late.

Chapter Fifteen

Tamara awoke to sounds of a battle at the bird feeder. Sitting up in bed, she laughed at the antics of the agile creatures of flight. She enjoyed watching the colorful finches, darting sparrows, and intelligent robins angle for position at the bird feeders.

Considering the upsetting confrontation at the bookstore yesterday, she felt good. In fact she fell asleep so easily last night that the journal lay unread beside her bed. Oh, well, there'd be time enough tonight.

She snuggled into the softness of the down comforter and flowered cotton sheets and fantasized, for a second, of lying in bed and having breakfast served to her. Dreams of the idle rich.

With a deep sigh of resignation, Tamara decided she better get up and face the day. She needed to prepare a list of questions for her appointment with Lady Divine. Breakfast waited for her out on the patio under the blue morning sky. There was no sign of Mrs. Harlow, something Tamara was grateful for. She ate her breakfast while being serenaded by songbirds. It seemed the siege on the birdfeeder been settled, and the birds were congenial again. She breathed in the fresh, pungent garden air and admitted that she would enjoy living here. The people were friendly, and the town was quaint, refreshing, and clean. Even the pace was a slower one than she was used to. Glastonbury's peace and solitude was far removed from New York. She found her desire to return to New York fading with each passing hour.

The morning passed in a blur and before she knew it, it was time for her interview. Her hopes of slipping out unnoticed were dashed as she closed the front door behind her only to turn and face Mrs. Harlow head on.

The squeal of delight from her hostess was about ten times as loud as the squawking at the feeder this morning. Dressed in flowery frills and dirt-stained ruffles, Mrs. Harlow presented quite the spectacle. Tamara laughed aloud at the gaudy gardening outfit worn by her hostess. An artist's rendition of great orange and yellow flowers adorned her oversized shirt, and a floppy hat of lavender perched atop her head.

"Child, I'm so glad to see you. Are you on your way out? Lunch is in the fridge, ready to be served. Can you stay?"

Amidst protests, Tamara was hustled into the kitchen and admonished that she looked skinny and needed to gain some weight anyway.

"Besides, I was talking to Lady Divine, and I happen to know you have an interview with her today, but not for another hour. Plenty of time to eat. I want to hear all about your day yesterday. Sorry, I couldn't be here for breakfast. Was everything all right? Now tell me, did you find the bookstore? Isn't Mac the sweetest man?"

Tamara couldn't even answer one question before another was being directed her way. Finally, when Mrs. Harlow wound down, Tamara was able to explain to Mrs. Harlow why she ended up not getting an appraisal on the journal.

"Well, I must say I'm surprised at Mac's lack of ethics. I mean really, what does he think he's doing letting someone read your personal property? No wonder you took the book back. I would have as well. By the way, if you're looking for some information on the Ceremony of the Stars, I can help out."

These last words captured Tamara's wandering attention. "You know about the Ceremony of the Stars?"

"Of course, any witch worth her salt knows all about this most sacred ceremony. It only happens once every couple of hundred years, you know."

"Yes, Mac explained it to me. Do you have anything to do with it personally?"

"No." A quick shiver accompanied Mrs. Harlow's exclamation. "I have the feeling I'd be a lot safer staying away from the Tor on that night."

"Why? I mean other people will be there, in fact, a big deal is being made of the Ceremony."

"Yes, but I think it's a big mistake."

Tamara's reporter instinct kicked into high gear. "A mistake, why?"

"I can't be specific, except to say that there have been stories and suppositions surrounding this Ceremony over the centuries. Since the event only happens every couple of hundred years, all that people know of it is what's passed down through word of mouth. Nothing ever seems to get documented. So, when the stars align themselves in the night sky, witches and Druids from all over find themselves drawn to the Tor to pay tribute to their ancestors."

"But what happens to cause these rumors?"

"Nobody ever sees anything, but still stories get spread about missing people and decapitated corpses, nothing specific."

"So you're avoiding the Ceremony more because of intuition rather than any solid reason?"

"Yes, and if you weren't so hell bent on finding out more about the Ceremony, I'd suggest you stay away as well. I don't suppose you would consider foregoing it altogether, would you?"

"Not on your life. I'm a reporter. It's what I do. Besides…"

"Besides what?"

"Well, my mother seems to believe that the journal has something to do with this approaching Ceremony. I owe it to her to check it out. Actually, she made me promise to approach this whole thing with an open mind."

"Then I guess you better do your checking around. You'll find that Lady Divine is quite popular. She's the one who helped me get going when I first became interested in Wicca. Now, if you're going to make your interview on time, you'd better get a move on. Time is passing."

Relieved to be free from the constant chatter of her hostess, Tamara beat a hasty retreat out the front door. Once outside, she took a deep breath and took a moment to appreciate the garden. Funny, it reminded her of her mother's garden, with the same sense of peace and oneness with nature. Birds flitted about, seemingly quite at home in the small Shangri-La. Rich, vibrant flowers grew in abundance amidst the pebble pathway that wound its way in and out of the lushness. In a brief flash she finally understood the Wiccan belief in harmonizing with nature.

Borrowing Tizzy, Tamara made her way to Lady Divine's home, which was only about ten minutes south of the bed and breakfast. When the house came in sight, Tamara realized the house would have been hard to miss.

The front yard resembled a garden of sorts, yet held virtually no organization. Between the ivy that choked out almost any view of the stone fence and the vibrant colors of azaleas, hydrangeas, tulips, and roses, Tamara could barely see the pathway that led to the house. In the midst of all this confusion stood a couple of tethered goats merrily munching on grass, a jersey cow with liquid brown drooping eyes, a couple of dogs of an indiscriminate breed, and a black cat.

Tamara couldn't believe her eyes. Was it possible someone worse than her mother existed on the face of the same planet? Lady Divine obviously loved animals. But in her front yard? At least Mom lived in the country and owned more than a few acres of property to maintain her pets.

She noticed two cars in the driveway and hoped Lady Divine didn't have another appointment. Able to pass by the menagerie with a minimum of sniffing and snorting from the exuberant dogs, Tamara knocked hesitantly on the front door.

Only seconds passed before the door opened to reveal the serene beauty of a woman whose long dark hair pulled back into a braid to reveal chiseled features of fine porcelain. She looked ageless. It was the act of brushing hair off her face that belied the age of the woman as more advanced than her features revealed. Her hand was dotted with age spots, and spider-veins showed an intricate blue pattern. When the woman spoke, her voice sang like the call of wind whispering through tall meadow grass.

"I assume that you're Tamara. I'm Lady Divine."

Able only to nod, Tamara felt gaunt and awkward in the presence of the woman. Embarrassed, she realized that Lady Divine's hand was suspended in the air before her, so she hastened to accept the customary handshake.

"Yes, that's right. I see you've got company. Should I come back later?"

"No, it's all right. Please come in."

Upon entering, Tamara let her eyes do a quick survey of the eclectic house. Furnishings were sparse but exotic. In one corner sat a rather large throw pillow embroidered with fine stitching depicting a dragon. There were also tables of marble and mahogany at either end of the chocolate leather couch. Upon the tables sat lamps with beads of crystal hanging from colorful shades. Tamara noticed that there were no rugs, just the dark sheen of cherry wood on the floor. The finely flowered, wallpapered walls boasted a couple of original paintings of voluptuous, nubile, faeries playing in a waterfall.

Tamara completed her appraisal of the surroundings and found her gaze drawn to Lady Divine's other visitor, Gavin. Eyebrows arched in surprise, Tamara demanded, "What the heck are you doing here?"

Firm lips curved into a sardonic smile. "I must say, that doesn't sound like much of a welcome for a friend."

"A friend. I would hardly call our encounter yesterday a start to a very good friendship." Tamara was tempted to really let loose on the arrogant man sitting in front of her, but good manners instilled in her by her mother kept her quiet. After all, she was a visitor and didn't want to make a scene.

"Lady Divine, I'll leave you to your visitor and come back later." Tamara's hasty exit was halted by the brief touch of a hand upon her arm.

"Please don't go. I think the two of you have something to talk about."

"There's nothing that man could say that would remotely interest me. I'm sorry to be so rude, but all I really want is an interview. If now is a bad time, I'll come back."

"Tamara, please forgive me for seeming so presumptuous, but Gavin has told me what happened yesterday. I think it's important that you put aside your anger at him and just listen to what he has to say."

"What is this, a conspiracy?"

A low rumble escaped from Gavin's throat as he stood to face Tamara. "Listen, I know you're not thrilled with me at the moment, but if you hadn't been so high and mighty and intent on reaming Mac out yesterday, you might have found out what's going on."

Flames of anger licked her cheeks as Tamara struggled to hold her temper. "High and might— How dare you!"

Tamara's tirade was cut short by a piercing whistle. Removing her fingers from her mouth, Lady Divine brushed her hands together. "Now, will you two stop acting like a couple of spoiled children and sit." Her commanding tone brought immediate response from both Gavin and Tamara. Warily they each sat down on the farthest edge of the couch from each other.

"Fine." Tamara conceded. "But only out of respect for you, and because I still want an interview."

"Well, the woman can listen to reason after all."

"Gavin, that's enough. If Tamara is willing to listen, the least you can do is behave and keep a civil tongue in your mouth."

"Sorry." Gavin's word of apology was somewhat negated by the tone of his voice.

"There. Now, would you two like a spot of tea before starting on a long explanation of events?"

"Look, I'm confused." She addressed her comments to Lady Divine. She wouldn't give Gavin the satisfaction of speaking directly to him. Besides, every time she looked at him, her pulse raced and her eyes wandered to the few dark hairs curling out from his shirt.

With a shake of her head, she questioned Lady Divine. "How do you know each other? What do you know of Nimue's journal? And what story is there to tell?"

Another gentle pat upon her arm and Tamara found herself calming down. "All in good time, dear. Now, Gavin, don't you have something to say to Tamara?"

"Fine. I'm sorry for yesterday. I guess Mac and I should have been honest with you right from the start."

"Honest about what? What is going on here?"

"I'll leave you both to it, tea will be just a few minutes." Lady Divine left the room amidst the swish of silk, taking her serene influence with her.

Sparks of tension and mistrust lit the air. Both Tamara and Gavin glared at each other until Gavin broke the silence. "Tamara...you don't mind if I call you Tamara, do you?"

"I don't really care what you call me. I would just appreciate getting let in on what's going on around here."

"Okay, okay, don't get all bent out of shape."

Frustration bubbled to the surface, but Tamara pushed it back, took a deep breath, and calmed the tone of her voice. "Look, I realize we may not have gotten off on the right foot, but I still can't see that anything you have to say would be of interest to me."

"Well, let's start with your journal."

"Key words—my journal."

Gavin's eyes narrowed and pinned Tamara with their intense gaze. His voice was slow and deliberate. "Do you think you can listen without interrupting?"

Clinking china signaled Lady Divine's return with tea. "Have you two settled your differences yet?"

"No, I was just about to tell Tamara the significance of the journals."

"Journals?"

"Now I have your attention, do I?"

"Fine, no need to gloat, I'm all ears."

"Look, this is all fairly new to me as well. It's only been a couple of days since I found the journal that's been passed down through generations of my family. According to my parents, I'm a direct descendant of Merlin the Magician. Go figure. I didn't really believe them until weird things started to happen."

"Weird things?" The familiar story piqued Tamara's curiosity. Maybe there was some kind of story here. She could call it "The Secret of the Lost Journals" or something. Heck, maybe she could even turn it into a novel.

"Weird like Mac finding out about some major misunderstanding between Merlin and Nimue, The Lady of the Lake."

Tamara gasped. "The Lady, that's who wrote the journal I have."

"Yes, I know. It seems that some kind of a curse caused the death of at least one of my ancestors. That's what Mom and Dad believe anyway. They swear to me they've tried to get rid of the book, more than once, but it keeps turning up like a bad cold."

"You have a curse on your family." Whispered lightly, the words were barely heard in the silence of the room. "But, so do we. At least, that's what Mom believes." Tamara's mind was spinning.

"There's more. The Ceremony of the Stars that's approaching seems to be the time when the curse is fulfilled. The alignment of the stars is such as it was on the night of the final battle between Merlin and Nimue, and it's the only time they can return to renew their battle for the sword."

"You mean the Sword Excalibur?"

"Yes. You know about it?"

"Nimue wrote about it in her journal. She was absolutely furious when Merlin stole it from Avalon."

"Merlin didn't steal the sword. She gave it to him."

"That's not what Nimue wrote."

"But Merlin's journal said Nimue gave him the sword to fulfill some prophecy begun by the former Lady of the Lake. He never understood what turned Nimue so evil and destructive. Poor man was stunned when the woman he loved vowed to kill King Arthur and take the sword back to Avalon."

"Do you even know what you are talking about? No ancestor of mine would do such a rotten thing. Merlin stole the sword and deserted Nimue and the land of Avalon. His lies and deceit devastated Nimue."

"Listen lady, that's my ancestor you're talking about and there's no way he would have deserted Avalon and the values and beliefs he grew up with."

Tension crackled between the two of them. Tamara felt the heat of anger but also a sliver of passion. No way. She couldn't be attracted to this man. He was arrogant and deceitful, just like his ancestor. Steaming insults ran through her mind one after the other, but before she could decide which one to use against Gavin, Lady Divine interrupted the melee.

"That's enough you two. Nothing will get accomplished by arguing about something that happened centuries ago. All you know is what is written in the journals. I think what you need to do is to start thinking logically instead of passionately. Who'd like more tea?"

She waited a moment apparently to allow the stress levels to lower. "Look, it seems to me that the source of misunderstanding is the true story behind the sword. Nimue's journal says Merlin stole it; Merlin says she gave it to him. How can there be such a discrepancy? One of them must be lying."

"But why would anyone lie in their own journal? It's for your own personal records. You'd know the truth, so why lie?" Tamara reasoned the situation out and didn't realize she even spoke aloud until Gavin answered her question.

"I don't think either one of them lied." A frown creased his forehead. "I'm trying to remember something...damn, I can't remember if Nimue gave the sword to him directly or someone else gave it to him."

"What difference would it make?" Tamara questioned.

Gavin's voice was building with excitement. "Don't you see? Someone else could have stolen the sword and given it to Merlin saying it was from the Lady. That would explain Merlin's belief that the sword was from Nimue."

"That same person could also have told Nimue that Merlin stole the sword, thereby turning her against her former lover."

"Yes, that would explain the story in both Merlin and Nimue's journal entries."

Tamara didn't want to be the one to throw a wrench in the workings, but her reporter instincts bubbled. "Whoa, slow down. This is all assuming someone else actually gave the sword to Merlin. We also need to figure out a reason someone would lie to them. Then, we need to figure out the source of the mythical curse and how to put an end to it. So far, everything is just supposition." Tamara threw her hands into the air. "I can't believe I'm talking like this, curses and stuff, I feel ridiculous."

"Maybe, but you're still finding yourself wanting to investigate further, aren't you?" Gavin teased with a twinkle in his eye.

"At this moment, I'm not exactly sure what I'm thinking. But my first suggestion would be to re-read your journal and see who Merlin says gave him the sword."

"A woman after my own heart. Mac has the book. I can call him and find out the answer to that question right away. Lady Divine, may I use your telephone?"

While Gavin was busy in the other room talking to Mac, Tamara absentmindedly sipped her tea, trying to make sense of circumstances so far. A curse that began centuries ago between Merlin and Nimue, secret journals, a magic sword...man, her mother would love this kind of stuff. Personally she still thought it was a bunch of bunk, but her investigative juices were flowing and that should count for something.

"Tamara," Lady Divine's voice broke her reverie. "I know it all seems unbelievable, but please don't discount anything. Before this is over I think you'll realize that sometimes forces are at work we may not see or understand, but that doesn't mean they're not around."

"You sound just like my mom. She's always trying to get me to open my mind. My whole life has been an education in magic, attuning oneself with the natural rhythm of life forces, and the power of the subconscious. As soon as I was old enough to understand that Mom was different, I put up with teasing from other kids."

"No doubt kids can be cruel, but I would bet now that your schoolmates are grown up, they aren't teasing you."

A memory of Mitch coming to her mom for a tarot card reading flashed through Tamara's mind. "Well, maybe not as much, but I'm sure people still laugh behind her back. She makes herself look foolish, and besides…"

"Besides what, Tamara?"

"Nothing."

"Come on. The true reason you resist so fervently is locked inside somewhere. Please share with me."

"I kind of think that the reason Dad left us was because of Mom and her ways." There, she'd said it. She'd always blamed Mom for Dad leaving, but never spoken the words aloud.

Before Lady Divine could reply to Tamara's confession, the sound of the telephone slamming back into its cradle interrupted them. Gavin burst into the living room, cursing aloud.

Lady Divine was quick to admonish him. "Gavin, no such cuss words in here, thank you. Now, tell us what's wrong."

Gavin's features were etched in anguish. The pain she saw jolted Tamara in a surprisingly personal way.

"Something's happened to Mac. He's in the hospital, but no one seems to know what's wrong. He's in a coma the doctors thought at first was caused by a heart attack, but there are no signs of that, so they don't know what to say."

"Who were you talking to?" Tamara questioned.

"The police were at the shop. They suspect it might have been a robbery, but have no idea if anything is missing. They figure I'll know, so they want me to stop by the shop and check it out. I'm sorry, I'm afraid our talk will have to be postponed."

"It's all right. Mac comes before investigating any supposed centuries old curse," Tamara reassured.

Gavin stopped with his hand on the doorknob. "What if…no, that's crazy."

"What if what?" Tamara prompted.

"I don't know. It's just that Mac seemed to feel I might be in some kind of danger because I had the journal, but he's got the journal. What if I put him in danger?"

"That's not even logical. Who would he be in danger from? Merlin?" A chuckle escaped, along with a hint of sarcasm, and Tamara felt instantly sorry for making fun of him after he received such horrible news of a friend.

"Don't laugh." Gavin pulled his car keys from his pocket and started toward the door. "There's something you don't know. Another journal was stolen from a museum about seventy years ago. Two guards were killed, the crime was never solved, and the journal never turned up."

"Another one! How many of those things are there? Whose journal was it? If you believe the same person is responsible, you'd have to believe some little old man or woman is running around stealing diaries."

"No, I'm just saying that maybe there is something to this curse after all. And, there are only three journals that I know of. The one stolen from the museum was written by Arthur's half-sister, Morgan Le Fay, or Morganna as some people called her."

Tamara's reporter instincts tingled on full alert at a possible story forming right before her eyes. She wanted to know more. But what about her interview and her plans to see the Tor? Quick calculations estimated there were still two days before the Ceremony.

She had time.

Chapter Sixteen

"**G**avin, I want to come with you." Then, just to make sure he couldn't resist, Tamara offered, "I'll bring my book."

Her words stopped Gavin halfway out the door. "You want to come with me? Why?"

"I can help unravel the mysteries of the journals. After all, I am an investigative reporter, so I have skills that could come in handy."

"Investigative skills, eh? I see. By all means, if you feel your skills will help, who am I to stand in your way?"

"Great. Lady Divine, can I come back tomorrow to interview you?"

"Yes, of course, you can. Just call first to make sure I'm home."

Tamara's unwanted assignment suddenly took on a new twist, and she looked forward to the challenge. Gavin followed her to the Will-o'-the-Wisp, where Tamara picked up her book and let Mrs. Harlow know she'd be gone for a while. Leaving Tizzy behind, Tamara climbed into Gavin's car and they were on their way to Glastonbury.

Gavin handled his Volvo like a pro, and Tamara found herself, unwillingly, drawn to his strong, tanned hands that caressed life from the steering wheel rather than demand it.

While Gavin's attention was focused on the road, Tamara took the chance to look him over. Surprisingly, she liked what she saw. He was a handsome man. Not in your usual Hollywood pretty boy kind of style, but more a rugged Marlboro man style. He possessed strong, granite-cut features, eyes of the deepest marine green, and dark hair that would rival the darkness of the midnight hour. Whoa, slow down, Tamara shook herself and focused her attention on the surrounding landscape.

"Is something wrong?" Gavin's voice startled her.

"No, no I'm fine, just thinking through everything you've told me today. Tell me, why weren't you honest with me, instead of trying to read my book behind my back?"

"If we told you the truth right from the start, would you have believed us? We were two strangers, still are for that matter, and we had some wild story about a curse and missing journals, and decapitated bodies..."

"Wait a minute, no one said anything about decapitated bodies."

"No? I thought I mentioned that to you."

"What you said was your parents told you about an ancestor murdered because of the supposed curse."

"Yes, well, I guess I neglected to mention he was found decapitated. His body and his head were found at the uppermost area of the Tor."

"You're kidding?" Tamara's antenna charged to full force. The Glastonbury Tor. Could this connect to her story somehow? "But who, how...Come on, you don't really believe in this curse stuff do you?"

"All I know is what I've been told and that my parents are scared half to death. They tried to throw the journal out, give it away, they even burned it, but somehow it kept showing up in their attic. When they couldn't dispose of it, they tried hiding it from me because they seem to think I'm in some danger."

"Why you and not them? If there's a curse, why hasn't it affected either one of them? Which side of your family is the journal actually handed down through?"

"You are full of questions aren't you?" Gavin took his eyes off the road for second to grin at Tamara.

With heart leaping strangely in her chest, she replied, "I told you, it's my reporter instincts."

"Okay, the journal and the curse have been handed down through my father's side of the family. The reason the curse hasn't affected him is because, at least according to him, the curse only takes effect on the night of the Ceremony of the Stars, and it affects the male of the family. My dad was adopted, so he inherited the book, but not the curse. I'm the only bloodline descendant of Merlin's."

"Oh. Why the Ceremony of the Stars? You know that's what I'm here to do a story on, don't you? You're not really worried about this supposed curse are you?"

"Slow down, one question at a time, woman."

"My name is Tamara."

"Sorry. Tamara. Look, I'm not sure why the Ceremony of the Stars is so important. Mac did some research and found out that Merlin and Nimue engaged in some battle at the Tor that took place on a night when the stars where aligned a certain way. Supposedly, they can only return when the stars are aligned in the sky the same way."

"Okay, now you've lost me. You can't expect me to believe that they can actually return from the dead?"

"Who says they're dead. Energy never dies, it only changes form, so maybe they return in a form other than human. All I know is there has been one coincidence after another. It's as if something or someone was orchestrating the whole situation. I've been raised to be open-minded enough to question and investigate before jumping to any conclusions."

"I'm sorry, but I can't believe that. It's too far-fetched. The whole curse thing is too far out there. What is the curse supposed to be anyway? You haven't made that very clear."

"That's because I don't know what it is. Mac was trying to find that out when…"

Tamara heard the pain in Gavin's voice. Reaching out she placed her hand on his arm and reassured, "I'm sure Mac will be fine. If the doctors can't find anything wrong with him, he's got to be all right."

"I hope so. He's more than just a friend. He's been like a second father to me. Not that I needed one. Dad and I get along great, but Mac is Mac and he's always there for me, so I need to be there for him. If his being in the hospital has anything to do with the curse, I'll find out and put things right."

"I'll help, Gavin. I promise I'll do anything I can to help."

"You and your investigative skills, right?" Gavin teased her.

"Laugh, but I'm good at my job."

"Actually, I'm kind of good at mine as well."

"Oh, what do you do for a living?"

"I'm a private investigator." A slight smile tugged at the corner of his Marlboro face.

Tamara felt the heat seep from her neck right up her face. She tried to remember what other remarks she made about her investigative skills. Gavin probably laughed up his sleeve at her bragging.

"I'm sorry, I don't mean to make fun of you, you were just so cute with your assurances that you could help me out," he said.

"Cute! Don't you dare call me cute. Why didn't you tell me sooner instead of letting me go on about myself? If you don't need my help, why are you letting me come with you?"

"There you go again. You really should try to limit your questions, it gets rather confusing when you string them all together like that."

"Oh, you are so frustrating." Tamara crossed her arms and looked out the window to the green countryside racing past.

"That's what people tell me. Look, all teasing aside, I let you come along because I think we need to figure this out together. I believe that's why we were brought together."

Tamara laughed and turned her attention to Gavin. "We weren't brought together by anything. It's coincidence that we happened to find out about each other and our prospective journals."

"Really. You're quite the skeptic, aren't you?'

"No, I just believe in tangible facts is all. For instance, this curse everyone seems so worried about, think about it for a minute. Sure, you say your ancestor was killed by the curse, but doesn't it make more sense that someone who wanted the book killed him? Look at how we found out about each other. Let's say someone found out your ancestor…what was his name?"

"Reginald."

"Fine, let's say someone found out Reggie owned a journal and thought it would lead them to the sword that seems to be the main focus of this dispute. Wouldn't it stand to reason that someone human killed him so they could get their hands on the journal and the sword? They decapitated him, buried his body, and then started some rumor about a curse to muddy the waters so to speak."

"So, what about the third journal stolen from the museum?"

"Another ancestor, yours, mine or Morganna's, found out it was there and, for the same reason as Reggie's murderer, stole it in an attempt to find the sword."

"Very logical, but I don't believe it for a second."

"Why not?"

"Let's just say I have a sixth sense that there's stuff going on here that can't be so easily explained. I don't believe in coincidence, and the fact that everything has come into place so perfectly just days before the Ceremony of the Stars makes me wonder what forces are at work we don't understand."

She couldn't win. No matter what argument she used, Tamara couldn't shake Gavin's firm belief that something mysterious and mystical was going on. Oh well, she'd just have to use good old fashioned investigative techniques to figure things out and prove to him circumstances were all humanly dictated.

As they neared the hospital, Gavin became quiet. Tamara felt the tension and she hoped, for Gavin's sake, that Mac was going to be all right.

"If you don't mind, I'd like to stop at the hospital first, then on to the bookstore."

"Sure, that's fine."

The visit to the hospital didn't yield anything more than they already knew; Mac was in a coma, but the doctors could find nothing wrong with him and gave no explanation for his unconscious state. Gavin and Tamara left with reassurances the doctor would call if there were any change whatsoever. The trip to the bookstore was short and silent. Tamara kept quiet and let Gavin worry in peace.

The silent chaos that greeted them was much different from the organized untidiness Tamara remembered from the day before.

"How will you know if anything's missing?" Tamara asked upon seeing the magnitude of Mac's personal collection of books in the upper room of the bookstore.

"Mac kept—keeps—everything well catalogued, despite the obvious disarray. Besides, I literally grew up in this room pouring over stories of war, fantasy, and even love. Trust me, if anything's missing, I'll know."

Tamara ran her fingers over dust-covered jackets and leather bound novels. The last couple of days must be getting to her, because she felt as if her body was soaking in energy from the vastness of the collection. A minor trembling started in her fingers and spread to her body. A deep breath of leather and ink set her senses to tingling. "This must have been a cool place for a kid."

Gavin laughed. "Some kids, I suppose, but not everyone can appreciate the knowledge and wisdom held within the pages of books. I was lucky enough to have Mac take me under his wing and share all of this with me."

A couple of minutes passed as Gavin shuffled through papers and books, comparing inventory lists to the actual books on the shelf.

"Where's Merlin's journal? Maybe I can do some reading while you're checking inventory."

"The journal! Oh my God, I hadn't even thought of it." Frantically Gavin ran upstairs to what Tamara assumed was Mac's bedroom. She followed only to find him pushing aside books and papers, searching for the familiar cover of his ancestor's journal.

"I can't find it." It has to be here. Mac was going to read it when he went to bed last night."

Tamara began pushing papers about in an attempt to help with Gavin's search. "I'm afraid I don't see anything, Gavin."

"No, neither do I. Dammit."

Her mind concentrating on searching for the journal, Tamara almost missed the paper that floated from the table down to the floor. She bent to pick it up and return it to the table, but found her eyes drawn to the spidery, barely legible handwriting scrawled across the page. Squinting, she could make out the word dagger, or was it danger? And what were the words that came before that one?

"Gavin, can you read this?"

"Let me see." Gavin took the paper over to the window and peered at the hastily written words. He must have come to the same conclusion as Tamara, because his eyes widened and face paled. "Danger, Mac's warning me about something. His being in the hospital wasn't an accident and he tried to write down this warning. That's the only thing this could mean. But I can't make out the rest of the words."

Tamara looked over his shoulder and tried to decipher the words with him. "It looks like dart lake or maybe day light. Is there a magnifying glass somewhere? It might help."

"Yeah, right over here."

With aid from the magnifying glass, the words suddenly became clear. Tamara and Gavin both spoke at once. "Dark Lady."

"Who's the Dark Lady?"

"How am I supposed to know?"

"Well, Mac's your friend, he wouldn't write something that couldn't be understood by someone."

"Trust me, I have no idea who he means. What I do know is this is a warning and most likely relates to the journals because that's what he was working on at the time this happened."

"And Merlin's journal is missing."

"Yes." Gavin clenched his jaw in suppressed anger. "Merlin's journal is missing, just like the one stolen from the museum so many years ago."

"So, now what?"

"Now, yours is the only journal we have, so we better finish reading it to see if we can find a clue as to what to do next. Otherwise, we have to wait and see what happens at the Ceremony of the Stars. Damn, that's what I forgot. I went to Lady Divine to find out if she knew anything about the stolen journal. She knows a lot of people, so she might have heard something. Once I tried calling Mac, I forgot all about asking her."

"I can ask her when I see her tomorrow. In the meantime, we should finish reading Nimue's journal for clues. We should probably show this note to the police and tell them a valuable book is missing. I'm sure they'd be interested in knowing this was a robbery."

"I suppose you're right. One thing for sure, we're not staying here. It's too dangerous. I'm not even sure if I want to let you out of my sight. How would you feel about a sleepover?" Gavin's green eyes twinkled at the suggestion.

All sorts of images flitted through Tamara's mind at the word sleepover. Before her imagination ran wild, she snorted. "Right! I don't think so. I'll be fine at the Will' O' the Wisp."

"Seriously, I want you where I can keep an eye on you. Besides, I have a feeling my parents haven't been totally forthcoming with information about this whole situation. Wouldn't you like to be there when I confront them?"

"That's not playing fair." Tamara considered the man beside her. So far, he'd proven loyal and caring toward friends, albeit lacking slightly in the respect for other people's property department. Other than that, she knew nothing about him. Well, not exactly nothing. He was gorgeous, in a masculine way. His cerulean blue eyes melted her resistance, and his body... Enough, already. The truth of the matter was, there was a story to investigate, and Gavin was handing her the possibility of furthering that investigation. Was it worth spending a night under the same roof as him? Probably not. But, she found she couldn't say the word no. The word just wouldn't cross her lips. Instead, she found her self agreeing. "As long as I have my own room that is."

"Don't worry, that won't be too difficult."

Not too difficult was an understatement. When Tamara got her first look at Gavin's family home she choked. "This is where you live? It's a castle."

"Yes, rather. Do you like it?"

"It's amazing. No, that's not an appropriate word for a place like this. Try majestic, noble, proud, and magnificent. That should about cover it."

Gavin's laughter warmed the cooling temperature of the late afternoon air. "I'm glad you approve of my humble abode."

"Nothing humble about this place. Gavin, are you sure your parents won't mind? What will they think when you bring some strange woman home to meet them, not to mention staying overnight?"

"They'll think I've fallen madly in love."

"What! Don't you dare let them think something like that."

"Relax, I was only kidding. Don't worry, as soon as I tell them what's been going on, they'll understand and welcome you warmly. My parents are very loving people."

"How nice for you." Tamara's tone was sarcastic but her thoughts turned to Gavin's remark about falling in love. She wondered what it would be like to be held in his arms, and feel the hardness of his body melding with hers. Her face grew warm as she imagined his lips claiming hers in a display of passion. Dear God, where was that coming from? She'd better get herself under control, especially if she was to spend the night under the same roof as this guy.

"Tamara, these are my parents."

Hardly even aware they'd left the car, Tamara was jolted hastily back to reality and immediately found her hand engulfed by a warm, welcoming one.

"Hello. I had no idea my son knew such a beautiful young woman or I would have insisted he bring you home sooner." The rather large man spoke in the teasing tone of a natural born flirt.

Gavin's mom put an end to the flirtation with a slap on her husband's arm. "Pay no heed to his teasing, he's all bluff and bluster. It's nice to meet you, Tamara. I'm Caroline and this beast of a man is Ruddy. We're pleased to meet you. Are you here for dinner?"

Put on the spot, Tamara didn't know how to respond. Relief washed over her when Gavin rescued her from an awkward situation.

"Tamara is actually spending the night."

Caroline and Ruddy stood in stunned silence, and Tamara cursed Gavin under her breath for leaving them with the wrong impression about their relationship. She shot daggers at him, her eyes silently insisting he tell the rest of the story.

Gavin laughed and his twinkling eyes made Tamara squirm with a memory of her earlier thoughts. Maybe she wouldn't mind sharing a room with him after all.

"Don't worry, she'll be staying in the guest room. Our relationship is just business."

"Yes, and that's the way it'll stay." The words were out before she could stop them and the shocked look on Caroline and Ruddy's faces made her sorry she spoke.

"I'm sorry, that was rude of me."

"What Tamara means is there's a reason she's here and it really is just business, kind of. I think we should sit down and have a serious talk."

Ruddy and Caroline looked confused, probably trying to figure out what was so serious they could possibly have to talk about with a total stranger. Shuffled into the living room, Tamara made a quick survey of her surroundings. The entrance hallway itself was almost larger than her entire apartment. Her gaze flicked across marble floors, life size paintings on the wall, a winding staircase, and a crystal vase filled to the brim with fresh flowers sitting on a round, hand carved antique table.

The living area itself awed her with the floor to ceiling velvet drapes of deep crimson and embroidered tapestry upon rose colored, painted walls. The furniture was the kind you would sit and disappear deep into. Rich, forest green, brushed velvet, and dark mahogany wood, the furniture exuded warmth and coziness.

Tamara's perusal was interrupted by Caroline's comment. "I'm not sure what's going on, but let's talk over dinner. I know I'm starving." All agreed. Declining Tamara's offer of help, Caroline left to make final preparations for dinner.

Gavin's dad made a light attempt at conversation, but every time he steered to the reason for the visit, Gavin assured him he wasn't talking until everyone was together. An uncomfortable silence ensued, causing all three of them to shift in their seats. Thankfully, Caroline took that moment to announce dinner and direct them to the dining room.

Caroline beamed a lightness that dispelled any awkwardness from the situation and everyone breathed a sigh of relief. Amidst the aroma of roast beef, gravy, and potatoes, Tamara found herself seated across the table from Gavin.

Caroline spoke first. Her voice like the gentle wafting of a warm summer ocean drifting into shore.

"Tamara...I like it, I think it suits you. Do you have any idea what it means?"

Damn. Tamara felt a blush rise in her cheeks. Here we go again. Maybe she should just lie and say no. She tried to avoid the question by filling her mouth with mashed potatoes.

"Tamara, you're blushing."

Great, Gavin would notice. "You're great at stating the obvious, is that the extent of your detective skills?" Again, Tamara wanted to bite her tongue for speaking like that to Gavin, right in front of his parents no less. What would they think of her? She shoveled some roast beef into her mouth, mainly to keep herself from sticking her foot in it.

"Gavin, don't be such a tease. Tamara, you don't have to tell us if it makes you uncomfortable." Caroline was quick to jump to her defense, which made Tamara grateful.

"No, it's okay. It's just that my mom named me and her reasoning was kind of weird. At least, I think so. When I tell people, they usually laugh."

Ruddy's voice was strong and reassuring. "We promise not to laugh. What kind of hosts would that make us?"

Tamara barely registered Ruddy's reassurance, something occurred to her and it made this whole situation seem even more surreal. What had Gavin said earlier about there being no such thing as coincidence? Maybe it wouldn't sound so strange if she just told the story aloud.

"Mom is a great one for the history of England. She just eats up legends and myths of the Druids, Celtic Gods, and Goddesses, that whole King Arthur and his sword story. You know, the usual." She hesitated, not sure what to say.

"Go on, we're not laughing yet." Gavin said.

"Yet you said you wouldn't laugh."

"No, my parents said they wouldn't laugh. I promised no such thing."

"Gavin, treat Tamara with the respect you were taught." Ruddy's words of caution to his son won him an affectionate pat from Caroline.

Tamara felt a twinge of sadness for the relationship they shared, one she had never been exposed to growing up. Not allowing herself to start feeling sorry for her lacking childhood, she continued her tale.

"You have to understand, my mom is slightly strange. In fact, she's a witch!" There, the words were out and she couldn't take them back now.

"Why, how wonderful. I'd love to talk to her. I've dabbled in the Wiccan religion myself, you know." Caroline sounded genuinely interested.

Tamara shook her head in surprise at the enthusiastic response. "Don't you think it's kind of weird, you know, her being a witch?"

"No, of course not. Many people these days are exploring the roots of ancient religions, beliefs, and traditions. Being a witch is not as much of a blight on a person's record as it used to be. They don't even burn you at the stake anymore." A smile twitched at the corner of Caroline's mouth.

"I know. It's just...it's not something someone should go talking about."

"Tamara, there's nothing wrong with learning to live in harmony with the elements of nature. It's what gives us life. We should show respect to Mother Earth." Caroline frowned at Tamara. "Don't tell me you hold it against your mother because she follows these ideals?"

Tamara squirmed under her hostess's pointed gaze. "I'll admit, we have our differences over the matter."

Gavin sat up straight in his chair, ran his fingers through his dark hair, and snapped. "Listen all this homey stuff is cute, but can we get to the point?"

"Gavin. Where are your manners? I asked our guest a question and when we've finished talking then you can hoard the conversation." Caroline turned back to Tamara with a raised eyebrow and a twinkle in her eye as if to say, There, that takes care of him for you.

Tamara shot Gavin a self-satisfactory smile and found herself liking her hostess very much. "When I was born, Mom had a vision. At least, that's what she says. Seeing the future or maybe the past, she saw me standing at the mouth of the Tamar River: the Goddess Tamara guarding the unofficial border between Cornwall and England. Supposedly I was guarding the land of Avalon from—here I quote her directly—'the encroaching beliefs of the thick-headed English and the weak-willed man who sat upon the throne at Tintagel.'"

The laughter Tamara expected from Gavin didn't come. Instead, he sat in his chair frowning. "You just made that up, didn't you?"

"No, I didn't." She knew what Gavin was thinking, probably a mirror of her earlier thoughts about coincidence. "It's really kind of weird isn't it?"

Caroline perked up in defense. "There's nothing weird about it, Tamara. I think it's a wonderful way to be named."

"Mom, you don't know the whole story. It is weird."

Ruddy sat quietly until now. When he spoke his voice was low with the slightest shake. "This visit has to do with that damned journal, doesn't it?"

"Good guess, Dad. Don't you think it's time you told me the whole story?" Gavin glared at his parents. "There is more than you've told me, and I want to hear everything."

"That isn't necessary. Gavin, just leave the cursed book alone and let the Ceremony of the Stars pass unnoticed," Caroline pleaded.

"That's not going to be possible."

"What's happened, son?" All sign of the flirt was gone from Ruddy now. Concern and worry were etched in his face and demeanor.

Caroline and Ruddy sat like statues of marble while Gavin related the events of the last couple of days. The strange appearance of the journals within a day of each other, the parchment written by the ancient Druid who witnessed the battle of Merlin and Nimue, as well as the birth of the curse, and Mac's findings to do with the deaths of their ancestors. It was the possibility of a woman glimpsed by the Druid priest that got the most reaction from Caroline and Ruddy.

Their gazes flew to each other and locked, their voices spoke in unison. "The Dark Lady!"

Tamara's heart jumped into her throat, and she saw that Gavin's reaction was much the same.

"What the hell do you know about the Dark Lady?" Gavin snapped at his parents.

"Don't talk to us like that. Gavin, you seem to be hiding secrets from us as well."

"Well, I'm getting around to telling you now. It's just that so much has happened since yesterday. Mac's in the hospital, and no one seems to know what's wrong with him. Merlin's journal is missing, and Mac scratched out a warning, something about a Dark Lady and danger."

"Dear God in heaven above," Caroline whispered in a voice full of fear. She clutched her husband's arm. "Tell them Ruddy. We have to tell them everything."

"Yes, yes, you're right." Ruddy sighed. "We only wanted to keep away from that damned book and that insane curse."

"You knew about the curse, too?"

"Yes. Reginald left a letter for his descendants, which stayed in the family for a couple of generations and then disappeared. Even though the letter disappeared, the story of the letter has remained a legend within the family. Your grandfather told me, his father told him, and so on. The letter told of the misunderstanding of Merlin and Nimue, the reason for the curse on your bloodlines. Reginald claimed there was a third person involved pulling strings and causing trouble, a Dark Lady of evil. He tried to put things right between Merlin and Nimue, but failed. He gave warning to all of his bloodlines to beware the curse and the Dark Lady."

"They fought over the sword, didn't they?" Tamara questioned.

"Yes, it seems that Nimue swore an oath to her predecessor, and all who had gone before, to give the Sword Excalibur to King Arthur and help him rule Britain as a United Kingdom. She reneged on the deal and ended up stealing the sword back to use as an instrument of Merlin's destruction."

Tamara reacted with indignation. "She did not. Merlin is the one who stole the sword from her bedchamber. He's the one who trashed the values and beliefs of Avalon, the place that gave him life, knowledge, and wisdom."

"Oh, here we go again." Gavin rolled his eyes.

"Whoa, what's going on here? Sounds like there's more than one side to the story." Ruddy tried to avert the tension.

"Yes, it would seem so, dear. It also seems that this whole sordid situation can't be avoided, so what do we do about it?" Caroline looked to her husband for guidance.

"I haven't a clue." Ruddy pointed to Gavin and Tamara. "Ask them, because I think this involves them more than us."

Gavin raised his hands, palms up, and remarked, "We have to find out the real story, find the sword, return it to where it belongs, return a sense of peace to Merlin and Nimue thereby negating the curse, all the while making sure the Dark Lady doesn't interfere. Shouldn't be too hard at all."

"You've got to be kidding." Tamara surprised herself by actually giggling.

"I'm kidding about it being easy, not about what we have to do."

"Fine, then how do we go about accomplishing these feats of wonder?"

"Hopefully, we can find a clue in Nimue's journal. She supposedly regained possession of the sword." Gavin stifled a yawn that set off a round of yawns around the room. Tension broke and they all laughed at each other until their sides hurt. Recovering from the round of laughter, Caroline put her hand upon Tamara's arm.

"Tamara, I have no idea what forces have brought us all together, but I'm glad that you're here. Together, I have a feeling we can work this thing out," she said.

"Oh, well, if my wife has a feeling then it'll be fine. Her instincts have proven themselves over the years."

"Maybe you have the sight." Tamara was only joking until she saw the look that crossed her hostess's face.

"I was only kidding. I didn't mean to insult you or anything."

"No, you didn't. I just wonder how much of the Sight you have yourself, because you hit the nail on the head. My ancestors were practicing Druids, and it's said that the powers can be dormant through generations only to rise once in awhile when you least expect them."

"You know, my mom would love to be here for all this." Tamara genuinely missed her mother at that moment and began to feel sorry for all the trouble she'd caused her over the years. God, when she looked back on how she snubbed her mom again and again, she felt shame.

Caroline must have sensed something. As they stood to retire for the night, she pulled Tamara into a brief but warm embrace.

"I'm sure your mom understands and will be waiting for you to return a much more open-minded person. It is all part of growing up, you know."

Tamara's only answer was a huge yawn that set off another round of laughter, more subdued this time, as everyone was tired and worried.

"Come on, Tamara, I'll show you where you'll be sleeping." Caroline led the way to the stairs but turned for one last remark. "Gavin, I'm sorry, with so much going on I didn't even ask about Mac. You said he's in hospital, but no one knows what's wrong?"

"He's in a coma, but the doctors have no idea why. I'll check in on him tomorrow. Hopefully, there'll be an improvement."

"I hope so too, dear. He's such a nice man and I know how much he means to you. See you in the morning."

"Goodnight, Mom, Tamara."

Tamara waved and followed Caroline up the stairs wondering all the way if she'd ever make it to the top. This place was huge. With feet dragging, they finally made it to her room where Caroline wished her goodnight with the urge to call if she needed anything.

"And by the way," Caroline spoke. "Gavin's room is just across the hall. He insisted that you have a room close to his so you'd feel safe, of course." Her eyes twinkled with motherly indulgence and not a small amount of hopefulness.

Tamara's heart raced at the thought of Gavin so close, and she was barely able to stutter a good night to her hostess. Once the heavy door was shut, Tamara browsed the room where she'd be spending the night. Looking around, she had no idea what else anyone could possibly need. The room was complete with television, books, fresh flowers, a nightgown, bathrobe, its own bathroom with bath bubbles, and thick towels. Talk about the lap of luxury, Tamara didn't live this well at home. Too bad she was so tired and couldn't enjoy her surroundings more. Without even the luxury of a hot bubble bath or time to read, Tamara dropped her clothes on the floor and crawled into bed only to fall asleep with visions of a flashing sword swirling its way into her dreams.

Chapter Seventeen

"I won't be long, unless something unexpected happens at the hospital. Are you sure you don't mind being here by yourself?" Gavin's question was a reasonable one, considering someone robbed Mac here only the night before last.

"I'll be fine. The front door will be open and it's the middle of the day. No one would try anything now," Tamara reassured Gavin as he fumbled with his key in the lock.

Earlier this morning, after a comfortable breakfast with Gavin and his parents, Tamara and he agreed to work together to figure out the mystery of the curse and the sword. Gavin would check on Mac at the hospital, and then join Tamara at the bookstore where she would be reading Nimue's journal.

Once the lights were on and the blinds pulled high, Tamara felt more comfortable. "This isn't so bad. I'll be fine. In fact, I'm looking forward to reading more of this journal. With all that's happened, I think I'll have a different viewpoint on what I do read."

"I hope you find something that'll help. By the way, if a customer comes in the prices are all listed inside the front cover of the book, and the receipts are just hand written, so it's fairly simple."

"You mean simple enough even for me to handle?"

A grin lit Gavin's face and Tamara's heart gave an extra beat. "I didn't mean any insult. Are you always so prickly?"

"Only with you. It must be an ingrained habit."

"We've only known each other two days."

"Then I should get over it quickly."

Gavin raised his eyebrow as if to say, Oh yeah? Tamara laughed at the comical expression on his face and tension was momentarily relieved.

"When I get back remind me to give Lady Divine a call. She may have managed to dig something up since yesterday."

"Good idea. See you later." Tamara saw Gavin to the door all the while fighting the urge to ask him to stay. She didn't know if it was because she was afraid to be alone, or she just liked the feel of him close to her.

"Gavin, all kidding aside, I hope Mac's all right."

"So do I. See you soon."

Tamara watched Gavin walk by the street level window, and listened to the sound of his footsteps retreating down the street. The heaviness of being alone in a store recently robbed made her uneasy, but she wouldn't allow it to overtake her. She had work to do. Eagerly, she took Nimue's journal to a well-worn, stuffed easy chair just under the window by the door. Sinking into the soft, brushed cotton cushion she folded her legs, and opened the cover of the ancient book that caused so much ruckus over the last while.

The moon rose high in the black of the starless sky. I shivered in the unnatural cold of the summer's night. Just more than a month ago, we lit the Beltane fires, preparing all as we have in the past. We gathered wood to burn, assembled twigs from the rowan tree to use for fanning the flames, and prepared special herbs for the fertility elixir. Lastly, we chose a ceremonial cow to be blessed and driven between fires of kindled wood, while we danced the dance of fertility and purification. The God Bel stayed foremost in our minds during the blessing.

Morganna was the chosen one this year. Her knowledge and powers placed her above all others, except I, therefore she was the logical choice. Since I could not be the Maiden to give her virginity to the God, I chose Morganna.

We gathered under the night sky, hands held high, and danced in harmony and unselfconscious abandon. We threw off our cloaks and allowed the moonlight to touch upon our flesh. Chanting to summon Bel, we swayed in unison, all as one. In our midst stood Morganna, offering herself to the God, giving of her virginity so our fields could grow strong and fertile, yielding herself to Bel, so our fields would yield to us.

Yes, all went as it should, so why did our fields lay barren and brown? Why did our livestock bear dead fetuses? Why did the stars disappear from the sky?

I ran my hand over the glassy smoothness of the pond, the moon reflected in perfect shape. My mind numbed and time slowed. I prayed to the Goddess Arianrhod for answers to my questions. As High Fruitful Mother, she could restore life to our lands. As Keeper of the Silver Wheel of Stars, ruler of time and karma, she could tell me where the stars disappeared and what debts needed to be paid for their return.

A ripple in the pond, a shiver in my heart, and visions began to appear. At first, I thought to have imagined, because what I saw could not be right.

Before my eyes, Morganna and Arthur were locked in a lover's embrace. I knew this was not a future vision because Arthur still bore the fresh face of youth. Since becoming king, he allowed his face to bush with blond hair.

But when, when could such a thing have happened?

If Morganna laid with Arthur, that would mean she was no virgin upon the Beltane, and that would explain why Bel withdrew his favor from our land. He was punishing us for the insult. How dared she to place us in peril with her own selfishness! She defiled the Sacred Ceremony of balancing the Divine female and male, our yearly rejoicing in the flowering of life.

My heart cried with the deception. What explanation could Morganna possibly use to defend her actions? I thought to call her from her monthly retreat early, but the fogging of the pond and emergence of a new vision stopped my action.

Before my eyes appeared a vision, so fast I thought it must have been my imagination. But there it was before me, Morganna with Merlin.

My mind recognized the familiar hill, with its terraced pathways laid out in a maze-like design. Like a sentinel to the heavens above, the stone monument rose. The place that signifies the central point of energy for lands that ceased to exist in the physical.

Below the Tor I saw a cave where no cave was supposed to exist. Within the dark entranceway stood Merlin and Morganna. The wind blew about my shoulders and leaves rustled around my feet. I shivered.

Energy unfamiliar to me tingled in the summer breeze, darkening the forest clearing until all I could see was the sight before my eyes. In a trance, not induced by myself, I watched Morganna reach out to touch Merlin's arm and plead with him with her pretty, pouting lips.

Pain and disillusionment distorted Merlin's face. What in Heavens was she telling him to thus bring about that look? Intensity grew within the pond, and settled deep in the roots of my mind until I felt ready to burst. In a final blinding flash of rainbow sparks and flames, the vision disappeared, clearing the pond for my final vision. Before my disbelieving eyes, and flashing brightly in the pond, the crystal depths slowly revealed the Sword Excalibur.

Unsteady, my hand quivered forth to touch the illustrious steel I knew so well, only to grasp at the air. Sobbing, I fell to the ground and let loose my sorrow in a keening voice. "Niobe, I have failed. Take me from this world and punish me with eternal banishment."

Upon my pain and sorrow, an unfamiliar energy slowly crept from the clearing, but even in my selfish pity, I sensed evil satisfaction in the dissipation. What was at work here? Was I being led falsely? I had no idea.

Once the air was clear and my emotions of failure and frustration settled, I felt a warm comfort tender itself to me.

Words were spoken, not aloud in a clear sound, but upon the wind that carried the sounds of songbirds and Cerunnos's earthly creatures. Like the warm breath of a loved one, the breeze ruffled across my brow, soothing my senses and imparting the remembrance of a basic priestess rule.

All is not as it seems, do not always trust your eyes, always trust your senses.

"Yes, I know, but my senses are so confused I need to see with my eyes."

Soothing warmth touched me again, infused itself within my limbs and I calmed.

"Niobe, I feel your presence. Help me, please help me."

Like leaves from the tree of life, words drifted into my mind. You are stronger than this. You must help yourself, you can help yourself. I believe in you; you must believe in yourself and in love. Then, like the receding ocean and the land we once knew, the words were gone, the energy was gone, Niobe was gone.

Unsteady on my feet, I stood to face my fate. I needed to think. What did the visions mean? Obviously, Morganna was not in her retreat, she was with Merlin, and they were working together. Deceived by the two closest to me.

In a heartbeat, I knew what the vision of the sword meant. I heard stories about Arthur's failing health, weak marriage, and battles he fought. If this were true, it would not be long before Sword Excalibur was without the hand that held it these past years.

Rightfully, the sword should be returned to Avalon and into my hand, but with Merlin and Morganna as one and the sword flashing before my eyes, I knew they were bound for Arthur's court and the sword.

I needed to act quickly, so I departed the clearing, called for Anthea to make ready my horse, clothing, and food for the trip. Startled glances greeted my dash as I disturbed priestesses in their daily rituals. I cared not. I had my own ritual to prepare for before leaving for Tintagel and the Sword Excalibur.

Excalibur had been forged in the fire of our ancestors from the land of enchantment, therefore I needed to set my ritual with fire. Since the God Bel was angry at the falseness perpetrated upon him at Beltane, I decided to call upon Brigit for my purposes. I would be well served with her occult knowledge and firepower. Casting my circle and raising my arms above my head in supplication, I recited my desire.

Goddess Brigit, I call upon thee
Your power of fire and magic
I call forth to me.

These lines I repeated until the litany became blurred into a never-ending chant. Visualizing, I stirred the cauldron and opened myself to the wants and needs of the Goddess. I was not sure that first my spell was working until I felt the first prickle upon my scalp. Like the fires I called upon, the prickly heat spread and became all that I was until I became consumed with the flames.

My mind flashed with images of screaming people fleeing in terror at the tremors of the earth beneath their feet. Amidst all who scrambled for waiting ships in a harbor of churning waters, one person made her way to the Temple of Apollo. A face masked in shadow, she knelt before the altar of the God Apollo.

Niobe taught me enough of the ancient Gods to know that this particular God was one of intellect, art, prophesy, healing, and light. She knew such things, because she herself came from this place and ruled over Avalon as the protector of the old ways for a time that could not be measured.

Leaning forward, the shadowy figure scooped water from the over flowing fountain and chanted a tune of reverence. As the first note passed her lips I recognized the voice of Niobe, but what was she doing?

Once the cask was filled with waters from the fountain of Apollo, Niobe stood and declared to an empty Temple, "This you owe me, Apollo, for the death of my children. These waters hold the powers of Atlantis. I will carry them with me to a New World and use them to help mankind on the journey that lies ahead."

I watched the wraith appear above Niobe's head. Spider-like, the mist reached out to touch her face and, in a glow of otherworldly love, engulf Niobe in an embrace of acceptance. In another blinding flash of light a sword appeared, suspended in the air, held fast by the hovering wraith.

Booming more loudly than the protesting earth, a voice spoke. "Your wish shall be, Niobe, but on the condition that you take this sword and guard it well. Forged by the powerful, beloved thunderbolt of Zeus, the Sword Excalibur embodies all that is and was Atlantis. Though the waters hold healing powers and certain properties of magic, the sword, wielded by the hands of one pure of heart and intent, shall ensure the ways of our land are carried into the future. Harmony and peace will reign and all will accept their oneness with the universe."

Niobe left the Temple and I could make out the island of Atlantis heaving and churning as the landmass disappeared beneath the darkened waters of the ocean.

Niobe was one of few who survived the disaster. I know from her stories to me that she made her way to these shores and, seeing the Tor upon the hilltop, knew she had found the place to settle the waters from the Temple.

With a mighty blast of her wand, she struck the ground beneath her feet. The earth shook, and the grass and dirt parted to reveal a hole, a well with no water.

Niobe upturned the cask she brought from the lost continent and poured the sparkling, crystal water into the newly formed hole.

Water fell from the cask into the earth and a cry of nature rang forth through the countryside. The darkening twilight sky suddenly became brilliant with displays of dancing lights and shooting stars.

I saw not much after that. The vision began to recede, and heat from the flames attacked my body again. Just when I believed my life form in this world perished, I was thrown to the ground. Sweating and panting, I'm sure I was a sight to behold. Brigit revealed her secrets to me, and I was in awe at the glimpse of powers, the Chalice Well. Based on Brigit's urgings, I was no longer on my way to Tintagel. Instead, I would defeat Merlin where my power would be the greatest. The place where I could call upon the Chalice Well and the ancient Gods to enhance my powers.

With the power of Brigit within me, and my purpose clear in my mind, I felt strong enough to withstand even Merlin himself. I held no worries of Morganna. She was like an annoying creature nipping at the heels of a mighty stag. If need be, I would destroy her. Though I would rather return her to Avalon and try to reconcile her to earning her position as Head Priestess of Avalon. In truth, no one possessed the ability to take my place. Morganna had been the shining star I chose to sit in my place. I would need to judge her participation in Merlin's deception. I hoped she was an innocent. I needed her to be innocent.

Avalon was the last bastion of the ways things once were, yet everything was falling apart, and the future of my home was in jeopardy. Avalon was the one remaining hope for people to understand all that they could be, the abilities that they shared, and the powers at their fingertips. If this place were lost, mankind may never realize so much again.

Why, oh why did all rest upon my shoulders? If I could only return the Sword Excalibur to a safe place, the power it held would remain, even if Avalon became nothing but mist in the memory of mankind.

My gaze took in the ashes of the circle and the disarray of my completed ritual. It was time. Over the protest of my faithful priestesses, I left Avalon.

I had no idea what was in store for me. I only knew I needed to regain my rights over the Sword Excalibur and in order to do so I needed to defeat Merlin, a battle which I dreaded. Not because I doubted my powers, but even with all that transpired, the thought of having to destroy the man I once loved struck deep in my heart like a deadly spike.

Wow! Tamara thought, as she raised her eyes from the parchment page and rubbed her tired eyes. She needed a break. Not only from the reading, but also from the emotions of the woman who wrote this extraordinary journal. If what she read could be believed, Nimue held the responsibility of a dying race and all their knowledge in her hands, and those closest to her betrayed her. Tamara could only imagine the confusion, sense of betrayal, and urgency in Nimue's actions.

No sooner had the thoughts entered her mind than Tamara felt a warm breeze drift across her arm. Strange, the wind chimes sat calm and hushed, so where was the breeze coming from? The whisper of a breath in her ear gave Tamara a sense of love...and gratitude?

Abruptly Tamara stood and sent the journal banging to the floor, but she didn't care. This was getting too weird. She didn't feel threatened, but she sensed an energy here that didn't belong, and that, alone, was enough to scare her.

A hint of breeze set the wind chimes to playing lightly, and Tamara imagined she could hear words within the tingling harmony. "Tamara, Taaamaraaa. Help me."

"Enough." Tamara snapped the word aloud. Now she knew she was imagining things. It was probably a good idea to stop reading altogether until Gavin came back.

Picking the book up from the floor, Tamara looked at the few remaining pages and decided she couldn't wait. She needed to see what happened between the star-crossed lovers.

With a deep breath, she settled into the deep armchair, opened the journal, and continued to read.

Thunder cracked deep in the night and lightning only outlined the form of Merlin as he stood upon the hillside of the Tor. Dipping into the Chalice Well, I called upon the powers of Niobe and the ancient Gods to help me right the wrongs perpetrated by Merlin.

In a brief flash, I wondered what happened to Morganna. In my vision she stood with Merlin, yet, I saw her naught. Time to deal with her would come later, after I finished with Merlin and retrieved the sword from Arthur.

Eyes blazing, heart pounding, and will unbendable, I faced the man I once loved. The man who betrayed our heritage and homeland with his deceit and manipulation

"Merlin, I call to you. Your time has come and I call you forth to settle what lies between us." In the power and strength of my ancestors, my voice rang out, echoing up the hillside to challenge the Great Magician and Seer.

"Nimue, I care naught to deal with you in this manner. Let me pass and go to Arthur. My duty lies in protecting him."

"I hear he threw you from his kingdom, why would you return?"

"You ask me such a question when you are bent on destroying him with your evil ways."

Those unfair words stabbed at my heart and made me blind. How dare he accuse me of being evil when he was the one to steal the sword and use it to better his position? How dare he accuse me when he left the Old Ways he promised to preserve?

He deserved naught to live.

I acted.

I summoned all energies to me, and threw my hands forward with fingertips directed to Merlin. I was hot, in flames. I began to vibrate so much I thought I might perish before the energy shot from my body. I need not have worried. I was protected by the ways of good. The Gods who came before the one God.

In a blinding array of sparks, bolts of energy shot from my fingertips and engulfed Merlin in an aura of crackling light. However, something happened, I felt him fight back with more ability than I would have believed him capable of. I thought these past years he retired and would be rather weak in his power. Instead, he grew. Maybe beyond my abilities.

"Merlin." I screamed in agony and frustration. "The Sword Excalibur belongs to the land of Avalon. I will take possession back from Arthur and return the sword where it belongs."

"No, Nimue, you will not. You have become corrupted. I will regain possession of the sword and enable its use as it should be."

The arrogance of his reply struck me into anger. I felt I was losing the battle and knew naught what to do. "Where are you Gods? Do not desert me now. My cause is right and just, you must help me."

Screeching in a final gesture of power, I gave all that was in me. Yet, it was not enough. Still, Merlin stood in arrogance upon the hillside beside the Tor. I thought my life ended, but as I stopped my flow of energy, Merlin stopped his as well. Was he giving in, or were his powers replete? I knew naught. The battle would begin again when powers replenished. The sword must wait. Before I left, I gathered energy enough to throw my final curse.

"Merlin, I curse all of your bloodline who come after you. They will yearn for the sword as you. When the stars are aligned as they are this eve, your blood descendants will search for the sword, yet they will be felled by their greed."

Merlin answered. His voice was deep and echoed like the booming of the surrounding storm. "And I curse you, Nimue. All your bloodlines will search endlessly for love never to find the need fulfilled. Their greed will overtake and blind them to what lies before them."

The curse barely registered in my mind as my body dissolved into the void of nothingness. I hope to guide my descendants with this journal and my energy to gently prod them. None can rest until the sword is returned to the Chalice Well to rest with the past. At least until one pure of heart and intent returns to hold the Sword Excalibur in his or her hands in the name of all, not One.

"So that's the supposed curse, is it?" Tamara gently closed the cover of the ancient book and sat in subdued silence. "I'm destined to go through my whole life and never find love because of my greed? That's ridiculous."

Overwrought with powerful emotions, Tamara sighed and stretched her fingertips to the sky as far as she could reach. Her self-satisfied groan of relief from stiffness was cut abruptly short by a gust of wind that sent the front door smashing against the wall of the shop. Swirling about in restless abandon the wind grasped loose papers in its jaws and whirled them to the ceiling.

Tamara ran to the door and pushed until the latch clicked in place. Though the door was shut against the natural elements, the wind acted alive, sending papers and dust on a macabre dance about the darkening bookstore. Shivers of fear prickled the back of Tamara's neck. Something wasn't quite right. She realized the small store was dark as twilight, yet a glance at the tiny street level windows showed the sun reflecting off heated asphalt. Her mind couldn't comprehend the contrast from what was to what should be. The otherworldly aspects challenged Tamara's logically motivated mind and scared her.

With her hand on the doorknob and full intentions to depart the shop immediately, she tugged hard.

The door didn't budge even an inch.

Her pounding heart became the only sound Tamara could hear, and the adrenaline rushing in her blood the only sensation. She tried the door again. It still wouldn't open.

A voice spoke from the empty room behind her. Tamara yelped and clutched her hand to her chest. Afraid, Tamara turned to face the sound that broke her peace. Before her stood a woman. Dark and menacing, yet possessing skin of alabaster white and eyes of vibrant blue.

"It will not open." Deep and vibrating, the apparition's voice shuddered inside Tamara's chest. Strange, she hadn't heard the words, merely felt them.

"I…who…what…"

Evil laughter filled the now deathly still air. "Yes, you are obviously one of Nimue's descendants. You are as stupid as she."

Tamara bristled at the insult to her ancestor and found her voice, as well as some small bit of courage. "Who the hell do you think you are bursting in here and insulting me and my ancestor?"

"What, you don't want to ask me how I got here? Or why I'm here?"

Actually, the entrance baffled Tamara. It must have been done with mirrors or some other magician's trick.

"Oh, I can assure you there was no trick involved. It was magic through and through."

Tamara was stunned. How could this strange woman read her mind? She couldn't have. It was just a lucky guess.

"All right, so who the hell are you? What are you doing here? How do you know anything about my ancestors?"

"I believe if you really think it through, you'll figure it out for yourself. Now give me the journal." The woman's voice rang deep and intense, causing Tamara's heart to pound.

"I'm not giving you the journal. It belongs to me." Her words were sure but her voice shook. She was afraid, but who wouldn't be? This woman shows up, practically out of nowhere, with evil oozing from her aura, and demands Nimue's journal. Okay, Tamara, she's just a thief. You can handle her with a good swift kick to the shin.

"Do not think your feeble attempts will stop me. I always get what I want." With these words, again reading Tamara's mind, the woman in black advanced on Tamara.

Tamara was terrified and found herself shrinking into the darkened recesses of the shop. The woman put her hand out, as if waiting for Tamara to place the book into it. Instead, a bright beam of light shot forth from suddenly transparent fingers and latched onto the journal. Off balance, Tamara tried to hold on to the book. Too strong for her, the unseen energy forcefully pried the book from her hands. For a brief moment the book hovered in the air, and then shot straight into the hand of the waiting woman.

Air became scarce in the small shop, and Tamara panted to enable breath to enter her lungs. Her ears hurt as any remaining oxygen was sucked from the air, and her heart pounded in her chest. Tamara knew she couldn't survive much longer. Black turned into mist, as Tamara's vision began to fog and her knees weakened.

The last thing she heard before passing out were the words, "I think I'll let you live. I will need your blood. By the way," like whispers in a nightmare, "my name is Morganna."

Morganna left the bookshop pleased with herself for acquiring the third journal. Now, with skill and luck, she'd be able to access the power of the Chalice Well and find a way to destroy both Nimue and Merlin, forever.

Mortals are so stupid, thinking they could come up against her and stop her from accomplishing what she had primed herself to do for centuries. They possessed not even enough brains between them to figure out what they were up against. She would manipulate from a distance, and they would never know that she was pulling the strings.

Oh yes, the legends called for a forfeit of blood in exchange for the return of the sword. She'd give blood. At least, she'd supply the blood to the forces of the ancient ones to finally have the Sword Excalibur in her hands.

Once she reached her loft, Morganna reached for the telephone. She needed to make her subordinate aware of the circumstances.

The female who answered the phone had been recruited by Morganna and trained diligently. Morganna found her to be useful in many ways and promised eternal life as a reward for her loyalty. The thought of eventual immortality made the stupid mortal obey Morganna's every command. Depending on how the plan went, and what kind of mood Morganna was in, she might fulfill her promise to the mortal woman. But then again, she might not.

Morganna answered the woman. "Yes, I have the book. The plan commences as planned."

"Have you read it? Do you know how to access the power of the Chalice Well?" The irritating female dared to ask.

"Do not question me. If the time becomes right, I will grant your wish, in the meantime, we think only of why I am here and what I want. Is that understood?"

"Yes, mistress." The woman answered quietly, sounding contrite and slightly fearful. Morganna liked the fear. It gave her a sense of power and control.

"The woman leaves the bookstore soon. Keep an eye on her. The Ceremony of the Stars is tomorrow night, and she will be our sacrifice. With the blood of Nimue's descendant, the sword will be mine."

"And eternal life will be mine," the woman proclaimed persistently.

"Yes, we shall see." Morganna's voice became vague as she began to plan for tomorrow. "I have much to do. Go, but make sure you keep your eyes on the woman. I will need to know where she is at all times."

Without giving the woman a chance to reply, Morganna hung up the telephone and lifted her scrying mirror before her eyes. She needed reassurance. She needed to see the vision again.

Eyes half closed and mind clear, she stared into the mirror. What she saw was not a reflection. Instead, she faced a bottomless pit of fog. Swirling and spinning, it made her dizzy, but she stayed focused and began to hum.

The vibration of her tone affected the fog within the mirror. Slowly, barely recognizable, a face appeared. Twisted and warped as it was, Morganna felt repulsed but quickly squelched the feeling. The demon made it clear he was not pleased with her negative reactions to his appearance.

"Why have I been summoned?"

"I need to hear one more time, just to be sure all has been arranged properly."

"Bah! Stupid woman. How many times must you make sure? If you have not got it right now, you never will, and I can kiss your soul to the bowels of Hell."

"I'll not be going to Hell or anywhere else. It is here I'll stay, and if you want to join me here, you will show me what I ask. Or do you not care if our mission fails?"

"Bitch. I will show you one more time, then you will leave me alone until the deed is done and I can see you face to face." Before his ugly face faded, the specter warned. "This time do not fail. I want no spectacle like the first time."

"That was not my fault. You promised that no one would be there, yet they showed up in packs. In order to keep the secret of my identity, I destroyed those who saw my face."

"Yes! In doing so, you almost destroyed me as well. Never again turn your powers away from me when I am in my vulnerable state. If I get destroyed, so do you."

With those words the mirror fogged and then cleared, this time revealing a different vision than a moment ago. Before Morganna's eyes swam figures darting in confusion and fear amongst fire and destruction. She watched, as she had a dozen times before, the single figure ascend to the altar and fill her cup with the water of the Ancients. The water she knew would end up bubbling and alive deep within the Chalice Well, giving life and healing energy to those who could access its powers.

This next part of the vision was the part that Morganna waited for. Darkness crossed the sky in her vision, coloring all in muted velvet. While sleep claimed Gods and people alike, one figure crept about in silence. Morganna watched as the God Hades shape-shifted his form to resemble Hephaestus and gained entry to the fiery pits of the God of Fire. Reverently, for he knew the power held by the sword, Hades took it into his grasp. The Sword Excalibur, forged in the fiery pits of the great God of Fire, blessed by the Gods of the Ancients, imbued with the ability to render great powers to the one who held the hilt. Upon finding out about the power of the great sword made by his son Hephaestus, Zeus needed to find a way the sword could never be used against the Gods themselves. He declared that only one pure of heart and intention could ever wield the sword and the powers inherent within its blade.

Hades knew the power of the sword and sought to use that power for himself. Chanting a verse of protection, he called the powers of Darkness to his side and cast a spell into the sword.

Demons of Night, Raiders of Evil
My request, I beg you fulfill
When one with goodness in his heart
Holds this sword of right, this sword of might
And seeks to fulfill his destiny of light,
One with darkness in his soul
And chaos as his goal
Shall gather the sword to his side
Instead of brightness to burn
The fires of Hell themselves will rage
A sacrifice of holy blood
Shall be the key that must turn

The words of the verse were simple, but deep within the sword, darkness now lay dormant to awaken at the right time. Stealthily, Hades melted into the darkness from whence he came, leaving behind a time bomb within the sword intended only for light.

"Thank you, my Lord." Morganna chuckled. "Thanks be to you for showing me the way." Her laughter rose to a fever pitch, fuelling her hunger for power. The time approached, and she felt the need inside her growing.

Soon, she would control the Sword She would destroy Nimue and Merlin, and then there would be none to deny her access to the Chalice Well and immortality.

Chapter Eighteen

Relief washed over Gavin. The doctors told him Mac was slightly on the weak side, but at least he regained consciousness during the night. Of course, Gavin wouldn't be happy until he saw the old codger for himself, but the doctors were with him now so Gavin paced the hallway outside his room.

Thank God, Mac was all right. Gavin hated to think that his old friend had been hurt because of him.

The sound of a door opening and approaching voices snapped Gavin's attention around. The doctors were leaving Mac's room. No sooner had they offered a few words of caution not to tire Mac out and Gavin was in the door.

Bright afternoon sun filled the room. Mac wouldn't like that. He was used to the dimness of his shop below street level. Mac's first words of greeting confirmed that thought.

"Do an old man a favor and close them damn blinds. Gets so bright a man can't think." Feisty words spoken in a shaky voice, enough to bring a shimmer of tears to Gavin's eyes.

"You got it, old man." His step now much lighter, Gavin strode across the room to close the blinds against the sun.

"Who you callin' old man, sonny boy?"

"You. Who else do you see in the room?"

Mac's deep cough brought the light, familiar banter to a halt. Gavin grabbed some water from the pitcher at bedside and offered it to Mac.

"You know I don't drink that stuff." A wrinkled hand pushed the glass away. "How about gettin' me some coffee?"

Gavin laughed. It began as a quiet chuckle at first, and then grew into a full-blown belly aching laugh that sent tears running down his face. "Mac, thank God you're okay. I'd really miss you if you weren't around anymore."

"Humph. Who says I'm going anywhere? I'm too curmudgeonly to die yet. Besides, we have us a mystery to solve."

With this reminder of circumstances, Gavin got serious. He slipped into his detective mode and inquired, "Mac, do you feel up to telling me everything you remember?"

Mac heaved a sigh of exhaustion. "I'll tell you everything later. Right now, I'm so tired. Those damn doctors have drugged me, curse their interference."

"Mac, they're only trying to help. If you're tired, I can come back later. I'm just glad you're all right."

Before Gavin could rise to leave, Mac grasped his arm in a surprisingly strong grip. "No! There's something I need to warn you about." Mac's voice wavered and his grip weakened. "It was no accident…Dark Lady tried to kill…damn doctors…so tired…beware, much danger. It's Morganna, Morganna."

Mac's words were barely decipherable, so Gavin leaned closer to hear. What he heard made him frown. Mac must be hallucinating, probably because of the drugs. The words were just a little too cryptic for Gavin to understand. If he believed what he was hearing, he'd also have to believe that a woman who lived centuries ago was still alive today. Mac's snores broke into Gavin's thoughts and attested to the fact that he'd get nothing more out of his old friend today. Gavin was

220 *Catherine Anne Collins*

relieved that Mac was all right. The mystery he could solve himself, with some help from an attractive woman named Tamara.

Even under the circumstances, Gavin enjoyed the drive through Glastonbury. Stretched out before his eyes, the scenery assaulted his senses from sight to smell to sound, and was enough to make a man happy to be alive. This was definitely were he belonged.

He glided into a parking spot just one door from the shop. Funny, the door was shut and the lights were out. Gavin frowned and pushed the door open only to be blasted with a surge of cold air hitting him squarely in the face. Mac hadn't said anything about getting air conditioning. Gavin adjusted his eyes to focus in the dim interior light and quickly surveyed the room. There was no sign of Tamara and the door was unlocked. Hair on the back of Gavin's neck prickled with unrestrained fear.

A stifled moan drew his attention and sent him scrambling to the corner where he was sure it originated. Framed with tousled auburn hair, Tamara's pale face greeted him. She reached a shaky hand to brush a stray wisp of hair from her face. Another groan escaped from between full lips.

"Mary, Mother of Christ. What the hell happened here? Tamara, are you hurt? Can you stand? Should I call a doctor?"

"Ouch!" She touched her fingers to her scalp. "My head hurts. Slow down with you're questions, you're starting to sound like me now." Tamara pulled herself onto the wooden bench and sat gingerly with her head in her hands.

"Sorry. You're obviously not hurt too badly." Gavin made sure to lower his voice in deference to Tamara's sore head.

"Are there any aspirin around?"

"Sure, just hold on. I'll get you some." Gavin rushed to the counter where he knew Mac kept the aspirin. "I know you don't feel great, but I need you to tell me what happened." He handed her a couple of aspirin and a glass of water from the tap.

"Okay, but I don't know if it makes any sense."

"Just tell me what happened and let me decide if it makes sense."

"Well, excuse me, Mr. High and Mighty. Who says you'll be able to make heads or tales of what happened any better than me?" Tamara grumbled.

"We won't get the chance to find out unless you tell me now, will we?"

Tamara snorted in return and remarked. "Men." Downing the last of the water, she quietly contemplated the glass.

"I'm waiting."

"I know." Tamara's voice softened, all signs of defensiveness and sarcasm gone. Her eyes glazed over and stared harder at the glass as if it held the secrets of the universe. "I just finished reading. I was sitting in that chair, over there." Her shaking finger pointed toward the easy chair by the doorway. "Suddenly, the door flew open and banged against the wall, startling me and sending papers flying everywhere. I shut the door, and when I turned around there was this woman just standing in front of me. I have no idea where she came from. She was dressed all in black and…it sounds silly, but evil oozed from every pore in her body. She had a powerful aura, so strong that I couldn't breathe. My heart began pounding and my knees became weak. She just laughed at me and asked for the journal. Of course, I told her no but she just held her hand out and…this is where it gets kind of weird." Tamara looked to Gavin, and he could see she was out of her semi-trance state and perfectly aware of what she was saying.

"Go on." He encouraged her. "I don't think it can get more weird."

Tamara laughed. Gavin was pleased to see she was returning to normal. "Wanna bet? This woman held out her hand and the book…well, I had no control, it was pulled from my arms with such a compelling force that I couldn't hold on for the life of me. It floated over to her hands, and that's when I began seeing spots in front of my eyes. I was having a real hard time catching my breath."

"Wait, you're saying the book floated in the air?"

"Yep, that's what I said all right, and that's not all." Her eyes looked into his warily as if uncertain whether or not to continue. She was waiting for something from him, but he wasn't sure what. She was suddenly so fragile looking, and Gavin sensed a struggle within her mind. What the hell happened to cause this strong independent woman to doubt herself? Doing the only thing he could think of to do, he offered some words of encouragement.

"Hey, tell me the rest of the story. I haven't called the men in white coats to come and cart you away yet, have I? Whatever you tell me stays between us, unless you say differently. Besides, how can we work this thing out together unless you tell me everything?"

Tamara sighed causing Gavin's attention to wander to her rising chest. His eyes then wandered higher, to the firm set of her jaw and the determination, mixed with apprehension, in her emerald green eyes. For some unknown and disconcerting reason, he found himself proud of the way she held herself together after what must have been a harrowing experience.

Tamara whispered. Her voice took on an eerie, otherworldly tone. "The woman called herself Morganna."

Gavin exploded from the bench where he sat with Tamara. The heavy wooden table teetered on the edge and then crashed to the floor sending books skidding into the darkest corners.

"She called herself what?" He knew his voice was demanding and loud, but couldn't help himself. The name Morganna crossed Mac's lips just before he drifted into a drugged state. Now Tamara repeated the same name.

The almost imperceptible withdrawal of Tamara's energy made Gavin aware of the fact that she wriggled herself to the edge of the bench. With a deep breath, Gavin mentally reminded himself that Tamara had been through an ordeal, and he should be more sensitive to her state. His latest outburst made her look like a deer ready to bolt, except her eyes weren't the liquid brown of a doe. Instead they were a shimmering green.

Christ man, get your blasted mind back to the matter on hand. Gavin took a steadying breath while Tamara peered at him from beneath her lashes.

"Sorry, I didn't mean to scare you, but you have no idea what a coincidence it is you said that name. Mac spoke the same name to me just before drifting off to dreamland earlier."

"He was awake? You spoke to him? Why didn't you tell me sooner? What else did he say?"

Gavin laughed. "I see you're back to your old self."

"Oh, shut up and tell me about Mac."

"He's all right. The doctors still have no idea what happened to him, but at least he's awake and in minimal pain. Of course, they want to keep him overnight for observation."

"Oh, Gavin, I'm so happy for you. Mac as well. But what's this about him and Morganna?"

"Talk about weird, just before the drugs took him he told me that the woman who stole the journal from him was Morganna. He also called her the Dark Lady and talked about there being danger."

Tamara's voice was barely a whisper. "The Dark Lady. She's Morganna. She stole your book from Mac and mine from me. I would bet she somehow affected Mac physically the same way she did me, except Mac is older and couldn't recover as quickly."

"Maybe. But who is she? I mean, we know her name is Morganna, but there's no way she can be the Morganna."

Gavin looked at the doubt in Tamara's eyes and her quivering lips. "What? You don't really think this woman has been alive for hundreds of years only to show up in our lives and steal our ancestor's journals, do you?"

"No, I guess not. But, Gavin, you didn't see her. She glowed, sparks flew off her body, and then there was the book, the way it floated right into her hands. God, it was so unreal. I have to tell you, it made me doubt a lot of things that I thought were fairly set in my mind about reality."

"You're right, I wasn't here, but I think you're reacting to a very unnerving experience. What we need to do is focus on finding out what's going on. My suggestion would be to find out about any descendants of the original Morganna. That will give us an idea who may be involved in stealing the journals. I mean, it stands to reason this woman has to be a relative."

"Yes, I suppose so."

"You suppose so, but you don't sound very sure."

A frown wrinkled Tamara's brow, and Gavin watched her struggle with her inner demons. He wasn't sure what her beliefs were but from remarks she made in regards to her mother the night before, he was certain that she held no stock with anything mystical. Her hesitation in accepting her attacker as an actual physical person surprised Gavin.

"Tamara, I said you don't sound very sure. Look, I think you're shaken from your experience, maybe you should go back to my parents' and lay down for the afternoon."

"Lay down! I do not appreciate being coddled like some simpering female. Let's forget about my morning encounter with whoever and focus on what we do next."

Gavin wasn't prepared for Tamara's reaction to his suggestion. Her words were barbed with anger, but it was her physical reaction that captured Gavin's attention. Tamara pulled herself to her full height and placed her hands on her hips. He enjoyed the indignant, yet gentle, flaring of her nostrils. The pulse that beat in the delicate hollow of her throat and gentle rise and fall of her chest sent his senses spinning out of control. *Jesus, there you go again, chap. Give it a rest and pay attention to business.*

Suddenly, like a jolt of awareness shot into her bloodstream, Tamara's eyes flew wide and her mouth formed a perfect O. "Gavin, with all the excitement I forgot about the curse. I read about it. It seems that during the final battle between Merlin and Nimue, they placed a curse on each other. Actually, not really each other, but each other's descendants.

"My family got off lightly. We're only supposed to go through life searching for love and never finding it because of our greed. Your family, on the other hand, is destined to desire the sword. Searching endlessly, one of your family will die for his greedy quest on the eve when stars are aligned properly, as they were on that night."

A shiver punctuated the end of Tamara's speech, and Gavin stood in a trance at the thought of such a curse. "You read that in Nimue's memoirs?"

"Yes. It's absurd though. It's just myth and mystery. No one can place a curse on anyone else. Although…" Tamara's voice drifted into a musing whisper.

"Although, what?"

"Although, no one in my family has ever been able to stay in a relationship. But that's silly. It's just coincidence."

"Maybe so, but people die in my family for no known reason."

They stood, in a state of silent pondering and misgiving. Gavin was the first to pull together and return them to reality.

"Listen, we can wonder all we want, but what we need to be doing is doing. As well as finding Morganna's descendants, I think we should check out the museum where Morganna's journal was stolen, maybe even check the police records of the crime. We might find something that didn't mean anything to the investigators then, but may mean something to us now."

"That's a plan, but do you know what museum the journal was stolen from?"

Gavin's face flushed. "Err, no, but it should be easy enough to find out. After all, that's what I do for a living—investigate."

"Fine, why don't you follow that lead, and I'll look for Morganna's descendants. We can meet back here tomorrow. Will that give you enough time?"

Tamara turned her cool gaze to Gavin, and he suddenly felt tongue-tied. On one hand, he admired her ability to think logically and calmly, on the other hand it bothered him. After all, investigating was his job. He should be the one giving orders and figuring out strategies.

"Gavin, you're wandering again. Is there something wrong?"

"What? No, no, what you suggested sounds great, I'm just not sure I like the idea of you being out of my sight. Maybe you should stay over at my parents' again."

Gavin meant what he said about wanting to keep her safe, but he also liked the idea of having this woman under the same roof for the night. Strictly selfish, masculine testosterone speaking here.

"I appreciate your offer, but if this woman, whoever she is, wanted to hurt me, she could have today. She could have killed me, but didn't. I honestly think I'm safe for now. There's nothing else she needs. She's got all the journals."

"I know, but still…"

"No buts, I'll be fine. So, you've got the museum, and I'll find out about Morganna's descendants. We'll meet back here tomorrow." Tamara turned her shimmering green eyes on him, and Gavin couldn't deny her anything.

"Fine. I'll see you tomorrow. Just be careful."

Heat from the afternoon sun hit them full-force as they stepped from the shop. The street was alive with shoppers, mostly tourists, and traffic on the narrow road. Although, traffic was minimal as most people chose to walk the streets and admire the sights offered by the quaint old town.

With a wave Tamara left Gavin standing in the middle of the sidewalk. He barely had time to call out another warning of be careful, before she disappeared around the corner. Damn, but she was an independent woman. Gavin wasn't sure if he liked that or not. He'd always been attracted to women who were soft and womanly. Now, he found his emotions set afire by someone soft and womanly for sure, but definitely not acquiescent.

Gazing down the street to where Tamara disappeared, Gavin realized how much he loved it here. He couldn't imagine whatever made him want to leave in the first place. Granted, his business never would have made it off the ground in such a place, but he could have found something else to do. It's not as if investigating was a calling or anything. It was just a way to make a living.

When all this was over, it might be an idea to look at his life and where it was headed. In the meantime, there was a museum to check out, a sword to find, and a curse to lift. Then, he could focus on the lips and body of the woman he couldn't get off his mind.

Chapter Nineteen

Driving back to the B and B, Tamara smiled at the occasional glimpse of sheep dotting the gently rolling green hills. What a beautiful country. She felt comfortable here amidst the cradle of surrounding hills and occasional stone ruins of an era long past, though she admitted that she missed home more than she thought she would.

Her gaze was drawn to the distant horizon and the single spear of stone that reached to the heavens. The beacon of ancient beliefs and powers, a sentinel for lifetimes lived and died.

The Glastonbury Tor.

She shivered at the sight. Thirty-two years old and only now could she appreciate the power and timelessness pulsating from nature. Whether it was the wind murmuring the songs of the ages, the rustling and dancing of leaves in weather-beaten trees, or the tumbling of the ocean waters into shore, Tamara's senses were awakening to the world.

Why had she never realized that before? She'd spent most of her life scoffing at her own mother for saying exactly the same kinds of things she had just been thinking and feeling. How could she have been so narrow-minded and judgmental?

Tamara's heart began to pound as her emotional moment of revelation turned physical. Eyeing a lookout stop on the side of the roadway, Tamara gave in to impulse and pulled her car over for a minute. Climbing out to stretch her legs, she let her gaze wander as far as she could see.

With her newfound awareness of nature's energy, Tamara sensed a waiting in the air, a history of passion, myths, and legends that soaked the surrounding countryside.

Shivering at the overwhelming sense of bittersweet longing she felt, Tamara slid back into the car. Inside her stomach, butterflies fluttered and her blood tingled with life giving energy. She felt weak with emotions, yet fully alive for the first time. Tamara thought of her mother and chuckled. This was the kind of thing her mother would just love, all the mystery of ancient curses, magical swords, and ghostly apparitions. Tamara tried to keep her mind focused on the situation in a logical manner. She just wasn't sure how successful she was.

Tamara missed her mother, an unusual feeling to be sure. She always made a point of keeping some distance between her and her childhood home. Maybe the reason she could never quite feel comfortable at home was because she wasn't exactly comfortable with her mother. Maybe that was changing. Tamara already felt as if she were a different person than the one who left her mother standing on the cabin porch in Vermont.

Turning the key to start her borrowed car, Tamara hesitated and took one last look over the surrounding countryside. This place made it hard for a person to remain aloof. The ancient land demanded attention. It invaded your senses until your mind ceased to function in a logical manner. The air pulsed with past beliefs and legends. Tamara raised her hand, as if reaching to touch someone. She tingled. For a second, she felt that anything was possible.

With a final brief shiver, Tamara ended the moment. Enough soul searching for today, there were things that needed doing. With a sigh of determination, Tamara made double time back to the B and B.

Upon arriving at Will-O'-the-Wisp, Tamara was smothered in a hug by Mrs. Harlow. "Ohhh, and I'm glad to see you back. I've been wondering how the bookshop fella's been doin'?"

Tamara laughed and pulled herself from the circle of Mrs. Harlow's arms. "Actually, Mac seems to be doing fine. The doctor's are keeping him overnight, but it's more a precaution than anything."

"What fine news. Your friend Gavin must be mighty pleased. And how are you doing? How is your little adventure going with the journals?"

"Well, if you're thinking of making some of your famous tea and following it with some scones, I'd be willing to fill you in on the details."

"Wonderful." Mrs. Harlow rubbed her hands together in anticipation. "I love a good story. Follow me into the kitchen and start talking, girlie."

After an hour of conversation, a couple of cups of tea, and twice as many scones between them, the two women sat in silence and listened to the birds singing outside the window.

"I must be sayin', that's some story," Mrs. Harlow remarked.

"Tell me about it. I'm having a hard time processing all that's happened. It just doesn't make any sense, you know."

"Well, I'd be thinkin' it all depends on how you look at the course of events." Mrs. Harlow threw a sly look in Tamara's direction. "I'm also thinkin' it would be in how open you're lettin' your mind be when considering all that's happened."

"I'm not sure what you mean."

Mrs. Harlow stood up and in a flurry of activity cleaned up the mess from the afternoon tea. Keeping her hands busy and eyes averted, she explained. "The truth of it is, I get the feeling you close your mind to things you don't understand. You need a logical explanation for everything, when in actual fact there isn't always a logical explanation. Sometimes, things are just what they are. Whether you understand or believe, it doesn't stop them from being what they are."

Tamara smiled. "Mrs. Harlow, in the short time you've known

me, I'm amazed at how well you understand me. But that way of thinking has always worked for me before."

A smack of biscuit tin upon the countertop snapped Tamara to attention, and the intense look on Mrs. Harlow face surprised her. "Well, maybe it's time you came across something you won't be understandin'. That's how people learn and grow after all. Come, Tamara, be thinkin' about all that's happened to you, and all you've seen, and then give me an immediate, obvious, logical explanation."

"I can't." Simple enough words, but they rocked Tamara to her core. Life-long beliefs were being rattled to the foundation, and emotions she wasn't sure how to handle were rising to the surface. She needed to solve the mystery and, in doing so, find herself again. The touch of a hand upon her arm snapped Tamara from her personal critique.

"Tell me, what are your plans now?"

"I need to find who this Dark Lady is. It stands to reason that she's a descendant of Morganna's, so I'll hit the public records and do some digging."

"Hmmm." The sound was plainly heard in the small kitchen.

"What, you don't agree with my reasoning?"

"It's seeming to me as if yer doing some more of that plain and logical thinkin'. I can save you some trouble and tell you that our Morganna has no living descendants." Mrs. Harlow plopped herself back into her chair, crossed her arms, and challenged Tamara with her eyes to explain that away.

A vice gripped Tamara's heart and squeezed. Breath became a commodity in short supply. Her words were whispered. "You must be mistaken. How do you know that?"

"Ach, anyone knowing of our history knows that she bore but one son, Mordred, who tried to kill Arthur, his own father, and ended up dead himself. Morganna never conceived any other children to carry on her name or beliefs." Smacking her lips in a smile, Mrs. Harlow directed her intense gaze at Tamara. "It still seems to me that you have some very real re-evaluating of your beliefs to do before you get anywhere in this mystery."

"But..."

"I see no buts, dear. Unless you want to waste time following the wrong path, you need to believe what your mind tells you can't exist. Now, I'm sorry but I do have one more question to sweeten your mood. Not that I want to be addin' to yer burden, but have you even done any work on the story you came here to write? I know how important tomorrow's ceremony is bein' to you."

Tamara's hand flew to her mouth and she stammered. "My God, Mrs. Harlow, I haven't done a single bit of research. I had a short conversation with Lady Divine, but it was mostly about the journals. Although, I did arrange to interview her today."

A quick look at her watch indicated that the day was fast passing. "I think I'd better get my butt over there before it's too late." Tamara jumped from her chair and gave Mrs. Harlow a brief hug. "Thanks for listening, and I promise I'll be back to sleep here tonight. No more running around. At least, for a day or two."

"A word of advice. Ask Lady Divine about the Sword Excalibur. She may be havin' some information to help you. And make sure to let me know if you discover anything new. I love a good mystery."

"I will, thanks."

Upon backing her car from the driveway, Tamara was abruptly waved back by Mrs. Harlow. Running from the house and yoo-hooing, the landlady came breathless to the car window. "Are you thinkin' that maybe Mac would be likin' a visit from an old lady like me. Maybe I could bring some homemade cookies or such to ease his discomfort?"

Tamara chuckled at the thought of Mrs. Harlow taking over Mac's hospital room like the whirlwind she emulated. "Yes, I think Mac may very much appreciate some company. But how will you get there if I've got your car?"

"I'll ring up a friend and get a ride over."

"Okay, if you're sure. Oh, by the way, don't take it personally if Mac's slightly abrupt. He can be quite a curmudgeon on occasion."

"Oh, and I'd expect nothing less from a person being forced to lay in a hospital against his wishes. If I don't make it back early, just help yerself to the kitchen."

"I will. Have fun and say hi to Mac."

With a brief wave of her hand, Tamara pulled out of the driveway feeling as if she was setting out on a life-altering journey.

Lady Divine's house was the zoo of chaos that Tamara remembered from the day before. She'd barely rung the bell before Lady Divine opened the door.

"Tamara, please tell me, how is your friend? I must confess I was getting worried when you didn't show up earlier."

"Sorry about that. It's been rather a hectic time. Mac's doing fine, and they should be letting him out of the hospital tomorrow."

"Wonderful. Now about yourself, I'm getting the feeling much has happened since yesterday."

"You got that one right." Tamara plunked herself down in an overstuffed chair and brushed her hand across her face. "Tell me, Lady Divine, how much are you really into this hocus pocus stuff? I mean, do you just go on gut instinct, or do you believe you really have some kind of connection to another dimension or something?"

"Well, that certainly is a loaded question. The answer is yes, and yes. I use my instincts. I also get direction from another source. The origin of that source is as much guesswork as anything. I do believe I have guidance from angels or guardians, I've even heard voices once in awhile when the direction needed was immediate and strong."

"Hmmm." Tamara chewed her lip in consternation.

"You don't believe, do you?"

"If you asked me that question a couple of days ago, I would have been sure of my answer, now I'm not so sure."

"The answers won't come overnight. It's just important you keep an open mind. Now, to the business at hand, the Ceremony is tomorrow night, what would you like to know beforehand?"

"Since I know nothing about it, why don't you just fill me in, and I'll ask questions as we go, is that agreeable?"

"Sounds fine."

Tamara took her mini recorder from her purse and settled herself deeper into her chair while Lady Divine shifted her position to sit cross-legged on the floor. All was quiet and the fading afternoon sun slowly found its way across the sky.

"The Ceremony of the Stars began after the legendary battle of Nimue and Merlin upon the hilltop of the Glastonbury Tor. They left business unsettled between them. Legend tells to this very day that they both vowed to return when the stars were aligned in the sky the same as they were that eve. Between times, it was assumed they would both work on their powers so they would be powerful enough to destroy the other. An observer to their struggle spread the story across the land. This same observer also told of seeing a mysterious woman he called the Dark Lady."

Tamara froze, her face must have shown her fear, because Lady Divine was quick to question her.

"Tamara?" Lady Divine took Tamara's hands between hers and began to rub heat back into them. "Tamara, are you all right?"

In a sudden gasp of breath, Tamara came back to awareness, for a moment she found herself back in the stifling bookstore being zapped by that woman.

"I'm fine, really. It's just that I had a run in yesterday with some woman who claimed to be the Dark Lady, or Morganna."

Lady Divine was shocked, her composure cracked. "My Heavens, what happened? Are you all right? What did she want?"

"I'm fine. She wanted the journal."

"Did she get it?"

"I'm afraid so. I didn't have much choice. She just took it from me."

"She took it from you? I get the feeling there's slightly more to the story than that," Lady Divine prompted.

"It was kind of a strange incident, but I still don't believe she was actually Morganna. People don't live for hundreds of years. It just isn't possible."

"The presence of the Dark Lady has been documented at different times in history and people say she is linked to Merlin and Nimue. She is real, and she is Morganna."

"Sure, and Nimue and Merlin supposedly appear on the night of the Ceremony of the Stars," Tamara scoffed. "But what happened when the two of them didn't appear on that night?"

"Who says they didn't appear?"

"Well, they were dead, they couldn't have shown up."

"Still a non-believer? Legends are sketchy and documents hard to find, but something did happen on that eve, something enough to scare all who were there to never speak a word of what transpired." Lady Divine's voice fell to a hushed tone, barely registering above the wind and the traffic outside. "The Dark Lady was there and she sent fire swirling from her fingertips. In anger, she destroyed many who were there to witness the battle between legends. Most were destroyed, but even those who lived to tell the tale, kept silent, almost as if they feared being struck down by an unseen force."

"But the Ceremony of the Stars continues on every couple of hundred years, have there been no disasters since the first time?"

"No. Seven times since that first time has the Ceremony been observed. It has been safe. Most people believe the massacre was just myths and fairytales." Lady Divine shifted in her chair, reaching out she poured more tea for herself and offered more to Tamara. "So, have I piqued your interest enough for you to come celebrate the Ceremony of the Stars with us tomorrow eve?"

Tamara almost choked on her tea. She been wondering how to approach the subject. "I thought it was a closed ceremony?"

"Glastonbury Tor itself is public domain, we can't deny anyone access. What we do is deny anyone access to our personal ceremony. There will be others around who recognize the evening in their own manner. I only offer you access to our practices."

"That would be amazing, thanks so much for trusting me enough to allow this. Is there anything special I need to do, or wear?

"No, just come as you are. Meet at the foot of the Tor around

11:00 p.m., and we'll take it from there."

"I'll be there, but for now I think I've taken enough of your time."

Lady Divine followed Tamara to the door and waved her away with assurances that tomorrow night would be worth the wait.

Tamara was thoughtful on the short ride back to the B and B. She found herself nervous about her adventure tomorrow night. She wasn't stupid or stubborn—not too much anyway—and she was beginning to believe there were mysterious forces at work. It wasn't so much herself she was worried about, because it was Gavin's family was the one cursed with death. All she would suffer would be a broken heart. Somehow, she would make sure to keep Gavin away from the ceremony tomorrow night. That way he'd be safe.

Frowning, Tamara recalled the granite cut of Gavin's jaw and determined glint in his eyes whenever he was challenged. She realized it wouldn't be easy keeping him from the ceremony. Especially since it was a personal matter for Gavin, and Tamara felt that he was very protective about those he cared about. The corner of her mouth lifted in a brief grin as she wondered what it would be like to have him care about her so much that he would risk his life for her. Not that she'd expect him to, of course. She was quite capable of taking care of herself.

The scenic view to the coast was spectacular, but Gavin had too much on his mind to enjoy it. Maybe later. Maybe even with Tamara. Hmm, there's a thought. Gavin shook his head. It wasn't going to happen. Tamara would finish her story and fly home. End of story. For him to think that anything else would happen only went to show how the woman messed up his mind as well as his emotions.

Illumination Point Lighthouse had been established in 1900, and to this day still shone its light as a beacon to passing ships. On the edge of the ocean's domain, the old lighthouse stood high upon a rocky cliff like a sentinel, a testament to the past, and a reminder to those who were tempted to forget those who lived before.

Somewhere along the way, a museum became a part of the lighthouse landmark. Through circumstances Gavin wasn't quite sure of, Morganna's book of memoirs found its way to the lighthouse that stood on the craggy cliffs of Bridgewater Bay.

Finding the museum had been no problem. Trying to get information from the museum curator was. Presently, Gavin and the grizzled old man were standing in the so-called lobby of the small museum, and Gavin was doing his utmost to convince the old man that the situation was urgent.

"All I want to do is speak with whoever's in charge."

A wrinkled face of worn leather worked itself into a frown and a deep, crackling voice replied. "He ain't here."

"Well, can you tell me when he'll be here, or where I can reach him, please?"

"Nope, can't say as I can." The old man pulled a dirty hanky from the pocket of his faded navy uniform and proceeded to blow his rather large bulbous nose. The sound echoed in the far recesses of the empty hallway.

Gavin was running out of patience. "You mean you won't tell me, or you can't tell me?"

Squinting crow's feet encrusted eyes, the old guy replied. "I'm supposin' I can't. You see, things run pretty much on their own here and the boss comes in when he comes in. In between times, he goes where he goes."

If Gavin hadn't been the person involved on the other end of this conversation, he would have found it extremely amusing. As it was, he found himself grinding his teeth to help maintain a polite demeanor.

The dim jangle of a telephone bounced about in a far off room somewhere. Without more than a glance, the guard hobbled off to answer the contraption. At least, that's where Gavin assumed he was headed.

Gavin took the moment to gather his composure and look around seeking a solution to his problem. Maybe there was someone else here, or a bulletin on the board with a number he could call. At this point, anything would help.

The hallway Gavin stood in was small, taking up only about half of the bottom floor. The light was dim, probably to conserve energy. Besides the bulletin board, which was empty, there was a rickety wooden table with a book for visitors to sign in, an old biscuit tin, Gavin assumed for contributions, and a braided rug of various colors that sat in the middle of the highly polished wooden floor.

The clearing of a phlegm-filled throat brought Gavin back to attention. The guard stood before him, waiting. Uncomfortable with the intense gaze of the old man, Gavin stumbled into another question.

"Can I look around at least?"

"Nope. We're closed." A smacking of lips as yellowed dentures chewed on gum.

"Jeez. Listen, I only have till tomorrow to find out what I need. This is really important."

"Important. Important, how?"

"Life and death," Gavin answered solemnly.

"Well, why didn't you say so? How can I help?"

Shaking his head, Gavin decided this was finally a step in the right direction. "I only hope you can help. I need to see records or something that deal with a book stolen from here in the 1930s."

Air whistled between the well-chewed gum and dentures. "Ahhh, I see. Why didn't you say so?"

"Well…"

"No matter, I can help you."

"You can, but…"

"My grandfather was the one killed when that there book was stole. My father took over the job, 'til I stepped into his shoes. I can tell you anythin' you need."

"Oh." Gavin hadn't been expecting to find someone with quite so close a connection. Caught off guard, he couldn't think of a question, so he remarked, "I'm sorry. About your grandfather that is."

"Oh, it's fine. A lot of years have passed. Never could be figurin' out why someone would steal a musty old book. Far as I can recall, weren't no treasure involved."

"How do you know? You didn't read it, did you?"

"Yep. Gramps brought me here on occasion when he was guarding or cleaning, as the case may be. Twasn't much for a young lad to do, so I found myself reading the book. I was disappointed. It was kinda boring, and so I made up my own stories and make believe ideas. Course, when it got stolen in such a way, I began to wonder what I missed in the reading."

"What did it say? Do you remember?" Gavin questioned anxiously. "Hmmm." The guard looked out the small porthole window into the distance. "Hmmm."

A worn black leather shoe tapped on the wooden floor until Gavin began grinding his teeth again to help stay calm.

Finally, the man spoke. "Can't say as I remember a whole lot. It talked mostly about a couple of people, umm, Merle and Nimrod or something such."

"Yes, that's it. It talked about the curse on the descendants of Merlin and Nimue, right?"

"Who…oh yeah, those were the names in the book."

"What did it say about them?"

"Not much, the person writing the book didn't like them."

"That much I know, is there anything else you can tell me?"

"Can't member much more."

Disappointment weighed heavily on Gavin's chest. He hoped for some kind of clue. He didn't know what, just anything more than what he already knew.

"You listenin' to me?"

"I'm sorry, what did you say?"

White, fluffy hair rustled as the guard shook his head. "I tell ya, no respect. You come in here askin' questions and can't even listen to my answer."

"Please, I'm sorry. I was just thinking about something. Can you repeat what you said?"

"Fine, if'n I must. I was sayin' there may be something else. I seem to remember words about a sword and a curse."

"Yes, the curse that Morganna put on the descendants of Merlin and Nimue."

"Nope, yer not listenin' again. I said the curse was on the sword."

"Can you be more specific?" Gavin knew his voice took on a high-pitched tone, but this curse on the sword was new to him, and he needed to clarify what was going on and make sure the old man wasn't remembering incorrectly.

"Tsk, tsk, young people, always wanting more. Can't you be satisfied with the facts as I tole you?"

"Please, it's very important. What can you remember about the curse?"

Sighing as if a great inconvenience, the guard squinted and considered. "Well, it seems that the curse was placed by some demon from Hell." The old man paused and glanced at Gavin as if waiting for some sign of disbelief.

"Go on."

Shrugging his shoulders, the guard continued. "The woman writing in this book was pleased as punch with herself, bein' as she was the only one that knew of this curse. You see the sword was supposed to be…what did she say…a beacon of light and goodness, yeah, that's it. Anyway, this curse only works if the sword is held in the hands of someone evil, and there's some kinda blood sacrifice." The guard paused to take out a stick of gum. With meticulous care he unwrapped the gum and placed it in his mouth. Chewing till he was apparently satisfied at the softness of the gooey mess, he snorted. "Can you believe that? I never heard such bunk in my life. Tell me, why is a story like this so danged important?"

Gavin couldn't reply. His throat closed up and his heart thumped in his chest. The guard just shrugged and, bidding good-bye, shuffled off in the dimming light of the lighthouse.

Gavin stepped from the dimness of the inner lighthouse and turned to face the wide expanse of ocean laid out beneath the cliff. Late afternoon wind buffeted and whirled around in reckless abandon. Gavin let the force of the energy cool his mind and body.

The sword was cursed. Gavin couldn't believe that the centuries held such a secret, with no inkling whatsoever that the Sword Excalibur was cursed. It was supposed to be the guiding light for the virtuous and right-minded, not a weapon for spreading evil and corruption. Could he even believe the guard, what was his name anyway? He'd never even bothered to find out. Oh well, not knowing his name didn't change the fact that the guard seemed to have some information not known by anyone else. He actually read Morganna's memoirs.

The question now was what should he do about tomorrow night? According to legends and history, he could quite possibly end up dead if he went anywhere near the ceremony. On the other hand, if he didn't go, how could he ever solve the mystery? Mystery aside, what about Tamara? If he insisted on attending the ceremony, there was no way she'd agree to stay behind, but he didn't want to place her in any kind of danger.

Sighing deeply, Gavin kicked a loose stone beneath his feet and sent it hurling over the edge of the cliff to land with a distant thump in the churning water below. There was no choice; the curse was his to deal with. He wouldn't put Tamara in any further danger, so he'd make plans to go to the ceremony without telling her. That way there'd be no confrontation between the two of them.

Startled from his musings by the ringing of his cell phone, Gavin almost lost his balance on the high edge of the cliff. Damn, I better pay more attention to what I'm doing. "Hello."

"Hi." The dulcet tones of Tamara's distinct voice greeted Gavin. "I'm not disturbing you, am I?"

"No, I'm just leaving the museum and heading for my car."

"Great. Did you find out any helpful information?"

Only the slightest pause gave any indication to Gavin's state of mind. "No, I'm afraid there was nothing here that was very helpful." Gavin reasoned that he wasn't lying. After all, there hadn't been any helpful information, just facts that confused the whole situation even more.

"Oh."

Tamara's disappointment oozed over the telephone, and Gavin felt like a heel for lying. Yes, he admitted to himself, he was lying, one of those gray area lies of omission.

"Well, I managed to find out that Morganna had no living relatives. Her only son, Mordred, was killed trying to kill his father, King Arthur." Tamara remarked.

"King Arthur? Morganna's half brother was also father to her son?"

"Yep."

"A little lax in the morals department back then, weren't they?" Gavin chuckled.

"I would say so. The thing is, we're no further ahead now than we were yesterday. We have three missing journals, a lost sword, two supposed curses to deal with, and some unknown enemy called The Dark Lady. Jeez, this just keeps getting more and more strange."

"You don't know the half of it, baby." Gavin didn't realize he mumbled the words out loud until Tamara questioned.

"Pardon me?"

Fumbling for words, Gavin spurted, "I said, you don't have to tell me."

"Oh. So what now? Any bright ideas rolling around in that empty head of yours?"

Gavin's plan was to try to distract Tamara from the whole situation until after tomorrow night. He could think of one surefire way. Over the years, various women he'd dated told him how good looking he was. Why not use his supposed good looks and the obvious attraction between Tamara and him to get her mind off things. Yeah, he'd bedazzle her with charm and woo her till she swooned. Once the ceremony was over, he'd let her know what he found out about the sword and the fact that he attended the ceremony. That was supposing he lived through tomorrow night. Gavin snorted. Of course, he would. No curse was going to be responsible for his death. Besides, he didn't feel ready to die. He wasn't even sure he believed there was a curse, or even a magical sword for that matter. That made sense. Why would some old security guard/janitor, in a crippled lighthouse/museum, know about a curse on a sword that probably didn't even exist?

"Gavin." Tamara voice pierced Gavin's ears over the telephone. "Gavin, are you still there? Are you all right?"

"Quit yelling, I'm fine. Sorry, my mind just wandered for a sec."

"Well, try to keep focused. What's our next step?"

"To be honest with you," Gavin cringed inside as he spoke those words. "I don't think there's any more we can do. I mean, we've exhausted all clues and checked out every angle. I think we're at a dead end." Gavin hoped she believed him.

"You know, this is one time I think I agree with you. I can't think of anything else we can do to find the sword or end the curses. I mean, who are we fooling? The whole thing makes for a fantastic story, but it boils down to some woman with an obsession for historic books, so she stole them."

Gavin was too relieved at her acceptance to follow his feeling of unease that Tamara's acceptance may have been out of character. Heck, he didn't know her that well. Maybe she wasn't as tenacious as he thought on his first impression . "That makes sense." In the mood now, Gavin embellished even more. "Then we, in our need for investigative fodder, started putting together a story from bits and pieces of information that probably have no relation to each other, just so we could have a story to follow. Man have we ever been fooling ourselves."

"But Mac did end up in the hospital, and you know that woman was more than a little scary."

"But she only wanted the journals. Now that she has them, the danger's gone. You said so yourself." Gavin reasoned with her. It sounded good to him anyway.

"You're probably right."

Looking for a change of subject, Gavin questioned, "Hey, what about your witches story? Did Lady Divine give you what you needed?"

"Yes, she gave me more than enough background. Couple that with other research I've done, and I think I've got all I need to write a great piece for the magazine."

Gavin was relieved. If she had her story, there was no reason for her to be around anyone, or anything, connected with this curse or the sword. "So you've got a couple of free days before you catch a plane home?"

"Yep. Two nights and two days before I head back."

"How about dinner tonight?" Dinner and some romance would keep her occupied. After all, what woman could resist candlelight and dancing?

"I suppose I have to eat, I may as well have dinner with someone who knows the good restaurants."

"Gee thanks. That's a shining acceptance for a dinner date."

"Oh, you mean a date. Sorry, I thought you just meant dinner."

"A man, a woman, candlelight dinner and soft music. Sounds like a date to me." Gavin was perturbed that she took his invitation so lightly. She should have been jumping at the chance to go out with him. Other women did. Instead, she seemed to be considering him as nothing more than a convenience. It didn't matter that it was just a diversion technique. She didn't know that.

"Do you think that's a good idea? I'm leaving in two days to fly across the ocean. We don't really want to start dating or anything. Why don't we just make it dinner between two friends?"

"Fine." Gavin knew frustration and sarcasm were threaded in his voice, but he couldn't help himself. This woman drove him crazy. "It's just dinner, but get dressed up. I'll pick you up at 7:30."

Gavin snapped his telephone shut without waiting for a reply from Tamara. Damn, she managed to frustrate him. Stomping across the pebble-covered parking lot, he yanked open his car door and got inside. It was only when he slammed the door shut on his ankle that he came to the realization that it wasn't really a date. It was only a diversion, so why was he letting himself get so upset? He consoled himself with the thought that his plan to keep her mind off the curse was working. Anyone with half a brain could see that all the clues tied in to each other and there was a heck of a story here. Maybe even a centuries old sword to find.

Starting his engine, he gave himself a mental pat on the back for his subtle success in manipulating Tamara. It was only for her own protection, of course.

Chapter Twenty

"What an idiot." Tamara mumbled as she hung up the telephone in her room. How could he be so blind not to see how all this was connected? The clues were right in front of them. They only needed to be put together in the right order, just like a puzzle. Tamara supposed it was a good thing that Gavin possessed looks, but no brains. It left her free to investigate on her own.

And what did he think he was up to with all that romance stuff he spouted about candles and music? Granted, the vision of a romantic evening with someone like Gavin... Okay, Gavin was a tantalizing vision, but she couldn't let herself get side-tracked by a handsome face. There was a sword to find and curses to debunk. Checked out all clues, exhausted all angles. Huh! He couldn't be very good at his business if he gave up so easily or if he thought she would.

A glance at her bedside clock indicated a couple of hours before Gavin got here, time for a bath and some relaxation. So far, it had been a very long day and tomorrow was going to be just as long.

Running the hot water full force and the cold only halfway, Tamara filled the tub with lavender scented bubbles. Easing into the steaming water, she reveled in the rush of heat through her body. She delighted in the purely golden silence Mrs. Harlow's absence afforded, and it gave her a chance to figure out tomorrow's agenda.

Mac would probably be getting out of the hospital, so Gavin would be occupied for part of the day, which would leave her free to do some research on her own.

An insistent ringing summoned Tamara from the bathtub. Bubbles trailed her into the other room as she answered the telephone.

"Hello."

"Tamara, dear, how are you? Did you find dinner in the fridge all right?"

"Mrs. Harlow, hi. Actually, I'm going out for dinner, but thanks anyway. Are you visiting with Mac?"

"Yes, I surely am sitting here right at his bedside keeping him company. What?" Mrs. Harlow's voice became distant, and Tamara assumed she was talking to Mac. "Tamara, Mac wants to talk to you."

"He does?" Before Tamara could tell Mrs. Harlow she didn't have time to talk, Mac's voice boomed over the telephone.

"Hey, girl, how are you?"

"I'm fine. You're the one in the hospital." Tamara wasn't sure how to act toward Mac. She hadn't seen him since she stormed out of his shop, journal in hand, and cursing him for daring to let a stranger read what was hers.

"Bah, I don't need to be here now. The doctors are holdin' me against my will. That doesn't matter, though. What does matter is Gavin. Have you seen him?"

"Yes, actually I'm having dinner with him shortly."

"Dinner." Mac gruff voice held a hint of surprise. "Well, well, well. Dinner you say?"

Tamara felt her face flush at the insinuation in Mac's voice. "Yes, dinner. You know, food and conversation."

"Sure, I do. I also know that my boy Gavin hasn't taken a person of the female persuasion out for dinner in, oh, I'd say about eight months."

The notion that Gavin didn't have an avid social life pleased Tamara. Realizing the direction of her thoughts, she gave herself a mental shake for even caring when there were more important matters to worry about.

"Mac, you said you needed to talk to me." She gently steered the conversation away from anything personal.

"Yeah. Gavin's in danger, but I don't remember how much I told him when he was here. Damn drugs, I think I passed out."

"I know you told him about the Dark Lady and that there was danger."

"Humph, don't even remember that much, damn doctors. Don't know what they're keeping me here for anyway. I feel fine." Mac's words were punctuated with a hacking cough and a wheezy shortness of breath. "Well, maybe I'm not one hundred percent but close enough."

Bubbles and cooling water slid down Tamara's legs and pooled on the rug beneath her feet. The air became chilled and goose bumps rose like pimples on her arms. With a shiver, she scuttled back to the tub and climbed in, thanking the powers that be for a long phone cord. "Listen, Mac, I don't have a lot of time. Was there something you needed me to tell Gavin?"

"Heck, yes, there's more. What's wrong with young people these days, no bloomin' patience. If you'd quit interrupting me, I'd get the words out."

Tamara chuckled at Mac's gruff manner and sank deeper into the heat of the scented water. "I'll keep quiet, I promise."

"Okay, then. It seems Gavin's ancestor, Reggie, found out something to do with Merlin and Nimue. He thought they were duped by the Dark Lady."

"You mean Morganna." The words were out before Tamara could call them back.

"I thought you weren't going to interrupt? How do you know about Morganna?"

Tamara hesitated. She wasn't sure if it was a rhetorical question and didn't want to face the wrath of an impatient Mac.

"Go on, girl, answer the damn question."

"I ran into her myself this afternoon, and she told me her name."

"You saw the Dark Lady? Are you all right? What did she want? What did she say? Jeez, girl, can't you stay out of trouble?"

"Mac, slow down, I can only answer one question at a time. She wanted Nimue's memoir. Unfortunately, when she left she took it with her, and I couldn't stop her."

"Good thing you didn't try. She's dangerous and evil. Reggie wrote about Morganna in a letter I found. The letter I didn't get a chance to tell Gavin about."

"You mean Reggie wrote about her ancestor."

"Girl, don't go getting logical on me now. There's too much at stake. The Dark Lady is the Morganna of King Arthur's time. I feel it in my bones."

"Oh, well then, it must be so if you feel it in your bones." Tamara was only half kidding. All this hocus-pocus stuff was getting on her nerves and making her question everything she believed all her life. She wasn't sure she was ready to start changing her ways, so she was still trying to find a logical explanation for everything that was happening.

"Don't be sassy with me, girl. Reggie felt that the Dark Lady, who we now know to be Morganna, duped Merlin and Nimue. He tried to warn them at the Ceremony of the Stars so they could put an end to their battle."

"But he ended up dead instead. Uh, Mac, what year did all this take place?"

"Seventeen eighty Six."

"Could you tell me how he could have warned two people who, at that time, had been dead for what, about 1200 years?"

"Yer bein' daft again, girl. Merlin and Nimue have been fighting for this sword for centuries."

"I see." Tamara didn't see. She couldn't believe that there were three people from centuries ago still alive, or even somehow still existing in this world. No doubt, there was something strange going on and some danger was involved. There must be a more reasonable explanation.

"No, you don't see and don't patronize me. Tell me, has Gavin told you of any strange dreams?

Tamara felt her pulse race. "Dreams?" she whispered. "Why do you ask?"

"Because…wait a minute, have you been having dreams? Your voice sounds funny."

"I've had a couple of dreams. Actually, I've dreamed the same dream a couple of times. But it's nothing. It's just a dream, probably inspired by all this talk of curses and magical swords."

"Tell me." Mac's voice may have been getting weaker as the conversation got longer, but his tone brooked no argument. "And don't leave out any details."

Feeling suddenly cold, Tamara ran hot water into her tub while she began to recount her dreams. "It takes place at the foot of some kind of hill, a circular hill surrounded in mist. I see two people, a man, and a woman, at the top of this hill. They're so angry, and as the sound of their raised voices reaches me, thunder rumbles across the land, and lightning snaps to light up the darkness of the sky. Funny, but the thunder and lightning seem to react to their voices and anger."

"Let me interrupt for a sec. Do you see anything else at the top of this hill?"

"Yes, how did you know? There's a stone monument of some kind, but for a brief second I also glimpse a circle of stones and some kind of temple made of what looks like marble. There are columns and statues, kind of a Greek feel to the whole scene."

"Damn, I thought your dream may have been at the foot of Glastonbury Tor, but the stone circle and Temple are out of place." Mac's voice broke off and Tamara heard him talking with Mrs. Harlow in the background. "Tamara, Mrs. Harlow says that there are myths of a stone circle and Temple on the Tor from centuries past. Strange."

"Look, Mac, it's only a dream. What's so strange?"

"Tamara, think, who do you think the two people are that are arguing with each other?"

"I…" Tamara was stunned. She'd never connected her dream with what was going on with the journals. "I don't know what to say. My guess would be that they're Merlin and Nimue. That would make sense. I'm only dreaming about what I've read in Nimue's journal."

"So, how do you explain seeing the Temple and stone circle?"

"Coincidence." Tamara infused her voice with hope.

"Nope. Tell me, is there more to the dream?"

"Some. I watch these two arguing, and I can also see another person watching from the shadows. She keeps herself well hidden."

"You said she. You know it's a woman for sure?"

"Yes, even though she's dressed in a long dark cloak." Tamara gasped. "The Dark Lady. God, what a coincidence. I must be more upset by this whole thing than I thought, if I'm dreaming about that woman."

"You're still not ready to admit that there's more going on than meets the eye. You chalk it up to only a dream, because that's what you want it to be."

"I'm not sure I'll ever be ready to admit it was anything but a dream."

"Humph. Whatever you believe, you have to at least make sure that Gavin doesn't go to the ceremony tomorrow night. His life is in danger."

"Well, in that we're in agreement."

"Good, so you'll find something to keep him busy tomorrow?"

"Ahh, I—"

"Wait a minute, you're not thinking of going yourself?"

"No, of course not," Tamara replied, but the hesitation was apparent even to her ears.

"Listen, young lady, I know Gavin's in danger, so there's a chance you are as well. You'd be smart to make other use of your night tomorrow."

"Look, Mac, this woman has all the journals. There's nothing I have of any interest to her. I'm in no danger."

"You don't know what else the bitch has planned. You'd be better off steering clear of the whole affair."

Tamara heard Mrs. Harlow in the background admonishing Mac for swearing. Funny enough, Tamara also heard him apologize for his foul mouth and promise to do better in the future. If one were to play matchmaker, those two would make an interesting couple.

"Mac, I need you to promise you won't tell Gavin I'm considering going to the ceremony." She wouldn't tell Mac that she'd already arranged with Lady Divine.

"I'll promise no such thing." Mac stated indignantly.

"If he thinks I'm going, you know he won't stay away. I'm sure you don't want to place him in danger, do you?"

"That's blackmail missy. Besides, if you know he'll follow you, and you go anyway, who's the bugger putting him in danger?"

Tamara's mouth twisted into a half smile at the self-satisfactory tone of Mac's voice. "Mac, it's not my ancestors who keep ending up dead. Gavin's the one in danger. If you don't tell him I'm going, I won't tell him what you told me about Reggie's suppositions or the fact that you're doing research tomorrow. Right now Gavin believes all avenues have been exhausted, and he's willing to let sleeping dogs lie. If he knows Reginald wrote about some misunderstanding between Nimue and Merlin, his investigative instincts would go into overdrive, and he'd feel obligated to check it out further."

"You mean like you are?"

"The differences are that I'm here to cover a story, I'm not in danger, and I'm looking at this whole thing from a logical point of view. Emotions aren't ruling my thoughts and actions."

"Right. But unless you let go of that logic stuff, you may not get anywhere, and you better not be in danger or Gavin'll have my head on a platter."

"I promise, I'll be fine. Let's just concentrate on keeping Gavin pacified and safe."

After a swift good-bye to Mrs. Harlow, Tamara jumped from the tub. There was only about fifteen minutes to make herself presentable for Gavin. Perusing herself in the mirror, Tamara decided she'd do more than make herself presentable. She wanted to stun Gavin with a sexy, provoking image. That way she could keep his mind from straying to tomorrow night. That way she could keep him safe, and keep him from getting in her way. After all, she was the one who was here to do a story and didn't need some private dick telling her what she could, and couldn't, do with herself.

Gavin's mouth literally fell open and settled into an expression of shock. Tamara knew she looked great. She swept her auburn hair up in a loose style that left tendrils of shiny, silken strands touching her cheeks. An azure dress clung to her curves in a way that made her decidedly uncomfortable and seductive at the same time.

"Gavin, you're staring."

"I am, aren't I?" A sexy grin illuminated and softened his features.

"Well, stop it, you're making me nervous." Tamara didn't usually feel ill at ease around men. She'd been told by enough of them that she was beautiful. But that didn't mean much, considering they were usually trying to get her in bed. Tamara stopped fussing with or caring about her looks long ago. With her busy and logical lifestyle, she adopted a look of "au naturelle," hardly ever wearing make-up or doing much with her hair besides tying in back in a ponytail. Bothering with her looks tonight gave her a small degree of forgotten pleasure, and the look on Gavin's face gave her a more intense measure of pleasure and satisfaction.

Gavin's reply was spoken in a deep drawl. "Lady, as long as you're looking like that, I'm going to keep looking."

The short drive to the restaurant was quiet, in a comfortable way. Tamara was pleased with Gavin's choice of restaurant, which was set in a rather unobtrusive back street in the downtown area of Glastonbury. The quaint building was built with ancient rough-hewn stones, and a cobblestone pathway led to a front door of scarred wood and ornate metal hinges that squeaked in protest when Gavin opened the door.

Inside it was dim, lit mostly with candles upon the scattered tables. Tamara inhaled the mouth-watering scents of various foods wafting from the kitchen. Her stomach growled in anticipation, which drew an amused grin from Gavin. Tamara's pulse quickened at the brief moment of sharing. Funny, but under the guise of two normal people going out for dinner, Tamara found that the two of them got along rather well. She also found her senses in tune with Gavin, in a sexual way. Thoughts of a sculpted chest and hard muscles melding with her soft flesh flitted on the edges of her mind. A blush crept its way up her face, and she was relieved to sit down in the offered chair and bury her face in the menu.

After placing her order for Beef Wellington, Tamara sipped her wine and contemplated Gavin's face in the flickering candlelight. Yes, he was definitely handsome with his rough-cut jaw and strong features. A shiver of appreciation tickled down low in her stomach. When she spoke, her voice trembled. "I didn't know this was going to be such a romantic dinner."

"You mean the candles? I guess you get to see another side of me, the one that appreciates a beautiful woman."

"And do you always wine and dine beautiful women?"

"Not all beautiful women, only the ones I share an ancient curse with." The orange-flamed candle sparked a twinkle in Gavin's ocean colored eyes and cast a shadow on the contour of his lips that were presently turned up in a chuckle.

Tamara gave herself a mental shake. Don't let yourself get caught up in the romance. This is strictly business. Although, if she wanted to keep Gavin's mind off tomorrow night, it wouldn't hurt for her to play along with the romance angle. Men were so easy to influence, a lick of the lips, a casual crossing of bare legs. Yes, Gavin would be no problem.

Conversation ran lightly, candles burned down only to be replaced by an attentive waiter, and the food disappeared in avid appreciation for the skill of the chef. Finally, Tamara sat back and pushed her plate away. "I don't think I can eat another bite."

"You have to, there's still dessert. The specialty is Creme Brulee."

Tamara moaned. "Oh, God, my favorite. Maybe I can force just a spoonful or two into my stomach."

"That a girl." Gavin motioned to the waiter to clear the plates and requested two of the house specialties for dessert. Looking at Tamara, he smiled and asked, "So, how's your story coming along? I don't suppose you've had much time to work on researching or writing."

Careful, Tamara warned herself as she reached for her wineglass and took a long leisurely sip. "Actually, I've got a fair amount of information, enough to spend time writing the story tomorrow." She hoped she sounded convincing, but she saw Gavin's eyebrows rise in a questioning manner.

"Surely, you can't write an accurate account without seeing firsthand where the ceremony takes place, and as far as I know you haven't paid the Tor a visit yet."

Damn, he's quick. She'd have to be more careful. "You're right. I was planning a quick trip first thing in the morning and then writing the story, of course."

"Of course."

An awkward silence descended in the almost empty restaurant. Tamara realized it must have been getting late, because they were one of only two couples remaining. Funny, time sure flies in the company of a handsome man.

"Would you like a tour guide?"

Gavin's question caught Tamara off guard because she hadn't really planned a visit until later tomorrow night at the Ceremony of the Stars. Now she'd have to cover her lie.

"You don't have to come with me. I'm sure you have better things to do, like pick up Mac for instance."

"Your friend, Mrs. Harlow, is giving him a ride home. So, what time do you want to leave?"

Not seeing any way out, Tamara realized she'd have to agree to a tour or get Gavin suspicious as to why she wasn't visiting the place she was writing about.

"Okay, but if we're leaving early in the morning it's probably a good idea to call it a night, so we can get a good night's sleep."

"If sleeping's what you've got in mind." Gavin's voice was low, suggestive, and teasing.

Tamara felt the blush spread across her face, more than likely clashing with her auburn colored hair. Even worse was the fact that she considered what a more intimate relationship with Gavin would be like. Heck, if she were honest with herself, she would admit that she imagined the heat of his skin, the pulse of the blood in his veins beating against her naked flesh, the throb of his…

"Tamara?"

Gavin's voice cut into the fog of Tamara's meandering mind. Realizing how she wandered, and what path her mind took, left Tamara tongue-tied. Gavin's teasing didn't help matters any.

"So, you were thinking about more than just sleeping the night away."

"Don't be absurd. I was thinking about something else all together."

"Uh-huh. That's why your pulse quickened and your eyes took on a dreamy look, right?"

Snatching her purse from the back of her finely carved wooden chair, Tamara stood and made her way to the door. "You have quite an imagination. Don't forget to tip the waiter well." She deliberately put a haughty tone in her voice in an attempt to regain her composure. Instead, she only succeeded in drawing a loud laugh from Gavin as he paid the dinner bill.

Tamara worried all the way back to The Will-O-the Wisp if Gavin would try to kiss her. Would she let him? Would she be able to control herself if he did? Of course, she could. She was an adult, not some young teenybopper whose head could get turned with the flattery of a handsome man. As they pulled into the driveway, Tamara wiped her sweaty palms on the seat. Here we go. She still hadn't decided if she'd let him kiss her.

The slamming of the car door interrupted her confused thoughts. Tamara's nerves caused butterflies to flit about her stomach while Gavin walked around to open her car door. Okay, he'd see her to the front door and try to kiss her there. With a gallant sweep of his hand, Gavin helped Tamara from the car, touched two fingers to his forehead in a quick salute, and returned to his side of the car.

Just before climbing back into the car, much as an afterthought, he remarked, "I'll see you in the morning. Goodnight."

The squeal of his tires left Tamara standing with her mouth open in shock. What the…he hadn't even tried to kiss her. In fact, the abrupt manner in which he'd left was extremely rude. Men! And here she'd been wondering about what it would be like to have him kiss her. With a shake of her head, Tamara stomped through the front door and up the stairs to her room.

Vigorously washing make-up from her face, she left the bathroom only to trip over the dress she'd thrown off in a fit of frustration. Stupid dress anyway. She'd been so sure in her ability to woo that stubborn man. Obviously, he was made of stone.

Once in bed, she rolled over and punched her pillow, mumbling about the unfairness of life. Why should she lose a night of sleep just because a handsome man flashed his smile and batted his eyes? Why should her restless dreams involve knights in shining armor rescuing damsels in distress just because she found herself attracted to a man who probably would have thrived in such times of jousting?

A brief grasp of a memory or emotion wriggled itself into Tamara's mind. A forgotten dream most likely, but the more she tried to remember, the more distant it became. For an instant, her ears rang and a fog of choking emotion clenched her chest into a tight ball. Just when Tamara thought the dream was within her grasp, it was gone, like the reflecting light of the sun in rippling water.

Damn! Oh, well, most people don't remember their dreams, so why should she be any different? Heaving a sigh of resignation and gauging the morning light streaming in her window, Tamara decided it was probably time to get up. She'd get no more sleep now. All she wanted to do was pull off her charade of touring the Tor and keep Gavin satisfied that she was researching her story. Then she would find another way to keep him busy for the day and away from Mac, who would be busy researching.

Mrs. Harlow was her usual sunny, cheery self at breakfast. Clucking about like a mother hen, filling Tamara's plate with eggs, sausage, pancakes, and home fries, until Tamara thought she'd burst. She listened politely while Mrs. Harlow rambled on about what a nice man that Mac is.

"Yes, he is."

"Tell me, dear," Mrs. Harlow stopped her fussing and looked at Tamara, "Are you going to the ceremony tonight?"

"Yes. Lady Divine has invited me to attend with her."

"What!" The single word snapped like a whip.

"Mrs. Harlow, is something wrong?"

Tamara watched her hostess flutter about the kitchen in a sudden display of nervousness. In fact, Tamara thought she detected a hint of fear in Mrs. Harlow's features. But that didn't make any sense. "Mrs. Harlow. Are you all right?"

"Sorry, dear, I just got distracted. Everything is fine. You should finish up. Your young man will be here any minute. Excuse me, I just remembered that I need to ring a friend."

Like a whirlwind, Mrs. Harlow stormed her way from the kitchen. Tamara heard the parlor door slam shut. "Boy," she mused, "that must be some important telephone call." Before she was able to wonder at the source of Mrs. Harlow's discomfort a honking horn signaled Gavin's arrival.

"Great. Isn't this going to be a fun morning?" Tamara muttered to herself.

Chapter Twenty-One

Tamara first glimpsed the Glastonbury Tor through the soft morning mists. Warm rays of sun filtered through the mist, touched upon the hilltop, and illuminated the stone monument in blues and violets of the early morning. Rising to the heavens, the ancient landmark stood like a sentinel between the two worlds of reason and magic.

Through her recent research, Tamara knew the Tor was considered a place of magic and power. Some people believed the forgotten entrance to the lost land of Avalon used to exist here. Now, the Tor exists only as a reminder of past ways and beliefs, a beacon of wonder and hope for those with distant memories of a restless past.

Realizing the mystery and atmosphere of this place were affecting her, Tamara gave herself a shake to clear the fanciful thoughts from her mind.

"This place is magnificent," she muttered. More to herself than Gavin, even though he stood beside her.

"Would you believe that this is my first time here?"

Tamara was stunned. "No way. How can you live so close and never check out what's here?"

Gavin kicked a stone with the toe of his sneaker, and answered. "I don't know. I just never felt the urge."

"So, I guess I can't count on you for much of a tour."

Gavin looked sheepish. After all, he suggested they come and he'd give Tamara the full tour. "Well, I do know some of the history. I'm not a total loss for a guide."

"The history lesson I can do without. I've probably read more about this place than you. Why don't we just hike up the hill and check things out along the way?"

"Sure, you're the boss." Gavin drawled.

Tamara just snorted in reply and made her way toward the first pathway she could see leaving Gavin to follow along.

Gavin gave himself a mental pat on the back for thinking about this morning tour. His gaze wandered to the woman walking beside him and the gut reaction he felt clawed his insides. Just the whirl of auburn hair dancing in the ever-present breeze and the reflection of full-bodied morning sun shadowing Tamara's face was enough to make Gavin wonder what depths this woman held. He wasn't used to being curious about any woman past the physical, but then he'd never been drawn the way he was finding himself now. A man of strong convictions and character, he'd always been the one in control of any given situation. Now he found he had no control over any part of his life. He didn't relish the feeling. Some unseen force propelled him toward tonight, even though he held no special interest in the events taking place. Of course, he was curious about the curse, but logically he chalked it up to myths and legends. Sure, a possibility existed that somewhere under the muddy waters of the situation lay the ancient Sword Excalibur. What a coup if they actually discovered the mystical artifact.

He decided his most likely purpose for continuing his investigation was to find out who hospitalized Mac, attacked Tamara, and stolen the journals. Yes, that was the logical reason for attending the ceremony tonight. The whisper in his mind, like a thousand voices nudging him forward down a path of nighttime shadows and dangers, had nothing to do with his stubbornness in pursuing the investigation.

"Gavin. Are you listening to me?"

Gavin shook himself from his morbid musing. "Sorry, my mind was wandering. What did you say?"

"Nothing important." Tamara stopped as if searching for the right words. "It's silly really."

Gavin waited patiently while Tamara continued her train of thought.

"There's an expectant energy in the air. I was just wondering if you felt the same thing?" Tamara's slender form shivered, as if to punctuate her words. She laughed. "I have butterflies in my stomach and my throat is tight, kind of like when I get nervous about something, you know."

Gavin knew all right, he was feeling the same effects himself. To have his feeling confirmed by Tamara surprised him, and he smiled at the coincidence. Big mistake. As soon as his lips curved into a smile, he was sorry.

Tamara put her hands on her hips and snapped at him. "Great, I finally begin to trust you enough to open up and share my feelings, and all you can do is laugh at me. So much for working together as a team."

The onslaught of anger that sparked Tamara's eyes stunned Gavin. He didn't even have time to defend himself, and Tamara was marching off up the pathway by herself. Women! They overreacted to everything.

Before he could follow her, his attention was grabbed by the scraping sound of leather upon the stones. Seemingly out of nowhere a man appeared and stood on the pathway leading up the Tor.

Investigative instincts clicked in place, and Gavin found himself sizing the man up. Something about the stranger was unusual. It took only a second for Gavin to realize what was wrong. The clothes didn't fit today's styles. In fact, Gavin didn't recognize them from any period in history at all. A long, black cloak of rough material adorned the stooping shoulders of the old man. Upon his feet were slippers with a thin, leather hide for a sole. Gavin looked twice to see that the hide of leather seemed original and not manufactured.

His gaze roamed up and was captured by eyes of the deepest black. Filled with emotion and turmoil, the man stared at Gavin's face. Wanting to speak, but frozen in place, Gavin stared into the depths of the man before him, and he felt a twinge of recognition. He watched thin lips open as if to speak, but heard no words. Instead, he sensed the urging of the man to follow.

Gavin looked up the pathway Tamara took. Strange, he could barely make out her form in the gathering mist. She seemed to be doing some investigating of her own. Prompted by the beckoning of the old man's spider-veined hand, Gavin found himself following the, so far, silent man.

Before him, the man seemed to glide up the gently sloped hill, deeper into overhanging tree limbs and thickening underbrush. Gavin gasped with exertion from the quick pace set by the old man. Every now and then, he thought he lost him, but the flash of black cloth through green leaves kept his course true.

The landscape was becoming unfamiliar, and the gently sloping hill of the Tor became a rocky ascent toward what looked like the darkened entrance of a cave. Gavin would have sworn there were no caves here, but then he'd never been here so he couldn't be sure. Breaking free from the stifling enclosure of lush growth, Gavin found himself in a clearing with the old man. The sticky silence was pervasive, cloying, and slightly on the eerie side. What happened to the birds, the wind, and the daily sounds of tourists on the Tor?

A corner of the old man's thin lips curled in a semblance of a smile. Was it supposed to be a sign of reassurance? Gavin couldn't tell, but he was tired of the mystery. He opened his mouth to ask what was going on, but his words halted in his mouth as the figure in black stepped into the mouth of the cave and disappeared.

What now? Did he follow? Who was this old guy anyway? What if he was some lunatic? Maybe he should get back to Tamara who was probably wondering where he was. Gavin tried to turn and leave the way he came, but his feet wouldn't move, at least not the direction he wanted. Instead, he found himself being led toward the foreboding cave entrance.

Heart pounding, unable to stop moving, Gavin stepped into the black hole and came face to face with the most splendid sight he could ever have imagined. From the extreme of dark to light, the cave was awash with crystals reflecting light into each other. Sparking rays of colors lit up the cave in a blinding array of crystalline beauty.

In the midst of this display stood the old man. He presented a figure of black in contrast to the light. On a pedestal before the man sat a black cauldron filled with water? Gavin stepped closer and looked again. Yes, water glistened from the depths of the cauldron.

In slow motion the man raised his arms toward the heavens. Loose sleeves slithered their way from wrist to shoulder and revealed faded tattoos of some ancient forgotten creature. Gavin's gaze fell to the marks on either forearm, and he wondered what would possess a person to mark his body in such a fashion. What kind of a creature did the markings depict? They brought to Gavin's mind visions of mythical dragons.

His musing was interrupted as the man lowered his hand over the cauldron. In a writhing display of bursting bubbles, the water churned. How was that possible? No fire burned under the large black pot. Gavin wondered if he was dreaming, because nothing seemed real.

The bubbling in the water ceased, and the surface became smooth enough to reflect his face. But something was wrong, the figure in the water began to move and Gavin realized he was seeing a man from another era.

It looked to be late at night. The stars sparkled high in the sky. Gavin watched the man running from someone or to something. He wasn't sure. In the background he discerned the unique outline of the

Tor. The mysterious man's face was etched with fear, and Gavin saw beads of sweat break on his forehead and run down his face.

Stumbling to the foot of the huge stone monument, the man fell to his knees. Gavin saw a brief glimpse of lips form in a final note of warning, and then the man was engulfed in a dark cloak of mist. To Gavin's eyes the man's actions were urgent, as if he knew some knowledge and tried to impart it just before disappearing in the black mist.

The old man spoke. His voice was deep and hypnotic. It oozed with knowledge and wisdom that Gavin was sure he could only imagine. For a certainty this man was one whose words held meaning.

"Your ancestor failed in his attempt to find the sword and end the imposed isolation of Avalon. You have been chosen to find the sword and banish the dark witch from existence, so Avalon may once again give sanctuary to the ancient ways of your ancestors."

Eyes with depths like a never-ending whirlpool pinned Gavin in place, and his mind only comprehended the words dark witch. His tongue felt like lead as he replied. "You mean the Dark Lady."

Those age-old eyes flickered a moment of confusion, yet the voice was steady. "The Dark Witch who hath stolen the sword and become the bain of my existence. She who ruled Avalon with words of peace, yet whose very actions spoke of deception and evil."

"You mean the Lady of the Lake, Nimue?" Gavin was confused by the man's use of Dark Witch rather than the Dark Lady he was used to hearing.

Emotion flared in near black eyes, and the old man's voice was no longer steady. "You know of her?"

"Yes. Who are you anyway?" Gavin felt his grip with reality slipping again. "The Lady lived hundreds of years ago, so how can she be the bain of your existence?"

"You are so very young." With these words, the old man waved his arms to create a new vision in the cauldron.

Stunned, Gavin watched himself fleeing from something. He ran up the hillside of the Tor toward an unknown destination. Just as the other man, Gavin appeared to be trying to warn someone. Up the pathway to the Tor he ran, followed closely by an invading fog of nightmare black.

Waving his arms again, the old man instigated a flash of brilliant light to reflect in the prisms of the cave. Gavin was blinded. When his vision cleared the old man was gone, but his voice echoed on in the confines of the cave. "Return the sword whence it came, beware the Lady of the Lake. Only you can remove the curse…or die."

Bubbles broke in the surface of the water and a vision of Gavin with sword held above his head vanished, leaving only a pot full of water. In a burst of energy, Gavin shouted to the now empty cave. "But it's not the Lady of the Lake. It's the Dark Lady. You've been deceived."

Gavin's voice echoed in the empty chambers of the darkening cave. The old man disappeared as if he never existed. Listening to himself trying to reason with a specter, Gavin wrestled with the notion he must be going crazy. No, someone's playing a trick on me is all. If that was the truth though, how did this person know about the curse, the sword, and the Lady of the Lake? And what would his motive be for pulling such a practical joke? It didn't make any sense. What did make sense was the old man really had been Merlin, and he was trying to help, trying to warn me.

Not able to come to any conclusion, but more firm in his resolve to attend the Ceremony of the Stars that evening, Gavin left the mysterious cave in search of Tamara. She must be wondering what happened to him.

Tamara was pissed at Gavin for laughing at her and re-igniting all her insecurities from her childhood. She knew she'd overreacted, but memories of being an outcast and having other kids laugh at her still ran deep.

Damn, why did all the good-looking guys have to be such jerks? Just when she'd started to think there might, just maybe, be something serious happening between them, he had to go and laugh at her.

She hated being laughed at.

Struggling to get her hurt pride under control, Tamara was startled by a snapping sound ahead on the footpath. Closer inspection revealed an overgrown path to the side of the downtrodden tourist path, and Tamara took an uncertain step on the strange path. She found herself nudging through lush growth of flower and herbs. Her nostrils quivered in reaction to the aroma of mint and thyme, while her vision was assaulted with vivid colors of pink and maroon geraniums. Her eyes drank in peach colored hibiscus, the flower of love. Wafting gently in the breeze, the hibiscus were a perfect contrast to the crimson red chrysanthemums, with their long petals reaching out in supplication.

Tamara pushed aside tree branches that brushed her face and heard the sound again. Someone was just ahead. It sounded like they were struggling through dense brush as well. Tamara paused for a breath and took a more intent look around. She was enthralled at the lushness of the growth, but surprised at the unfamiliarity of some of the plants. There were flowers and plants growing here that she'd never seen anywhere. God, it's beautiful, she thought.

"Yes, it is beautiful."

The voice, so close by, startled Tamara and caused her pulse to beat a rapid staccato in her veins. Peering into the underbrush, Tamara could see the form of a woman.

"How did you know that's what I was thinking?"

"Just my intuition."

Mollified, Tamara turned to look about again. "I've never seen flowers like these before." She reached out to touch the velvety soft petal of a luscious peach colored flower. "I don't remember reading anywhere that the Tor offered such a display of plants."

"The Tor does not. At least not now, but in ancient times the beauty to behold was supreme."

"I'm sorry, I don't understand. The flowers are here now." Tamara was having trouble placing the accent, so unlike any she had ever heard.

Amidst the rustle of leaves and with a lightness of movement, the woman stepped into the clearing. The ethereal beauty of the strange woman bewitched Tamara. She looked strange because of her unusual manner of dress. Tamara frowned at the full-length dress worn by the woman. Simple and unadorned, the pale blue dress exuded richness in material and style.

Comprehension dawned on the woman's face, and she remarked. "I am dressed different than you are used to seeing?"

Tamara snorted, and then blushed in embarrassment. "Yes, just slightly on the eccentric side. Your dress is beautiful, though." Her gaze touched upon the flowers. "But like the flowers, it doesn't fit."

"This place is not what you think. Few here have ever seen this plane of existence, but you are special."

Uneasiness settled in Tamara's stomach. Was this woman just crazy or dangerous? Deep blue eyes pierced into Tamara and cut her with their intensity. "You know who I am. Think."

Tamara squinted and fought against a growing awareness. "I must be dreaming. Are you reading my mind?"

"Of course, I am. It's easy if you know how. Now stop foregoing the inevitable. You know who I am, say my name."

"But—"

"Say my name." The mysterious woman insisted in a breathless tone.

In a breath of a whisper, terrified lest anyone hear how crazy she sounded, Tamara spoke. "Nimue."

"See, you do possess the intelligence I credited you with. The question is will it be enough to finally outwit my nemesis and return the sword to where it belongs?"

"Okay, now I know I'm dreaming. I think I should leave." Tamara turned to leave, but her feet wouldn't move. Her panicked gaze flew to the woman, Nimue. "What's happening?"

"Nothing more than a stillness spell. Relatively basic actually. Something the most average novice can master. I just need you still for a moment while I warn you about the deception of Merlin. He will be dangerous tonight, so you must be careful."

"Tonight. You mean at the ceremony?" Tamara was busy trying to move her feet, but she was asking questions through habit more than anything.

"Yes, the ceremony. You need to take the opportunity to find the Sword Excalibur and return it to where it belongs."

Those words returned Tamara's full attention to the woman before her. "The Sword Excalibur? Don't be ridiculous. The sword has been missing for centuries."

"I know that. I was there the night it disappeared. Merlin is the one responsible. Now he is also after the sword for his own purposes. He intends to use the power of the sword and the Ones Who Came Before to bring about the return of Avalon. Of course, with the sword in his hand, he will rule in absolute power. This we cannot allow to happen, because he has become ruthless and greedy. He is dangerous, so you must be careful."

Tamara's eyes rounded in disbelief. "You were there? Come on, don't you think this joke has gone far enough?"

Was she trying to convince herself? Tamara didn't get a chance to ask any more questions, because Nimue's form was shimmering to a dim mist in the late morning sun. Tamara's mind barely registered the haunted whisper spoken by the strange woman.

"You must find the sword, only then will the past be put right. Trust no one." Nimue's voice drifted into the shadows of the surrounding gardens.

Chapter Twenty-Two

Frustrated, Tamara attempted to stamp her foot and realized she couldn't. This frustrated her even more. "Ohhh, let me go!"

In a flash, the ethereal world she stood in a moment ago disappeared. Looking up, Tamara saw she was standing on the pathway she had been on with Gavin a short while ago. The manicured path, green grass, and trees of the Tor replaced the exotic flowers of a moment ago. "What the…?"

"There you are. I've been looking for you." Gavin's greeting stunned Tamara into complete silence. She must have looked silly standing there like a statue, but couldn't help herself.

"Tamara, are you all right?" Gavin sounded worried.

Barely able to put words together, Tamara replied. "I'm fine, I think. What time is it? Where have you been? Did you see that lady? Man, she was weird."

Gavin's sharp tone startled Tamara. "What lady?" As he spoke, Gavin glanced at his watch to check the time. His exclamation jolted Tamara. "Holy Mother of Christ, that can't be right."

"What?" Tamara inquired.

"Do you have a watch on?"

"If I did, I wouldn't have asked you what time it is." Tamara replied, rolling her eyes at Gavin's lack of deduction.

"No need to get snippy." Gavin took her by the hand and pulled her back the way they came. "Maybe they have a clock at the gate."

Tamara tried to resist Gavin's rough treatment, but he was far too strong for her, so she just stumbled along behind him. She protested verbally instead. "What are you doing? I'm not made of glass, but I like to be treated a little bit more gently than this."

Suddenly realizing how rough his grip and long his stride, Gavin slowed and apologized. "I'm sorry, it's just that the strangest thing happened, and now…" he looked at his watch as if it offended him. "Now, my watch tells me that two hours have passed since we got here."

"Well, obviously it's wrong. We've only been here for a few minutes at the most." Frowning, Tamara questioned Gavin's statement. "What do you mean something strange happened?"

Emotions of uncertainty passed across Gavin's sturdy features. Tamara enjoyed the masculine line of his jaw and the shadow of stubble on his chin. Her heart pulsed as Gavin's cerulean eyes flashed in the afternoon sun. She wondered what was happening to her, as unfamiliar feelings of lust and passion warmed her limbs and sharpened her senses.

This whole day was filled with surreal qualities, right from her meeting with the woman to her burgeoning feelings for Gavin. Drawn to him like a magnet, she fought the urge to reach out with her fingertips and soothe the frown from his brow. In a way, she felt powerless against forces that seemed intent on sending her down a path that she herself did not intend to follow. Nimue warned her to trust no one. If that were true, then why did she feel herself wanting to share with Gavin? Of course, the Lady of the Lake was under a misconception about Merlin, just as he was about her.

Whoa, slow down, Tamara, none of this is real. She cautioned herself in an attempt to come back to some sense of logic.

"Tamara." Gavin's eyes were fixed on her face in a calculating manner that caused Tamara to feel uncomfortable. Whatever happened now could change everything. She was sure of that, but wasn't sure if she was ready.

"Yes."

"The last couple of days have been hectic and confusing, right?"

"To say the least." Tamara kept her voice neutral.

"All this stuff with the memoirs, ancient curse, magic swords, and people living for hundreds of years. What do you think about the whole thing?"

Tamara stammered. She wasn't sure what she believed, but she didn't want Gavin to know she was wavering. She remembered this approach from school when the other kids would pretend to go along with her, and then when she actually began to believe and confide in them, they'd laugh at her. For Gavin, she wanted to appear logical, none of that silly mythical, mystical stuff.

When she spoke her voice was strong and sure. "It's obviously some kind of fairytale mixed in with totally unrelated coincidences to make it seem as if something more were going on." Satisfied with her answer and ignoring what she just experienced with the lady claiming to be Nimue, Tamara stood face to face with Gavin, daring him to disagree with her.

"I see you've got the whole thing figured out logically."

The tinge of sarcasm in Gavin's voice, or was it taunting, put the bristles up on Tamara's back. She snapped at him. "Of course, there's a logical explanation for everything. None of it can be true. It's all fake and if you believe any of it, then you're crazy." She put the vision of the Lady from her mind all together, because if she were to analyze her confrontation, she'd have to re-evaluate her whole way of thinking.

"Me thinketh the lady doth protest overly much."

Yep, there it was, a hint of laughter in his voice. Tamara spent her whole childhood being laughed at by other kids, and there was no way she'd spend her adulthood the same way. Snorting in disgust, she turned her back on Gavin and strode toward the car. "This is getting us nowhere." Grabbing the door handle, she swung it open, plopped onto the seat, crossed her arms, and waited.

From the corner of her eye she saw Gavin standing where she left him, studying her. Well, she wasn't moving until she got an apology.

Damn that woman is prickly. What's wrong with her anyway? Here he was doing what came naturally to him. Investigating and enjoying himself in the process. Sure, he was confused, but he was at least willing to question and leaf through the circumstances before jumping to conclusions. Yet, there Tamara sat with arms crossed and a stubborn look on her face. She wasn't willing to explore any avenues except the logical, and she got her back up any time he tried to steer things another direction. What kind of investigative reporter could she be anyway, being so close-minded?

Personally, after his recent experience—whatever it meant—he was willing to explore the mythical. His parents raised him to believe that there was more to the world than what was visible to the naked eye or reasonably explained away. Tamara's face was staying stubbornly set in place. This wasn't going to be easy, but he had to loosen her up, and it looked like he'd have to be very diplomatic.

Sliding gently into the driver's seat, Gavin turned the key and checked out the dashboard clock. The time didn't surprise him, but it did set his pulse to racing. His reaction must have shown, because Tamara looked at him in a questioning manner. He didn't bother telling her the clock read the same as his watch, and two hours passed. Instead, he decided to address the situation as a whole.

"Okay, so you want to look at things the logical and analytical way?"

"It's the way I've learned to investigate," Tamara snapped.

"Funny, I've always found my intuition stands me in good stead."

"I'm surprised you're still in one piece then."

Gavin had enough verbal sparring. It was time to get some things settled. The Ceremony of the Stars was only a matter of hours away, and there was a lot to do in the meantime.

"Let's do things this way then. Let's pretend we're in a world where anything can happen, and there's no reasonable or logical explanation for anything. Now, with that in mind, let's go over everything that's happened and see where it leads us, no matter how fantastic it sounds. Can you handle that?" He deliberately used a tone of voice one would use if talking to a child.

"Don't speak to me like I'm a simpleton. I'm the only one that seems to still have full use of their faculties around here."

"Yes, well, that's debatable isn't it?" His words earned him a slap across the arm. "Ouch. What'd you hit me for?" It was a rhetorical question. Gavin knew he'd pushed her buttons. He found enjoyment in the light verbal sparring.

"Quit fooling around."

"I'm not fooling around. I'm quite serious. Do you think you can handle throwing caution to the wind and fantasizing for a few minutes?" For a brief flash, Gavin imagined a different situation for fantasizing. In his mind, he imagined Tamara naked and lying in his arms while he ran his hands over her body. Hearts beating in unison, chests rising in passion, lips...

"Gavin, I said I'm willing. Are you listening to me?"

"Oh, yes, you're willing all right." Gavin was still locked in his vision of lust until he noticed Tamara looking at him like he'd lost his mind. Focusing his attention back to the matter at hand, he remarked, "Good, then let's get started. I'll begin by recapping the last couple of days. We have two, actually three, journals written hundreds of years ago by Merlin, Nimue, and Morganna. Both journals we've been able to read tell of a battle over the Sword Excalibur."

"There was more going on than just a misunderstanding over the sword. They disagreed on religious beliefs and the direction of the country's future."

Gavin rolled his eyes. "You just can't let go of the logical for two minutes, can you? Those issues may have been the driving force, but the sword was the culmination of all the beliefs and battles of opposing forces. Without the whole mishap over the sword, the final battle may never have happened. Would you agree with that?" He fixed his gaze on Tamara, willing her to let go of her staunch logic. She was obviously struggling with inner emotions, trying to stay in some semblance of reality, yet Gavin sensed a part of her that longed to explore in unfamiliar alter realities.

"I guess I could agree with that, just for the sake of this conversation."

That's a step in the right direction, he thought. "Great. Now, we have a history in my family of mysterious deaths, all focusing on the Ceremony of the Stars, and actual written facts by Reginald stating he was in the midst of some kind of struggle with forces beyond his control. Would you agree that this coincides with the supposed curse placed by the Lady of the Lake on my family?"

Tamara gritted her teeth and replied. "Yes, it fits."

Gavin smiled, actually it was more of a self-satisfactory smirk. He couldn't help himself. "Good. Now, your family, as you've said, is notorious for remaining single most of their lives. Searching for that perfect soul mate to share their lives with, never able to remain with one person for long. This coincides with the curse placed by Merlin, right?"

"Yes, but it's all coincidence."

Gavin raised his hand in objection. "We agreed to leave logic behind. Now, Reginald talks of a Dark Lady. We've encountered a Dark Lady. The journals speak of curses, and our families seem to be living examples of those curses. So far, pretty simple. Where things get murky is with the Sword Excalibur and its relation to Avalon. If we believe in the existence of Avalon, we have to wonder how the disappearance of the sword is responsible for the disappearance of Avalon."

Gavin was so caught up in his recital of the facts that he almost didn't catch Tamara's half-finished sentence or the red spreading across her face. Frowning he asked. "What did you say?"

"Nothing. Sorry, I was just thinking out loud."

"Don't give me that. You're covering something up, now tell me."

"Really, it's nothing."

"Tell me." Gavin infused as much energy into those two words as he could. "Now is not the time for secrets."

"I just started to say that Mac was doing some research into the Sword Excalibur. He was going to call some friends about it." Tamara finished her explanation and sat quiet.

"I see. When did you and Mac start planning behind my back?" He narrowed his eyes in contemplation at Mac's betrayal.

Tamara shivered under his gaze. "He called last night before you picked me up for dinner."

"I see."

"No, you don't. Mac cares about you and only wants to keep you out of danger. He wanted me to keep you busy tonight, so you wouldn't go to the Ceremony of the Stars."

"He wanted you to keep me busy and you said no, right?"

"Right." Tamara hesitated. "I'm going to the ceremony. I've already made plans with Lady Divine."

"Really." Gavin let sarcasm infuse itself into the word. "So, I'm not allowed to go, but you are. Where's the sense in that?"

"The sense is that if anyone is in danger it's you, not me."

"Not good enough. I'm going tonight, and neither you nor Mac are stopping me. What about the research he's doing on the sword?"

"He's trying to find out the connection between the sword, the curses, and the disappearance of Avalon."

"That's good. I know for sure there's a connection, but it would be nice to know what it is." Gavin spoke before thinking. He hadn't wanted to say anything about his encounter with the man in the cave, and he hoped Tamara wouldn't catch his slip of the tongue. No such luck.

"Now, you know for sure? How do you know? What are you keeping from me?" Tamara balled her hand into a fist and drove it into Gavin's arm.

"Jesus, woman, take it easy." Gavin rubbed his arm and considered how much to tell. Seeing the dark look on Tamara's face, he figured he'd better spill it all. He'd been the one to speak about honesty.

Sighing deeply, Gavin let his gaze wander to a group of departing tourists laughing and chattering their way past the car. Not a care in the world, packed with picnic basket and camera, the family piled into their van and drove away. Had his life ever been so simple? Gavin didn't think so. There had always been a yawning, dark place filled with longings for something he could never quite identify. Now, with all that happened over the last few days, the longing was replaced by a certainty. A certainty of ancient roots and forgotten beliefs inherited from his ancestors and flowing in the hot blood of his body.

In a burst of understanding and faith, the path of his life became sure, and his reason for being concrete. He felt blessed with an understanding of destiny that eluded most people in their pursuit for enlightenment.

Shifting his position in the seat of the car, Gavin faced Tamara. He settled his unwavering gaze on her face and spoke. "Okay, Tamara, I'm going to tell you something. First of all, I believe in the memoirs, the curses, the seemingly endless energy forms of Morganna and Merlin."

Tamara frowned. "Merlin. Now, what are you up to? We haven't seen anyone impersonating Merlin."

Gavin chuckled at Tamara's insistent logical approach. "No, we haven't seen anyone impersonating Merlin. But, I have seen Merlin himself." Indicating the natural wonder of the Tor rising like a sentinel to the sky, Gavin continued. "When we were up there, I was approached by an old man who shouldn't exist, led to a cave that shouldn't exist, and shown things that I shouldn't be able to see. Merlin showed himself to me in an effort to warn and guide me." Gavin felt he imparted enough to Tamara to start the onslaught of questions. He was right about the questions; he just wasn't prepared for the sarcasm in her voice.

"You saw Merlin? What did he do wave his hands in the air and do magic tricks? This cave, was it filled with forgotten treasures of gold and jewels?"

Gavin was stunned by her reaction. Better yet, overreaction. "Lady, what is your problem? What do you need to happen before you start to question your staunch moral logic? Who do you think you are to belittle me with your arrogance and holier than thou attitude? Basically, who died and left you the only one with a brain?" His words flew from his mouth in a charge of sharpened anger. The look on Tamara's face told him his attacks were striking vulnerable areas. He didn't care. He meant every word.

Trembling in emotion, their gazes locked in a silent battle of wills. Gavin wasn't giving in. There was too much at stake. He watched emerald green eyes turn to forest green and glaze over with tears. Damn her, why did she have to start crying? As if that wasn't enough, she turned her face from him and her shoulders began to shake. Sure, she was attempting to hide the fact that she was sobbing, but he wasn't fooled.

Unthinking, Gavin reached his hand out to rest on her trembling shoulder. No, I'm not giving in. Just before the traitorous hand laid itself on Tamara's shoulder, she spoke.

"I'm sorry." Her shoulders settled into a dejected calm making Gavin feel even more a heel.

"You don't need to be sorry." The words escaped his mouth with a will of their own, just like his hand. Damn, he'd given in to the tears. Oh, well, his mom would be proud of his chivalrous attitude.

Tendrils of auburn hair tickled Gavin's face as Tamara turned and faced him with intense anxiety written all over her features. "Yes, I do need to be sorry. I was doing to you just what kids did to me for years. I belittled you in the most arrogant manner possible. How could I do something like that? You'd think I'd know better?" Tamara brushed her hand across her forehead. "Believe it or not, I'm so tired of being mature and logical. God, I wish I could be more like my mom. Now there's a woman you'd get along with."

"I get along fine with you. Tell me about the kids who teased you."

"Oh, it's nothing really. It's just that when I was growing up, being a witch wasn't as accepted and common as it is these days. That didn't stop Mom. She proclaimed herself a witch and psychic before the whole town. Halloween was the worst. Our house always seemed to be the center of practical jokes. It never bothered Mom, but it did me." Tamara gave a small, bitter laugh. "I kept to myself all through school, because it was better than getting laughed at by other kids. Funny, though, just before I left to come to England, one of my former classmates showed up at the house for a reading. I couldn't believe my eyes. There he stood, telling me how my mom gives the best tarot card readings he'd ever been given. This came from one of my worst tormentors." She laughed in irony. Hmmm, maybe if Mitch can change his ways, I can do the same. Besides…"

Gavin narrowed his gaze. "Besides, what?"

Tamara's skin flushed a delightful shade of pink as she answered. "Besides, I had a strange encounter today as well." Tamara's voice lowered to hardly more than a whisper. "I met the Lady of the Lake."

Gavin was stunned. He grabbed Tamara's arm and pulled her to face him. "You what?"

"Ouch!" Tamara yanked her arm from his grip. "I said I met the Lady of the Lake."

"And you're just telling me this now?"

"Well, you just told me about Merlin." Her gaze narrowed and pinned Gavin in place. "You weren't going to tell me about him, were you?"

Gavin looked sheepish.

"I knew it, so don't you dare give me heck for holding information back when you were doing the same." Tamara's gaze challenged Gavin to deny the facts.

Gavin considered the situation and realized that Tamara probably had more reason than he did for not talking about the incident. Her past would be enough to haunt anyone into remaining quiet about strange and unusual occurrences. With that in mind, Gavin decided to be as tactful as possible.

"All right, I think we'd both agree that neither one of us has been forthcoming with information. I also think we both agree that there is something going on here beyond the explainable. Right?" He looked to Tamara for confirmation on this last statement, knowing she'd have a hard time admitting this.

Tamara's struggle was obvious. Her face wrinkled in concentration. Gavin worried she would be too ingrained in her past to open up her mind. Thankfully, she replied in the positive.

"Yes, I don't know how I can bring myself to admit it, but what's going on here goes far beyond the logical." A deep sigh of acceptance accompanied the sentence.

Gavin was relieved, because Tamara's acceptance of the circumstances could possibly be what could save them both. That is, if you believed in the curse that there might be danger.

"Tell me about your encounter with Nimue."

"The whole thing was surreal. She came out of nowhere and disappeared the same way. She showed me a place in a time that I'm sure doesn't exist anymore, and she told me about Avalon."

Gavin listened as Tamara related her story, and he found the similarities to his encounter startling. When Tamara was finished, he proceeded to tell her about his trip to the crystal cave and Merlin's warnings about Nimue. When he reached the end of his story, he related what he considered the piece de resistance.

"To top it all off look at the clock." Gavin waved a flowery salute to the car clock that gently ticked away the time.

Tamara's gasp was worth Gavin's intentional theatrics. "My God, two hours really have passed. I wouldn't have believed it, and I'm still not sure I believe what I'm seeing."

"Now, don't go getting logical on me again. That would be a step in the wrong direction."

"Okay, wise and weasely one, since you're so smart, what's our next step?" Tamara's tone showed her words to be light teasing, so Gavin took no offense. He was glad Tamara was loosening up and was going to try to keep her on the right track.

"We're both partners here, so we both have a say. But, my vote would be to pay Mac a visit and see what he's come up with."

"Hmmm, that does seem the logical thing to do."

"Woman, you're trying my patience. And speaking of trying my patience, I have a thing or two to say to Mac when I see him. I don't like him manipulating behind my back."

"He only did it because he cares about you. He really believes you're in danger."

"I know. But there's no way he's keeping me away from the ceremony tonight."

"Us. You mean us, right?"

Gavin's forehead wrinkled in thought. Before he could comment, Tamara spoke. "I'm going. We already agreed that I'm not in danger."

"No, you said you weren't in danger, but I never agreed."

Tamara turned to Gavin, fixed her gaze on his face, and stared. Although he was in the middle of backing the car from their parking spot, he sensed her glare.

"What? What are you giving me that look for?"

"I'm not getting left out tonight."

Gavin put the car in gear, stepped on the gas and squealed from the parking lot. "It's too dangerous for you. Besides, you already told me you had all you needed for your story."

"I lied. I was trying to make you believe I wasn't going to do any more investigating."

"Fine. I'll take notes tonight and fill you in."

"I told you, I'm not getting left out."

"Tamara."

"Gavin."

"You're trying my patience."

"And you're trying mine, but I'm still going to the ceremony." Gavin turned the full heat of his energy on Tamara. She ignored him and wasn't giving an inch.

"Fine, we'll talk about it later," Gavin said.

"I don't think so." Then Tamara chuckled. "Don't think you're going to get Mac on your side. He was the one who didn't want you to go, remember?"

"He'll see it my way once I've talked to him."

"Even if he does, and I'm not saying he will, he has no say over what I do, or don't do."

"No, but with him on my side, we may be able to convince you to stay away from the ceremony."

"Funny, I was thinking that he and I could convince you to stay away." Tamara smiled sweetly, innocently.

Gavin raised his mouth in a half smile and glanced briefly at the defiant woman seated next to him. Her deceivingly sweet demeanor didn't fool him. It only served to help him imagine her turning that sweetness toward better use. In a brief flash, he imagined her lips running up and down his body. He flushed warm at the thought. Where had that thought come from? His attention was brought back to focus by Tamara's questioning voice.

"What are you smirking at?"

"Nothing, really, just the idea that Mac would side with you against me."

"He already did. Remember the telephone call last night where he asked me to keep you busy so you wouldn't go tonight."

"Well, trust me, that won't be happening again." Gavin punctuated his remark with a burst of speed that set Tamara back against her seat.

Chapter Twenty-Three

Mac adjusted his position and groaned loudly at the pain in his shoulder. "Damn, stupid thing." He mumbled to himself while pushing a well-worn book across the bookstore's one and only table. With a beleaguered grunt, he made a feeble attempt to stand.

"Now, what are you thinkin' to be doin?" Mrs. Harlow questioned, as she rushed to his side.

"Don't fuss, I'm just stretching my legs some. See, I'm fine," Mac crowed proudly as he stood on his own two feet. "Besides, we're not finding a darn thing here, and I think it's time to collect some outstanding favors." Mac wobbled over to the ancient, scratched desk that held his dial telephone. Dusting off a cracked leather book, he leafed through yellowed pages until he came upon a name sprawled in spidery handwriting. "Yes." He jabbed the name in exclamation. "Ray is just the person to help me out on this one."

"And Ray would be?"

Dialing the phone, Mac replied. "Ray used to be one of the young punks roaming the streets here about who happened to get himself in some minor trouble with the law. I stepped in and became his alibi.

Rotten kid pulled his boot straps up after that scare and actually made something of himself."

Still dialing, Mac silently cursed himself for not having the initiative to get one of those newfangled push button telephones. It sure would save time, but he just figured that the number of telephone calls he made didn't warrant the expense of a new telephone.

"As circumstances would have it, Ray has grown up and become the head curator of the Museum of Ancient History."

Mac listened to the insistent ringing until it was answered by a disembodied female voice. After a minute or two of conversation, his call was redirected. The hearty male voice that bellowed a greeting over the telephone made Mac wince.

"My Lord," Mac exclaimed. "This has to be Ray. That voice of yours'll be one I'll not soon forget."

"Don't tell me…it can't be. Is this, Mac?"

"Well, well, I see you've not forgotten yer old pal." Mac joked, but his heart tightened ever so slightly at the thought that the young lad grew up and away, but hadn't forgotten his old friend.

"Mac, how could I ever forget you? It's mainly because of your insistence that I remain respectable, that I've actually made something of my life. I'll never forget the times you chased me down the street and hauled me back to your store. By the ear, I might add. No, Mac, I'll not soon forget your lectures on respect for others or the times you sat me down with some musty old book and forced me to read cover to cover."

"Humph!" Mac could hardly talk as the band around his heart tightened a notch further, and his eyes became mysteriously blurred. He was aware of Mrs. Harlow frowning at him in concern, so he took a deep breath and cleared his emotions away. "I'd say you couldn't hate musty old books too darn much, considering you spend a good part of your life with them."

Ray's bellow echoed into the dim recesses of the bookstore. "You are so right. Now, I'm sure you're not calling me after all this time because you miss my voice. What can I do for you?"

Mac felt a twinge of guilt at how mentor and protégée drifted apart over the years. It seems that of all his pet projects, Gavin was the only one still hanging around. Maybe it was time for him to find some of the young waifs who plunged into life's current only to be swept away on their journey forward. No doubt about it, after his recent brush with death, Mac found himself uncharacteristically nostalgic.

"Mac, are you there?" Ray interrupted his reverie.

"Yes, sorry. My old mind hit a snag and stopped working for a second. I'm back on track now."

"You're all right, aren't you? I mean, you're not calling to tell me bad news or anything?" Ray's former booming voice lowered to a more reverent pitch.

"No, I'm still alive and kicking for a long while yet. I'm calling you for some information, if you can help me?"

"For you, anything. What's up?"

Mac paused to marshal his thoughts. He wasn't sure how much to tell Ray, as the events over the last couple of days were enough to make him wonder at his own sanity. Probably better to keep things as simple as possible.

"To be tellin' you the truth, I need information. Not only facts, but legends, myths, suppositions, and so on."

"Sounds interesting. What, or who, exactly are you looking for?"

"A sword, a special sword."

"Great. Swords I know well. Are you looking for information on sabers, katanas, broadswords, foils, daggers?"

"Whoa. Slow down. I'm looking for one sword in particular, the Sword Excalibur."

Silence met Mac's words. Sounds of noon hour traffic whooshed outside and a train whistle moaned in the distance. Mac's stomach crawled with unease. "Ray?"

When his friend spoke, his voice shook with a hint of unexplained anger. "What's this really about?"

"Like I said, I need all the information you can find on the Sword Excalibur as well as anything that may have been written on some old journals, supposedly written by Merlin, Nimue, and Morganna."

Mac wasn't ready for the onslaught that greeted his words. He held the phone away from his ear, rather than risk loosing his hearing.

"What is this all about? I don't appreciate your insinuations, and I'd like to know how you found out after all these years. Damn it, I never would have thought it of you. Why don't you just come out and ask what you want instead of beating about the bush?"

Ray took a pause in breath long enough for Mac to get a word in. "Settle down, boy. What I want is exactly what I asked for. Nothing more, and nothing less. How in blazes could you assume any kind of insinuation from what I said? And what am I supposed to have found out after all these years?"

Silence again. Confusion seeped over the telephone. When Ray spoke, resignation replaced anger.

"Sorry, I should know better than to think you'd have an ulterior motive. It's just that I grew up under a shadow of accusations, and I thought I'd left all that behind. I guess I was wrong."

"Why don't you tell me about it," Mac prompted his friend.

"I suppose I owe you that much." He sighed. "I never told you why I hung around your place so much when I was a teenager. Well, things weren't great at home. My Dad was obsessed. His world was ruled by a book and a sword."

As soon as the words were spoken, Mac's memory came crashing back. The words exploded from his mouth. "Of course. Your dad's uncle was the guard killed at the museum when the journal was stolen."

"Bingo," Ray retorted. "Dad's uncle's dying words were, 'The sword is evil, it must never be held by one whose heart is not pure or else...'"

"Or else what?"

"Or else, nobody knows. That's what Dad spent the rest of his life trying to find out. He scoured old museums, bookstores, and archives, always looking for some kind of reference to the stolen journal and the sword. He didn't even know what sword, only that the journal referred to the sword. His feelings were that the book was responsible for his uncle's death, and Dad was going to solve the mystery, or die trying."

"Did he ever find out anything?" Mac knew the answer to the question.

"No. He died trying. He committed suicide when he couldn't stand the failure anymore."

"Ray, I'm sorry. I had no idea."

"I know. Everyone believed he died in a boating accident, which was fine with Mom and me. There had already been enough gossip about our family."

"Ray, is it possible your dad found out something? Did he keep a journal or have a place where he collected information or ideas?"

"I don't think so. At least, not that I ever knew. I do remember an argument between he and Mom. It seems Dad was mumbling something in his sleep about a lady, and Mom took offense."

Cold water might just as well have been thrown in Mac's face. "The lady. Ray, was it the Dark Lady?"

"I don't remember. It was too long ago."

"Please, this is very important."

"I suppose it could ring a bell. I can't be sure, though."

"One more thing, Ray. How did your father take his life?"

"We aren't sure. We just found him one morning laying in the attic. He was peaceful looking, and there was no sign of the cause of death. I do remember the mess of the attic. The police thought Dad surprised a burglar and was killed, but there was a suicide note. We assumed Dad must have gone crazy or something."

"How can a man kill himself and leave no trace behind of the method?"

"Gee, Mac, I don't know." Sarcasm crept into Ray's voice. "I was only a kid. I didn't really care at the time. All I knew was that my father was dead."

Mac hastened to make amends for being insensitive. "I'm sorry, Ray, so much is going on I can't even begin to let you know how important my questions are."

"No, I'm the one who's sorry. Dad died a long time ago, and I should be past it by now. I can't get past the waste and senselessness of it all. Mac..." Ray's voice became quiet and uncertain, "...you're not in serious trouble, are you?"

"Not really, but a good friend of mine could be, and it all centers around the damn journals and the Sword Excalibur."

"Excalibur, you think that's the sword my Dad was looking for?"

"I sure do. Ray, can I throw a supposition your way?"

"Sure."

"What if your father didn't kill himself? Do you think maybe someone was lookin' for something and when he wouldn't tell them where it was, they killed him and searched for it themselves?"

"Come on. That's kind of stretching things a little, isn't it?"

"You tell me. I know you where young, but was your father the kind of man to kill himself?"

"I always carried doubts, but, as you said, I was only a kid."

"Yeah, well, what about the attic lookin' like it had been searched? Why would your father mess it up and then kill himself? And how did he kill himself? Don't you think these questions should have answers?"

"Mac. I was a kid. I went along with what the police said. Now I'm beginning to wonder myself. Damn it!"

"What's wrong, son?"

"What's wrong? All this was behind me. Now you're making me face it all over again."

"I'm sorry."

"Well, the least you could do is tell me what the hell this is all about."

Twenty minutes later, Mac ran out of breath and was thirsty. He wouldn't have bothered with the whole story, but he felt he owed it to Ray. He also had a feeling that Ray was going to be able to help him.

"So, you see why I'm so intent on getting to the bottom of things?"

"That's a strange story. You're not pulling my leg, are you?"

"Come on, Ray, give an old man some credit. I wouldn't dig into your past like this if it wasn't important."

"Sorry. Of course, you wouldn't. So, what can I do to help?"

"I think you should have a look in your attic. I know it's been years, but if your father hid something and if someone was looking for it, there's a chance they may not have found it."

"Well, I guess it's possible. I'll have to wait until Mom's not home. I wouldn't want to upset her when I go over to search."

Mac hesitated. He didn't want to pressure Ray, but there was no other choice. "The ceremony is tonight, Ray."

"Oh." Silence echoed over the telephone. "I'll see what I can do."

Mac sighed in relief. "Thanks, Ray. Let me know."

"Will do. Talk to you later, Mac."

Mac gently placed the telephone in its cradle. He hoped he hadn't upset Ray's world for nothing. Somehow, though, he knew Ray held a missing piece of the puzzle. Everyday sounds of life slowly returned him to the present.

Mrs. Harlow's voice was the final snap back to reality. "So, was your friend able to help you?" The clink of teacups accented her question.

"Kind of. He's working on it anyway." Finally noticing the steaming tea, he smacked his lips in appreciation. "Ah, just the way to ease these old bones." His words were light, but his mind was wound around the suspicious suicide of an obsessed man.

Chapter Twenty-Four

The drive from the Tor to Mac's store was a silent one. Tamara was aware that Gavin was not in a mood for conversation, which suited her fine, since she was lost in her own musings. Her original story of covering a harmless ceremony carried out by a coven of witches was whirling out of control. Somewhere along the way, her story ceased to matter. Instead, this was now a personal journey of self-discovery. She was changing, and her mind was opening up to possibilities. Granted, she still had trouble admitting unexplainable forces existed, but she wasn't as opposed to the idea as she used to be.

For a brief flash, she wished her mom were here so she could ask her some questions and confide her feelings. The truth was that she didn't know what her feelings were. They were as out of control as her story.

She sighed deeply, rubbed the back of her aching neck, and leaned her head on the headrest. She sensed rather than saw Gavin's eyes on her. It was disconcerting that she didn't have to see him looking at her. The fact that she could feel him unnerved her. Without opening her eyes, she spoke. "You should really keep your eyes on the road, you know."

"Don't worry about my driving. I've been doing it for years now." His teasing voice softened. "Are you all right?"

Tamara was touched. She even found herself welcoming the fact that he cared enough to ask. It was beyond her why she cared, but she did.

"I'm fine. I could use a bucket of steaming hot coffee though."

Gavin laughed. Tamara's attention was drawn to his mouth, again. Fine lines that creased the corners enhanced the masculinity emanating from the man, and his square chin was only enhanced by the shadow of stubble. Tamara's gaze wandered from his chin, which she ached to kiss, and then lower still to the hint of chest hair barely visible at the V of his unbuttoned shirt.

"You're staring at my chest again."

Embarrassed, Tamara felt the heat of a blush. "Sorry."

"Don't worry, I know how irresistible I am." His eyes sparked with teasing light.

"Oh, really. And you know this, how?"

"It's what all the girls tell me."

"Girls? Oh, that's sweet, your neighbors have kids."

Gavin looked slightly confused, and then realization dawned. "I mean, that's what all the women tell me."

"I see."

As teasing as Gavin's remark was, Tamara didn't doubt the validity of it for a second. Most women were drawn to raw masculine power. Especially when it was only barely controlled and bubbling just below the surface. They usually oohed and aahed over well-defined muscles and a tight butt. Only when she found herself opening the window to cool herself, did Tamara realize that she somehow became one of those women. This had never happened to her before, she usually prided herself in her control around men. What is it? You hit a certain age and suddenly everything starts changing? Truth be told, though, she'd never met anyone quite like Gavin, except in her dreams.

"Are you listening to me?"

With a guilty start, Tamara looked at Gavin. "I'm listening. What did you say?" Gavin's deep laugh made Tamara realize the contradiction of her words. "Okay, okay. I wasn't listening."

"I was only telling you that there's a great coffee place a couple of shops down from Mac's. You can grab a coffee there to satisfy your urge."

"My urge?" Tamara closed her mouth quickly. *He meant your urge for coffee, you idiot.* Gavin's expression reflected bland nonchalance. Maybe his comment had been meant as a sexual innuendo. Damn, what was it about this man that kept her so off balance?

"Yes, coffee would be great." She was able to remain acceptably business like. "I think I'll head there first, and then meet you at Mac's."

"Okay." Gavin wheeled his car into a free parking spot. "Grab some sticky buns for Mac. They're his favorite."

"Sure." Tamara slammed the car door in an attempt to relieve her frustration. Gavin climbed from the car and flashed her an innocent smile which only frustrated Tamara further.

"See you in a couple of minutes." Gavin threw the words over his shoulder as he headed to the bookstore.

"Sure." Tamara couldn't think of anything else to say. Her mind seemed stuck on the comment about her urges, especially in the face of the swaying butt headed away from her.

Hypnotized by the warm afternoon breeze and the quaintness of surrounding shops, Tamara found herself relaxing for the first time in awhile. She inhaled deeply of the wafting summer scents of flowers, fresh cut grass, and laze inducing heat.

Her shoulders gradually settled down from her ears into a more natural posture. With relaxation came hunger, and Tamara found herself craving a homemade cinnamon roll to go with her coffee. Just a few doors down, the aroma from Heavenly Delights promised just what Tamara was craving, and she could pick up sticky buns for Mac at the same time.

Stepping over uneven stone sidewalks, Tamara's gaze wandered from the picturesque shops to the multiple church spires that dotted the horizon. History and character abounded, and Tamara found herself thinking how comfortable she felt in this town.

Subconsciously following her nose to the bakeshop, she let her mind fantasize what kind of life she would have here. She could see herself living in a small manor house, not the castle that Gavin lived in. Something older, built with silver-gray block stone, a prominent chimney rising to the sky, and a front column porch. A low-rise, stone fence would encircle the property and engulf the garden that would abound with flowers. She could almost see one or two children playing in the yard.

Lost in her reverie, Tamara was slow to become aware of her surroundings and the flash of black that tickled the corner of her eye. Something about the movement made her heart pound. There it was again. This time, she saw a flutter of dark material disappear around the corner of Annie's Antiques.

It couldn't be, Tamara reassured herself. Why would the Dark Lady be at the docks? And what business would she have in an alleyway? A squeeze in the pit of Tamara's stomach compelled her forward.

It took all Tamara's courage to step from the safety in front of the antique store and peer down the mouth of the alley. The sun shone brightly, yet the narrow alley loomed dark and foreboding in front of Tamara. She didn't see anyone, which was even more confusing. Someone had come down this alley. There were no doors anywhere and only a bricked wall at the far end. Maybe her imagination had been working overtime. Maybe she should just get her coffee, sticky buns, cinnamon rolls, and go to the bookstore.

The muffled sound of laughter echoed off the well-worn brick walls of the alley. Bouncing off one wall, across to another, high then low, the laugh started quietly, but increased with each echo until Tamara was almost deafened. She covered her ears, but the vibration of the laughter echoed deep inside. Panic rose, competing with the overwhelming intensity of the laughter now all around. Inside and out, the laughter vibrated. How could no one else hear the sound? Why was no one coming to investigate? Tamara looked behind, expecting, hoping, to see people from the surrounding stores.

Like the crescendo of an opera, the intense laughter took over senses and emotions. Tamara became dizzy. She took one staggering step, but wasn't sure if it was forward or backward. Nausea tightened her throat as she fell to her knees. Her hands still desperately held themselves over her ears, although it did nothing to relieve the echo.

Suddenly, there was silence. Silence and darkness descended into the alley, creating the sensation of being alone. Tamara was able to rise to her feet just as a gray, cloying mist swirled about her. Dizziness returned, along with a sense of floating. Her legs became like rubber, and she knew she was about to faint.

Just before her eyes closed, Tamara saw what drew her to the alley, and it terrified her. Before her stood the Dark Lady, at one with the mist. But, it was the vaporous apparition floating above the Dark Lady that evoked terror in Tamara's heart. The vision was unrecognizable as anything remotely human.

Tamara fell to the cobblestones with visions of sharp teeth, dripping saliva, a horned skull, and eyes...oh, the eyes; they'd shine in her nightmares for eternity. Deep and bottomless, the eyes mirrored the torture of a thousand souls in agony. Twisting features and soundless screams on reflected faces sent Tamara over the edge to her own dark oblivion.

Hands on hips, and peering through the late afternoon sun barely managing its way in the dingy windows, Mrs. Harlow watched Mac and Gavin. Hunched over old books and yellowed papers, the two of them were in their own world of history and supposition. "Don't you men seem to think it's taking a long time for Tamara to get her coffee?" she questioned, only to receive a mumble sent her general direction.

"See, I told you I remembered some reference to a sword. Now call an old man senile, will you." Mac shoved the dusty, leather bound book under Gavin's nose. The action elicited a sneeze.

"Keep that thing away from my nose. You know I'm allergic to dust."

"Yer just allergic to hard work," Mac grumbled. "Let me read it for you instead."

Mrs. Harlow stamped her foot. "I'm thinking that Tamara is taking an awful long time with her coffee. Should someone maybe go looking for her?" Both men waved her direction in a dismissive way. "Fine. I guess I'll take it upon myself. See you in a few minutes." The stairs creaked, the door slammed, and Mac and Gavin shook their heads.

"Women!" A nod of understanding to each other, and Mac began to read the passage he found.

"Forged from Earth, Wind, Fire and Water
The sword of Truth shall shine its power
Within the hands of one who to reign
So long as he strives not for false gain,
On the day the King's blood ceases to roar
The sword and its power shall return once more
Deep to the elements in which it was forged."

"Return to the elements in which it was forged." Mac pondered for a moment. "Popular historical belief is that the sword was given to Arthur by the Lady of the Lake. Legends tell of the sword rising from amidst froth and bubbles to float across the air into Arthur's hands. It also states that the sword was returned to the Lake when he died. We know differently, at least about how Arthur received the sword. Merlin's own words specifically say that Morganna gave him the sword, supposedly on orders from the Lady, and he in turn presented it to Arthur. Based on this, we can't be sure what happened to the sword when he died."

"Yes, but if I remember the battle right, both Merlin and the Lady thought the other was in possession of the sword at the time. I also remember that King Arthur died around the same time as this battle took place." Gavin found himself caught up in the history and possibilities.

"Yep. You'd be right there, lad. And as for the sword, no one ever saw it again."

"Is it possible the sword was stolen by one of his knights or someone else with access to the inner sanctum of Camelot? Maybe even Guinevere herself."

"Possible, but…"

Just then the door shot open and was abruptly accompanied by the whirling of afternoon breezes winding down the stairs and rustling papers on the table. Grasping for flying parchment, Gavin snapped at the inconsiderate intruder.

"Close the damn door would you."

The door was slammed shut and accompanied by a demand given in a throaty voice.

"Where's my daughter?"

"Your daughter?" Gavin and Mac both spoke and exchanged a questioning glance.

"Yes, my daughter. Tamara."

"Tamara." Again, Gavin and Mac spoke at the same time. Gavin felt a little foolish. He took a moment to recover and study the woman standing inside the now shut door. Long silver hair was swept into a loose bun. High cheekbones, probably hollow once, were softened with the addition of weight that comes with age and a slowing of the metabolism. Dark blue eyes sparked and her full, coral colored lips were set in a line of impatience. Tall and regal, the woman was dressed casually in an embroidered denim shirt and jeans. Even so, she managed to exude sureness within herself. The woman obviously possessed self-confidence that her daughter still lacked. Gavin liked the honesty in her eyes and the naturalness of her appeal.

"Have you finished staring? Can you tell me where to find my daughter?"

Mac was the first to speak. "Please," he waved to her, "come in and have a seat. Can I offer you a drink?"

A heavy sigh trembled on the lips of the woman. Her shoulders dropped just a smidgen, but enough for Gavin to see how tense she had been.

"Look, I appreciate your offer, but I just need to know where I can find Tamara." A moment of uncertainty flitted in her eyes. "You do know Tamara, don't you?"

"Yes. Yes, of course we do. She's just out getting coffee and should be here any minute," Mac reassured.

"Oh, thank God. I wasn't sure I'd get here in time."

Fingers of fear clenched Gavin's heart into a rapid staccato. A glance at his watch and he realized how much time had gone by since Tamara left for coffee. Where was she? Some of his worry must have shown because the woman stiffened.

"What's wrong? There's something you're not telling me, isn't there?" Her voice rose.

"No, nothing's wrong. Mac's right, come and have a seat. What is your name by the way?"

"Diana. You can call me Diana." Gracefully, she made her way to the bottom of the stairs and stood hesitantly.

Gavin extended his hand. "I'm Gavin and this is Mac." He stood aside while Mac and Diana shook hands. "I didn't know that Tamara was here with her mother."

"She's not. I just got here. I went to the bed and breakfast where she was supposed to be staying, and a note on the door said the place was closed for a couple of days due to an unexpected event. It gave this store as the place the owner could be reached. Mrs. Harlow is her name, right?"

"Yes. She's gone to look for Tamara." No sooner were the words out and Gavin wished he hadn't spoken.

"Why does someone have to go looking for her?" Strain and worry were evident in Diana's voice. Her fingers wrung around the leather strap of her purse.

Distraught women were not Gavin's forte, so he was relieved when Mac stepped in.

"Now, now, sit yerself down here." Mac took Diana's arm and gently led her to the overstuffed armchair. "Tamara's gone for coffee is all, and Mrs. Harlow has gone to help her carry it back."

Mac's eyebrow twitched, a sure sign he was telling a whopper. Gavin knew the sign, but Diana would have no idea she was being smoothed over. At least, that's what he thought.

"Don't try to pacify me." Diana refused to sit. Instead, she stared Mac down. And look down on him she did. In fact, she towered over him by a good six inches.

Mac wasn't intimidated. Gently, but firmly, he set Diana into the chair. "I'm sure your day has been busy, so why not be lettin' me fix you a cup of tea. Tamara'll be comin' through that door any minute. Until then, why not tell us why you're here."

With a sigh and a brush of a weary hand over her brow, Diana gave herself over to Mac's ministrations. "Tea would be good, thank you."

Gavin took a deep breath. One emotional scene averted, now it was time to find out where Tamara was. Mrs. Harlow should have returned with some news by now. As unobtrusively as possible, Gavin meandered over to the bookshelves by the door. Pretending an interest in a book, he watched Mac expertly put Diana at ease. The flow of homey conversation permeated the room, and the low tone of voices and laughter created a cozy atmosphere. Gavin took the opportunity to creep up the stairs and into the sunlight.

A few long strides and he stood in front of the Café Coffee. The rich aroma of fresh ground beans assailed his senses along with the tantalizing scents of baking that hinted at cinnamon and chocolate. He glanced around, but saw no sign of familiar auburn hair, no Tamara. She wasn't here. Damn!

Conspicuously absent as well was Mrs. Harlow. Maybe they'd gone shopping together? Right! Don't be such an idiot, Gavin scoffed to himself. His bones tingled, and that was a sure sign there was trouble.

Mac found himself fascinated by the warm energy Diana's presence stimulated. She was recounting her trip, but the words were meaningless to Mac. Instead, he found himself lost in the depths of her flashing blue eyes and the slightly crooked corner of her full lips. Inside, he felt a flutter in the pit of his stomach. Gentle at first, the flutter grew to an all out attack of energy that exploded through his limbs in a blinding flash.

Through the haze and confusion, Mac saw the object of his fascination looking at him in a questioning manner. Oh, God, she probably asked him a question and here he was sitting like a mute idiot. Heavens above don't fail me now. Like a schoolboy, Mac struggled to find a way out of the awkward moment. He was saved by the vision of an angel in front of him.

"I'm sorry," she said. "Here I am rambling on about myself and you probably have work to do."

"No." Mac practically yelled. He cleared his throat and settled himself down. "I mean, it's my slow time of year, and I'm happy to entertain you, being Tamara's mother and all."

"I'm glad to see she found friends here so quickly. Tamara can sometimes hold people at a distance more than she should." Diana hesitated, and then appeared to come to a decision. "Mac, what's going on here?"

"What makes you think anything's going on?" Even to his ears, his voice sounded higher than normal. Maybe Diana wouldn't notice.

"Come on, Mac. You may own a small bookstore in the middle of a quaint village, but you and I both know you've got more on the ball than most. You just choose to play the country hick. Level with me."

Her gaze locked Mac to his seat. An exchange of thoughts, emotions, and energy brought them to an understanding of each other that could never be reached by mere words. A hint of a smile touched his face and was shared by Diana.

"Yes. I think Tamara is very lucky to have a mother like you."

"She may argue with you on that score. According to Tamara, I'm her flaky mother who embarrassed her to her friends and drove her father away."

Mac felt the sadness and melancholy in Diana's voice. Without needing to be said, he knew what Diana was, what she believed, and how she lived. The natural wonder of her abilities shone from her aura like the energy of life. Animals would flock to her, and people would seek her out for advice. She would accomplish seeming feats of magic with her understanding of the energy surrounding her. Someone like Tamara, so intent on the logical and physical world, would have a hard time understanding her own mother.

"You're here because you know there's trouble, don't you?"

"Yes. I felt the tug of my daughter needing me. I know it has to do with the curse. You know of the curse, don't you, Mac?"

"Yes. And there's so much more you don't know."

"All the way here, I prayed I wouldn't be too late."

Mac gave in to the urge to put his hand on Diana's and console her with the physical contact. They shared an unspoken understanding of each other. The room echoed with the softly sung songs of faeries and angels, happy with the merging of two souls finally finding each other.

Abruptly, the mood was shattered as the door flew open and banged against the wall. Books on shelves trembled, releasing dust to hover in the air and fall to the floor.

"I can't find her anywhere." Gavin stood on the stairs, intense and obviously shaken. "I looked all up and down the street. Mrs. Harlow is missing, too. Damn, why didn't I pay more attention to where she was and how long she was gone?"

Unaware of the effect his words were having on Diana, Gavin kept bemoaning his own stupidity. Mac felt the warmth leave the hand he held. Diana tensed, but remained calm. When she spoke, her voice was strong, holding only a hint of fear.

"Well, I guess I was right. I am needed here after all."

The three of them shared a look of camaraderie and cemented a silent pact to work together. Mac smiled and thought of the Three Musketeers. But he would guess that the musketeers never came up against what they faced on the dark night ahead.

Before anyone could speak, the telephone echoed an ear splitting shrill through the bookstore.

"Damn, I keep meaning to turn that darn thing down." Mac mumbled as he snatched the offending thing from its cradle. "Hello." He snapped.

"Mac. Mac, I'm so excited. I can't believe what I found. Are you ever going to like this? I had no idea."

Mac barely recognized the excited voice of his friend Ray. "Whoa, Ray, take a deep breath and let me know what in the dickens yer blatherin' on about." His words drew the attention of both Diana and Gavin who now stood, one over each shoulder. Mac was distracted by the closeness of Diana. He found himself liking the distraction.

"I'm sorry, it's just that I found something in the attic that could possibly answer a lot of your questions."

"Well, maybe you better tell me what it is you found my friend, because the life of someone very important may depend on the information you give us." Mac used his free hand to pat Diana on the shoulder in a gesture of reassurance that everything would be all right.

Chapter Twenty-Five

Cotton? Why did she have cotton in her mouth? Tamara tried to spit it out, but couldn't. She reached up to pull the offensive substance from her mouth, but her hands wouldn't move. She must be dreaming. Usually, a little prompting on her part would send her nightmares into oblivion. Concentrating, she focused on opening her eyes and regaining consciousness.

Finally, managing to open her eyes, she was confronted with Mrs. Harlow's looming above her. What was she doing here? And who was standing beside her? Why was it so bright? In a sudden flash, full memory returned of the moments before her black out.

Shit! Morganna, the laughter and the ghastly apparition all became clear. But that didn't explain where she was, or what Mrs. Harlow was doing here.

"I see our company wakens." Morganna's voice held none of the evil laughter from the alley. Instead, it was full, rich, and hypnotizing.

Tamara struggled to gain some kind of control of her situation. Her attempts to sit up were met with a sneer from Morganna.

"Do not bother struggling. You are a slave to my powers, and your weak will can do nothing to overcome what I have spent centuries developing."

In a desperate attempt to move, Tamara realized the Dark Lady's words were true. She was able to move her head, so she took an inventory of her surroundings. Not an easy task considering the blaze of radiance impeding her vision. Light shone everywhere. It reflected off the slick cave walls and rebounded back into itself to create an illusion of brilliant fire. Could it be a dream? But, no, it was the cave. It was formed of crystal. Solid, hard, unforgiving, the cave crystals still managed to exude warmth with their glimmering glow.

The crystal cave. Merlin's cave. Gavin told her about it from Merlin's memoirs. What was Morganna doing here? God, her head ached with the multitude of questions buzzing around inside.

Tamara's eyes adjusted to the brilliant light and she risked another look around. She knew enough from her mother's ways to recognize the elements of magic that surrounded her. Morganna closed her in a circle with elements of earth, air, fire, and water simulating the four directions, and black candles guarded the circle all around. When used for black magic these were good for binding and shape shifting.

Pungent in the air were he scents of ginger incense to enhance vibrations and mugwort to increase psychic ability and promote astral travel. The aroma of myrtle, an herb reputed to help maintain youthfulness, also tickled Tamara's nostrils. Deep in the corner of the crystal cave, an altar in a small alcove revealed itself to her gaze. Familiar, yet ancient looking tools of magic adorned the natural stone crevice that served as the altar. The blade of a black handled athame streaked silver in the flickering firelight. Also visible were an ornate chalice, small black cauldron, a crystal wand that glowed with energy, and silver and gold candles to signify the Goddess and God.

Then she remembered. Her voice croaked. "Mrs. Harlow, I'm sorry you got involved. Are you all right?"

Confusion wrinkled the familiar face of her landlady.

Morganna's laugh filled the crystal cave. "Is she all right, you ask? You are a stupid woman." Morganna brushed a strand of auburn hair from Tamara's face and leaned close enough for Tamara to feel hot breath on her cheek. In a delighted whisper of evil, Morganna whispered. "Mrs. Harlow belongs to me. She's been watching you and reporting back to me from the beginning."

"Mrs. Harlow?" Tamara searched the familiar face for confirmation, and the blush readily apparent in the flickering candlelight was all she needed.

"I'm sorry. I was told no one would get hurt." Fearfully whispered words squeaked from tight lips.

"Be silent, bitch. I will not tolerate your insolence. You knew what was involved. If you turn from your duties now, I can easily use you as a sacrifice as well."

"Sacrifice," Tamara whispered. "What does she mean?" The petrified look on Mrs. Harlow's face answered her question. "Dear God in Heaven above, she can't be serious."

"Your God cannot help you. I have the power of the ancient Gods behind me, and once I use your blood in sacrifice to them, I will also have the power of the Sword Excalibur." Morganna's voice held a touch of hysteria. This scared Tamara almost as much as the wild look in the woman's eyes.

"Oh, Mom, where are you when I need you? All your hocus pocus would come in handy about now." Tamara surprised herself with her whispered plea. She actually believed in all this stuff. Somewhere along the way, she'd adopted her mother's beliefs. Her head suddenly ached with the beginnings of a whopper of a headache, but her thoughts were clear and her senses sharp. She struggled to move her limbs, but couldn't despite the fact there were no ropes or bindings.

What about Mac and Gavin? They would be worried about her by now, but even if they searched, they wouldn't be able to find her. Where would they start? Even if Tamara tried to guide them with her mind—yes, she was beginning to believe—she had no idea where she was. She was in this all on her own, or maybe not.

Mrs. Harlow huddled in the deepest, darkest recess of the cave, and she looked miserable. From her earlier statement, Tamara could only assume that her landlady had been misled. But was Mrs. Harlow upset or scared enough, to help Tamara out of this bind? Could she be a possible ally for Tamara? How much power and control did Morganna have over the woman?

Questions galore, but no answers.

Low chanting distracted Tamara from her thoughts. Morganna settled in front of the altar and was performing some kind of ceremony. Although many of the offerings and motions were similar to a ritual her mother might perform the result was not. Her mother always created an atmosphere of warmth and love. Her rituals drew the surrounding energy of the earth and air to her in a gentle blend of nature and mankind. Morganna, on the other hand, created a tumultuous frenzy of unleashed energy. Heavy, stifling, and intense, it rushed through the cave like a mini hurricane. Tamara felt sick. Mrs. Harlow looked terrified, yet impressed at the power Morganna called forth so easily.

Then it happened. Tamara became aware of a new presence palpitating within the cave. Dread made its way down her spine. Her heart pounded in rhythm with her increased breathing, as a familiar form slowly began to take shape. Morganna's chanting intensified, and the now distinct form leaped about in a frenzy of teeth, drool, and putrid stench.

Tamara gagged and struggled against her invisible chains, while terror and the need to escape fueled her attempts. A sense of survival tore through all pre-conceived beliefs, and she searched her memory for any piece of information she could remember from her upbringing as the daughter of a Wiccan witch. Fight fire with fire. In light of the scene playing out before her, Tamara gave her mother a quick, silent apology for doubting her.

Now the three of them, Morganna, Mrs. Harlow, and the beast, were locked in some kind of ritual dance. To Tamara, it looked a little obscene as they cast off their clothes and writhed around in a display of flesh and morbid eroticism.

"Please, someone help me," Tamara whispered in desperation.

Suddenly, all sound stopped. Candles and flame flickered and sizzled. Morganna approached Tamara, paced the enclosing circle three times, and then spoke.

"Your friends will follow you in a feeble attempt at rescue. We'll make sure they find you, but only when the time is right. Just think about it, blood from descendents of both Nimue and Merlin can bless my ritual this eve. The sword and its power will surely be mine to command."

"If you're talking about the Sword Excalibur, everyone knows it can only be held and its powers used by one pure of heart. I'd say that pretty much leaves you out of the picture." Although she spoke defiantly, Tamara was quaking inside. Why hadn't she listened to her mother when she was growing up? Then she may have an inkling what to do against the power of the Dark Lady.

"Stupid wench," Morganna spat. "Would I trouble myself with centuries of manipulating and align myself with vile creatures such as this," her hand waved toward the beast hulking in the corner, "unless I was sure of what I do? The curse placed on the Sword Excalibur by one many years ago is little known by any. But with your blood and that of the spawn of Merlin's descendants, I will take the sword as mine and rule."

Tamara knew of no such curse, but Morganna was sure of herself. Tamara looked into eyes of deepest black that reflected emptiness, and for the first time, she truly doubted everything she'd ever believed. The woman before her was Morganna, the real Morganna. Beliefs ceased to be defined, and logic held no place in this cave. Tamara knew the danger was in the unknown, not the known. The question was how did she battle this age-old virago of ancient beliefs and rituals?

Still unable to move, she let her mind relax and recalled every tidbit of information her mother ever instilled in her, either through intent or osmosis. Her mother's credo had always been that half of any battle was the belief in yourself. If you believed and put the thought into the world, it became a form of energy itself. That much she could do, but the other half of the battle would need to be won with the help of her friends. She needed to focus her energy their direction and pray to God they knew the seriousness of the situation facing them. This was no crazy lady with delusions of some forgotten history. This was Morganna herself manifesting history into the present and using the Ceremony of the Stars for her own evil purposes.

Chapter Twenty-Six

Mac was pensive as he placed the telephone back in its cradle. Gavin gave him a second, then pounced. "Come on. What's up? We don't have all day."

"My boy, yer still in need of learnin' some of that patience I keep tellin you about."

"Later. Tamara and Mrs. Harlow are missing. This is no time for patience."

"You might be right, just this once." Mac heaved a sigh and shot a glance to Diana who sat silently through the entire telephone conversation.

"Don't worry about me. I'm a lot stronger than I look. I came here because I knew there was trouble. I think the only way to get through it will be to work together."

Gavin was perplexed at the look that passed between his long-time friend and Tamara's mom. Mac patted Diana on the shoulder and left his hand there while he recited the gist of the conversation. Where they falling in love? They only just met. Gavin smiled briefly. Life sure found ways to work its own magic.

"Ray searched the attic where they found his father. One of their attic windows leaked last spring and warped some floorboards. To make a long story short, he found something under the floor that he missed before. Ray's dad researched for years, taking extensive notes. There were notebooks filled with rambling pages of supposition and references to certain books and passages. He wrote about the Dark Lady, your ancestor Reginald, the journals, and something else that clears Morganna's motives up somewhat."

Gavin frowned. "I thought she wanted to destroy Merlin and Nimue for revenge and power. We know she can't gain control over the sword itself. She's kind of stepped over the line of good versus evil."

"That's where you're wrong. She can gain control over the sword. When the sword was forged in Atlantis, there was a curse placed on it."

"Atlantis." Gavin frowned, but noticed that Diana smiled at the inference to the supposed lost continent.

"Strange or not, the Sword Excalibur can be as powerful a weapon for evil as it is for good." Mac cleared his throat and whispered, "For the sword to be wielded by one with a sinister heart, it requires a sacrifice of the blood from someone descended from the Ones Who Came Before."

"The Ones Who Came Before. Who are they?"

Diana answered Gavin's question. "The people of Atlantis are the Ones who Came Before. When Atlantis was destroyed, or cast into another dimension, some of the people made their way to Britain and founded the land of Avalon, which in turn became another lost land cast into a dimension beyond our grasp. With them, they brought certain artifacts that were revered and cherished as sources of ancient power and wisdom. The Sword Excalibur was one such artifact, although, I never knew anything of a curse." She frowned.

Gavin and Mac were stunned at the story. Gavin was the first to speak. "How do you know all this?"

"I see many things through my meditations, but until today I never had confirmation any of it was real."

"Oh." Gavin was disbelieving but he saw Mac smile as if in total acceptance of Diana's story.

"Okay, so what's with the curse? What are we facing tonight? How are we going to get Tamara back? What…"

Mac raised his hand to stem the flow of Gavin's questions. "One thing at a time. The curse can only be fulfilled with a blood sacrifice, either yours or Tamara's."

Diana's face turned ashen and Gavin's heart clenched with fear, whether for himself or Tamara, he wasn't sure. Probably both.

"It also needs the Sword Excalibur to be in the hands of Morganna when the sacrifice is made. Her frantic search for the journals make me assume that she doesn't have her hands on the sword yet. According to Ray's father's notes, 'Cast from this earth by The Powers That Be, Sword Excalibur shall reign for the hour at midnight only when the stars line in the sky.' If we can find out where the sword will appear at midnight tonight, we can snatch it before Morganna has a chance to get it in her greedy paws."

"That's your plan? This woman has powers we can't even fathom, yet she's going to let us walk up and take the sword before she can? That's assuming we can even figure out where it is."

Diana's voice was low in the tenseness of the room. "I know where the sword will appear."

This forward statement of fact, shocked even Mac. He and Gavin spoke in unison. "What!"

"I told you I see things when I meditate. I've been getting visions for my whole life, but never knew what they meant, until now. The Sword Excalibur will appear at the Chalice Well at Glastonbury Tor."

"You don't know that for sure, do you?" Events were moving too fast and, as flexible as Gavin's beliefs were, he had trouble staking Tamara's life on the supposed visions Diana spoke about.

Diana pinned him with a gaze as assured and confident as any he'd ever seen. "She's my daughter. Believe me, I'm sure."

Not one to argue with that kind of logic, Gavin acquiesced, although his stomach churned at the chance that Diana might be wrong.

With Tamara's life on the line, Gavin's feelings for her pulsed through his veins like a drug. He needed her to be safe, because without her he'd be missing part of himself. He knew that, as surely as he knew he needed air to breathe.

Diana's hand brushed his cheek, and she spoke. "You love my daughter, don't you?"

"Yes." The word wasn't necessary, but Gavin said it anyway.

"Good, I think you'll be good for her."

Mac cleared his throat. "Can we maybe get back to business here?"

"Fine." Gavin replied. "So, what's our next step? Mac, any ideas?"

"Nary a one, except to beat Morganna to the sword so she can't use it for her blood lust sacrifice."

"That sounds good, but what if she gets to the sword first?"

"Well, then she'd have the sword and the sacrifice she needs to fulfill her centuries long desire for ultimate power and eternal life."

Silent until then, Diana spoke. "We need to be well prepared for our eventual confrontation with the Dark Lady. And there will be a confrontation. That has also been part of my visions."

"Great. Did your visions show you how this whole fiasco turns out?" Gavin was frustrated with his lack of control over the situation. Having to rely on visions, myths, and magic went against his natural instincts of survival.

"No, the outcome is unknown. What I do know is that we have to work together in total trust and belief or all is lost. Have you ever heard of the power of three?" She looked to Mac and Gavin who both shook their heads in the negative.

"The number three is a powerful one in many cultures. You have Father, Son, and Holy Ghost in the Christian religion. Wiccans tell of Maiden, Mother, and Crone, which relates to three cycles of the moon: waning, full, and waxing. Oriental cultures believe the number nine is the number of completion, three times three. These are just a few examples, but many cultures have different myths woven into their history, all dealing with some representation of the number three."

"Okay," Gavin agreed. "We work together, but I'm afraid Mac and I are amateurs when it comes to magic."

"Not to worry, I'll give you a list of supplies. Since you know the area you'll be able to collect the items together quickly. Mac and I can stay here and go over a plan of attack. We'll fill you in when you get back. Oh, one thing before you go. I'd almost forgotten, but now I know why I was led to do this." Diana reached into her purse and pulled out a couple of bags on a string. "I need for each of you to wear these." Before her, she held two silver bags on leather ropes.

Gavin frowned. "I don't think now is the time to be worrying about accessories."

"Cute, but I'm not kidding. Put them on." Diana commanded and thrust the silver bags closer. "They have powerful energy, they link us together, and they may just save our lives."

Without protest, Mac plucked one from her hand and put it around his head to settle with a light thunk on his chest. Gavin hesitated and then, with a roll of his eyes, did the same.

"There, now, are you satisfied?"

"I will be as soon as you promise not to take them off, no matter what." Diana crossed her arms and fixed an intense stare at them.

"I promise, and so does Gavin." Mac gave his word.

"Not good enough. Gavin has to make his own promise."

"Fine, I promise not to take it off. Now can we please get going?"

Diana flashed a bright, if somewhat tense smile. "Thanks. Now I need paper and pen to write out a list for Gavin."

Gavin waited while Diana wrote her list. He watched Mac watch Diana and was bemused by the look on his friend's face. Mac was obviously smitten. Any other time, Gavin would have teased, but not now.

His stomach curled at the thought of what lay ahead. Deep inside, he sensed Tamara's fear. It seems that somewhere along the way, they stopped being two separate entities. Her emotions were wrapped up with his, and his with her. Keeping this in mind, Gavin took a moment to focus his mind and send his intentions to Tamara.

Sweetheart, we're coming to get you. Hold on.

A tendril of hope and love warmed his heart, and Gavin took that as a sign that maybe Tamara was returning his feelings. Could it be possible? He chose to believe so.

God, he hoped Diana knew what she was doing. She knew more than Mac and he combined, and she was right that together they made a great team. At least he hoped so, for Tamara's sake.

Chapter Twenty-Seven

Morganna caressed the smooth stone of the sacrificial altar. She knew first hand the killing stone had seen many long years of disuse. In fact, she had probably been the last person to use the altar for its intended purpose. Over time, the once illustrious stone had become nothing but an attraction for any tourist hardy enough to wander off the guided pathway.

Located just below the crystal cave and close to the Chalice Well, the altar clearing sat on a line of energy. Further above, like a beacon to the heavens, stood the Tor itself. From well to clearing, to cave to Tor, the line ran straight; a line of energy that connected past and present, this world and the other world. Some would even say the connection ran to the stars themselves.

Morganna knew the power held in this sacred place of reverence and mystery, and very few remained that knew how to access the power. Soon, people would lose the ability to wander from one state of vibration level to another. Strange happenings and sightings would cease, and mysteries wondered about would no longer matter. Once she gained possession of the sword and retained its power, Morganna would be the most powerful of all.

Visions of rule and domination were interrupted by the whining voice of that stupid wench who served her. "Mistress, all is ready."

"You are sure? There must be no mistakes this eve."

"Your tools are laid out as you requested. The resting place lays ready to receive the sword, and the altar is prepared to absorb the sacrifice of blood you will offer."

Mrs. Harlow's voice shook. Morganna was scornful of the woman's weakness, yet she derived pleasure bending others to her bidding. The woman had no choice but to accept the fact that blood would be spilled that night. Yesterday, she had been aghast at the fact that someone would get hurt. Such stupidity, no wonder the human race was losing the powers that were once so much a part of their daily life.

"Fine, you may leave and return to the cave. Make sure our guest is comfortable," Morganna commanded.

The order was given, and Mrs. Harlow ceased to exist for Morganna. Her mind was too busy with thoughts of the approaching ceremony. Shadows from treetops passed across her face and danced in the clearing as the sun descended below their peaks. The warm afternoon breeze drifted away, leaving a muffled stillness and only the occasional twitter of a songbird. That suited Morganna just fine, as she hated birds anyway.

A sensation of being watched pervaded the surrounding air, but Morganna recognized the energy. Without turning, she said, "After tonight, we will be unstoppable."

"Yes." The rasp of the beast's voice grated across Morganna's spine. "Our pact will have been fulfilled, and you will give me the power you promised so long ago."

"Yes, of course." No way, she swore to herself. She hated the beast, and she hated the fact that he sapped her energy to boost his. Over the years, she became weaker, and he more substantial. Maybe she made a mistake with the words of chant when she called for him so long ago. She couldn't remember. She hadn't meant for him to be so forceful. Originally, his presence was supposed to have been a link to the evil ways. Instead, he took over every breathing, waking moment of her life until she could not escape him. Oh, he was in for a surprise tonight. Once she held the sword in her hands, her power would reign supreme, and she would send him back to the depths of the underworld where he belonged.

For now, she would smile and play his game, because soon she would need him no longer. His voice invaded her senses again.

"Are you sure of your visions? Will you be able to gain possession of the sword?"

"Do not bother me with stupid questions. I have told you the sword will appear for us when the time is right, so do not waste time worrying over what will be provided for us," Morganna said.

"The altar is prepared for the sacrifice of blood?"

She ground her teeth. The beast was persistent in his manner, but she must remain calm and keep him on her side, for he could still ruin her plans. If all did not go well this eve, she would perish. Her strength and powers were not what they had once been. She hid the fact well, but her powers faded fast, and she would not live the centuries to see another ceremony.

When she spoke, her voice was restrained. "All is ready. Nothing can go wrong, so stop questioning me, and let me focus my energies."

Fetid breath scraped across her neck. The beast moved closer. His detestable voice growled in her ear. "You will live up to our bargain, will you not? When the sword appears, it will become mine."

A shiver of loathing tingled up Morganna's spine. She could not stand his sickly presence. "Damn you, creature, hold your tongue. I need peace and concentration for the task ahead. Now leave me."

With an effort, she gathered her powers and shot a ball of energy at the beast. The screech of pain and anger that echoed in the clearing gave Morganna a bead of satisfaction. At least, she still possessed enough power to scald her nemesis.

Bound together by the ancient ritual, the two glowered at each other, neither willing to be the first to break. Morganna was the first to speak.

"Tonight, the Fates will decide all. Until then, we need each other, so let us not cause any more disruptions in our energy forces."

Nostrils flared and eyes rolled, but the beast contained his anger. With a nod of agreement, he dissolved into a wisp of smoke and disappeared. Morganna was alone in the clearing. She would not be sorry to be rid of that creature. Now, though, she needed to take a moment to recharge her energy in the stillness of dusk. Her favorite time of day, dusk allowed the veil between worlds to become passable. It also signaled the approach of darkness. Soon, the sun would set and the stars would begin to appear like speckles of light on a canvas of black.

Anticipation was a tonic to her blood, bubbling and boiling. She tasted the need. She craved the power. Nothing could go wrong tonight. Tonight would be the culmination of her dreams.

Chapter Twenty-Eight

Tamara didn't know the time, but she sensed anticipation hovering in the air. Mrs. Harlow returned from somewhere, and she knelt in a hollowed corner of the cave chanting. The loathsome beast disappeared, and then returned in a foul temper. Not too surprising, as it matched his foul looks.

No time to get cocky, Tamara warned herself. Night approached. Unless she did something, she'd find her blood spilled to fulfill some ancient curse. At that point her mind was the only thing she still controlled, as Morganna controlled her body. Fine. Mom always said the mind was stronger than the body, so maybe it was time to see the extent of her own powers.

She needed to let Mac and Gavin to know where she was. She needed to rely on them to save her, as she obviously couldn't save herself. She took a deep breath, blew gently outwards, and gradually became aware of each muscle in her body. Silently, she began to recite to herself. Relax one muscle at a time, let your body float, and your mind become one with your surroundings.

The cave and its sounds receded into the background, and a rushing sensation made her head light. Another minute or two of relaxation and Tamara felt her limbs begin to tingle with a floating sensation. Good, now she needed to picture Mac and Gavin and try to connect her mind with theirs. She imagined their faces and focused all her energy on reaching them. She then envisioned the path leading up the Tor and to the crystal cave.

Focus! Concentrate! Relax! The litany repeated in her mind to mingle with her images of Mac and Gavin. Damn, something wasn't working. In a hazy display of wavering colors and images, her mother's face kept interfering.

It made sense that her connection to her mother would be stronger than to a couple of virtual strangers, but Gavin and Mac were the ones to help her, not her mother. Come on Tamara, concentrate. Strangely enough, images were becoming clearer. She felt as if she were standing on the hilltop looking down on Mac, Gavin, and her mother. Her mind's eye showed her the three of them standing in a circle in the middle of a clearing, but the details were hazy.

Wait a minute. The path looked like the one that led to the Chalice Well. She'd seen it earlier today. In her vision, Gavin shifted from one foot to another, and Tamara saw the ornate wooden lid that served as a cover to the well.

Tamara knew she must be dreaming, or was it just wishes put into thought? She was no good at this ESP stuff. Her mother would know what to do, but she obviously didn't inherit any of her mother's abilities. And, yes, she was willing to admit that her mom had some kind of natural born abilities. With her own stubborn, close-minded attitude, Tamara realized she probably damaged any close relationship she may have had with her own mother. Now, it was too late.

Her thoughts wandered off course, and she no longer felt the sense of any familiar faces in her mind. Her senses became foggy, and new visions began to clutter her mind. Just like her dream, she could see the Tor, but it looked different. Swirling with mist the monument rose to the skies, but this time there were figures moving about the hilltop. Thunder and lightning crashed about and muted the voices echoing from the dream figures. A gleaming flash of light reflected into her eyes, and suddenly, everything became clear.

Gavin.

Gavin held a sword in his hands. The Sword Excalibur? He held it high and threatening toward an advancing figure, the Dark Lady. He didn't see the beast approaching him from behind. Tamara screamed a warning, but her words were caught in the gusting storm. Two bodies melded into one, and Tamara lost sight of Gavin. The sword sparked and danced with a life of its own, using Gavin as a mere pawn to its ancient power.

There was a man and a woman, she didn't recognize them, or did she? The woman was the same woman from earlier today. The man must be Merlin. Unaware of the battle ensuing near them, Merlin and Nimue spoke no words. Instead, they manipulated the energy of nature and the surrounding storm. Flashes flew from their fingertips, leaves and debris raged about their feet, and the earth trembled with their anger.

Chaos reigned, as Tamara struggled to wake from the nightmare. At least, she prayed it was only a dream. She wasn't sure about anything. In the storm's fury, she heard Gavin call out her name. Mac appeared and joined in the melee, while Nimue and Merlin raged on in their battle.

The chaos peaked.

A flutter of movement drew her attention to the edge of the clearing, beyond the beast and Gavin. She saw herself; she looked dead.

Tamara screamed.

Movement from the back of the cave shocked her to stunned awareness. She was still in the cave. Morganna and Mrs. Harlow were packing some items into a wooden box of sorts. Tamara swallowed in fear. It must be nighttime.

Tamara's panic rose a notch. This couldn't be happening, yet it was. Was this how her life was going to end? As some sacrificial lamb for a demented, centuries-old, evil ghost? Just a few days ago she was going about her day-to-day life, minding her own business, safe in her ignorance.

Morganna's face loomed in Tamara's vision. The flickering firelight highlighted her high cheekbones and created a grotesque mask of light and dark. With a wave of hands and rustle of silk, Morganna released Tamara from her imprisonment.

Stunned at first, Tamara quickly realized she was free to move. Though her limbs were stiff, she stood and faced her tormentor. Morganna stood complacently, giving Tamara a chance to turn and make a dash for the cave entrance.

Unfortunately, as she turned and took a step, she found herself smacking into the immovable brute of a beast that appeared from nowhere. Her nostrils were pressed against scaly, tough, skin and assaulted with a foul aroma quite unlike anything she ever encountered. Her arms were gripped in a long fingered grasp, and she was lifted until she came eye to eye with the beast.

She stared him head on, barely. His eyes were depthless and empty of any soul. If she didn't know better, Tamara would have figured herself to be an early dinner. She knew she was safe only because Morganna wanted to make her a human sacrifice instead. Wasn't she lucky?

Morganna spoke. "Your fate has been sealed, and any attempt to escape will prove futile. Now come, there is not much time. We go to the altar." With a toss of her head, Morganna swept from the cave and disappeared into the night. Mrs. Harlow followed, and then the beast with Tamara still locked in his grasp.

Tamara began a prayer that she would continue until she could no longer speak. Her words were soft and quiet in the night. "Please, God, help me. Please, God, help me."

Chapter Twenty-Nine

A sliver of mist drifted across the face of the moon and left a wispy trail in the clear, starry sky. A beautiful night in stark contrast to the desperation of the situation.

Mac, Diana, and Gavin stood in a small, enclosed courtyard adorned with lush vegetation and surrounded with old growth forest. Colors were hard to distinguish in the fading light, but Gavin knew from his earlier visit that the clearing was alive with shades of pink, lavender, gold, and green.

The energy here was different than earlier. He remembered a feeling of tranquility, a sense of time standing still, and worldly problems ceasing to exist. Now, the air was cloying. It felt like a feral creature waiting in the dark, somewhere just beyond the edge of the trees. Subdued, expectant, it prowled the forest and weaved a spell.

Gavin shivered. He turned to Mac and uttered. "How soon before we can get this over with?"

Diana's voice echoed in the cool night to answer his question. "Not much longer. We just need to wait for the moon to crest the trees so we can use the light and the moon rays for the ritual."

Mac just shrugged. "Don't bother askin' me any questions." Gavin saw him pat Diana's shoulder. "Our resident expert is in charge for now."

Gavin studied his old friend's face and smiled at the force of love and peace he saw reflected there. The same look glowed on Diana's face.

Gavin's insides quivered. He was jealous. And he was scared. He began to feel the same way for Tamara, and now her life was in jeopardy. Gavin wasn't sure if he was up to the task of saving her. What did he know of mystical stuff? Somehow events passed far beyond his understanding and knowledge of occult. How well did they even know Diana? Granted, she was Tamara's mother, but how much did she really know of the events of tonight?

Gavin looked at her and saw a soft, feminine face reflecting silver moonshine. Eyes of blue sparked with electricity, determination, and just a hint of uncertainty.

"Damn." Gavin muttered and drew attention his direction.

"What's wrong, Gavin?" Mac and Diana questioned.

"This isn't going to work, is it? You really have no idea what to do next, do you?" Even to his own ears, Gavin sounded on the wrong side of hysterical. There went his tough p.i. reputation.

Diana only smiled. Her lips gently rose in one corner, and she spoke just as gently. "No, Gavin, I have no idea what to do next." Before he could protest, Diana continued. "But I have faith and a certainty that we will be shown the way. Trust me, I know I have powerful guides and energies surrounding me. I always have."

Mac looked as if he'd believe Diana even if she told him the world was flat, but Gavin could only picture the last time he'd seen Tamara. The smile she threw over her shoulder as she went for coffee. Dazzling, sexy, and trusting. That was the kicker. She finally began to trust him. He couldn't let her down.

"Gavin." Diana rested her hand on his arm. "I know you're worried about Tamara, just imagine how I feel, she's my daughter.

The thing is, we have no choice but to deal with whatever the Fates throw our way."

Her words were strong, but Gavin heard the quiver in her voice. They were all so scared, so he could only imagine what Tamara was feeling. Wherever she was.

"Gavin, Diana." Mac's raised palm stilled their chatter. "Can you feel that?"

"Feel what?"

"Pay attention lad. Stop using yer emotions and use yer senses instead."

"I feel it," Diana whispered in awe. "It's Tamara, she's calling to us. I can feel her." Diana's voice rose with each word until she was almost shouting.

"I still can't…" Gavin paused. "Wait. Yes, I can. She's close, but she's in trouble."

"Well, we knew that lad. At least, now we know she's still alive. Oh, sorry, Diana."

"Don't be sorry. I've known for a long time something like this was coming. I just pray to the powers that be, I'm prepared enough to save my daughter."

Excited and anxious, Gavin swore that if—no, make that when—they saved Tamara, he'd make sure she never left his side.

"Come on, guys, we need to join hands around the well." Diana held her hands out, one each toward Mac and himself. Not knowing what else to do, and needing to believe, Gavin extended his hands and they were clasped by the others. One soft, feminine and firm, the other, slightly more hesitant, but just as firm.

Gavin took a deep breath, looked both his friends in the eye, and spoke. "Together we have the heralded power of three."

At first, nothing happened. Their hearts slowed, their minds mingled with the night, and the wind began to rise. Leaves rustled, flower petals tumbled on the breeze, and dark clouds rumbled in the distant sky.

Overcome by the strangest sensation he'd ever felt, Gavin's feet felt as if they no longer touched solid earth, his body tingled, and he became so infinitely aware of each beat of his heart. The wind whirred in a state of frenzy, and a deep howling began in the distance. Gavin no longer felt the hands that only a moment ago grasped his so tightly.

He was scared and not too proud to admit the fact. The howling came closer, but not close enough to cover a scraping sound that rose from the middle of the human circle.

In a blaze of color and flash of blinding radiance, the Chalice Well opened itself to their gaze. Gavin felt his hands. Each of them was being held in a strangling grip. The pain didn't matter, because his eyes were locked on the cover of the Well as it hovered at eye level then, as if by human hands, moved to the side to lower slowly to the ground beside him.

The show wasn't over yet. Vibrating and dancing, vibrant colors shot from the Chalice Well, reached to the Heavens, and then fell back to the Earth. Spectacular was not magnificent enough of a word to describe the display. Gavin was entranced.

Fading and sparking, the colors sizzled back into the Well, leaving the three of them open-mouthed at what they just witnessed.

Mac's whispered voice broke the stunned silence. "Lordy, will you feast yer eyes on what the Heavens have left for us."

Three pair of eyes fixed on what hovered in a blanket of mist in the center of the circle. Three voices spoke in awe. "Sword Excalibur."

Resplendent in its simplicity, the ancient sword inhaled the luster of the moon and glowed with nature's energy. Onyx carvings of a dragon were embedded in the silver handle, and the double edge steel of the polished, silvery blade gleamed to a pointed tip.

Afraid to move, Gavin stared. He was aware that the trio no longer held hands. Instead, they stood like statues. He looked to Diana for guidance. "What now?" he whispered in fear and reverence.

"Take the sword in your hand. You are Merlin's descendant," Diana whispered, probably afraid to speak out loudly and break the spell woven by the appearance of the sword.

"But…" The thought of plucking the shimmering sword from the unseen force holding it steady was a little intimidating to Gavin.

"There are no buts, Gavin. Your destiny is intertwined with Tamara's, and both your destinies lie with the Sword Excalibur. Take it in your hand."

Gavin raised his trembling hand and felt the world around him stand in hushed silence. Mac and Diana stopped breathing, and the breeze that had blown so fiercely now lay in stillness on the forest. The only sound Gavin was aware of was a tranquil buzz emanating from the sword itself.

The closer his hand came to the sword, the faster his heart beat, the louder the buzz vibrated until his hand touched the warm hilt of the ancient sword and all hell broke loose.

Fire shot from the depths of the well, thunder rolled across the sky accompanied by streaks of lightning that lit the heavens. Suddenly, wind rose to a deafening roar causing Gavin to take hold of Mac and Diana as the force of the gale whipped them about.

The sword. Ah, the sword felt steady in his hands. It pulsed in tune with his heartbeat and gave him a sense of such strength and total well-being. A wave of soft, gentle, warmth spread through his limbs, and he smiled. Amidst the danger and chaos, he actually smiled.

Memories from times long past hovered on the edges of his mind. Battle cries and mourning howls, echoed through his soul, and the sword sang to him songs of deeds forgotten and yet to be. Tingling with overwhelming power, Gavin held the sword high and hollered for all to hear. "The Power is mine."

He became aware of Mac and Diana's worried looks. With an effort, he lowered the sword, took a deep breath, and focused his mind on the present.

Strong and powerful, his voice rose over the force of the thrusting winds as he urged to others. "Let's go find Tamara."

The point of the sword led the way and cleared a path through the swirling leaves and dust. Gavin held on to Mac, who, in turn, held on to Diana, and the three of them made their way to the footpath leading to the Tor.

The way was hard. The wind blew strong, and now they needed to contend with the thicker vegetation of the forest. Gavin used the sword as much as he could to make the way easier for them, but the forces of nature seemed intent on raging with all their mighty powers.

A voice drifted to Gavin over the slapping branches and wildly racing debris. "What? I can't hear you!" he bellowed.

A tug on his sleeve made him turn to see Mac's finger directing his attention to the top of the Tor. Expecting to see the familiar stone monument outlined by lightning he was stunned at the scene that was being played out before him.

All he could do was repeat the words. "Oh, my God. Oh, my God."

Against the dark backdrop of the midnight sky and billows of menacing clouds, the Tor was visible, but an unfamiliar structure punctuated the horizon. Reminiscent of Greek Temples Gavin remembered from books, the structure shone opalescent in the moonlight. Glimmering and translucent, the Temple wavered, seemingly trapped in a timeline outside its own.

Gavin's gaze was drawn to two figures visible in the surreal quality of the hilltop. With the Temple as a backdrop, the man and woman were locked in mortal combat. Thunder and lightning crashed about in wild array in time with the furtive motions of the bearded man and beautiful woman.

"It's Merlin and Nimue." Diana's voice carried through the night.

"Oh, my God." Gavin was stuck in the moment, not able to believe what his eyes were seeing. A stinging smack across his face broke him from his trance. "Ow! What the hell?"

"We don't have time for you to get all flabbergasted now, lad. Git yerself together, and let's go find Tamara." Mac's words were the incentive Gavin needed to make his feet move forward.

As they climbed over fallen trees and debris, words tumbled from Gavin's lips. Spoken to no one in particular he had no idea what he said. He knew the appearance of the two figures on the Tor held some significance. "What does this mean? What happens now? Is it midnight yet? Will Tamara still be safe?"

No one answered him. Probably because no one knew the answer. They just made their way as quickly as possible. Diana was behind him now, motioning the way as if she knew exactly where they were headed. At least Gavin prayed she knew.

A tug on his sleeve stopped him, and Diana indicated for the three of them to get close. "We're here," she yelled. "The clearing is just ahead. Remember that we need to keep in physical contact with each other to amplify the power of the Sword Excalibur. Morganna will be very strong, so it's the only chance we have. Most important of all, don't let yourselves be misled by anything you may see. She's known for conjuring up hallucinations. Just remember, that's all they are—hallucinations."

Gavin was terrified and not too proud the fact. So many lives depended on what happened in the next few minutes. Yes, he held the sword, but so what, he had no idea what to do with the weapon. The steely taste of panic rose in his throat, and his palms began to sweat. Before he could lose it all together, the same wave of warmth and total well-being he had felt earlier washed over him. The sword worked its magic.

Gavin took a deep breath. Lives depended on him holding it together. He grasped Diana's hand and squeezed. "Let's save your daughter."

He waited until Diana took Mac's hand in hers and he felt the connection of energy sparking through them and into the sword. In the fervor of the storm, they stood in silence. Trembling, yet strong, scared, yet sure, they turned to take their final step from forest to clearing.

Chapter Thirty

Smooth, cool rock pressed against Tamara's back, and her mind kept envisioning the dark stain of blood she'd seen when Morganna lay her upon the worn altar. She shivered, but more from fear than the coolness of the night.

Tonight she was the sacrifice.

Hopes of rescue receded into the distance. If no one came by now, there would be no rescue. Her last moments on earth would be as a prisoner of some fanatical, centuries old woman.

High above her in the night sky, Tamara looked to the shimmering stars and sent a prayer to her mother, who would never have the chance to see her irritating daughter again. She focused on the luminous moon, knowing that Diana was probably looking into the same sky, soaking in energy from the same moon.

She choked back a sob.

"I'm sorry, Mom. I should have listened to you." Tamara whispered the words, willing them to voyage through the night. With any luck, her mother would sense them and, when she heard the news of her daughter's death, know that Tamara's last thoughts were with her.

Tamara risked a glance about the clearing, not sure if she even wanted to know what was going on. Ignorance was bliss, so they say. Morganna meditated in her robe of black silk, the beast grumbled and drooled in the background, and Mrs. Harlow stood beside the altar in a trance imposed by Morganna.

So far, not much to worry about. The position of the stars and moon let Tamara know that midnight was either here or fast approaching. Damn, was there nothing she could do?

Tamara looked to Mrs. Harlow, hoping for some help. Just before being placed into an induced trance, Mrs. Harlow whispered, "I'm sorry. I had no idea." Tamara felt no pity for her. After all, Tamara was the one glued by some unseen force to the stone altar. She was the one whose blood would soon be shed for some crazy scheme of ultimate power and eternal youth.

Oh, Gavin, where are you? A tear slipped down her cheek.

"Stop it." The words slipped from her mouth to be snatched by the wind and thrown away into the void of the storm. "You have to do this yourself," she whispered. "Think. What would Mom do?"

Tamara gave a self-patronizing laugh. If her mother were here, she'd know just what to do. Why hadn't she listened more to her when she was growing up instead of being worried about what others thought?

Now, it was too late.

Although, she might still have one chance. So caught up in plans for the night, the witch bitch hadn't noticed Tamara partly conscious on the way from the cave to the altar. Tamara learned enough from her mom to know the power of elderberries, so, upon seeing some growing wild just outside the cave, Tamara grabbed a handful. It wouldn't save her life, but it would give her some protection and help repel negative entities. At least, for a moment, but that moment might provide Tamara with surprise enough to break free and run. She needed to wait for the right moment, if there was one.

Tamara worked on relaxing and trying to regain control of her limbs. So far, she was able to move her head and one of her hands.

With any luck, her mind could conquer the unseen power holding her in place.

The fury of the storm whipped about the clearing as Tamara focused on the proceedings. Morganna began to chant, and that couldn't be a good sign. The chanting increased in pitch, and a strange light glowed higher up the hill toward the Tor.

Tamara looked to the very top where she saw two figures locked in a display of forces involving fireballs. That wasn't all. The Temple from her dreams wavered in a mist atop the Tor as well. It couldn't be!

Even the clearing itself took on an ethereal, surreal quality. Some kind of a time shift? Was it even possible? And could it really be Merlin and Nimue battling it out on the Tor? "Don't be so stupid. It's not possible." Tamara shook her head. "But, look at everything that's happened. Of course, it's possible. It's Merlin and Nimue." Her mind was jumbled and emotions confused. She had no idea what to believe anymore.

Her time of death was obviously approaching. Morganna stopped chanting. What did that mean? Tamara wasn't sure, but it couldn't be good for her.

The repulsive beast danced with glee and snorted with desire. Tamara prayed his touching her wouldn't be any part of the forthcoming ceremony. Morganna advanced toward the altar with a far away look in her eyes. Tamara could almost see the past, maybe the future, in the depths of her black eyes. Naked figures danced and writhed in a morbid display of rapture, and then melted away. Morganna advanced and her eyes began to focus in the present. Tamara became aware of movement, as Morganna drew her hand from beneath her silken robe.

Glittering in the light of the hundred candles, miraculously still dancing their fire in the wind, appeared a knife. Not just any knife. Tamara sensed the energy of the jewel-studded weapon. It wasn't a positive energy.

Her heart beat within her chest, and she realized that if she there existed any chance for escape, it needed to be soon. The knife rose above her head, and Morganna looked into Tamara's eyes with evil satisfaction.

"Wait." The word screeched from Tamara's throat in an attempt to halt the sacrifice. "Aren't you missing something? Aren't you supposed to have the Sword Excalibur in order for my blood to fulfill the curse and give you the power?"

"Yes." Morganna sounded amused.

Tamara was confused, was she missing something here? "Well, then, you can't kill me yet. You need the sword."

She wasn't ready to die. She needed to tell her mom how sorry she was for never believing in her. She needed to write a novel. She needed to take Gavin in her arms and make passionate love. Whoa, where had that thought come from? It didn't matter. The fact was she wasn't ready to die, so there was no way she was going to let this bitch in black get the better of her.

Morganna laughed. Deep and vibrant, it rumbled through the clearing and dissipated amongst the roaring and crashing of the storm. "I have the sword, wench. Did I not tell you all would come together for me? Look to the edge of the clearing."

Tamara looked and thought she was dreaming. There stood Gavin, Mac, and her mother. My God, where had they come from? Tamara's heartbeat quickened and her hand clenched on the herb she held in palm. She didn't have time to question what was going on, as Gavin's voice split the tension.

"Let her go or I'll use the Sword Excalibur to destroy you forever."

"No, I do not think so." Morganna didn't sound worried.

In a daze, Tamara watched the three advance into the clearing. She noticed they held hands and the sword glowed with their combined energy. Wow, if she weren't about to become a blood sacrifice, the sight of the mystical sword would have enthralled her.

She noticed that the sword distracted Morganna. The beast slobbered in the background waiting for a chance to pounce on the intruders, and Mrs. Harlow was useless in her hypnotic state. As soon as Gavin and the other came closer, she'd be able use the elderberries on Morganna and give them the edge to take her out with the sword.

The sweet sound of her mother's voice rang out strong and sure. "You may be powerful, but you know you're no match for the power of the sword. Even you can't stand against it and succeed, witch."

"Well, that may be true, if you fools possessed the intelligence to wield the power of the sword. You are like children playing with fire. You will lose the game and get burned in the process."

"Morganna, I have been preparing for you my entire lifetime, as well as my ancestors before me. Are you really so certain that we are ill-prepared to battle with you?" Diana taunted.

Morganna hesitated. Tamara chose that moment to use her weapon. Throwing the berries directly into Morganna's face, she chanted the rhyme she had come up with. Three times, she repeated the words.

With these berries, I curse your Fate
Consume yourself with your own hate

Morganna screeched in pain and anger. In a flurry of movement, Gavin, Mac, and Diana ran to Tamara's side. Together they stood with the sword between them and Morganna.

Surprised, the hovering beast screeched in anger, and Morganna raised her fists skyward, joining her screeching with the beast's.

Tamara watched her mom withdraw something from her pocket and place it around her neck. Strangely enough, whatever it was released her from her imprisonment. Ecstatic at her freedom, Tamara rose stiffly to sit on the edge of the altar and hug her mother until they both choked.

Tamara smiled at Mac, and then looked to Gavin who held the sword. He was too busy to look her way, but that didn't stop her from soaking up his rugged good looks. He looked downright heroic standing there holding the sword between them and Morganna. Her heart did a triple leap.

She touched her fingers to her throat and they tingled with energy. "What did you give me, Mom?"

"It's an amulet of protection, dear." Her mother smiled and kissed her cheek. "Now grab hold of my hand, so we are all linked with the sword. We're protected that way."

By now, Morganna had been able to throw off the spell of the berries, just as Tamara figured. But it had been long enough, and Tamara felt proud of herself for her accomplishment. She gave her mom's hand a quick squeeze in silent thanks.

Morganna and the beast stood in unison between the four of them and the pathway to safety. Gavin raised the sword. The ground trembled in time with crackling energy generated from the ancient object of steel.

Thunder rumbled as the battle between Merlin and Nimue increased in tempo. Words of anger between the two were barely discernable over the noise of the storm. The air became suffocating, as all surrounding energy was drawn into the battle above and the sword below.

Beads of sweat broke out on Tamara's forehead, and she found it difficult to breath in the heavy air. Morganna became visibly agitated.

"Give me the sword, or you will all die. And, be assured that I will make your deaths long and painful."

Beside her, the beast snapped in their direction. But both were afraid of the sword. Morganna no longer looked sure of herself. She even looked more ravaged and older than a few minutes ago.

Gavin still held the sword steady and strong, linking the four of them together.

Morganna screamed. "This is not how it was meant to be. Give me the sword."

Her scream drew forth a beam of energy from the sword. A stream of light from the point of the sword struck her in the shoulder and caused a thunderclap of immense proportions. Gavin's face showed shock. He didn't seem to be in any kind of control of the sword. It acted of its own volition. A certainty grew in Tamara that they may get out of this alive.

Morganna wasn't about to stand for the turn of events. In a blaze of hand motions and chanting, she brought the fury of the storm to her fingertips and shot a blast of fire into their midst.

They did the one thing they weren't supposed to do. They broke the link between them by raising their hands to their faces in a natural gesture of protection.

Chapter Thirty-One

Morganna couldn't believe her luck. Those mortal peons with their inflated sense of justice, those arrogant creatures who tried to take on the great Morganna in matters of the occult, made a fatal mistake.

They broke their circle, and there they stood with dumbfounded looks of fear on their hateful faces. Morganna savored the taste of her victory, and her enemies' total defeat. Yes, her power would reign supreme over all energies in the Universe. All she needed was the sword that now sat useless in the hands of that stupid man.

Streaks of lightning smeared across the sky bringing to Morganna's attention two figures locked in eternal battle. Merlin and Nimue. Surely, they would have felt and recognized the energy of the Sword Excalibur. At one time or another, they both held the sword in their hands and used its power for their own ends. Time ran short.

With an age-old gesture used to maneuver objects at her will Morganna spiraled her hand once, and then again. The sword leapt from the hand that held it, hovered in mid-air for a second, and then flew across the glade to yield itself to Morganna's outstretched hand.

Defiant, triumphant laughter bubbled in her chest and spewed from her mouth at the same time as Morganna thrust the sword deep into Mrs. Harlow's chest. The hypnotized woman stood no chance against the sword and Morganna's evil intent. Amidst screams of pain, blood gushed from the fatal wound, which only added to Morganna's overwhelming sense of power and completeness.

One twist of the sword and she felt the power flow through her veins as the curse became a living, writhing animal within her very soul. She withdrew the sword, reveling in the sensation. Crimson blood dripped from the tip and trickled down the blade to warm her hands. With a sneer, she held the sword in both hands and slammed the point to the heavens.

"I declare the power of the sword is mine."

"Dad blast! We're in deep trouble now." The old man's voice reached Morganna, and she felt powerful.

Now that she activated the curse, Morganna needed to reinforce it with blood from either Nimue or Merlin's descendant. The blood of the slain woman would be weak, just as she had been.

She turned to the four who reassembled at the edge of the glade and sneered at their attempts to re-establish their circle. Dolts! Didn't they realize that nothing could stop her now? At least, with the sword they stood a chance. Without it, they were dead.

But, there was still a way she could be stopped. She needed to get to them before they got to Merlin and Nimue. In her moment of glory, she had been ecstatic enough to forget about her lifelong enemies. If they came together against her…the thought did not bear finishing. She would ensure that event did not take place.

Her calculating gaze turned to the two familiar, hateful, figures at the top of the Tor. The attention of the others focused on the hilltop of the Tor as well. Idiots they were to think they could reach the Tor before she killed them.

With a single thought, she called the beast to her side and instructed him to dispose of the two men and the older woman, and then return the younger woman to the altar.

Amidst slobbering and grunting, the beast lurched across the clearing. Morganna had total faith in his ability to fulfill his orders. After all, they were dealing with mortals. Unversed, untrained, unaware even, of the powers at their fingertips, they would be easily handled.

She couldn't have been more wrong.

The older woman, the one with hair that shone the color of silver moonlight, disrupted everything. How could that mere mortal possible know the Rhyme of the Avalon? But she did. The ancient words to encircle oneself with the protecting virtues of nature were being spoken in harmony with the surrounding vibrations of the storm.

One by one, words Morganna long ago ceased to even remember, fell from that woman's lips as if she had been speaking them her whole lifetime.

> Nature's wonders, strong and true
> I give my heart in keeping to you
> From the shining stars of heaven
> To the fertile soil of the earth
> I give my very soul as your due
> With these gifts, I ask in return
> The bounty of your endless power
> The force of your boundless vigor

The storm calmed, an aura of gossamer brilliance circled the woman, and was punctuated by pinpricks of flickering golden lights that Morganna knew to be the woodland fairies. A gesture of the woman's hand sent the other three people scampering up the hillside. Morganna would have to get through the woman to seize her prey.

Rage exploded in her mind. "Nooooooo!" The woman needed to die. The sword jumped in her hands, almost in protest to the required task. Her control was slipping. She needed to spill the proper blood to fully activate the curse.

It was now or never. Only one of them would come out alive

from this encounter. And she wasn't planning to make this horrible little clearing her deathbed.

With a lunge of fury, desperation, and exasperation, Morganna flew across the clearing, with sword pointed at the woman she quickly came to hate.

Chapter Thirty-Two

Tamara tripped over a branch only to be quickly pulled up by both Mac and Gavin. Adrenaline pumped and the taste of fear in her mouth was equaled only by the panic that rose in her chest.

"Sorry." Was the only word she spoke before they were on their way. She reached up to wipe away a trail of blood. She must have cut her face when she fell.

Mac was leading, as he said he knew the fastest way to the Tor. Tamara was in the middle, and Gavin brought up the rear.

It's a good thing Mac and Gavin were guiding her, because Tamara was still stunned by what happened in the clearing. Her mother saved the day. She had been amazing, standing like some avenging Goddess and reciting that verse. Tamara was enthralled as she felt the warmth of circular energy spiraling around, and then seen the radiance of energy flowing from the earth.

Her mother used herself to delay Morganna and give them the time they needed to make a run for the Tor, Merlin, and Nimue.

A whimper mingled with her ragged breathing. Chances were that her mom saved their lives or at least given them a fighting chance at survival. But at what cost? Tamara would never forget the sacrifice made, and she would never again doubt her mother. Tamara ached that she might not have the chance to sit down with her mom, have a heart to heart talk, and tell her how sorry she was about all the years wasted in disbelief and shame.

The whimper turned to a sob and warm tears fell down her face to mingle with the warm blood from her cut. Gavin must have sensed her state of mind. He motioned Mac to hold up for a second.

"Tamara," his voice was soft, but urgent. "Your mom most likely gave her life for us, don't let it be in vain. We need to hold it together long enough to see this through." His hand brushed her tears away. "You can do it. I know you can."

"But…my mom…I never understood. I—" She couldn't say anymore. Her heart ached for what had never been and now never would be. She turned beseeching eyes to Gavin, but he just shook his head.

"We have to go. Pull yourself together."

"Come on, you two, I think I hear that beast approaching." Mac's voice urged them on, but Tamara saw the sympathy in his eyes.

The palpable sense of danger from below them grew stronger, and sounds of crashing underbrush enforced the fact. Gavin's gaze connected with hers and created a small spark of energy that grew into the heat of a blazing fire.

She smiled. Gavin put his hand out to her.

No way would she let Morganna get away with her plans, not now. When she spoke, her voice took on a new strength. "Let's go, we have a bitch who needs to be put in her place. Hopefully, that place is Hell."

"That's my girl."

"Come on, people, we need to hurry," Mac urged. "We just have to get around the bend up ahead, and we should be in sight of the Tor."

Tamara ignored the stitch in her side as they dodged swinging branches and flying leaves. Her heart and mind came together to give her a purpose; that purpose was revenge. The storm may have calmed in the clearing below, but it raged full force in her heart. It also rang across their path and the closer they got to the Tor, the more they fought the wind.

"What do we do when we get close?" Tamara could hardly hear herself. The words were ripped from her mouth. The shrug of Gavin's shoulders meant he either didn't know, or he couldn't understand her words.

They were so close, but so was the wave of evil following them up the trail. Just when Tamara felt stifled with the stench of evil, they turned the bend and stood only about twenty feet from the crest of the hill.

Tamara was awed.

The stone monument that was the Tor was lit up by alternating streaks of lightning and bolts of light energy flashing from the fingertips of Merlin and Nimue. A historical monolith, the Tor was believed to quite possibly be the gateway to past, present, and future. Maybe even to other worlds beyond mankind's grasp and understanding. It was hard not to stand in awe and wonderment.

But there wasn't time.

Tamara turned her attention to Merlin and Nimue. A figure in black and a figure in white. Did Gavin feel the same as her? Their ancestors, supposedly dead these hundreds of years, stood before them.

Merlin and Nimue became aware of their presence.

Silence reigned upon the hilltop. As Merlin and Nimue ceased their battle, so the storm ceased its intent. Five pairs of eyes scrutinized and assessed.

At that moment, the beast broke from the forest. In a frenzy of anger, the creature bee-lined for Mac and Gavin. All they could do was evade his attacks. Tamara screamed as immense claws ripped into Gavin's shoulder and blood ran dark down his arm.

She turned to Merlin and Nimue and beseeched them. "Do something. Please, you're the only ones that can stop him."

Snarling and snapping of teeth were the only sounds that broke the silence. The beast was preparing another attack.

"Please," Tamara begged.

Merlin and Nimue exchanged a confused glance.

Merlin spoke first. At least, Tamara thought he was speaking. She became aware of words, but didn't see his mouth forming any.

"Who dares show their faces? Be gone or you will pay with your lives."

Sounds from the beast raised the level of urgency.

"I'll explain later, just kill the beast," Tamara screamed once more in a plea for help.

The beast attacked. Mac was the object of the frenzied efforts. With one mighty swipe of a scaly arm, the beast catapulted Mac across the clearing and crashing into the dense brush of the surrounding forest. His wiry body sprawled, unmoving and bloody.

Tamara sobbed, and Gavin yelled his anger and frustration.

In a single flash of power and energy, Merlin and Nimue waved their hands at the beast. With a howl of pain, the hoary beast writhed in anger, but stood no chance against the power of the Magician and the Lady. With a final scream, he disintegrated into a hundred flickering sparks of light, and then nothing.

Tamara had a chance to breathe. Gavin ran to Mac's side and gingerly lifted his friend's head to his lap.

"Leave this place," Merlin shouted. "You are intruding on what does not concern you."

Gavin was busy tending to Mac, who seemed to still be alive, so Tamara answered. "Mighty Merlin, do you not recognize your own blood?" She waved her arm toward Gavin and spoke again. "Lady, you should recognize your own kin as well."

"I know who you are, but now is not the time."

"Please, listen to us. Lives depend on your patience and understanding," Tamara pleaded.

"Whose lives?" Merlin and Nimue questioned in kind.

"Ours and yours," Gavin answered. He and Mac rose to stand together with Tamara. "Let us come closer. Danger approaches quickly."

"The only danger is what you will find if you come any closer. You have allowed yourself to be beguiled by the eyes of the woman, therefore, you are no good to me now. Be gone." Merlin bellowed. "We have unfinished business and do not need interlopers such as yourselves."

"Wait," Nimue demanded. "I have need to find out what these people speak of, it may pertain to the disturbance in the lower clearing. You, yourself sensed the familiar power. Do not deny it old man." The Lady of the Lake beckoned them forward with a rustle of silk and wind.

"I will listen, but this only delays the inevitable between us, Nimue." Merlin acquiesced.

An outburst from below the Tor drew the attention of everyone. Glittering, glowing, and larger than life, stood Morganna, sword in hand.

The surrounding air tightened as oxygen was sucked from around them and pulled into the light surrounding Morganna. Tamara had trouble breathing and saw Mac and Gavin gasping for air as well.

"Morganna." Both Merlin and Nimue whispered the name in disbelief.

"The Sword Excalibur." Again, they both spoke. This time, they turned to look at each other and then back to Morganna.

"How come you to have the sword?" Merlin demanded.

"It matters not. What does matter is that you two will perish in this place, tonight. I now rule the power of the sword."

"Do not be ridiculous. The sword can only be used for good, not to destroy at the whim of the person who holds it in her hand."

Literally bursting with all that happened over the last while, Tamara screamed. "Yes, yes she can use it to destroy. We've been trying to tell you that there's a curse on the sword. She's the one who lied to you both, and neither one of you was betrayed by the other. She planned all these centuries for your destruction so she could have supreme power."

"Enough," Morganna screeched and the light around her dimmed. "I will finish this here."

Morganna reached behind the stone Tor and, in one wrench of strength, pulled someone to her side.

Tamara screamed. The person was her mother, and she was alive.

"I offer you your mother's life for yours."

"No." Her mom grabbed Morganna's hand and pulled the sword to her own throat. "If you need blood to spill, take mine."

"You will not do. As strong as you are, your daughter bears the full power of the ancient blood. I need her."

Without even thinking of the consequences, Tamara took a step forward, but Mac stopped her with a surprisingly strong grip on her arm. He then strode toward Morganna with the most determined look on his face.

"Mac, no. She'll kill you," Tamara screamed.

"Not if I kill her first," Mac snapped.

It all happened so fast, Tamara barely saw the streak of light shoot from the sword and send poor Mac flying through the air to land with a thud. Tamara winced and prayed that he was still alive.

Obviously furious and desperate, Gavin beseeched Merlin and Nimue. "There lies the cause of your anguish. Morganna lied to you both about the sword. Think back, and you will see the truth. Now, Nimue, she wants to take the life of your descendant so she can ignite the curse that lies in the sword and take the power for herself. The only way she can be stopped is if you two reconcile and use your powers against her."

"Morganna, what say you to these accusations?" Merlin questioned his protégée.

"I say all is true. I lied to you both, and you were too stupid and self-centered to see the truth." Disdain tainted her words. "You were so easy, both of you. Now, I hold the sword, and neither of you can stand in my way."

With these words, she held the sword to Diana's throat. "Come here now, Tamara, or your mother's blood will spill on this soil and you will be responsible."

"No!" Nimue raised her hand, and her voice pleaded. "Merlin, if this is true, you and I have done each other a grave injustice. We must put this right."

"Now, Tamara. I want you here now!" Morganna screamed. Her face took on a deathly pallor and her shoulders developed a slight stoop. In desperation, she pressed the sword hard enough to pierce skin and set off a dark trickle of blood.

"Mom!"

"No, Tamara, stay there." Her mom was barely able to choke the words out.

Gavin wrapped both his arms around her, fighting her struggles and preventing her from running to her mother's side. His voice shook, ragged with emotion and fear. "Merlin, Nimue, look into your hearts. See what's before your very eyes. You are not each other's enemies. You never have been. The Dark Lady is your enemy. Please save us all, bind together and destroy the evil."

Morganna screeched for Tamara and angled the sword another inch lower. Mac was stirring in the bushes, and Tamara struggled against Gavin's arms.

Through her haze of emotion, Tamara was only barely aware of the moment that Merlin and Nimue joined hands. When their hands touched, the air sparked and Morganna screamed in outrage.

The Lady and the Magician began to chant in an unfamiliar language, and Morganna released her hold on Diana who fell to her knees. Gavin's arms released Tamara, who stumbled, sobbing, to her mother's side. With gentle care, she wiped away the trailing blood and made sure her mom was all right.

There was no time for teary reunions because Morganna leveled the point of the sword at Merlin and Nimue and begun to chant in the same unfamiliar language they were speaking.

The trio advanced toward each other. Merlin and Nimue against

Morganna and the sword. Tamara saw the power of the sword was fading fast and a tremor marked the level of Morganna's voice.

Incensed, Morganna's chanting turned to a scream and her features contorted into a mask of horror. With each passing second, it became obvious she was losing. Merlin and Nimue glowed in a spiral of golden light that stretched down from the sky above. Together, they raised their hands and intoned, this time in English, for the powers of the Ones Who Came Before.

"We call to the ancient powers of the Ones Who Came Before,
Bind together to smite the evil from the sacred sword
Give us your energy, oh beloved Ancestors of the Light
Use us as a vessel to set events once again right."

In a beautiful tone, their voices melded one with another, then became one with the forces of nature, until the trees around them sang the song of Merlin and Nimue.

It's what Tamara would have imagined the songs of the Sirens sounded like. So beautiful, she was enthralled, yet so powerful, her ears hurt.

But it was working.

Before the eyes of everyone in the clearing, Morganna's form became transparent. She must have realized what was happening, because she broke from her chant and screamed in frustration and rage.

"No. You cannot do this to me. I have the sword."

But the sword quivered from her hand and hung as if suspended on the wings of the wind. Morganna grasped one final time, her face contorted in a death mask of agony, and her form became nothing but an empty black hole in the clearing. After a moment, even the hole disappeared.

The chanting of Merlin and Nimue slowed to a stop, calmness settled over the hilltop, and everyone stood, or sat, shell shocked.

Chapter Thirty-Three

For a brief moment, the Sword Excalibur, in all its glory, hovered in the air before them. Brilliant and powerful, it glowed with a magnetic force felt by all. Merlin and Nimue joined hands, raised them to the Heavens, and with one word—a word from another time—they sent the sword flying skyward and then streaking to the earth. Just before the final moment of impact, the Sword Excalibur disappeared. Not amidst flashes and lightning as one would expect. Instead, the sword fell into a gentle blend of rainbow colors and left behind a tranquil serenity wafting on the gentle winds.

The storm passed. The Tor, which witnessed so much over the centuries, finally witnessed the conclusion of a centuries old battle.

Gavin looked about the ravaged, but triumphant, group of people who stood in the midst of the debris that scattered from the storm and the ensuing battle between legends.

Merlin broke the baited silence. "I desire an explanation of these events, as I find myself quite at a loss."

Tamara, Gavin, Mac, and Diana looked at each other. None of them were too sure how to begin.

Merlin directed his gaze to Gavin and demanded. "You. You, who are of my blood, I warned you of the Dark Lady, but I see I was mistaken."

"Yes. I tried to tell you of Morganna, but you left the cave before I could. She gave you the sword and said it was from Nimue. She then took its powers and made you doubt Nimue in your dreams. All along, she manipulated and planned."

Tamara spoke to Nimue. "Yes, and it was she who told you Merlin stole the sword and was using it against Avalon. She needed to make you doubt each other and destroy you both so she could rule supreme."

"How do you know all this?" Nimue questioned.

"We read your memoirs." Tamara and Gavin spoke together.

"So much hate, Merlin." The Lady whispered as she touched her hand to his cheek. "So much time wasted. So many lives affected. It is all my fault." Her whispered voice turned to a sob. "Righteous hate ruled me because I felt betrayed, and as a result I became what I was preaching against. I judged and condemned people for their beliefs, forgetting the vital fact I was raised with: that there is light and dark in anything. Because of my hate, I condemned all Christians when I should have embraced the good."

"My love." Merlin comforted Nimue by taking her gently in his arms. "I am as guilty. I believed Morganna's tricks, and I did not have enough faith in you. That was one mistake. I also was too willing to give up on the Old Ways for the Christian ways. I should have realized that they both offered much, and with acceptance and love that is prevalent in both beliefs, they could have worked together so well. Avalon did not have to perish."

"I fear that Niobe placed the Land of Avalon in the wrong hands. Oh, Merlin, what have I done?" Overcome with grief, Nimue fell to her knees.

"My Lady, is Avalon really gone?" Diana spoke for the first time since being released from Morganna's grasp of death. She looked radiant in spite of her closeness to death. "With the sword where it belongs, and you two reconciled, does it not stand to reason that Avalon may return one day when understanding and acceptance come to the mankind?"

Nimue frowned and looked to Merlin. "I do not know. Merlin what think you?"

"From the dust of Atlantis rose Avalon. I think sometime in the future another place will rise in the place of Avalon. The names may change, but the premise remains true through the years. Memories of past times lay in the souls and hearts of people, and understanding comes full circle."

Nimue nodded, then smiled at Merlin and Diana. "You are a wise woman, mayhap you were one of my priestesses in Avalon."

Obviously flustered, Diana stuttered. "It would have been my honor, Lady."

Merlin took Nimue in his arms and held her close. "Come, my Lady, we have much time to make up for, and many plans to make for the future."

"But what happens now?" Tamara protested. "You can't just leave. There are so many questions."

Merlin smiled. "Life is a quest my child. You must search for the answers to your questions. Nimue and I must leave. Our time is done, but yours is just beginning."

Slowly, their bodies took on the quality of fine mist. Shimmering and crackling, the mist entwined into one form and rose skyward until no longer visible. Just before the mist was gone, Nimue's voice reached their ears.

"We will always be here for you. Just look to the flowers that bloom and the birds that sing in the trees. We are all around you."

Tamara choked back a sob and wrapped her arms around Gavin. "Is it finally over?"

Gavin brushed an auburn strand of hair from his face and assured her. "Yes, our lives can get back to normal now."

"Normal." Tamara chuckled. "My life will never be normal again, not after everything I've seen. Do you realize I now have to re-think everything?"

"Well, I could say I told you so, but I'm your mother, so I'll be nice," Diana quipped. She'd made her way to Mac's side, and they stood arms entwined as if it were the most natural thing in the world. Strength and beauty shone from Diana's eyes, and Gavin glimpsed Tamara in the future.

"Gavin," Tamara whispered in his ear. "What's up with Mom and Mac? Granted, we've all been through an unbelievable night, but the two of them look like they're in love or something."

"I think they are."

Gavin met Tamara's gaze and smiled in understanding at her confusion. At least, he'd adjusted to the instant attraction between Mac and Diana. He watched acceptance dawn in emerald green eyes, and Tamara left his side to go give her mother a hug.

"Mom, I finally get it. I'm sorry I doubted you."

"Tamara, you don't need to be sorry for anything. Everyone has to believe in something. It's just not always the same thing, and that's all right."

"So, what happens now?" Gavin stepped over and took Tamara in his arms. He liked the feel of her body shaped to his.

"I have no idea," Tamara stuttered. "What does happen now?"

The woman on the loudspeaker was talking again. Her distorted voice interrupted Tamara's good-bye to her mother. Tamara rolled her eyes and repeated herself.

"I'll miss you, Mom. It's kind of hard to say good-bye when we've only just found each other." A single tear formed and she blinked it away.

Diana laughed and folded Tamara in a hug. "Dear, it's not as if we'll never see each other again."

"I know. It's just that so much has changed."

"Cheer up, here come the boys and if Gavin sees you crying, he'll probably blame me. Last person who made you cry got thrown into another dimension you know."

"Mom." Tamara laughed and automatically reached her hand out to take Gavin's as he approached. It amazed her how quickly touching became such a natural part of their relationship.

Mac went to Diana, put his arm around her shoulder, and smiled into her eyes. "I don't remember the last time I was so excited. Gives an old guy a rush to know there's still life left in him."

Diana laughed and struck his arm. "Don't try and fool us with that old man bit. And don't get too excited either, I'll be putting you to work in the gardens as soon as we get home. After that, the front porch needs repairing."

Mac slapped his hand to his forehead and moaned, "What am I lettin' myself in for? Maybe, I'll just stay here in my safe little bookstore."

Tamara responded quickly. "No way, your little bookstore is now mine and the bank's, so there's no turning back, Mac."

"Maybe Woodstock is in need of a quaint little bookstore with an eccentric old proprietor?"

"Let's just get home before you start making plans, Mac. There's so much I want to show you. Besides, there's a wedding to plan for."

Just the word wedding made Tamara's chest tight. She couldn't believe her mother was getting married at her age. Before jealousy got a total hold on her emotions, Tamara gave one last hug to Mac and Diana. "They're calling your flight. It's time to go."

Amidst the flurry of good-byes, Tamara felt heartsick, she was worried that maybe she'd made the wrong decision to stay in Glastonbury. After all, what did she know about running a bookstore?

Silence reigned as Tamara and Gavin watched the silver streak of the plane disappear into the horizon.

"I'll miss them," were the only words spoken by Tamara as Gavin wheeled the car through the airport traffic and onto the open highway.

"I guess you want me to drop you off at the bookstore? You must have a lot to do."

When had things gotten so impersonal between them? Tamara wondered. "Yes, that would be fine, thank you."

The lush green countryside flashed past, but Tamara saw nothing but a blur. She squeezed her eyes tight to prevent the threatening tears from falling.

"By the way, I have some exciting news."

"Yes." Tamara was able to speak the single word without her voice shaking too much.

"It seems that Mrs. Harlow didn't have any relatives, so her estate went to the government. With the help of someone I once did a favor for, I was able to put my name in to purchase her house. I'm a soon-to-be home owner," Gavin proclaimed proudly.

Tamara's heart did a triple thump in her chest. She loved the Will-o-the-Wisp. The thought of Gavin living there without her brought tears back to her eyes.

"That's nice for you." She managed to choke out.

"Hey, are you all right? You're not having second thoughts about staying here, are you?"

Tamara's eyes flew open. The question sparked tendrils of worry to tickle her stomach. Maybe she was alone in her feelings. Oh, God, what if Gavin didn't want her here? She'd changed her whole life and for what? For the first time in her life, she'd done something not logical, and it looked as if it were going to bring her nothing but heartache.

"I don't think so." Even to her own ears, her voice sounded weak.

"You don't think so. Well, that's hardly a resounding endorsement, is it? Personally, I would prefer a stronger declaration of your feelings than that."

"I'm not sure I understand." Tamara was confused, and she noticed that Gavin turned on the road leading to the Tor. "Where are you taking me?"

"You know where we're going."

"Yes, but why?" Tamara's confusion grew.

"I decided it was the best place," was Gavin's cryptic reply.

Tamara's frustration rose. Her voice reflected her state of emotion. "Would you stop being so damn stubborn and just tell me what the hell is going on?"

"There you go. That's the Tamara I know and love."

"Love?"

Gavin brought the sleek BMW came to a halt at the base of the Tor. Since it was late afternoon, the place was nearly empty. Rays from the setting sun bathed the Tor and the surrounding hill in a golden aura of light.

Tamara barely noticed the beauty. Instead, she faced Gavin and whispered, "What are you talking about?"

Gavin reached out and swept his hand across her cheek. The feel of his skin on hers made her tingle. Their eyes connected and sizzled with desire.

"I think you know what I'm talking about, Tamara."

Bubbles of delight rose rapidly in her throat. Within Gavin's blue eyes, she saw the answers to all her doubts. "I need to hear the words."

"What words, my love?"

"Dammit, Gavin, must you be so pigheaded?" Tamara accented her remarks with a slap on Gavin's arm.

"Ouch!" Gavin moaned. "If you want me to marry you, I'm afraid I'm going to have to insist that you stop hitting me on the arm all the time."

"Marry you!" The words squeaked from Tamara's mouth. "Marry you." She couldn't think of anything else to say.

Gavin laughed. Moving his seat back, he reached across the console of the car, wrapped his arms around Tamara, and pulled her to his lap.

Still unable to speak or think, she took the moment to enjoy the feel of Gavin's muscled body as she settled into his lap. Knots of uncertainty unwound, and she felt the love radiating from the man she had known for such a short time. She sighed deeply.

"I'll take that as a yes." Gavin nuzzled her neck and ran his tongue over her lips.

"I suppose I have to marry you since you saved my life and all. But do you think you could ask me properly?" She took the time to enjoy the feel of his lips with the tip of her own tongue.

"Woman, if you keep that up, I won't be able to ask you anything. I'll just throw you in the back seat and have my way with you."

"Sounds good, but…"

"But what?" Gavin halted his fingers, which had been intent on unbuttoning Tamara's shirt.

"It's just I'm worried that maybe we're getting caught up in the emotion of the past week. My buying the bookstore is one thing, but committing to each other for the rest of our lives is something else entirely."

A hint of a smile touched Gavin's mouth and softened his face. "My ever practical Tamara, have you learned nothing over the last while. You know how you feel, and you know how I feel. Can't you just accept that without bringing logic into the equation?"

The words were in her heart, but Tamara wasn't used to impulse, so her mind wouldn't let her speak. The struggle within her brought about a moment of silence. She looked to the Tor, as if looking for an answer. Subconsciously, she acknowledged the beauty of the ancient stone structure, which now stood out in bas-relief against the fiery orange ball of the setting sun. A gentle breeze blew the trees and rustled the leaves. Life was wonderful. Her relationship with her mom was stronger than ever. She had an interesting new career. And she was in love with the man who saved her life and wanted to marry her. What more was there?

Eyes bright and heart full, she turned to Gavin. "Okay, let's get married."

Gavin laughed. "Great, but aren't you missing something?"

Tamara frowned. "I don't think so."

"Aren't you going to say the words?"

"The words? Oh!" Adjusting her position, Tamara swung herself around so she was facing Gavin. Wrapping her arms around his neck, she looked directly into his azure blue eyes and said, "I love you."

Gavin's grin stretched from ear to ear. Placing one hand on either side of Tamara's hips, he pulled her close enough so that Tamara could feel the physical effect she was having on him.

She blushed.

Gavin whispered in her ear. "I love you, too."

"Yes, I kind of get that feeling," she teased.

Gavin claimed her mouth with his and time stood still. Tamara could have sworn that she heard the songs of the Sirens whispering in the background. Liquid fire ran through her veins as Gavin's hands found their way inside her shirt and touched on bare flesh. Damn, but it felt good to go with emotions rather than logic.

Whimpering, she wriggled herself closer to Gavin.

"Wait. Tamara, wait, " Gavin demanded in a ragged voice. "I was only kidding about throwing you in the back seat." He carefully pushed her away so there was breathing room between them. "I want our first time to be memorable, complete with wine, flowers, dinner, a bed. You know the routine."

Tamara brought her senses back into focus. She swallowed and took a deep breath. "You mean you didn't bring me here to make out?"

"No."

Tamara watched Gavin reach into his pocket and take out a small velvet box. Yikes! It couldn't be. But it was. Gavin opened the box to reveal the most beautiful square cut emerald Tamara could ever have imagined. Entwined in a Celtic design of glimmering gold tendrils, the emerald glittered. Regal and exquisite, it emanated passion from its very depths. Hesitantly, Tamara touched her fingertip to the smooth surface.

"It's been in my family for generations. Who knows, it may even have belonged to Merlin at one time."

"I couldn't possibly wear it. It's too valuable."

"Yes, you can." Gavin slid the ring onto Tamara's finger. It fit perfectly. "See, it's like it was meant for you."

"Oh, Gavin. I love you so much." She threw her arms around Gavin's neck and hugged him close.

"I love you, too. For now and always."

"Across time and any other dimension that we may not know about?" Tamara teased.

"You got it, woman."

Tamara smiled and was about to seal the promise with a kiss, but a flicker high on the Tor caught her attention. "Gavin, look."

Beneath the darkening Tor shimmered a reflection of an ancient Temple. On the steps of the Temple, two figures entwined together in an embrace. One brief flash of light and they were gone.

"Yes," she whispered, as her heart filled with joy. "Across time and forever."

~End~

About the Author

Catherine Anne Collins lives in a small town in Ontario, Canada with her husband, two dogs, cat, and bird. She has been an avid reader since childhood, many times waking up early in the morning in order to have time to read before going to school.

Currently Catherine and her husband Fred own and operate a martial arts and wellness centre that keeps them both busy. Her hobbies include photography, kayaking, horseback riding, reading, and hiking.

Sword Across Time is Catherine's first published novel, but the urge to write keeps her going strong, and she has more manuscripts in the making.